Also By Abbie Williams

The Shore Leave Cafe Series

Summer at the Shore Leave Cafe
Second Chances
A Notion of Love
Winter at the White Oaks Lodge
Wild Flower
The First Law of Love
Until Tomorrow
The Way Back
Return to Yesterday

Forbidden

 The Dove Series

Heart of a Dove
Soul of a Crow
Grace of a Hawk

Wild Flower

a

SHORE LEAVE CAFE

novel

Abbie Williams

central
avenue
publishing

2017

Published by Central Avenue Publishing, an imprint of Central Avenue Marketing Ltd.
www.centralavenuepublishing.com

WILD FLOWER

978-1-77168-109-4 (pbk)
978-1-77168-018-9 (epub)
978-1-77168-058-5 (mobi)

Published in Canada

Printed in United States of America

1. FICTION / Romance   2. FICTION / Family Life

To those of you who are able to recognize
and appreciate the wildflowers present in your life...

Prologue

CAMILLE'S VOICE WOKE ME WHAT SEEMED MINUTES AFTER I fell asleep and I sat up too fast, reeling, reaching blindly into the humid darkness of a July night. The blood in my veins thundered like water over a cliff. Only a second earlier, my niece had been clutching my arm, screaming and frantic, and now all I could hear in the silence surrounding my eardrums was the violence of my heartbeat.

Oh God, what is it, what's wrong? Camille and Mathias were still in Montana; I hadn't spoken with either of them since earlier today. I closed my eyes and concentrated for all I was worth, trying to discern a shred of an answer. Sending the thought with as much force as I could muster, I pleaded, *Camille, tell me!*

Beside me, Justin woke and rolled to wrap an arm over my lap.

"I'm here, baby." His warm hand curved around my right thigh. "I'm right here."

"I'm scared." My voice was high and hoarse. The only time a sense of foreboding had ripped through me so fiercely was the long-ago winter night my first husband, Christopher, had died.

Justin was wide awake now, sitting up fast, the sheet falling away from his hips. He collected me close, his protective embrace easing the rigid tension in my body. "I'm here, Jilly-honey, it's all right."

I clung, feeling the worried pace of his heart against my cheek, slowly regaining a sense of calm. I whispered, "It's not that."

He smoothed loose hair from my flushed face. "Is it Rae? Clint?" Before I could answer, he said, "I'll check them."

The hall light clicked into existence as Justin assured himself that our children were both safe in their bedrooms down the hall; seconds later he was back, gathering me against his warm, bare chest. Even in the dimness of our room, I could see the tangible force of his concern. He stroked my pregnant belly in small, comforting circles. "What is it, Jills? What's happening?"

"It's Camille." I pressed all eight fingertips to my forehead. I moaned, "Oh God, I was just dreaming of her and Mathias. Something's wrong…"

Justin knew me well enough not to question my words. "I'll call Jo and Bly."

Against the backdrop of my closed eyes a picture wavered into existence, a horizon in the distance, etched with the outline of a low-slung, jagged-edged mountain. For a fraction of a second, I could see Camille through misting rain; despite the dark night around her, she was momentarily highlighted by a rending in the cloud cover and a milky spill of moonlight gilded her long, wild hair. She was screaming one word, in a refrain of hysteria.

"*Mathias.*" I was helpless to prevent the vision from disappearing, rippling away as swiftly as a reflection in a lake when disturbed by motion.

Justin caught up the bedside phone and was already dialing.

Hold on, I tried to tell them, sending the words as hard as I could through the night. *Oh God, hold on.*

Chapter One

Sultry June heat, sticky as fresh honey and manifesting as sweat upon my temples and a thin trickle down my spine. The sky appeared quilted with clouds, low and sullen on this late Saturday afternoon, and I was crabby as hell. I'd just scraped the driver's side fender of the Shore Leave work truck against the headlight of a pristine little Audi with Michigan plates, clearly belonging to an out-of-towner. Though my father-in-law, Dodge, would offer to fix it as good as new, the owner would undoubtedly be annoyed at this destruction, best case scenario; the Audi's headlight was in pieces at my feet.

I stood in the hot parking lot scribbling a note on a piece of lined paper torn from my order pad, which I'd plucked from the passenger seat of my mother's truck, my daughter tugging on the hem of my tank top and fussing that she was thirsty. I didn't voice it but I was also craving a drink, something ice cold and about fifty-proof; because I was pregnant, this possibility was unfortunately out of the question.

"Rae-Rae, give me just a second," I told her with as much patience as I could manage to inject into my tone, trying to brace the note I was writing against my thigh. Rae bumped my leg with her belly and the pen jerked in my hand, creating a long scribble across the paper.

"*Dammit,*" I muttered in an undertone, flipping it to the other side and starting over.

I could feel the gathering edges of a headache and wished that my husband would magically appear and take our child off my hands, at least until I could collect my thoughts. Rae was just past two years old and though she resembled a golden-haired, brown-eyed angel, she could be hellaciously temperamental; I supposed I shouldn't have been surprised, given her genetics, and at that thought I almost smiled, finally successful with the second attempt at an apologetic note. I stuck it under the windshield wiper on the driver's side of the Audi, thinking that I wouldn't feel *too* terrible if the wind just happened to blow it away before the owner finished shopping...

Jillian, I scolded, hitching my purse strap over my shoulder and collecting Rae by her hand. She continued complaining as we made our way across the parking lot of Farmer's Market, though upon entry into the familiar old grocery store she brightened considerably, breaking from my grasp and darting for the red-painted carts.

"Mama, can we get cake?" Rae asked as I lifted her into the basket seat, angling her chubby legs so I wouldn't get inadvertently kicked.

"There's cake at Shore Leave, sweetie." I paused to select apples.

"Let me help!" Rae insisted and I indulged her, unable to keep from smiling, passing the fruit piece by piece into her small hands and letting her drop it into the plastic bag.

"Can we get cookies?" Rae asked next. "Daddy gets oatmeal cookies!"

Justin was such a sucker when it came to our kids, Clint and Rae both, but most especially Rae; he was definitely the softie of our parenting team, but again I smiled at the thought.

"We'll see." My favorite parenting line of all time.

"*Please*, Mama," she wheedled, already starting the begging campaign.

"Maybe," I hedged, kissing her nose and then turning to choose bananas. At the same moment, Rae leaned from the cart like a little monkey and plucked an orange from the bottom of a pile, displacing about seven thousand other pieces of fruit. I squeaked in alarm, dropping the bananas I'd grabbed.

"Uh-oh, Mama!" she cried delightedly, bouncing in the seat.

I sighed and looked around, hoping to catch a glimpse of a "real" adult who would come take care of the problem, before kneeling carefully, mindful of my six-month pregnant belly, to collect the errant produce. I retrieved the last orange and stood to tuck it back on its stand when a female voice behind me drawled, "Well, hello there, Jillian."

I looked over my shoulder in semi-annoyance which changed at once to a burst of consternation, suddenly confronted with the sight of Aubrey Pritchard. More specifically, my husband's ex-wife.

"Hi, Aubrey," I managed, pleased at the relative calm of my voice. Aubrey looked much the same as when I'd last seen her, tall and willowy, her skin a deep, glowing bronze from the summer sun. I noticed small wrinkles webbing her eyes and felt a spurt of purely vindictive glee. I couldn't truly claim to hate this woman but I still disliked her way down deep in my bones; I was reminded of this fact as her gaze roved over Rae.

"Congratulations," she said after an uncomfortable silence. Her eyes swept down to my belly before returning to my face and she studied me with unapologetic appraisal for the space of two heartbeats. There were many things she might have said, but she chose, and I was not mistaking the bite in her voice, "Your hair's gotten so *long*."

The situation was surreal, facing off here in the produce department, Rae watching with unblinking fascination; Jim Olson called hello to the both of us as he pushed by with his cart. As though in response to my silence, Aubrey flipped her auburn hair over one shoulder, an old, self-affirming gesture I recalled from our teenage years. Throwing me a nasty, unexpected curveball, she said, "He always had a thing for you, you know. Yet, *I'm* the one everyone blames."

My eyebrows lifted, my chest went tight; she really wanted to get into this now? In the grocery store?

When I didn't take this bait she pressed the point, shifting her weight to the opposite hip. "He used to talk about you all the time, how *worried* he was about you. And yet when *I* step outside our marriage, *I'm* the cheater, *I'm* the—"

"Aubrey." I kept my voice low but allowed an unmistakable note of warning.

She bit back further comment with real effort, I could tell, her sparkly, mauve-shadowed eyelids lowering. Flipping her hair to the other shoulder, she settled for, "Like it matters anyway. I'm just in town for a few weeks. Like I could ever live in this shithole again."

"Come on, Rae-Rae," I murmured to my daughter, clutching the cart handle. Aware that I was running away, I pushed the cart around Aubrey without another word.

"Tell Justin I said 'hi,'" she called in a singsong and I just barely resisted the urge to flip her off over my shoulder.

"Aw, baby, I'm sorry," Justin said later that night as I lay over his chest on our bed, my cheeks hot with frustration as I related the story. He tucked a strand of hair behind my ear and let his warm hand linger on my jaw. We were virtually alone; Rae had been in bed for an hour and Clinty was sleeping over at his best friend, Liam's. Justin added, "If she knew you were upset it would only make her that much happier. She's that way, mean-spirited. Jilly-honey, I'm sorry. I wouldn't have let her talk to you like that."

"*I* shouldn't have let her talk to me like that." Tears broiled and wet my eyelashes, which made me even more furious. "She totally caught me off guard. And Rae was right there, J. I'm just so pissed."

Justin grinned at my use of the letter as a nickname. It was a joke between us; his full name was Justin Daniel, shortened by some to J.D. – which didn't suit my husband at all, but this didn't stop his sister and her husband from using it. I'd started using "J" to tease him, and the habit had stuck. He shifted and used both thumbs to brush away the tears that spilled onto my cheeks. "I'm sorry, sweetheart."

"It's not your fault," I said, tenderness displacing the swell of my anger. In the amber-tinted lamplight, I studied this man I loved beyond all else, his strong jaws stubbled with dark beard a day past shaving, framing the sexy mouth that routinely kissed every inch of my skin. His straight nose and incredible, long-lashed eyes of rich brown, the shade of coffee without cream and just as hot. His black hair that was as unruly as ever, through which I spent most every night stroking my fingers. The planes of his cheeks, the squint-lines in the outer corners of his eyes, the shape of his firm chin.

I let my hands glide from his muscular chest to frame his face with its livid scars that I never noticed anymore, moving so that my breasts rested flush against his bare chest. I was wearing an old, periwinkle blue tank top, so threadbare that it was nearly worn through in spots, and absolutely nothing more. Justin's eyes kindled with a familiar heat and his lips curved in the wayward grin I'd come to know so very well in the past three years.

"Jilly," he murmured, sliding both hands slowly over my ribs, continuing downward along my hips, at last taking firm anchor around my ass, which he cupped and used to settle me atop his nearly-naked body.

I spread my thighs over his boxers, smoothing my hands over his collarbones and then to his wide shoulders, so solid and warm beneath my palms. I sighed a little, in pleasure, a jolt of heat between my legs as he shifted. His fingertips teased the juncture of my thighs and I arched my spine, skimming the tank top over my head.

"God, you are a beautiful woman." His voice was hoarse with desire. "Come here, woman, and put your nipples in my mouth."

I curled my fingers into his chest hair and shook my head. Justin caught my hips in his hands and his dark eyebrows lowered menacingly, like a pirate who was intent upon having his way with a captive. My smile widened at the thought; we'd played that little game on more than one occasion. Justin kept an old red bandana in the nightstand on his side of the bed, which had done its fair share of duty as a headscarf, a garter, and sometimes to bind my wrists. And there was truth to the rumor about the second trimester of pregnancy, of which Justin took wholehearted advantage; to be fair, I couldn't get enough of him as it was.

"We're so naughty," I reflected as Justin cupped my breasts, heavy against his broad palms, and told me with his eyes that I should bend forward and let him have his way.

"Hell, yes," he agreed, and I giggled, then moaned as he tipped me into his mouth and lightly bit my nipple before taking it sweetly between his lips.

A soft thump from the bedroom across the hall; I murmured, "Dammit."

Justin rolled me beneath him, growling against my neck as he tugged the sheet over us. Not a moment too soon, as Rae pushed open the door and came straight into our room, dragging her tattered elephant by its trunk. She stood regarding us with her eyes squinted in the bright light of the lamp.

"Mama," she implored, rubbing her nose with her free hand, just like Clint used to do.

My heart melted and I reached for her. "C'mere, little one, what's wrong?"

Justin leaned and caught Rae under the arms, hefting her effortlessly atop the mattress and smoothing a hand over her soft golden hair. His wide palm bracketed her head. Rae burrowed against Justin with a happy grunt, her little feet churning to get beneath the covers with us.

"Daddy, I had a bad dream," she whispered. "Elephant, too."

Justin tucked Rae into the crook of his arm and rocked her close. My heart was undone for the countless time since giving birth to our daughter; Justin was an amazing father, as I always knew he would be, and tears wet my eyes as I snuggled against them, sandwiching her between us.

"Tell Daddy all about it," Justin soothed, but Rae's long eyelashes were already fluttering closed.

I kissed Rae's forehead, feathering her downy hair. She sighed and popped a thumb into her mouth, and moments later fell fast asleep. I leaned and kissed my husband's forehead, whispering, "Now get this girl to bed and get back in here. And *hurry*."

Justin grinned and covered Rae's ears. He added, "Don't start without me. Wait…on second thought…"

"Hurry," I ordered again.

"Holy shit, baby," he said upon reentry a minute later, locking the door behind him. I had started without him.

Justin was out of his boxers and braced over me before I could blink, and I muffled a shriek, giggling and struggling, but he held his ground, dark eyes lancing heat right through me. He cupped the flesh between my legs, displacing my hand and biting my shoulder. I groaned, lacing my arms about his neck, lifting my hips into his touch.

"You're so…incredible at that…" I whispered, growing ever more breathless, my head bent back against the mattress. I told him this at least twice a week.

"Fuckin' right," Justin replied in his usual poetic fashion, licking along my throat, closing his teeth around my earlobe; I shuddered and gasped, feeling his grin against my neck.

"Don't you dare stop," I ordered, and he deepened his touch at once. I clung to his back, leaving nail marks, biting the firm muscles along the slope of his shoulder as I came against his stroking fingers, reaching immediately to grasp his cock. I shifted and took him within the slick, heated wetness he'd created.

He groaned, "Holy *Jesus*, woman…"

I arched upward and Justin slowed his pace at this wordless request, grinning down into my half-closed eyes as I quivered beneath him. He pressed soft, suckling kisses upon my chin, whispering, "I know you've got one more…c'mon, baby…"

"*Justin*," I moaned, as turned on by his words as his touch, as he bent to my breasts and lifted my hips in his big hands. No more than minutes later I tightened in bursting waves and he shuddered, overcome, sweat trickling along his temples as he plunged one last time.

"See?" he murmured, forehead bent to my shoulder. "I knew it."

"You *always* know it." I was utterly content, my fingers sunk into his hair. I kissed his jaw, scratchy with stubble. "You're the world's best lover."

He laughed, tickling my skin, and gently shifted us, turning so that my spine fit against his chest.

"I aim to please, that's all."

"That's the secret," I giggled.

From behind, he slipped one hand over the sloping curve of my belly and murmured, "How's the boy?"

"No doubt traumatized."

Justin's chest rumbled with laughter. "Nah, he must be used to it by this point."

As though in response, our son poked what was either a knee or an elbow just beneath my belly button. I caught Justin's hand and maneuvered it to the spot. He smoothed his palm over my skin and said with quiet reverence, "Hello there, son. Did we wake you?"

"I'd say that's a big *yes*," I responded. The baby pushed against our joined hands and I snuggled closer to my husband.

"G'night, my sweet little woman," he whispered, leaning to click out our bedside lamp. He was snoring within a minute but I lay awake while the baby moved in gentle somersaults, content to watch the waning moon as it inched diagonally across our bedroom window on its journey westward. Though we hadn't officially confirmed that I was pregnant with a boy I knew my prediction was correct, just as I'd known with Clint and Rae.

Since childhood, I'd experienced these inexplicable flashes of absolute knowing; my great-aunt, Minnie Davis, had also been endowed with such illogical (but no less real) abilities, and it was from her that I learned, if not when, at least *what* to expect when a Notion overtook me. Notions were unpredictable; spontaneous, they often occurred in the form of dreams, though a dream containing a Notion was different than the regular, disjointed jumble of images from any other night. I had learned to accept and even appreciate these strange instances of precognition, and thanked the powers that be for Minnie's presence in my early life; without her, I'd probably have assumed I was crazy—or eventually become so.

Great-Aunt Minnie foresaw my first husband's death when Chris and I were still teenagers and only dating; he'd gifted me with a promise ring for my birthday less than a year before this particular Notion struck Aunt Minnie. I could even pinpoint the moment the Notion overtook her thoughts—a warm spring evening in 1985 as we sat together on the porch, along with Gran (my grandmother and Minnie's little sister), while Minnie fixed my hair. I'd sensed the sorrow flowing from her fingertips, the briefest of pauses in the motion of her gentle hands. She refused to divulge anything that evening except for the fact that I would be all right; though it took me over a decade and a half to fully realize it, Great-Aunt Minnie was correct in this prediction. When I was twelve years old she'd said, *You'll never see more than you can handle, Jillian. My grandma had the gift. It stretches far back in our family. Trust it, doll, always trust it, even when you don't understand exactly what it shows you.*

And I always had.

This autumn would mark mine and Justin's three-year wedding

anniversary. I'd been so blissfully happy on the night of my birthday, three years ago, when Justin asked me to be his wife. Not so much as a flicker of a Notion warned me of Gran's impending death or the car accident that nearly killed me just days later; I clung to the belief that all things (joyous or dreadful) happened for reasons not always revealed, and struggled not to blame myself too harshly for the instances when a Notion failed to alert me to danger. Minnie had never spoken the words but I sensed that a Notion was a *sign* of what was to come—but not necessarily something capable of being changed. Fate or destiny, or whatever one wanted to call the forces beyond anything's control, were entities moving outside of my reach. If, at times, I was allowed a glimpse of a future event, I understood that I must recognize this as something fixed, something I could not change. As a result, though some people suspected that I possessed an uncanny sense of observation, very few people outside our family actually knew the truth.

My older sister, Joelle, didn't tell me until later just how terribly Justin had suffered to see me in the hospital bed those unending days and nights, unmoving and unresponsive, knowing I was pregnant but not if I would survive. The thought made me cringe even now. I still hated driving a small car after dark, preferring either Justin's oversized truck or the work truck from Shore Leave, besieged by the memory of being broadsided that night. Since we'd been married, Justin sold his old house a few blocks from Fisherman's Street, where he had lived for the duration of his marriage to Aubrey. Working over a period of a year, we (with considerable help) cleared out a section of woods on the property about a quarter-mile to the east of Shore Leave, where we proceeded to build our own cabin. It wasn't grand on the scale of some of the places ringing Flickertail Lake like majestic pearls on an expensive necklace, but instead cozy and functional.

I'd been insistent on a few small luxuries, such as a master bathroom and a decent entryway, spacious enough to accommodate our messy outer gear during the average six months or so of winter we routinely experienced in northern Minnesota. Our cabin also featured a gorgeous picture window, complete with a bench seat, and a stone fireplace that Dodge helped Justin craft, piece by piece. Our cabin was built with three bedrooms; the baby would sleep with Justin and me for probably the first year of his life; Clint's room would eventually become the new baby's. The thought of my oldest son moving away for college was like the throbbing ache of a new bruise, though it wasn't as excruciating as it would have been without Justin and Rae.

I remembered where I'd been three years ago, lonely as hell, in love with Justin without fully realizing it. I'd been adrift back then, Justin so bitter from both the terrible accident that scarred his face and the embarrassment of a cheating wife; in a small town like Landon, everyone had known within twenty-four hours that Aubrey not only left him, but left him for someone else. Recalling that summer when we'd at last admitted our feelings for each other made me scoot closer to my sleeping husband, shifting to press a soft, lingering kiss to his chin. Even in sleep, his arms tightened around me.

Aubrey's barbed words in the grocery store returned to me as I lay in continued sleeplessness, along with her clear intention to elicit guilt. I sighed a little, considering what she'd said. Beneath the surface a strong connection had always existed between Justin and me, there was no denying; even unacknowledged, it raced along, swift and powerful. As much as I'd once loved Clint's father, Chris Henriksen, there was a part of me that had always belonged to Justin. Even Aubrey, who was shallow and petty, discerned this, so perhaps I deserved to feel the sting of guilt, at least a little.

You still hate her, admit it.

Fine, I still fucking hate her. Even if she has a tiny little bit of a point.

Wouldn't Aubrey be justified in her anger after observing that her husband expressed undue concern over another woman? I considered anew, chewing my lower lip, increasingly troubled at my own culpability in this matter. But then my thoughts strayed to even more unwelcome territory; Aubrey and Justin had dated in high school, marrying shortly thereafter, and as his wife she'd therefore been the recipient of his love, his kisses and his incredible passion, for many years.

Jilly, quit it.

The blaze of jealousy overtaking my blood was, of course, ridiculous. Nevertheless, I gritted my teeth as I imagined all the way back to the days when Justin was a lanky football player and Aubrey a popular cheer-leader. She'd intimidated me to no end back then; though we'd been in the same grade she always possessed an attitude of being worlds ahead of the rest of us. The only person not snowed by Aubrey's behavior was my sister, Joelle, who was (and still is) a complete knockout, and was at that time dating the most over-confident and notorious boy in Landon High, Jackson Gordon. Jo had married, and later divorced Jackie; their three daughters were the only good thing that came of their union. As though conjured by my thoughts, the phone suddenly rang; I knew it was Jo. I kept the ringer turned off on our bedside cordless but heard the one in the kitchen jangling. I eased from beneath the covers and hurried down the hall before both Justin and Rae woke up. The microwave clock read 11:37.

"What's up?" I asked my sister, settling carefully upon my chair at our table, leaving the room encased in darkness. I propped my feet on the chair opposite, Clinty's usual spot. "I was just thinking about you."

"Jilly Bean, sorry to call so late." Jo sounded hushed and apologetic. "But I knew you were up. I didn't wake anyone, did I?"

"No," I assured her. Joelle and her new husband, Blythe, lived just a stone's throw from Justin and me, in a similarly-styled cabin, though they'd built theirs with four bedrooms to accommodate their son Matthew and two of Jo's three daughters; Joelle's oldest, Camille, lived in my old apart-ment above the garage at Shore Leave, along with her fiancé, Mathias Carter, and her little girl. I asked my sister, "You want to come over and sit on the porch for a while? I can't sleep, either, and it's gorgeous out."

"Yeah, I was hoping you'd ask." I could hear the smile in her voice. "I'll be there in a sec."

I plucked Justin's worn flannel shirt from the peg in the entryway and stepped into my red flip-flop sandals before heading out under the stars. Justin and Clint hung a wooden swing from the porch beams the first week we'd lived here and I claimed my usual place on it, listening with pleasure to the sounds of the night. The air was warm and the humidity had been swept away by a whispering breeze. A pair of great gray owls lived in the woods just beyond our yard; their haunting calls made me long for my grandmother, dear Gran, who also loved the sound of owls. Jo appeared from the path that led to her house no more than a minute later, wearing cut-off jean shorts and wrapped in a hooded sweatshirt of Blythe's, carrying a candle lantern that I recalled from our childhood, which Mom claimed had been in the Davis family for over a century. The nail holes punched into the tin threw apricot light in a thousand tiny pinpricks, as though Jo was being preceded by a flock of dancing fireflies.

"God, I wish we still smoked," Jo said as she climbed the porch steps, hanging the old lantern on a cast-iron peg near the front door. I scooted over so she could join me on the swing.

"You can say that again," I murmured, not even attempting to disguise the longing in my voice. Gran and Great-Aunt Minnie would have scoffed at us, as both of our menfolk (rather than ourselves) had driven the decision to abandon the bad habit. I recognized that it was the right choice but I still truly missed the feel of a burning cig in my hands. I missed blowing smoke rings; I missed the way a cigarette helped me slow down, gather my thoughts. I knew there were healthier ways to do so, but shit, I was a creature of habit.

"How's my nephew?" Jo bent a knee on the swing, smoothing her palm over my belly.

"He was doing acrobatics just a minute ago."

"Matthew finally nodded off. We can manage to get him into his toddler bed, most nights anyway, but he'd still rather sleep with us." She added, with soft affection, "Bly just can't refuse him anything."

"He's as much of a marshmallow as Justin when it comes to the kids," I agreed. "We have to be the disciplinarians, Jo, we can't back down."

"Yeah, that's a scary thought. It is hard to say no to Matthew, I admit. He's so darn adorable. And Bly just worships him, can hardly let him out of his sight." Jo shifted a little, tucking her loose golden hair behind her ears. "You know."

She meant the fact that years ago, when he still lived in Oklahoma, Blythe's ex-girlfriend had become pregnant and then proceeded to have an abortion, without telling Bly. The ache of this would always be present in Blythe's sensitive soul, Jo and I both realized, and so I understood that she couldn't be too irritated with him regarding their son.

"So, I have two things," Jo said then, and in the lantern light I studied my sister's face, its graceful contours more familiar to me than just about any other in my life. I was so glad she lived near me again that it was difficult to express in words; I knew she felt the same. I waited patiently for her to continue.

"First, I'm worried about Camille." She leaned to grip my knee. "Jills, have you seen anything?"

I curled my hand over hers. "I would tell you immediately, you know that. And besides, Camille is so happy it radiates off her like a beam of sunshine."

"I know, and I'm grateful for it. They're so in love." She paused to sigh, tapping her lips with an index finger. "Though, on that subject, I'm worried she's going to get pregnant before their wedding. *Seriously…*"

"They are pretty…active," I giggled in agreement, shying away as Jo flicked her finger against my bare leg. "But come on, they're engaged, and Mathias is very…" I bit back additional laughter at all of the adjectives popping around in my mind, words a mother may not really want to hear in conjunction with her daughter's lover, such as *virile, sexy,* or *studhorse-like.* I finally settled for, "It's that Carter magnetism."

Joelle rolled her eyes, knowing I was right, setting the swing into gentle motion with one foot.

"Like *you* should talk," I pestered, letting suggestive innuendo flood my tone. "Your own man is awfully…*magnetic.* In fact, if I don't mistake myself, I'd guess he proved that to you this very evening. Probably more than once!"

Jo snorted a laugh, elbowing my ribs.

"So, what's worrying you, exactly?" I asked. "Do you want a drink? If I can't have one at least I can watch you enjoy. I've got gin…or a beer…"

"No, Jills, I'm fine, just relax. Mathias told me just yesterday that he's worried about Camille's nightmares. You know…"

I did; Camille and I had discussed it. Further, I could sense that something very real *was* wrong—but nothing more. But I knew better than anyone that a Notion could not be forced. Camille had never experienced Notions that I was aware, but I felt strongly that her nightmares were indicative of something different, connected with the past rather than the future, centered around an old photograph she'd found two years ago, a picture with tremendous energy surrounding it; I'd held it in my hands for only seconds before recognizing this.

The photo showed a man named Malcolm and a horse named Aces, the man one of the first Carters in the Landon area, both of them standing in the light of a long-ago sunset. The back of the image was scribbled with the words *Me & Aces*. Camille was obsessed with discovering what had happened to Malcolm—there was a troubling but unsurprising (given the amount of time that had passed between his life and hers) lack of information. The dreams to which Jo referred had plagued my niece since last winter, dark dreams of loss and terror, of wandering without end. I knew at the heart of her deepest fear was that she would somehow lose Mathias, utterly unable to prevent this loss from occurring. The worst of it was, as Camille had said, that she was certain she'd lost him before now, maybe in another life. *Or maybe I'm just crazy, Aunt Jilly*, she'd moaned. I simply held her that night; words of comfort seemed hollow.

"And with everything last Valentine's Day..." I muttered, trailing to silence, thinking of the strange and terrifying night last February when Mathias had been attacked in the woods on the north side of Flickertail Lake; he'd been walking his trap lines at dusk and someone had not only struck him in the head, but then proceeded to drag his unconscious body through the snowy undergrowth. If not for Camille experiencing a premonition that he was in serious danger, and her subsequent swift reaction, Mathias might have been hurt far worse, even killed. Months later, none of us possessed satisfactory answers. No trace of the perpetrator was discovered, no hint as to why anyone would use a weapon to strike an unarmed man in the woods. The only clue were two bars of solid gold, stamped with their minting date of 1876, found in the woods near the scene of the attack. I wished for the ability to reassure my niece, to tell her that everything was all right in the aftermath—surely Mathias was no longer in danger—but my gut suggested otherwise. And I was not one to ignore gut instinct.

What sort of danger? I wondered for the countless time. *And in what form? Who would want to cause him harm?*

I had no answers, and remained aggravated by this; further, I understood that Camille likewise had none, despite her intensifying dreams. The past spring had proved relatively calm and I tried to be reasonable. Camille and Mathias were planning a trip out to Montana, in addition to their October wedding, and there should have been nothing but sunshine on their collective horizon.

"For Mathias to come to me means he's really worried." Jo's voice pulled me from my thoughts. "I hope they find some answers on their trip, Jilly. They leave in just a week or so."

"Is Millie Jo staying with you or at Mom's?"

"At Mom's," Jo confirmed. "Camille said they plan to be back within a week. I hope that's enough time. I think if she could find out exactly what happened to Malcolm Carter, she might rest easier."

"It's important, I don't know *how* exactly, just that it is." I gazed into the darkness of the woods. The lantern threw a sphere of light that was broken by its impact against the house. The spruces rustled as though offering suggestions I didn't understand; we both were startled as a crow called from somewhere near, raspy and insistent, invisible in the dark. I rolled my eyes at my jumpiness and changed topics. "It's pretty wild that our ancestors might have actually known the Carters. Why else would something of theirs be stored in a Davis trunk in our attic?"

"Wasn't that interesting?" Jo reflected. "I'm so glad Mom found all that stuff. Seeing those pictures from the Civil War. And the letters."

"I know, I just wish there were more of them. Most must have been lost, or destroyed, or what-have-you. It's crazy that our relatives migrated all the way from Tennessee back then. God, I wish I knew that whole story. How long would that have taken?"

"Months, at the very least," Jo said, tucking hair behind her ears. She abruptly straightened. "Shit. Before I forget, Dodge was at Shore Leave earlier. Did you by any chance break off someone's headlight today? I should have called you right after supper, when I found out, but I got busy. And then Dodge was going to call you guys, but I said I would take care of it."

"What?" I'd almost forgotten that particular incident. "How did you—"

"It was Aubrey's car," Jo interrupted me to explain and I stared at her in disbelief, surprised into silence. "Apparently she's in town for a few weeks, without her hubby, and she was all in a tizzy, stopping out at the filling station and bitching at Dodge. He calmed her down, but she was demanding to see Justin."

"That bitch! What the hell? Where does she get off? Demanding to see *Justin?*"

"She wants him to fix her car. She was acting like you'd done it on purpose." Jo shook her head. "Dodge told her he'd fix it and basically to shut her trap, but you know how she is."

My skin prickled with restless irritation; I forced myself to relax the fists I'd unconsciously made. I all but growled, "Well, she can fuck right off. Dammit, I wish I would have flattened her stupid car. And here I was all *nice* in that note."

Jo laughed, unconcerned by my bristling anger. "Jilly Bean, calm down. I know it sucks, but what do you do? What about your car?"

"I was in the work truck." I sighed. "I don't know if Mom even keeps that insured." Normally it was only ever driven on Shore Leave property; I'd borrowed it to drive into town for groceries because the trunk of my own car was loaded with cast-offs I'd been meaning to donate.

"Dodge will take care of it," Jo said. "Don't worry."

I was sure she was right. There was no reason to feel an additional swell of uneasiness.

Chapter Two

"OH, I LOVE HOW THAT LOOKS," I TOLD MATHIAS, WHO was leaning over the schematics spread all over table three at Shore Leave. He looked up and winked, taking a sip of his root beer at the same time, then grinned as I flushed.

"I love how *that* looks," he said, his familiar voice full of suggestion, and I flicked his shoulder with one finger. I would not be distracted by him, no matter how sexy his lips, with their cupid's bow curve and flanked by a dimple in his right cheek. His eyes were the same color as the deep-blue irises growing in profusion around the porch outside, flecked with gold, his black hair flattened from having been tucked under his fishing hat all day. His stubble was thick, a good three days past shaving.

It was a lazy Sunday three weeks into the sunny, humid month of June and we felt justified in taking it easy today, after a crazy-busy week. Mathias had been working weekdays at the township forest fire station while I did lunch duty at Shore Leave, leaving us evenings and Sundays together; late yesterday afternoon, he'd helped me hang a hammock between the two oaks growing a few yards from the front porch of our cabin. Simply the words 'our cabin' filled me with promise and possibility; Mathias had obtained a permit from Beltrami County to start renovation on the little homestead back in May and we'd spent nearly every free moment there since, working our asses off. One of the first Carters to arrive in Minnesota had built the original structure in the late 1860s and it was our greatest hope to make the little place livable year-round—for the both of us, my two-year-old daughter, Millie Jo, and any babies that may join our family in the future.

"Honey, you're giving me those eyes," Mathias said, and I moved around the table, unable to resist him; he shifted so that I could sit on his right thigh, hooking an arm around my waist and resting one hand against my belly. I looped my elbow around his neck and kissed his bearded jaw.

"I'm just thinking of what we talked about last night."

"Me, too." His lips were against my neck. "I haven't thought of anything else all day. You can't know how happy it makes me, honey."

"To have a claw-foot tub and a king-sized feather bed?" I teased. We'd also discussed these things, hoping to acquire them for our cabin before our wedding night, but what I truly meant was the way we'd decided that as of this week I would stop taking birth control pills.

Mathias shook his head, a smile deepening the dimple in his cheek. "Yes. A king-sized feather bed. Where I plan to lay you down and make you my wife. That thought makes me the happiest man on the face of the earth, yes."

I slipped my hands down along his sides. "That sounds so traditional, almost biblical. 'Make' me your wife. As in, by brute force?"

Mathias tried for an innocent tone. "I don't think force will be required. If this morning was any indication, you seem fairly willing... excited about it, actually..."

I giggled and stole a kiss.

"God, you guys, get a room," my younger sister, Tish, complained, coming up to our table. "You *have* a room, now that I think about it."

As of early spring, Mathias, Millie Jo, and I had been living in the apartment above the garage, which had been Aunt Jilly and Clint's place before they moved across town to live with Justin Miller, back in 2003. Since then, Uncle Justin had built them a new house closer to Shore Leave, just around the lake, near the service and filling station where he worked with his dad, Dodge Miller; the service station had long been the Millers' family business. Much like Mom and Blythe's cabin, Aunt Jilly's wasn't large in scale; instead, as Aunt Jilly said, it was *thoughtfully laid out.* According to her, there were certain things you should never compromise on, such as an accessible laundry room, in which you could move with a laundry basket and avoid bumping your hip.

Mathias grinned, acknowledging the way my sisters, Tish and Ruthie, and his—Tina, Glenna, and Elaine—often complained about our public displays of affection. He squeezed my waist before we turned to face my younger sister, who stood watching us with an air of long-suffering, arms folded. Tish's thick, curly hair was stuffed into a messy bun and she lifted one dark eyebrow to emphasize her sarcastic statement. She was wearing a dark blue, halter-style bikini that exactly matched her eyes, but I knew she hadn't intended that; Tish could not have cared less about clothes or cosmetics, barely knew the difference between her hair straightener and the hot-air dryer. Despite my best efforts to persuade her otherwise, she still wore sports bras, embarrassed by her breasts that wouldn't seem to stop growing.

I dearly loved my sisters and could not help but smile at her obvious irritation, earning another eye-roll.

"Mom *made* me come get you guys," Tish complained. Behind her, the screen door clacked as our youngest sister, Ruthie, and our cousin, Clint, followed in Tish's footsteps.

"Pontoon's heading out!" Clint announced, resettling his baseball cap over his dark hair, shaved military-short for summer. "If you two are coming, that is."

"God, I can't believe you guys graduated high school this year," I said. We'd held the celebration just last weekend here at the cafe, for both Clinty and Tish. My dad, a successful lawyer named Jackson Gordon, and his pretentious second wife, Lanny, even flew in from Chicago; it hadn't been the most pleasant experience for either Dad or my mom. At first, Dad had been his usual charming self, making smooth conversation and smiling at everyone (everyone except Blythe, that is), but as the evening wore on, he continued drinking and things took a gradual turn for the worse.

Uncle Justin had stepped in and led him outside after Dad started slurring and referring to Blythe as 'Jo's ex-con.' Probably to save face, Lanny collected their things and hustled Dad to their rental car.

"Lanny's clearly had her breasts enlarged again," I'd told Mathias in an undertone that afternoon, before Dad proceeded to get drunk.

In response, Mathias started humming our favorite Dolly Parton song from *The Best Little Whorehouse in Texas*; he adored finding any excuse to break into song, and did so whenever the urge overtook him. People thought he was crazy, and he was, a little. But he was also mine, and I loved him so much, so totally insanely completely, that it still stunned me. But nothing in my entire life had ever felt more right.

"We're coming," I told my sisters, but didn't budge, reluctant to move from Mathias's lap.

"It's so pretty out, you guys should hurry," Ruthie said, though she came near and began playing with my hair. "Uncle Justin is taking the motor boat, too."

"Dad said we could waterski for a while before full dark," Clint explained.

Everyone seemed to have a soft spot for Clinty, well deserved; he hadn't an inconsiderate bone in his body. Over the past year he'd grown another four inches or so, edging up on Blythe, who was the tallest in our family. At present, Clinty's frame was so lanky and lean he resembled a heron, all elbows and knees. Hearing him call Uncle Justin 'Dad' made my heart melt; I knew it meant a great deal to Justin, who wasn't actually Clint's father. I wished for Millie Jo to be able to call Mathias 'Daddy' but understood that it wouldn't be fair to Noah Utley—as much as I truly resented considering the concept of fairness when it came to him.

Three summers ago, Noah had been my first real boyfriend. I understood clearly, despite precautions intended to discourage it, that I was just as much to blame for getting pregnant. What I was unable to accept was the way Noah instantly retreated after I'd told him the news; for all practical purposes, he had abandoned me and our baby. I was not being overdramatic in that statement, as Noah wanted nothing to do with either me or Millie for nearly the first two years of her life. It was only since last Christmas, after dropping out of college and being forced into a rehabilitation center for his drinking that Noah began trying to see his daughter more regularly. But lately I was suspicious that he was drinking again; I'd told his mother last week, wondering if I would feel a spurt of retribution at this revelation, only to realize I felt nothing but pity and disappointment that my child's biological father was choosing to make his life into a train wreck.

"Hell yeah, that sounds great," Mathias said at this announcement about waterskiing.

"I get first dibs!" Clint said, earning a snort from Tish. She cried, "No way, you went first last time!"

Ruthie was still busy braiding a few strands of my long, tangled hair, slim fingers flying. Ruthann was the baby of our family (not counting Matthew, Mom and Blythe's son). It startled me sometimes to realize that Ruthie was hardly a baby anymore, having outgrown her preteen awkwardness. At fifteen, she was sweet-faced and softly beautiful, her gentle demeanor the exact opposite of Tish's. Ruthie possessed the same hazel eyes as most of the Davis women, a cross between cedar-green and dusty gold, and the brown curls that all three of us had inherited from our dad.

"When you get married your name will be Camille Carter. That sounds like a country-western singer," Tish observed, as though just stumbling to this conclusion. She snapped her spearmint gum, hands planted on hips in an unintentionally belligerent pose, as though facing off with a jury. She demanded, "Don't you guys think?"

"I think it sounds like all my sweetest dreams coming true," Mathias said, low and sincere.

"Oh, *barf*," Tish said.

"No, it's so sweet," Ruthie countered, her tone adoring and wistful at once. She bent and kissed the top of my head, as though she was the big sister. "You guys are adorable. But we gotta go!"

At that exact instant, Dodge blew the air horn down by the dock, sounding two elongated honks. The noise drew Tish, Clint, and Ruthie like the Pied Piper; seconds later I was alone with my man, and a second after that I was in his arms and we were kissing in a furious rush of need to be joined as closely as two people are able.

"The bar," I gasped between kisses, and he made his throaty, lovemaking sound in agreement, catching me up into his arms, my bare legs threading around his waist. Clumsy, stumbling against chairs, he carried me through the arch and into the semi-darkness of the bar, settling me atop a stool that was the perfect height for such things, skimming my swimsuit bottoms down my thighs; I was wearing a sundress over my bikini, and I freed one leg without breaking the contact of our lips.

"Hurry," I commanded, gasping as he slid all the way inside with the first thrust.

He groaned, "You're so wet, *oh my God*, you're gonna make me come already—" and held himself deep, unmoving.

He felt so good and I could never get enough of him; the hunger, the onrushing need, only increased with every touch. He drew out and plunged back within, and I moaned; he muffled the sounds with his kisses. I clutched his powerful shoulders and held fast. He growled against my neck as my body tightened convulsively around his and seconds later he came in a hot rush that could have very well led to our second child. My heart swelled at the joy of such a notion; Mathias was thinking the same thing, I knew; and he nuzzled my neck, whispering, "I'm so excited."

His tone was one of reverence but I could not resist the urge to tease, whispering, "You are *so* excited, love. I can feel it all through me."

His eyes opened and flashed into mine; his laughter threatened to uncouple our bodies and I giggled all the more, clinging tighter.

"Camille!" Mom called from the porch, her footsteps rapidly approaching, and I squeaked, fumbling as we raced to scrape our clothes back into place.

"I feel like such an animal," Mathias muttered hoarsely, kissing me one last time. His blue eyes, flecked with gold, caressed mine as he thumbed a stray strand of hair from my lips. "No control whatsoever. Jesus, honey, I love you so much."

"Camille! Mathias! We're leaving!" Mom insisted, inside the cafe now, and I tried to appear as not-guilty as possible as we reentered the dining room. Though she gave us a knowing look, Mom politely refrained from commenting on what was exactly what it looked like. Instead she announced, "Final warning!"

Outside, the air was calm and perfect. Flickertail Lake lay like an unwrinkled silk tablecloth under the peach-tinted evening sky. I paused on the porch and observed the scene just down the incline from Shore Leave, where my family was gathered at the dock and in the water. Mathias stood behind me and hooked his arms around my waist, bending to tuck his chin against my shoulder. For a flicker of an eyelash I felt once-removed from time, struck with a sense of knowing even deeper than instinct, a sense that I was on the right path and, for this one moment, the universe had allowed me to glimpse it.

But at what price?

I shoved that icepick of a thought from my mind. I hated feeling like I couldn't trust my own happiness. Was there a limit to the amount any one person was allowed? I couldn't help but wonder. And what happened when the limit was reached, the tally marks totaled?

Mom walked along the dock boards toward the pontoon, leaving wet footprints. Her long, golden hair hung in a thick braid; in her cut-off shorts she looked about twenty-five or so. Dodge, Grandma (corralling Millie Jo and Rae into their lifejackets), Aunt Ellen, Aunt Jilly, and Blythe were already on board, ready to chug around the rim of Flickertail at a top speed of about five miles an hour, a summer Sunday-evening tradition. Blythe was toting their son, my little half-brother Matthew, in a baby sling against his chest, and he caught my mom close for a kiss as she climbed aboard. Blythe's hair was long again, because Mom liked it that way, and he had grown a goatee; we all teased him that he just needed to learn to play acoustic guitar to complete the look. (So far he'd progressed to strumming the G-chord that Eddie Sorenson of Eddie's Bar had taught him). Blythe was my stepdad but I never thought of him that way. I considered him the man who made my mom happier than I'd ever seen her in my life, and though he wasn't my father, I did love him for that.

Aunt Jilly looked as pretty and pixie-like as ever despite being nearly seven months pregnant, curled into a lawn chair on the pontoon; she caught sight of us and waved, blowing a kiss. Uncle Justin, shirtless and darkly tanned, a red bandana tied over his black hair and his hands stained with motor oil, knelt to monkey with the outboard motor on his boat, which was anchored about thirty feet off the dock. Two pairs of water skis stuck out like misplaced branches from the stern. Ruthie, Tish, and Clint were in the process of swimming out toward it, their hair slicked back, laughing as their pale arms, not yet bronzed with summer tans, cut through the water like trout.

"Carter! You want to ski you best get your ass down here!" Dodge yelled in his big roaring voice, wiping sweat from his forehead with the back of one hand, clutching a silo-sized can of beer in the other. His aviator sunglasses were settled like a headband over his bushy hair, as usual, and I sensed Mathias's grin. We linked hands as we made our way down the lawn to the lake, Mathias lifting mine to kiss the ring on my third finger, the slim gold band that functioned as my engagement ring, engraved on its inner rim over one hundred and thirty years ago. Both of us believed the words inscribed there were originally chosen by Mathias's ancestor, Malcolm Carter, though to whom the ring was originally intended to belong, we had not yet discovered.

"I'll hitch a ride on the pontoon," I said, as Millie caught sight of us and barreled down the dock, her enthusiastic bare feet making the boards shudder with the impact. Her curly hair was tied into two pig-tails, her small, plump torso buckled into a lifejacket that was patterned like a ladybug's wings.

"Hi, darlin'," Mathias said, catching her into a hug as she raced to him with arms extended. Love has many guises, a lesson I'd learned over and over again since becoming a mother. Watching my man as he cuddled my daughter, bouncing her on his strong forearm, listening with rapt attention as she rambled on in her cheery, high-pitched voice, a nearly unbearable sweetness caught me directly in the heart. Tears prickled in the corners of my eyes but I blinked them away.

"You gonna ride on the big boat?" Millie Jo asked Mathias.

"Not right now." Mathias kissed the end of her nose. "I'm going to ski for a little while," and he pointed at the motor boat, where Uncle Justin had finished his ministrations and stood wiping his hands on a grubby towel. Clint reached the boat and climbed up the rope ladder draped over its side, Tish and Ruthie not far behind.

"We'll clap for you!" Millie said, and then looked my way, ordering, "Mama, you ride with us!"

Mathias handed her over to my waiting arms and kissed my forehead before stripping his shirt and jumping into the lake to follow after my sisters and Clint. I slipped out of my sandals, leaving them on the damp, grassy shore.

"Camille, you want a burger?" Aunt Ellen asked as I stepped carefully onto the deck of the swaying pontoon, holding Millie; Aunt Ellen and my grandma were also stationed in lawn chairs, while Mom, Blythe, and little Rae sprawled on the starboard bench seat; I claimed the port side for Millie and me. Rae scampered across the bow to join us. Millie Jo wriggled free of my arms and immediately began roughhousing with Rae. One of Grandma's dogs, Chief, lying quietly on the deck, barely stirred as the girls tumbled over him, used to such antics. His tail thumped twice.

"Yes, thank you, with extra cheese," I told my great-aunt. I beamed at little Matthew, who reached his chubby arms my direction. I begged Blythe, "Can I hold him? Pretty please?"

"I'm too nervous to let him out of my arms when we're on the water," Blythe said. "Sorry, Milla."

"It's all right," I assured, hiding a smile, touched by his just-slightly-overzealous devotion. Blythe was so protective of his son that I was surprised he didn't make the little guy wear a helmet at all times. The expression in Mom's eyes was both tender and amused as she smiled and tucked loose strands of hair behind her ears. She slipped her hand under Bly's elbow and leaned to kiss his temple.

"He hardly lets *me* take him when we're out here," Mom said.

"Tilson, he's about the age when you just pitch 'em in so they learn to swim," Dodge said, with no trace of a smile. I knew Dodge was only teasing, but the look of horror that crossed Blythe's face effectively ruined the joke.

"He ain't kidding!" Uncle Justin called over from the deck of his boat, using both hands to shade his eyes, bare feet widespread to maintain balance. "I think I was about that age. It was all sink or swim for us in the Miller house!"

"Not helping!" Aunt Jilly called to her grinning husband. "Bly is turning green over here."

Mathias reached the motor boat and I admired from afar the way the powerful muscles of his back and shoulders bulged as he climbed the rope ladder, black hair sleek from the water. I went all weak-kneed and shivery-hot at the sight of him, thinking about how later tonight I would glide my hands and mouth all over those muscles. His fireman's hat was still on the floor on the far side of our bed, from last night when he wore it while I—

"Camille, you want a beer, hon?" Grandma asked, and I jerked instantly from my daydream.

"Sure," I said, and Grandma passed it to Aunt Jilly, who passed it to me, with a wink. I almost held the icy-cold can to my neck.

Clint and Tish whooped as Uncle Justin fired the outboard to growling life. He goosed it a little as he hung a sharp left and took the five of them out toward the widest part of Flickertail. Dodge hauled in the anchor rope and got the pontoon rolling, and we followed in their wake at a much more sedate pace, the engine issuing a comforting, purring *putt-putt-putt*. Millie Jo and Rae crawled onto the bench, settling themselves on their knees, facing the water and clutching the top railing.

"Those two," Aunt Jilly said fondly. "Camille, that may as well be you and Tish, once upon a time."

"It seems like yesterday you were that little," Mom said, sitting cross-legged on the bench seat. "And now look at you, a big girl getting married."

I knew she chose her words to make me smile, but even still I heard the note of wistfulness in her tone. I noticed things like that now, an extra-perceptive set of senses I'd inherited along with motherhood. I longed, suddenly, to confess to the womenfolk that Mathias and I were no longer attempting to prevent pregnancy.

Soon, I thought. *Maybe after our road trip.*

"I can't wait to see the progress on your cabin," Aunt Jilly said, ruffling her golden hair with both hands before resting them on her growing belly. "I remember partying out there back in high school, with Tina and those guys. But you two will make it a home."

"Everyone has been so wonderful about pitching in," I said. Mathias's father, Bull Carter, was so happy that we were restoring the cabin that he'd shed tears on numerous occasions. I dearly loved my future father-in-law, with whom I shared a deep bond; he and I, after all, had worked together to save Mathias last Valentine's Day, the agonizing night I'd known something was wrong and demanded that Bull leave White Oaks in the midst of a busy dinner crowd to help me find Mathias. And Bull had listened to me, without thinking I was crazy, without questioning. We'd very nearly been too late—even now, months later and with no reason to believe anything was currently wrong, my eyes swept after the motor boat, seeking reassurance that Mathias was all right.

When I looked back at Aunt Jilly, I found her gaze more speculative than normal, and worked to sound calm as I offered, "We brought the blueprints over. We can look at them when we get back to Shore Leave."

"Camille, sweetheart, I know you're doing what's right, but we'll miss you something fierce at home," Grandma said, leaning to pat my knee.

"Oh, Gram."

"*Mom*," Aunt Jilly scolded Grandma. "It's not like they'll be far away. Just a canoe ride away."

"But Millie Jo has lived with us since she was born," Grandma said, with a deep sigh, pushing her yellow sunglasses to the top of her head. Her silver hair hung in its customary braid over her left shoulder. "I don't know what I'll do with myself if I don't see her every day."

"I'll bring her over all the time," I promised. Grandma's steady presence was one of the main reasons I'd survived the first two long years of single motherhood. She and Aunt Ellen had helped me immeasurably; worlds better than any help I would have received from Noah, errant drunk that he was. And then I thought, *Stop that. You're being unnecessarily mean.*

"Lookit, there's Daddy and Clinty!" Rae yelped, pointing at the boat skimming the waves, now across the lake from us and no bigger than a toy as it flew along the gleaming surface. Clint gripped the tow rope, skiing slalom-style, as he'd been practicing since the moment the water was warm enough. Rae and Millie giggled as Clint jumped the wake and landed as smooth as whipped cream.

"Wave to them!" Aunt Jilly said, giggling at the excitement on Rae's face, mirrored on Millie Jo's.

"Are you leaving on the fourth?" Mom asked, referring to the trip Mathias and I had been planning since last winter, when we'd learned that one of Bull's cousins out in Montana had a potential lead on Malcolm Carter. Though I was reluctant to be away from Millie Jo for the week that we planned to be gone, I would be lying through and through if I didn't acknowledge the intensity of my elation at the prospect of all that time alone with Mathias. We kept calling it our "pre-honeymoon."

"July fifth," I reminded Mom.

"We can't wait to have Millie Jo all to ourselves for the entire week," Grandma said, reaching for my daughter, who ran and burrowed into Grandma's hug. Grandma smoothed tangled hair from Millie's cheeks. "Isn't that right?"

"Can we make cinnamon rolls?" Millie asked.

"Every morning!" Grandma said.

"Here, hon," Aunt Ellen said, handing me a plate. As Dodge was busy driving the pontoon, Aunt Ellen was taking care of grill duty.

Dodge used the back of his free hand to swipe at sweat on his forehead. "Nothing ever came of those gold bars from last winter?"

"No, unfortunately," I said. "I wish there was a logical explanation. I might be able to deal with everything a little better, if so."

"It reminds me of a story about Bull's grandpa, Grafton Carter, and the stories he'd tell about lost gold," Dodge said.

"Justin has mentioned that story a time or two," Aunt Jilly said, shifting to a more comfortable position.

"Bull, too. One night after…" I stumbled even still over the words, finally concluding, "After the attack, Mathias and I were talking late one night with Bull and Diana, over at their house." The pontoon was currently putt-putting past White Oaks Lodge, as grand as ever on the far shore, the setting sun caught in its windows and throwing sizzling rectangles to dazzle our vision.

"Gold lost from where?" Blythe asked, gently bouncing Matthew in his carrier, feathering the baby's downy hair. "And when?"

Aunt Ellen explained, "It's a Carter family legend. Dodge, you tell it best."

Dodge assumed his storyteller voice, the one we'd all listened to a thousand times sitting around the fire. I was certain that behind his aviators, his dark eyes had taken on a faraway sheen. "I heard the tale for the first time when I was just a boy. My pa was still alive then and he knew Grafton Carter well. Grafton was Pa's second cousin, on the Jacob Miller side, that is…"

"No, for the love, don't get into family connections," Jilly scolded. "We'll never get to the point!"

Dodge draped his wrists over the top of the big steering wheel, gazing into the middle distance as he considered—surely he was seeing into the past rather than the gleaming surface of Flickertail. In that familiar, half-dreaming tone, he continued, "Grafton swore that there was a legend in the Carter family about a letter scribbled with a map, with directions to a stolen haul of gold from sometime back in the 1870s. Not that the Carters would ever admit to thievery, being an honest lot, so surely there was a good reason for the theft. That is, if the story had any truth to it. Somewhere out west was all Grafton knew."

"Does it have anything to do with Malcolm?" I asked, hearing the reverence in my voice as I spoke his name. The old, fading picture of Malcolm Carter and his horse, Aces, was still in the top drawer of my nightstand. I'd found it over two years ago; fate, I was certain, as the discovery led me to White Oaks, and eventually Mathias.

Speculation ripe in his tone, Dodge said, "The time frame would be right. From everything I know, Malcolm was the boy who disappeared from the family history, but I don't know if he's directly connected to Grafton's story or not."

"There's no record of Malcolm after the telegram from 1876," I affirmed, heart increasing in speed at the thought; I saw the way Mom's eyebrows drew inward as she worried over what I was saying.

Aunt Jilly leaned forward, bracing her fingertips to her forehead. "There may be no record, but he lived beyond 1876, I'm certain."

"We've searched through everything that Bull could find in the attic at home and at White Oaks," I said, goosebumps shivering over my arms at Aunt Jilly's words. I believed wholeheartedly in her Notions, which she had once explained as striking her with all the unexpectedness of lightning on an otherwise clear summer night. They were often enigmatic, but when she told you something you'd do well to heed it.

"But there's more, I know there's so much more. That's what we're hoping to find in July," I added, catching my ring between the index finger and thumb of the opposite hand; just as I touched it, part of my dream from last night sprang forth, as though breaking from a leash in my mind. The disjointed flash struck me almost like a blow, and the memory of a voice, a girl's terrified, pleading voice, sent discomfort racing with little cat-feet up my spine.

"Lookit, Mama!" Millie Jo cried, pointing, and I turned to see that Mathias was skiing now. Uncle Justin angled the boat our way, cutting close enough so that the pontoon swayed with the aftershocks of the waves stirred up by the speedboat. Mathias waved to us and Millie Jo shrieked as they roared away. I refocused all my attention upon my daughter, willing away the sense of unease; I hadn't even remembered dreaming last night, until this moment.

Later, after we'd eaten our fill of burgers and chips, and the last of the day's light receded into a mauve sunset, Uncle Justin maneuvered his boat back to the dock, catching up with us. Mosquitoes grew increasingly annoying but the air was warm and soft, and we were all reluctant to retire. It was so lovely on the water, a waning half-moon crisp against the indigo sky; long fingers of translucent pink light stretched from the western horizon. Uncle Justin cut the motor and the quieter sounds of the lakeshore again took precedence in the evening, the peepers and crickets, the gentle lapping of water against the hull of both boats. Grandma and Aunt Ellen were laughing about something Dodge was saying, Aunt Jilly was collecting lifejackets from Clint, who swam over to the pontoon with an armload of them. Above our heads, little brown bats swooped through the air with their strange, choppy flight patterns, feasting on insects. A few trees down the shoreline, a crow rasped at us.

"Honey, you should come swim!" Mathias called to me, flopping into the water with both arms extended. Millie Jo and Rae shrieked and clapped as he made a gigantic splash. I hadn't wanted to get my hair wet again today but I shucked down to my swimsuit and climbed onto the bench seat to hop feet-first into the water; no belly flops for me.

"Yay, Mama!" Millie Jo cheered as I surfaced, smoothing back my hair with both hands. The water felt warm and murky this close to the dock. I kicked quickly out of the marshy weeds that waved from the bottom and ducked under as I swam, loving the feeling of submersion into this liquid existence which muffled sounds and amplified the beat of blood in my veins. Tish jumped in no more than ten feet from me, creating a maelstrom of bubbles beneath the water. I broke the surface and inhaled the evening air, kicking out my toes so that I could float on my back, hair streaming in ribbons around my head. Mathias swam close and grinned down at me as he tread water.

"I'm so glad it's summer again," I murmured, my voice sounding distorted to my ears, both under the water.

"Same here," he agreed, resting one hand on my belly, before joining me on his back. "It's so pretty out here. *Look* at that moon."

"I'm excited for our trip." I tilted my face his way, our arms making continuous, languid fluttering motions under the water, fingertips brushing.

"July can't get here fast enough," he agreed. "I can't wait to have you all to myself for a whole week, selfish or not."

I grinned at his words, tasting lake water. "Camping out, roasting marshmallows. I can't wait to see the mountains. I never have."

"They draw you in like magic, it's a little dangerous. I remember thinking as a kid when we'd drive out there that I didn't want to drive back home."

We would be following the exact route the Carters took in summers past; I thought, *Maybe this can be our family's annual trip. Wouldn't Millie love it?*

"Daddy! Catch me!" Rae begged from the deck of the pontoon, as Uncle Justin leaped gracefully into knee-high water to draw the speedboat to its lift on the far side of the dock.

"Rae-Rae, not now," Aunt Jilly said, catching the back of her daughter's lifejacket.

"Listen to your mama, teddy bear," Uncle Justin said. "We'll swim tomorrow."

"We better get out before Millie decides to jump in, too," I said, righting myself in the water, swimming for shore.

Mom and Grandma helped Aunt Jilly herd the girls away from the temptation of the lake and up the bank toward the cafe; Aunt Ellen elected to ride with Dodge over to the filling station, just around Flickertail, where the pontoon was stored at night. I covertly studied my great-aunt and Dodge, who was more a grandfather to me than anyone I'd ever known, as they chugged away, wondering when they would openly admit that they harbored feelings for each other.

"Who took my towel?" Tish yelped, hefting herself onto the dock, Ruthie on her heels. Clint waded directly to shore, bypassing the dock altogether. He found Tish's beach towel crumpled on the bank and made a show of wrapping it around his dripping body.

"Clint!" Tish yelled, and he ran, Tish in pursuit, Clint's hee-hawing donkey laugh trailing in his wake. It was somewhat reassuring to realize that despite being high school graduates, they hadn't changed much in the past few years.

Ruthie was polite enough to wait for me; I wrapped one arm around her shoulders, squeezing out my hair with the other hand, droplets falling to the dock boards like a miniature rainstorm. Mathias helped Uncle Justin grab the last of the gear from the speedboat. Up on the porch, Mom lifted Matthew out of the baby sling while Millie Jo tugged on the hem of Blythe's t-shirt, begging to be tossed into the air.

"You doing all right?" I asked my little sister as we walked through the purple twilight, keeping my voice low; I knew she'd recently broken up with her boyfriend of the past few months. Though we didn't live in the same house anymore, I tried my best to keep up with all of the matters in my sisters' lives, important or trivial. And this was far from trivial. Ruthie had been the one to end the relationship, but still. Both of my sisters had for a time "kind-of" dated Aunt Liz's sons—Aunt Liz was Uncle Justin's little sister; between Aunt Liz and her husband, Wordo, there were five kids, Lisa and Jeff from Wordo's first marriage, and then his and Aunt Liz's triplets, Fern, Linnea, and Hal—but because Ruthie was good friends with Fern and Linnea, she'd been reluctant to seriously date Hal, and decided they should just be friends.

Ruthie nodded rather than answering, hugging a little closer to me, which told me more than any words. I squeezed her more tightly in response. Both Tish and I were protective of Ruthie in a way that we weren't exactly of with one another; I wouldn't hesitate to stand up for Tish if the need arose, it was just that Tish had never required my protection, and vice versa. Tish was opinionated, quick to go on the offensive; she relished arguing her side of any issue, longing to be a lawyer like our dad since I could remember. I used to tease her about the way she felt compelled to inform people within minutes of meeting them that she was bound for a career in law.

"But?" I pressed.

"It's not about that," Ruthie said, knowing what I was thinking. "Truly."

"Then what's wrong? I could tell something was even before we left on the pontoon."

I sensed Ruthann was reluctant to admit to whatever troubled her; our footsteps carried us ever closer to the cafe and we'd subsequently lose any hope of privacy. At the last second, she admitted, "It's Tish. I'm just going to miss her so much."

Tish and Clint had both been accepted to the University of Minnesota; though the university was only a few hours' drive from Landon, I understood that Tish's departure in August would signal a change of some magnitude; both Ruthie and I knew Tish planned to return to Chicago and work in a glamorous downtown law office, just like Dad. Tish's departure at the end of summer meant she was leaving life as we'd known it, in the relative peace and contentment here at Shore Leave, for good. It would never be the same.

Before I could respond, Ruthie said, with quiet passion, "I don't want her to go. I know it's selfish, and stupid, but I can't stand the thought. I'll be so lonely without her."

"Aw, Ruthie." I stalled our progress. "I'll miss her, too. I wish she'd stay around here but you know you can't convince Tish when she's set her mind."

"I know," Ruthie sighed, swiping at stray tears before they fell and embarrassed her.

"I'll be here," I reminded her, trying for a smile. "I don't plan to go any farther than our little cabin."

Ruthie burrowed close, the same way she had since she was a little girl. I wrapped both arms around my sister, breathing the familiar scent of her shampoo, the hint of lake water clinging to her long wet curls. She and I were a little shorter than Tish, closer in height to each other. I rubbed her back, over which she'd slung her damp towel. She whispered, "But you'll be busy with your family."

"Never too busy for my sister," I amended, a little shocked that she would think so; but then again, Millie Jo and Mathias were my daily life—I focused nearly all of my attention and energy on them. I drew back enough to see Ruthie's face, studying her serious, long-lashed eyes that shone brightly even in the gathering grays of night. Her skin appeared dusky. "I know I get busy but I am always here for you, please remember that."

"Thanks, Milla," she said, and hugged me one more time.

An hour later, everyone had headed home, even if home meant just a quick walk through the woods; after talking to Ruthie, I was reminded anew how much I appreciated that my family all lived so close. Mathias, Millie Jo, and I climbed the steps to our little apartment above the garage and I managed to get my hyperactive child into bed in Clint's old room, now hers. Millie was bug-bitten, her nose and cheeks sunburnt a light pink despite my best efforts to keep her skin protected throughout the day. Millie's complexion was the only reflection of Noah in her little face; my skin was olive-toned and tanned quickly, like Dad's, while Millie had inherited her peaches-and-cream fairness from the Utleys.

"G'night, Mama," she whispered as I tucked her into bed. Mathias was in the shower, singing as he always did when there, but Millie was so used to this that her eyelids fluttered toward sleep despite the sound. I smoothed curls from her forehead.

"Good-night, baby," I whispered. "See you in the morning."

"Say 'don't let the bedbugs bite,'" she reminded me, half-asleep.

"Don't let the bedbugs bite," I repeated dutifully, kissing her nose. Millie settled her right arm on the pillow over her head and was snoring almost immediately after this statement.

I eased her door to within two inches of being shut and then proceeded to the bathroom, stepping over and subsequently ignoring the piles of dirty clothes shed on the tile floor there, the shambles of combs, brushes, gels, toothpaste, and cosmetics strewn over the miniscule countertop. Since living together as of last February, Mathias and I had discovered that neither of us was particularly organized, neat, or concerned about household messes. It was a relief that we were both relaxed in this regard, though our place wasn't exactly company-worthy at any given moment. I unhooked my bikini top and slipped from the bottoms, still damp from the lake, letting both pieces fall to the floor atop Mathias's swim trunks, already smiling as I drew aside the aqua-blue shower curtain to join him.

Mathias stood facing me, head tipped back in the spray, singing even as water purled over his face. At my entrance, he opened his eyes and grinned, dimple flashing, beckoning to me as he continued crooning the chorus to an old Travis Tritt song, "Drift Off to Dream." We were hooked on old-school country. I shivered with undiluted pleasure, my nipples tightening and swelling at the sight of him, my man in the steamy shower, powerful and gorgeous, his black hair dripping down his neck, all of the dark, curling hair on his body riotous in the shower's steam. He wrapped me close, already growing hard, strong hands gliding down my back, pulling me flush against him, still humming the song.

I dug my fingers into his hair as he licked a path down my neck. He lavished attention upon my breasts, his tongue swift and hot on the swell of my flesh, both hands spread wide on my ribcage as the showerhead poured hot water over us. He went next to his knees, grasping my hips.

Hi, I said with no sound. I cupped his face, his handsome, unshaven face, moving my fingers tenderly over him, even as desire beat fiercely between my legs.

Hi, honey, he said back, pressing an open-mouthed kiss to my palm, caressing my hipbones with his thumbs. I traced the outline of his sensual lips and shivered again, as he grinned knowingly and rested his face against my belly. He let his tongue make patterns over my wet skin before bracing his chin against my belly button and looking up at me, eyelids slightly hooded.

Yes, I said, again without sound, and with no further encouragement he bent his face between my legs, taking me over the edge and then beyond, holding me upright when my legs would have given out in the desperate need to spread around his hips, reduced to primal instinct for the countless time since the night we first made love.

"I need you...*right now*..." I ordered when I could bear no more, and Mathias surged to his feet, lifting my legs around his hips and entering my body with all the force I needed and craved, right down to my bones. He braced me against the yellow shower tiles and I bit the top of his shoulder to keep from waking my daughter with my cries, my fingernails creating deep crescents in his back. He groaned, his tongue reclaiming my mouth just as possessively as his cock claimed me, lower down.

"*Yes,*" I gasped, over and over, and swore I saw stars from the intensity of our lovemaking.

We clung together in the steaming shower for some time after, our bodies still joined. Mathias smoothed wild, tangled hair away from my cheeks and studied me somberly, his eyes replete with love. He kissed the scar on my top lip and then licked water droplets from my mouth and chin. He asked quietly, "Do you know how much I love you?"

I tightened my arms and legs around his strong, wet body, whispering, "I do know," and tears of joy gathered in the corners of my eyes; one trailed down my left cheek, and he nudged it away with his nose.

He said, "It only gets stronger every day. I wake up and see you and it hits me all over again. I never imagined I would feel this way in my life. I can hardly bear to be apart from you long enough to go to work." And then he grinned a little, making fun of himself. "God, I don't mean to sound crazy. You know what I mean."

His words, crazy or not, pleased me immeasurably, and I felt just the same. The second I saw his truck coming up the driveway toward Shore Leave in the jewel tones of evening light, all was right again in the world. I held him by both ears and said what I'd been thinking earlier. "You *are* crazy. But you are also mine." My throat choked around a lump of intensity as I called him by my special nickname, the one no one but me used, "You are my love, Thias. I need you so much."

Against my lips he murmured, "Honey, let's get dried off and in our bed. Our full-size, non-feather bed in which I am going to practice making you my wife."

I giggled as he kissed me, already nodding agreement.

Chapter Three

"JILLY-HONEY, YOU WANT ANYTHING?" JUSTIN CALLED FROM
the kitchen, where I imagined him standing in the wedge of light created by the open fridge, hoping just like I often did that something delicious and easy to prepare had magically appeared on its clear-plastic shelves. I wasn't much of a cook and neither was Justin, but somehow we managed. We'd arrived home from Shore Leave a half hour ago, the kids drooping with exhaustion from an evening spent on the lake.

Early this morning I'd told Justin everything Joelle told me while sitting on the porch swing. By the dawn's light, which painted the log walls of our bedroom with a cheerful rosy-orange glow, my rage over Aubrey's words seemed misplaced, even ridiculous, though I nearly writhed with embarrassment as I explained that the person whose expensive little car I'd crunched in the parking lot belonged to his ex-wife, and that she was...unhappy about this situation.

Justin's expression went from mildly concerned to outright amused as I related this particular part of the tale. He tucked an arm under his head, still relaxed on his pillow, and teased, "Are you sure you didn't realize it was her car? God, it's actually funny, in its own way."

Irritation instantly replaced all other emotions. "*Funny?*"

He repeated calmly, "Yes, funny. Don't spend one second worrying about Aubrey and her endless need for drama. It's what she would want, Jills."

I flopped to my back and pressed both hands to my forehead, closing my eyes, probably irrationally upset, but upset nonetheless. Justin rolled to his elbow; I could sense his grin and it angered me all the more. Just to be a pain in the ass, I grumbled, "Doesn't it bother you *at all* that she demanded *you* fix her car? That she thought she had the right to drive over to the shop and accost Dodge?"

Maintaining a reasonable tone, my husband said, "I can't believe it bothers you this much, baby. I shudder at the thought of even hearing her voice. God, I wasted too many years with that woman as it was."

"But she wanted to see *you*," I pressed, digging the heels of my hands into my eyes and rubbing.

There was a moment of total silence before Justin, with an air of dawning awareness, asked, "Jillian Rae, are you *jealous?*"

Because he'd hit the nail so close to the head I rolled away from him, mortified that I'd pushed it this far. Of course I wasn't jealous. I knew better than that.

"*No,*" I muttered, as though insulted.

"I don't know if I should be shocked or flattered," Justin said then, and I could tell he was grinning now, relishing this opportunity to tease me. He decided, "I have to say, I'm pretty damn flattered."

I snatched a pillow and thwacked him across the head. He blocked my next shot with crossed forearms, laughing.

"You should be so lucky!" I bitched, and then contradicted myself in the next moment as I pretty much yelled, "*I'm not jealous!*"

He was rendered almost breathless by his laughter, and with disgust I threw aside the pillow. My eyes had teared up and before he could notice, I struggled from the bed and stormed, as much as a pregnant woman is able, to the bathroom. The slam of the door was particularly satisfying. Attempting to sound contrite, Justin called, "Baby, come on!"

I heard Rae in our room then. "Daddy, can you make pancakes?"

Clint must have been on her heels, as he followed up with, "And bacon? Please, Dad?"

I knew it meant the world to Justin that Clint called him Dad. I'd never asked Clint to do so; it was something he started on his own. Once, not long after my car accident, Clint explained that he loved Justin because Justin made me so happy; in that conversation, Clint had teared up admitting how glad he was that Justin was going to be his father. Just considering those truths dissolved my anger in a burst similar to an exploding firework. Even so, I soaked in the hot shower for a good fifteen minutes to calm down before joining my family in the kitchen for a breakfast of blueberry pancakes (one food item Justin could manage to prepare).

Now, twelve hours later, Rae was asleep in her toddler bed and Clint on his phone; I could hear the muted sound of his voice from behind his closed bedroom door. Lying on the bed, I slid my bare legs over the softness of our top sheet, luxuriating in the fact that most of the day's humidity had dissipated. The bedroom windows were propped open to the pleasantly cool air. I was not in favor of shutting out the sounds of the night, even if it meant keeping the air conditioner from running. We kept a small fan near the bed and I loved the tinkle of the wind chimes strung at Rae's height in our blue spruces, the peaceful breath of an occasional breeze, the sigh of it through the lush summer leaves. From our bedside table, the trailing bouquet of honeysuckle blossoms I'd picked this afternoon scented the entire room with rich sweetness.

"No, I'm not hungry!" I called back.

Seconds later Justin appeared in the bedroom and just like that I felt a jolt in my heart. I smiled in a lazy fashion at my sexy husband, who remained shirtless, his swim trunks riding low on his lean hips. One little tug and he'd be completely naked. He let his dark, smoldering gaze travel down my body before coming back to my eyes.

"Those flowers smell so good," he said, holding my gaze in his. He leaned on his forearms over the end of the bed and caught my ankles in his hands. He slid his palms up the backs of my calves and tilted to kiss the inside of my left knee. His lips were warm and the lightning bolt in my heart zinged at once southward.

"You're not hungry…at all?" he questioned quietly.

"Maybe just a little," I allowed, and he climbed over the end of the bed and cupped my belly, smoothing his broad palms in gentle circular motions, as someone stroking a crystal ball.

"Hi, son," he murmured, resting his chin on the crest of my rounded stomach. Love for him, and for our children, both the two down the hall and the one yet within me, flooded my soul, and I berated myself for how I'd acted this morning. I reached to tuck a strand of his black hair, even wilder than normal from the evening on the lake, behind his ear.

"Justin," I whispered, a catch in my throat. Outside, one of the gray owls called and Justin moved with fluid grace, bracing carefully over me and taking my face in his strong hands. He traced my lips with his thumbs before lowering his mouth to mine and kissing me so softly that I shivered.

"I know, baby," he whispered, reading my eyes. "I know it."

"I was just thinking of the summer you started calling me 'Jilly-Anne.'" I twined my arms around his neck. "You must have known how much I crushed on you, even way back then."

"I wasn't observant enough that summer, but subconsciously maybe I had a clue." He kissed my nose and then my chin, which he bit lightly, sliding one hand down my ribs as he ran his tongue along my bottom lip. "You're so soft. Soft as silk, baby, I can't touch you enough."

"I need your mouth…right here…" I pressed my breasts against his bare, hairy chest. Justin nipped my collarbone, easing the soft, stretched-out white tank top I was wearing over my left shoulder. My nipples nearly sliced through the material. Pregnancy made my nerves, my skin, so very sensitive that I could hardly bear the teasing. I clarified breathlessly, "Right now, I mean."

Justin skimmed the tank top over my head without further ado. Tenderly, expertly, he caressed with his tongue, taking me between his teeth, suckling by turns, knowing exactly what I needed. He lifted his head, voice a little hoarse as he observed, "It's kinda like palming basketballs, these days."

I giggled. "Basketballs with nipples, you mean."

He murmured, "You taste so good, baby…"

At that moment our son landed a kick on the inner curve of my belly, strong enough that I gasped in surprise and Justin raised his head, eyebrows lofted high.

"Holy shit, that was a big one." He studied my stomach as though imagining the baby boxing his way free of the confines.

"He's not done yet," I said, rising to both elbows and observing what was surely a tiny heel pressing outward just beneath my ribs, distorting the roundness.

"Oh, wow." Justin laughed a little, following the baby's movements with his fingertips. "I love when I can see him. Look there."

I smiled at his expression. "I *feel* it, believe me. Wow, he's on a roll now."

"It doesn't hurt you, does it? I don't remember Rae kicking you so hard when she was in there."

I shook my head and admitted, "It's uncomfortable, but it doesn't hurt. He's definitely more active than his big sister. Clinty was that way, too. Maybe it's a boy thing."

"Whoa!" My belly subtly changed shape with each new kick and his tone was that of someone on the sidelines of an athletic competition.

"Shoulda had a beer before bed," I teased, which was exactly what Gran would have told me to do, and Justin laughed, resting on one elbow near my hips.

"I can just hear Louisa saying that," he recognized, pressing a kiss to my stomach.

"He was quiet all afternoon," I said, settling comfortably on my left side. "When I'm moving he sleeps and then when I finally lie down he thinks it's a free-for-all."

Justin stroked my skin, almost lulling me to sleep. After a time he said softly, "I'm sorry I teased you this morning."

"Don't be sorry." I opened my eyes. "I was being ridiculous."

"No, you weren't," he said, shifting back up the bed. He caught my hip in his right hand and aligned his much longer body so that we lay face to face. "I wouldn't like it either, if the situation was somehow reversed."

He always tread gently when it came to an even indirect reference to Clint's dad, Christopher, who died in a snowmobile accident the winter Clint was three. The aching sadness that had permeated my every movement for years after finally let me be, replaced by a sense of fading sweetness at the memories of the time Chris and I spent together.

I whispered, "I was so jealous of Aubrey once, I guess it's still in the back of my mind."

"There's nothing to be jealous of, not ever. You know that."

"I do," I murmured. "It's just that she…the way she talks…"

"I know," he acknowledged. "She loves to make a scene. She's not content unless she thinks everyone is paying attention."

"Like Jackson," I said, referring to Joelle's ex-husband. Justin's thumb moved in slow circles over my bare thigh and I squirmed, desire sparking along my nerves.

Justin agreed, "Exactly like him."

I admitted, "I still hate her!"

"Aw, honey, don't waste your time."

"I know it's stupid…"

"Jillian Rae Miller, my wife, my sweet little woman, it's not stupid, and I don't mean to change the subject, but I have a problem right now…"

I snorted at this pronouncement. He had a "problem" that needed my attention at least once a day. I smoothed my left hand down his powerful torso, curling my fingers into his chest hair.

"I really am flattered that you were jealous," he couldn't resist, and at that I pinched his belly.

He smothered a laugh even as I sputtered in a whisper, "You really want to talk that way to the woman who planned to help you with this?" My hand had reached its destination. "It seems like a pretty gigantic problem to me."

He made a sound deep in his throat and pressed against my palm, covering the back of my hand with his own. His dark eyes blazed, and he kissed the outer corner of my mouth, promising in a whisper, "I'll stop talking."

"You do that," I said against his lips, and felt him grin as he got us both completely naked almost before I could blink.

Monday morning dawned clear and fresh, the scent of dew-spangled grass and blue spruces flowing in the open window. Justin usually got up for work around seven-thirty and Rae rolled out of bed around the same time; Clinty, my night owl, rarely appeared in the kitchen before ten. I still worked lunch shifts a few days a week and even though the cafe was closed today, Rae and I walked through the woods to Shore Leave after breakfast. I knew Aunt Ellen would have a fresh pot of coffee perking and probably something delicious just coming out of the oven, and I craved the company of the womenfolk. We waved to Justin as he headed for his and Dodge's mechanic shop. He blew us a kiss, and I collected Rae's hand and let her lead the way among the familiar trees.

"Lookit, Mama, a blue jay!" she said as we ambled along the path through the woods, sun dappling our shoulders with little leaf-cutout shadows. I smoothed my hand over her golden hair as she grinned up at me with her long-lashed brown eyes that were exactly like Justin's. I thought of how she liked to kneel on his lap and pat her hands and trace her little fingers over the scars on his face; she had never been afraid of them, calling them 'Daddy's scratchies.' She asked him once if they hurt, to which he'd replied, "No, sweetheart, not at all," prompting Rae to promise, "But if they do, Daddy, I'll kiss them for you."

Justin was once so self-conscious of his scars that it had almost ended our relationship before it even fully began; it took some damn hard convincing on my part that they didn't bother me at all, that he didn't look like a monster. I realized that other people might not share this opinion; I bore witness to the way people who did not know him, out-of-towners in Landon for example, would do a double-take when they caught sight of his face. I saw only the man I loved, the stubborn, passionate, loving man who'd staked a claim in my heart back when we were little kids. An accident in his repair shop led to the red, rope-like scars that crisscrossed the right side of his face and continued down along his neck. But as I'd told him years ago, it was this accident that eventually led us to one another.

I breathed deeply of the fresh morning air, smelling the lake, a scent as dear and familiar to me as any I knew. I didn't want to let the thought of Aubrey Pritchard ruin the morning in even a small way, but she intruded despite my best efforts. I acknowledged that if Justin's face had never been scarred he may very well still be married to Aubrey; though they'd weathered problems in their marriage prior to the accident, it was the catalyst that finally ended their relationship and Aubrey left him for another man.

God, Jilly, you're being completely ridiculous. It's not like you to get so ruffled.

But just the idea of Justin still somehow belonging to that smirking snake of a woman made me nauseous. Shore Leave came into view through the trees and Rae darted ahead, effectively refocusing the direction of my thoughts.

"Don't run into the parking lot!" I yelled after her, even though the cafe wasn't open. Other than Dodge, who stopped out every morning for coffee, only Mom, Aunt Ellen, Camille, and Millie Jo would be around and about, but still. Supply trucks often rumbled through the lot on early Monday mornings like this. Rae changed course and trotted back to me as I continued at a more sedate pace past Mom and Aunt Ellen's white clapboard house, the one in which I'd been raised, and then the detached garage with its second-floor apartment, painted a cheerful yellow, where Clint and I had moved when he was just a toddler, shortly after Chris died.

"C'mon, Mama!" Rae ordered, standing with hands on hips. She wore a pair of orange shorts and a matching tank top, dotted with multicolored flowers. I smiled and wondered if any child, ever, looked so adorable.

"Mama's coming," I assured her as we reached the cafe, Flickertail Lake a muted indigo blue, still mostly in shade as the sun slowly crested the trees on the eastern shore. Mathias's work truck was the only vehicle in the lot. I heard Mom and Aunt Ellen chatting through the open window, and then Millie Jo raced to the screen door.

"Rae!" she squealed.

I loved how they always acted as though they were being reunited after months apart. The door sang on its aging hinges as I entered the warm space, smelling coffee and cinnamon rolls, just as I'd been hoping.

"Hi, sweetie," Aunt Ellen said; she and Mom were situated at table three, as usual.

"Jillian, Dodge told us about Aubrey's car," Mom said without preamble.

Dammit. It was the last thing I wanted to talk about, but in our family nothing was ever a secret for long.

"Yeah, how stupid, huh?" I asked, joining them, trying for a self-deprecating tone.

"You know I don't insure that damn old truck," Mom said. "Why ever did you drive it into town?"

"My trunk's full," I explained shortly, fetching my coffee mug. I poured a steaming cup and added two sugar packets. Stirring with just a touch more force than necessary, I added, "I didn't figure you'd mind."

"I don't mind. I just wish you hadn't taken off someone's headlight with it."

"Joanie, let it rest. Dodge will fix it up and we'll be done with it," Aunt Ellen scolded. It had always been their dynamic; whatever Mom cast out of proportion, Aunt Ellen reeled back into perspective.

"Jo told me about how Aubrey stormed out to the shop on Saturday, like I'd hit her car on purpose," I said, and now I was the one not letting it rest. "As though I could have known it was *her* fucking car."

Aunt Ellen hid a smile behind a sip of coffee while Mom frowned at my cursing. Ellen and Mom looked as much alike as older versions of Jo and me, with fair hair going gray, pale skin prone to cinnamon-colored freckles in the summer months, and eyes of a rich golden-green. I was the oddball, having inherited my father Mick Douglas's blue eyes instead.

"Jilly, the kids," Mom complained.

"They aren't paying attention," I muttered, only half-apologetic.

"Dodge was more concerned than he let on about Aubrey causing problems if she could," Aunt Ellen admitted, and she knew Dodge better than anyone, even if she would not openly acknowledge this if confronted. She patted my hand. "But don't you worry, Jilly, there's nothing that ridiculous woman can do except bluster."

"I was a little bit upset yesterday," I said on a sigh, still downplaying. "Justin talked me out of it."

"Good for him," Mom said. She called to the girls, "You two want a treat?" and they scampered over.

"Aunt Jilly, I helped make these," Millie Jo told me, pointing to the cinnamon rolls, and I ran a palm over her soft curls; she looked so much like Camille.

"That's nice of you to help Grandma."

"There's the lovebirds," Mom observed as she dished out rolls for Rae and Millie Jo. I followed her gaze out the front windows to spy Camille and Mathias in the parking lot, kissing good-bye near his truck. I was amused by the sight of them even as I considered Jo's words from last night; Mathias Carter was, as Jo and I would have said in high school, a total fox. He was hunky, with a killer grin and the kind of powerful shoulders that drew second glances like a honeysuckle blossom drew bees. And yet, despite his undeniably strong and capable physical appearance, there was a sweetness, a vulnerability, about him—that spurred within me a sense of need to protect, aggravated by the bizarre events in the woods last February, when he'd been struck and dragged over the frozen ground by an unknown assailant. I knew Camille was plagued by this sensation as well. As though the loss of him was somehow inevitable.

Just relax, I thought, clamping down upon such thoughts. *Quit worrying so much. You're letting your imagination run wild, same as always, instead of paying attention to what is right before your eyes.* And I couldn't help but smile as I observed, *He's plenty fine, right out there.*

The way Mathias looked at her, Camille would probably be pregnant by nightfall. Probably I should call Jo.

"Hi, guys!" Camille chirped when she breezed into the cafe a minute later, as Mathias drove away. "Hi, Aunt Jilly! How's the baby?"

"He's all tired out from keeping me awake half the night," I said, cupping her elbow as she caught me in a quick, one-armed hug. She smelled sweet, like lilacs, or maybe lily-of-the-valley. The long ripples of her hair brushed softly against my cheek.

"Millie Jo-Jo," Camille scolded, trying and failing to catch the little girl into her arms. She called after her daughter, "Wipe your fingers before you touch anything!"

"What're your plans for the day, sweetie?" Mom asked Camille. "You and Millie heading over to White Oaks later?"

"Yep," she said, finding her coffee mug and joining us. "We're helping Bull varnish the porch. Or," she amended, "We're keeping him company while he varnishes."

Bull and Mathias would likely complete ninety percent of the renovation on the old cabin, rather than relying on hiring out the work. Much like Justin and Dodge, who were actually related to Bull and his family through a second-cousin connection, the Carters tended to be self-sufficient.

"Can Millie sleep over tonight?" I asked Camille. "Rae has been begging."

"She'd love to, but Noah is picking her up this evening for a few hours. Maybe tomorrow?"

"Now who's this?" Mom muttered, peering out the window. "I don't recognize the car."

We all watched as the unfamiliar vehicle, a small green canoe strapped to its roof, came to a halt near the porch, its bumper scraping the raised cement strip separating the parking lot from the grass. A man climbed out, straightened his sunglasses, and then cast his eyes toward the cafe.

"Lost, maybe?" Aunt Ellen wondered aloud.

He climbed up the porch steps and either didn't notice or totally disregarded the CLOSED sign on the screen door, stepping inside without so much as a courtesy knock.

"Can we help you?" Mom asked in her most contrary voice, the one I recognized from my high school days, pruning up her lips. We all studied this intrusive stranger with varying degrees of irritation. He was wiry and darkly tanned, and as he removed his sunglasses I saw that his eyes were just slightly too close together, giving him a vaguely eerie appearance. Maybe this was an uncharitable observation, but as his gaze skimmed over all of us and decided to rest on me, I felt a distinct flutter of misgiving.

"Sorry to interrupt you, ladies," he said in an easy tone, immediately causing me to second-guess my apprehension. He sounded normal, even nice. "Ed Sorenson directed me out this way. I'm over from Moorhead State, collecting water samples in the county. Ed said your place has the best coffee on the lake."

Mom allowed a grudging smile. "Well, we aren't technically open this morning, but I suppose we could offer you a cup."

"Have a seat, young fellow," Aunt Ellen invited, and he grabbed a chair from an adjacent table and joined us, plunking down between Camille and Aunt Ellen, which put him almost directly across the table from me. He smelled rather strongly of aftershave, not pleasantly so, settling his sunglasses so they fit like a headband. He was probably in his late twenties, with close-cropped hair, a lean face and those odd eyes that gave him an impression of something vaguely reptilian, even as he smiled at me with apparent friendliness. Maybe it was the mascot image of the curling, fire-breathing dragon on his Moorhead State t-shirt that put the thought in my head.

Camille rose and poured him a cup of coffee; he accepted it with a polite thanks.

"Zack Dixon," he said by way of introduction.

"Joan Davis," Mom said, shaking his hand and then indicating the rest of us. "This is my sister, Ellen Davis, my daughter, Jillian Miller, and my granddaughter, Camille Gordon."

"And you guys run this cafe?" he asked Mom, taking a sip of his coffee.

"It's been in our family for decades," Aunt Ellen explained.

"That's great." He leaned back and tipped the chair on its hind legs. "Ed Sorenson spoke highly of you guys. He said you're one tough family."

Mom and Aunt Ellen laughed at this, rolling their eyes. Mom replied, "We prefer 'wise' to 'tough,' don't we, Ell?"

"Eddie's been on the receiving end of your temper a time or two," Aunt Ellen reminded Mom, who laughed a little in agreement. "It's a fair statement."

"Are you staying long in town?" Mom asked Zack.

"I drove over yesterday from Moorhead and got a room at the Angler's Inn," he explained. "I plan to hit Itasca and Tamarac on the way back."

"Do you teach at the university?" Aunt Ellen asked.

"No, I'm doing grad studies." His eyes again flashed over to me though I sat silently, not contributing to the conversation at all. He kept his gaze steady as he added, as though speaking just to me, "I have a month or so to do some research around here. I plan to fish and do a little hiking in these parts. It's great here. You guys are lucky to live here year-round."

I poured myself a second cup of coffee.

"Winters aren't easy in these parts," Mom said. "But you're right, it is beautiful here. Summer makes it all worth it."

"I'm from St. Louis, originally. I moved up here to go to college and haven't left yet," he said.

"Well, feel free to stop out for coffee a time or two while you're in town," Aunt Ellen said. "Ours is the best on the lake."

"I will, thanks. Do you care if I leave my car out here when I put my boat in?"

"That's fine," Mom said. "Just park farther out in the lot when we're open, if you don't mind." And then to Ellen, "Here comes the truck."

"You live around here, too?" Zack asked me as Mom and Ellen were distracted by the rumbling arrival of a supply trailer. He braced forward on his elbows, abruptly enough that I leaned just slightly away. His eyes were a pale silvery-blue, with pupils that appeared smaller than normal, hardly pinpricks.

Emphasizing my words more than necessary, I replied, "Yes, my husband and I live near here."

He nodded at this information, studying me without letup.

Mom said, "Excuse us."

Zack said immediately, "Thanks for the hospitality. Nice to meet you."

"You, too," Mom said, distracted as she and Aunt Ellen stood to go and meet the truck driver at the back entrance, around behind the kitchen and the stock pantry.

"Come on, Millie Jo-Jo," Camille called to her daughter, also planning to head out for the day.

Left virtually alone with Zack Dixon at table three, I opened my mouth to take my own leave when he indicated Rae and Millie. "So, are those your kids?"

"One of them," I said, a little stunned at the clipped hostility in my tone. I wanted him out of here, it was that simple.

He replied with, "You seem to be a pretty fertile family," directing a nod at my belly. I wore an old green maternity tank top that Jo had lent me, and was further stunned that he let his eyes linger on the rounded curve of my breasts; pregnancy gave me a considerable boost in the chest department, but still. It was undeniably suggestive and outright rude for him to be so obvious.

"Walk me to my car?" he asked when I didn't respond, setting his cup on the table and offering me a smile. I was reminded at once of a shark.

I straightened my spine and managed to keep my voice low. "Are you fucking kidding me?"

His eyebrows lifted at my words. And something shifted in his eyes, buried instantly, almost before I recognized the threat; I blinked, so discomfited by him that I felt a curl of nausea across my gut. But nothing more. Where there should have been a flash, a sensing, the usual vibrant, unseen cord that connected my awareness to everything around me, there was only emptiness. It was this more than anything that caused the next breath to lodge in my lungs.

"Touchy," he said lightly, casting his eyes to the table, his tone conveying unmistakable embarrassment. "Sorry I asked."

I was compelled to say, "It's all right."

"Thanks for the coffee," he said, meeting my gaze once more. This time he seemed nothing but friendly. He added, "See you around," before rising and heading outside, and seconds later was unloading gear from the backseat of his car. I stood and observed as he unstrapped his canoe and hefted it over his head, before proceeding to the lake without a backward glance. I stood watching a moment longer, second-guessing myself, while behind me Camille teased Millie and Rae.

He's harmless, and you're being unfair.

His eyes are fucking creepy though.

That's hardly his fault.

It's everything with Aubrey, I decided. *You're just more worked up than normal.*

"You have a second to talk before you go to White Oaks?" I turned around to ask Camille.

"Of course. I've been wanting to talk to you, too."

"Let's go sit on the dock," I suggested. "It's cooler out there."

By the time we'd buckled the girls into their lifejackets and made our way down the incline to the water, I was relieved to see that Zack Dixon was well on his way across Flickertail, no more than a speck as he paddled. Camille and I settled on the end of the dock, letting our feet dangle into the water, as the girls held hands and jumped in together, proceeding to play and dog-paddle near our legs. Camille stooped to pick a few of the long-stemmed daisies that bobbed near the south side of the cafe and trailed these along her neck, her eyes fixed meditatively on the far shore.

"Your mom and I talked for a while last night," I began, stirring up the water with both feet.

"Mom's worried, I know." Camille let the flowers rest upon her lap. Her loose hair hung down her back in waves; the lake breeze plucked at it like gentle fingers. I was reminded suddenly of a conversation we'd shared almost three years ago now, sitting at a booth in the cafe, Camille newly pregnant and terrified at the prospect of caring for an infant. She'd come so far since that afternoon, had discovered within herself a well of strength and capability; she now had a sweet daughter and a fiancé who would do anything for them. The Camille from three summers ago, lonely and disillusioned, would never have believed it possible, and so I understood her fear of it all being swept away—the whole idea that something too good to be true often proves just so, that somehow she didn't deserve this much happiness.

"Not about Mathias," I clarified. "We all love him, I hope you know."

Her entire face lit like a candle at my words. She rested her chin against her shoulder to look at me and said softly, "I do know. Isn't he amazing?"

"He is." Mostly to keep the buoyant smile on her face, I tattled, "But Jo is worried you're going to get pregnant before your wedding."

Camille giggled, sounding momentarily like a younger version of herself, scooping her hair into one hand and drawing it over her shoulder. Beneath her tan, I saw the heat that spread like a wine spill across her cheeks. In a tone that suggested a major confession, she asked, "Aunt Jilly, can I tell you something?"

"Oh my God, you're *already* pregnant," I realized. "I should have known, you have that glow about you…"

Camille fluttered her hands in the air, still giggling. "No, no. Not yet. But we decided to stop using birth control, just this week."

I nodded at this announcement, debating whether I should tell Jo or let it rest. Camille saw the indecision on my face and hurried to say, "Don't worry, I'll tell Mom soon."

"I'm not worried." I folded her hand in mine. Her fingers were long and slim, but strong as they curled around mine, holding fast. "I think it's the right decision for you two. It just seems so right thinking of that little homestead cabin full of babies, you know?"

Tears spangled her long lashes as she nodded, squeezing my fingers. "Oh, I do. I *so* do. I've thought that since I first went out there to see it, that spring with Bull, before I even met Mathias." Her gaze moved to Millie Jo, busy splashing and shrieking with Rae, and she whispered, "I was so sure that Millie would never have a brother or sister."

I let go of her hand to smooth my palm over her back, as I had when she was a little girl. "I know exactly how you feel, I really do. After Chris died, I figured Clinty would always be an only child."

"Clint's such a good big brother. And I love that he calls Uncle Justin 'Dad.' I wish…" She paused, clearly torn, before admitting, "I wish Millie Jo could call Mathias that. He's so much more a father to her than Noah will ever be."

"Does Millie call Noah 'Daddy?'" I asked.

"Not in front of me. I guess I don't help that very much…I always call him 'Noah' when I talk about him to her. That's probably shitty of me." Her tone was carefully hopeful that I wouldn't agree.

I said gently, "If Noah's trying, which he seems to be, then probably that's a little shitty, hon."

She sighed, studying the far shore. "I know. I should be grateful that he's trying. I think he's drinking again, though."

"He looks pretty rough every time I've seen him lately. But that doesn't necessarily mean he's fallen off the wagon."

"He was at Eddie's with a couple of friends, Eddie told me," Camille said, shading her eyes as the sun increased in intensity. In a few more minutes, we would have to tote out the sunscreen. "When I confronted him about it last week he said he was the sober cab for his friends. But I think it's just plain stupid to put yourself in a situation like that when you've clearly got a problem."

"You, and friends and family of alcoholics everywhere. At least he's trying to be a part of Millie's life now. That's an improvement."

"It is, I can't deny it," she said, in a tone that suggested she wanted badly to deny it, and more than likely, simply deny *him* and his potential role in Millie's life; I struggled to muster up any real sympathy for Noah Utley, whose behavior toward Camille and their child, especially that first year, could be described as nothing short of pathetic. But considering the way Noah had appeared lately, I felt a twinge of pity for him—not that I'd admit this to my niece.

Instead, I changed the subject, remembering my actual intent. "Your mom told me last night that Mathias came to ask her what he could do about your nightmares. He's worried about you."

Camille murmured, "I didn't realize he'd talked to Mom."

"I wish *I* knew how to help you. I know that there's something unresolved, something much older than you or Mathias, something from the past. But I don't know if you have the power to change it. Or mend it." I wished for the countless time since she'd passed away that I could somehow speak directly with Great-Aunt Minnie. Although she came to me in dreams, it was hardly the same thing as a real conversation; I longed for her stern, reassuring presence, and had since the day she'd died. Of all the womenfolk in our family, no one understood me the way Minnie had, and I ached with missing her, even still. I shifted on the dock boards to relieve the pressure on my tailbone; I finally admitted, "I can't get a better handle on it than that, not yet. But I'll keep trying."

Camille caught her engagement ring between the thumb and index finger of her right hand, studying it in the sunlight. "If I understood what happened last winter, I could rest easier," she said, pale at the remembrance. "We have absolutely no answers, no idea what would have motivated it. Whoever attacked Mathias is still out there and all we have are those stupid gold bars with fingerprints that weren't in any database. What in the hell?"

For a split second I thought, *Zack Dixon…*

But he'd only just arrived in Landon—he hadn't been here last February.

So he said.

Camille continued, "If we could find out what happened to Malcolm, I feel like that might be a start. Who was Cora? What was he searching for? Sometimes I feel like I'm so close to knowing, right in that moment before you fall asleep, you know, when your leg jerks all of a sudden and wakes you up?"

I nodded, forcing myself to set aside these new fears bubbling inside of me since Zack's arrival at Shore Leave.

"I feel like the answers are right there, and then when I come fully awake they get snapped back up inside my mind. It's exhausting." Camille brought her left hand to her lips, kissing the ring there as though invoking a talisman. "I love Mathias so much, Aunt Jilly. That picture of Malcolm led me to him, and I will be thankful for that, for always. But a part of me is scared…I don't even like talking about this… I'm so afraid that something might happen. That I can't possibly be this happy without some sort of consequence…"

With as firm a tone as I could muster, I ordered, "Camille, *stop*. You know what you sound like?"

She looked my way with the exact expression that graced my son's face when he didn't want to hear what I intended to say. I explained softly, "You sound like someone who hasn't had enough sleep. You need rest. It's tough to be rational when you're overtired."

She finally nodded agreement. "You're right, I know you're right. But it's almost like…"

"Like what?" I encouraged.

Her eyes darted across the lake, in the direction of White Oaks. She whispered, "I feel like…I *owe* Malcolm. I know it sounds crazy."

"It's not crazy. Would discovering what happened to him fulfill what you owe?"

She used the back of her wrists to swipe the tears away. "I'm counting on that."

Later, Justin drove over from the filling station to have lunch with Rae and me, like usual. After Camille and Millie Jo left for White Oaks, Aunt Ellen and I made bacon cheeseburgers and coleslaw, and Rae sweet-talked Mom into stirring up a batch of brownies.

"It smells amazing in here," Justin said. I met him halfway and he scooped me into a hug. I kissed his jaw.

"I hope you're hungry." Though he'd shaved this morning, he already had a five o'clock shadow going; he wore his typical work attire—an old t-shirt with the sleeves torn off and faded jeans. He looked better than dessert.

"Always," he said.

"Daddy!" Rae barreled through the swinging door that led to the kitchen.

"Hi, teddy bear," he said, catching her up into his strong arms. Rae giggled and Justin planted a kiss on her nose. "You been listening to Mama today?"

She nodded with vigorous enthusiasm.

"Whose car?" Justin jerked a thumb over his shoulder to indicate Zack Dixon's; in a small town, we all knew one another's vehicles, and no one parked out at Shore Leave that he didn't know, not when we were closed. He clearly saw something in my eyes, as he asked in a different tone, "What is it, Jills?"

Rae squirreled down and galloped back to the kitchen before I could answer, and Justin straddled a stool at the counter, reaching for me. Like a magnet to its mate I moved into his embrace, hooking my arms around his neck, my belly cushioned safely between us. He studied me, unblinking, and asked again, softly, "What?"

"There's something about him that bothers me." Even if I was being irrational, it was the truth.

Justin's eyebrows drew slightly together. "About who?"

"The guy who owns that car." In Justin's arms, what distressed me about Zack Dixon seemed insubstantial, even ridiculous. I explained, "Eddie directed him out here. At least that's what he said. He's a grad student at the college in Moorhead and he came in and had coffee with us this morning."

"And?" Justin spoke lightly, but beneath the surface his tone resounded with protective concern. Even if I hadn't said it in so many words, he could tell I was more troubled than I was admitting.

"I can't explain it exactly." I ran my fingers over the back of his neck, where his hair formed slight curls.

"Anything else?" I knew he meant, *Did you have a Notion about him?* I loved how he had always simply accepted my oddly-timed Notions, that he trusted in them implicitly, as I did. I debated telling him that I still felt oddly disconnected from my usual self, but I hadn't slept well last night and decided I would take my own advice and get some rest.

"No. I'm probably overreacting," I allowed.

Justin bracketed my hips with his hands. "So where is he now? What's his name?"

"Dixon," I said. "Zack Dixon. He's out in his canoe. He asked Mom if he could park here when he puts in the water. He's collecting water samples for something."

"How about I beat the shit out of him, just for fun?" my husband asked, gliding his hands along my ribs. I knew he was just kidding, trying to coax a smile.

"Because you're not seventeen anymore. Getting into fights with Jackson, just for fun."

"We never fought each other. We just had each other's back. That's funny, I ran into Brent Woodson this morning and it got me thinking about the time Jackie fought him after the homecoming game, senior year..."

"I remember that night. Jo was beside herself with worry. Fucking Jackie. Brent was pretty tough back then..."

"Now he's just got a beer gut from hell," Justin interjected.

"What did he do again...he said something about Jo..."

"I don't remember anymore, but Jackie was offended, of course. God, that was a beauty of a fight," Justin said, half-smiling at the memory. "I jumped in because Brent brought along Mikey Mulvey. I cleaned his clock. Shit, and now he's a cop..."

"And you busted your knuckles on Mikey's jaw," I reminded him. "I remember Jo and I got there just in time to see the aftermath. You two were the triumphant victors and Jo was ready to kill Jackson."

"I remember you being there that night." He stroked his fingers through my loose hair. "I always knew where you were, even back then. I wasn't entirely aware of it, but then I'd be watching you out of the corner of my eye. My sweet little woman."

"I watched you, too," I said, recalling well. I slipped my palms over his broad shoulders and slowly down the muscles of his back. I murmured, "But back then I couldn't touch you."

"What about now?" he asked, low and throaty.

"Now," and I smiled into his eyes, pressing my breasts a little closer to his chest. "Now, I can touch you anytime I want."

Later, Dodge joined us and we all ate on the porch before Justin and his dad headed back to the shop. I spent an hour helping Mom weed the garden, picked strawberries until my back was aching, then walked Rae home for a nap in the early afternoon and ended up sleeping alongside her. Clinty woke us up an hour before dinner to remind me that he was biking into Landon to play baseball. Justin and I tried to get to as many of his games as we could.

"Love you, Mom!" Clinty called as he left, my sweet son who would still burrow on my lap if he wouldn't squash me in the process.

By the time Rae and I walked back to Shore Leave along the forest path, the quality of the light had altered, now that evening was approaching. I never failed to take pleasure in the long summertime beams. Rae scampered ahead and I noticed Mathias's truck in the lot. And Zack Dixon's car, still in the same place he'd parked it this morning.

"Jilly, are you having supper with us?" Mom poked her head out the door to ask. "Dodge is bringing Ruthie and the triplets."

"No, we're heading over to the athletic field to watch Clint's game," I reminded her.

I'd forgotten my shoes on the side of the cafe and headed that way to grab them, collecting a pile of lifejackets along the way, intending to return them to the shed. I bent, with great care, to catch my flip-flops by their straps when my arms broke out in sudden cold gooseflesh.

"Jillian!" I heard someone herald, and turned to see Zack jogging up the incline. He'd drawn the bow of his canoe onto the shore. I wanted him and every piece of equipment associated with him off of Shore Leave property as soon as humanly possible, but wasn't entirely sure how to express this without sounding slightly crazy. He was lean and athletic, catching up with me long before I had a chance to disappear inside the cafe. Reaching my side, he asked, "That's your name, right?"

In the afternoon light he appeared sweaty and disheveled, normal-looking, a sunhat shading those eerie eyes. Without waiting for me to respond, he added, "I feel like we got off on the wrong foot. Sorry. I have a big mouth, and you are really, really pretty. It threw me for a loop."

I stared at him without a word, clutching the lifejackets to my belly in a protective gesture, also very much thrown for a loop.

It's an act, I realized. *He's selling you something. But what? Why?*

"Just keep your opinions to yourself, all right?" I said at last, shifting the burden of the lifejackets to my other arm. Without asking permission he swept them from my grip, his fingertips brushing my tank top.

"You're pregnant," he said. "I'll carry these for you."

"Mama! Millie's daddy is here!" Rae announced from an open window.

"Where's Camille?" I called, grateful for this excuse to leave Zack behind. I climbed up the porch steps and entered the cafe to see Noah Utley standing awkwardly near the till, hands in the pockets of his khaki shorts. Even if I wasn't particularly fond of him, it was easy to see why he'd once appealed to my niece; he was tall and fair and angelically handsome, if slightly worse for the wear these days. He offered me a polite, impersonal smile.

"Hi, Noah," I said. "Are you waiting for Millie Jo?"

"Yeah, she's coming to Lilly's birthday," he explained, naming one of his brother's children. "Is Camille around?"

"She's up at her place," I said. I knew he didn't want to encounter Mathias, and tended to avoid their apartment if at all possible. Too late for that now, as Mathias and Camille ambled along the path, each of them holding one of Millie's hands, the picture of an intact, loving family—mother, father, daughter. Noah bit his bottom lip, hard enough to leave dents, as he observed this. His chest rose and then fell as one drawing a fortifying breath. He looked like a man who desperately needed a drink and I felt a splash of sympathy; he'd matured very little since the summer that he first dated and then impregnated my niece, currently a college dropout who lived with his parents and relied upon them to foot his monthly child support bill. But it had to sting to watch your former girlfriend looking so blissfully happy in the company of another man. Noah drew a second deep breath and then, seeming to have gathered courage, headed outside to collect his child.

Chapter Four

NOAH LOOKED ROUGH IN THE EVENING LIGHT, THERE WAS no denying. Sometimes I couldn't believe I had ever found him attractive. Strain seemed to have aged him; he appeared much older than the past three years would warrant as he stood watching us approach. Before I could say anything, the graduate student from Moorhead walked around the far side of Shore Leave, carrying his canoe portage-style, and asked Mathias if he'd mind helping him strap it to the top of his car; Millie was still up on the porch saying good-bye to Rae and I seized this moment of relative privacy to confront Noah.

"You haven't been drinking today, have you?"

There was no way in hell I would let my child go with him if I even suspected, but for all that he looked pale and rather drawn, I didn't think he appeared under the influence. I could smell his cologne, no hint of booze, but still felt compelled to ask.

He sighed and offered me a resentful look, eyes narrowing, mouth twisting. Matching my quiet tone, he said, "Of course I haven't. *Jesus*, Camille." And then, though he sounded more exhausted than accusatory, "I know you called my mom."

"Because I actually do *worry* about you." And it was true; I did feel concern for him, along with a large slice of resentment and irritation, but there was no need to mention that.

"Well, don't waste your time."

Mathias finished lending the grad student a hand and sent me a message with his eyes.

Everything all right?

It is, I said in return.

Noah looked over his shoulder at Mathias, following my gaze, and this time there was a flash of angry resentment in Noah's eyes, no mistaking. As the Moorhead guy's car rattled out of the parking lot, Noah cleared his throat. "I'll have Millie home by ten or so, is that all right?"

"That's fine," I said, not about to argue, just wanting him to leave. I called to my daughter, "Come give me a hug!"

Aunt Jilly stepped onto the porch as Noah and Millie Jo drove away, shading her eyes against the glare of the evening sun. "You guys eating here this evening?"

"No, we're heading to Bull and Diana's."

"Mom's been complaining that we don't come for supper enough," Mathias added.

"God, I'm jealous," Aunt Jilly said. "Diana's an incredible cook."

Five minutes later, we were headed around Flickertail in Mathias's truck. I'd changed into a soft sundress, patterned with sunflowers, my hair in a braid that hung over one shoulder. I felt relaxed, better after having talked to Aunt Jilly on the dock, and Mathias was whistling softly, in tune with an old Randy Travis song on the radio, his right hand warm on my bare thigh.

"Aunt Jilly told me that you talked to Mom," I said, studying his profile. Summer sunshine had darkened his skin, making his eyes all the more blue by contrast. His black hair, fresh from the shower, was drying with a slight curl on his nape and along his forehead.

He rubbed his palm over my leg. "I worry about your nightmares."

"I know," I assured him. "I'm not upset. I just wish they'd go away so I could sleep all night without waking you. And that I could remember exactly what I dreamed. It's like the second I wake up it gets snapped away. I know I'm missing something important. If I could just talk to—"

"Malcolm?" he supplied, completely serious. We'd talked about it many times before. He saw the worry knitting my brows as I continued to study him, and said softly, "Honey, I'm all right. I swear."

I didn't want to bring up what had happened in the forest last winter, as it made me too ill, and likely always would. If I hadn't trusted my instinct that night—if I hadn't insisted that Bull come with me...

"If I felt in danger, I would tell you. I'd tell my dad, I'd tell Charlie," Mathias assured me. I'd been furious when he resumed walking his trap lines only two weeks after being attacked, before the stitches on his forehead were even removed, terrified that whoever struck him out there, who'd dragged him over the snowy ground for some purpose unknown to us, would return to finish the job. I'd insisted that he stop going alone, that he take better care of himself. Mathias insisted that he'd walked his trap lines since he was a boy and would not be afraid to do so; he stayed home after our first confrontation over the issue, but would not allow fear to dictate his actions and had resumed his usual routine with the winter lines. To be fair, nothing dire had occurred since—but my worry refused to be as neatly destroyed.

"I know," I allowed. A small but potent rush of gladness filled me as I said, "I can't wait for our trip."

His answering grin could have lit the entire sky at the dark of midnight. "I can't wait either, honey. I want to show you all the places we'd stay when I was little."

"I am excited for that." I loved his characteristic enthusiasm. I confessed, "But mostly I just can't wait to have you all to myself."

His grin deepened and his hand crept higher on my thigh, edging beneath my hem. "Why's that?"

"Because I like the way your jeans fit," I said, giggling as his expression grew increasingly wayward. "And how your shoulders move when you walk. And I like the way you need to shave about ten minutes after shaving. And..." I gasped as he caressed a particularly sensitive spot beneath my skirt. "And the way you...do that..."

We'd reached his parents' sprawling cabin. Mathias parked in his usual spot on the long, curving driveway bordered by towering spruces and wasted no time hauling me close. I linked my arms about his neck and kissed his jaw, then his ear, where I whispered, "The way you do everything."

"I gotta confess," he whispered, lips brushing mine with his soft words. "I want to do *everything* with you. Right here."

I giggled at the urgency in his teasing tone and kissed his sexy mouth; he groaned, grasping my jaws, and it was at that exact instant that someone rapped on the windshield with curled knuckles. We broke apart to see Mathias's oldest sister, Tina, and her husband, Sam, who was shaking his head at us.

"You two trying to scare the kids?" Tina teased through the open driver's side window. Heat stormed my face even as Mathias grinned and kept me close.

"We are in love," he told his sister in the tone of voice you would use as the class know-it-all. He started singing "Forever and Ever, Amen," one of the Randy Travis songs he'd perfected in the shower. I giggled, loving him so much that a familiar ache formed at the juncture of my ribcage.

Tina groaned, opening the truck door for us. She invited, "Come on, lovebirds, get your asses moving. Mom won't let us eat until we're all here."

The Carters lived just a few minutes from their family business, White Oaks Lodge, in a spacious log home overlooking Flickertail; from their wide, second-level back porch, I could see Shore Leave across the lake's silken surface, just to the left. I smelled charcoal from the grill and heard the radio on top of the fridge, tuned to the local country station. Diana appeared at the open screen door to greet us, smiling widely. Mathias's family reminded me a great deal of my own, as there was always an air of gaiety to their get-togethers, tons of food, kids running everywhere and making a mess, but no one really minding. Diana hugged me, her soft hair brushing my cheek; she smelled good, a combination of her perfume and whatever she'd been baking. "Hi, hon. No Millie Jo this evening?"

"She's with Noah," I explained. I loved Mathias's parents; I'd met them even before I knew him, when I worked at White Oaks last winter. Diana was petite, with lovely auburn hair she'd passed on to her three daughters, while Mathias resembled his father, who well deserved the nickname, "Bull." They treated my daughter like one of their own grandkids, and Millie adored them, more than I could have ever hoped.

"Son, you look happy," Diana noted as Mathias caught her close and kissed her cheek. He was a mama's boy, the baby of his family after three demanding sisters. He called himself spoiled but he really wasn't, not by any definition of the word. She added, "It does my heart good."

"Ma, I've never been so happy," Mathias said, all smiley and sweet, grabbing me around the waist.

"Milla, you're going to be pregnant long before the wedding," Tina said, also kissing her mom on the way inside.

I admitted, "That's the second time I've heard that today."

"Did Jilly call it? If she did then you know it's true," said Tina, who had graduated with Aunt Jilly. "Nobody bets against Jillian Davis."

"When would our baby be born, if you get pregnant tonight?" Mathias asked, true excitement and anticipation in his tone, and the flush on my face overtook my entire body. I had long ago realized that the Carters were open and honest, not great at secret-keeping in general, but I hadn't even told *my* family about our decision to stop using birth control. Well, at least not anyone besides Aunt Jilly—which probably meant Mom would know by nightfall.

Despite everyone's good-natured laughter, I felt compelled to scold, "*Mathias Carter.*"

"You're just like your father," Diana said to him, snapping a kitchen towel at his backside.

"Around the end of March," Glenna, the middle sister, supplied cheerily, from where she stood at the counter shaking salt into a bowl of noodles. The house was chaotic in the wake of the granddaughters running from the kitchen to the patio and back again; between Mathias's three sisters, there were eight girls.

As though reading my mind, Diana added, "I'm counting on grandsons, you know. I've got you two pegged for that."

"Six or seven, that's what I'm thinking," Mathias said. "Boys, I mean. Then we can get started on more girls."

"You've wanted to be a daddy since you were little," Diana said, reaching up to smooth his hair, with maternal affection. "You told us you wanted a baby for your fifth birthday, remember? And not a little brother. You wanted your *own* baby, you said."

Even though I'd heard that story before—the Carters being story-tellers of the highest order—my heart melted all over again. I made my way to the antique curio cabinet in the corner of the dining room, upon which Diana had arranged numerous framed pictures of the family. I sought my favorite and held it close, sending my man a smile over one shoulder as I teased, "I could handle having a half-dozen little boys just like this."

He grinned. "I *was* adorable, wasn't I?"

In the picture he stood near Flickertail in the heat of summer, eight years old, knobby-kneed and brown from the sun, dark hair cut into shaggy bangs that hung in his eyes. He was smiling widely, proudly holding up a stringer of bluegills. I resisted the urge to kiss the picture as I still sometimes kissed Malcolm Carter's, and then lifted another image from the bunch. In this shot, he posed with his hockey stick, leaning over it, clad in his blue and white Landon Rebels jersey, number ten.

"Do I hear Camille and my boy?" Bull called as he came inside. I loved my future father-in-law and had no trouble at all imagining him as someone from an earlier century. It was partially his gruff voice and par-tially the tendency to speak like he was in a Clint Eastwood-era western. He rumbled into the house for hugs all around, then caught me by the shoulders and gave me a quick, speculative perusal with one eye squint-ed. Looking at Mathias, he concluded, "Son, I remember Jackie Gordon real well. I feel I oughta give you a punch in the nose on his behalf."

I giggled and Mathias lifted both hands in surrender. He justified, "We're *in love*."

"As even a blind man could see," Bull agreed.

We headed out to the porch, where the view of the lake was un-encumbered. Even having lived on its shores for the past three years, Flickertail never ceased to amaze me with its sheer beauty; I could live here forever (and planned to) and never take the sight of it for granted. Now, as evening cast its apricot-tinted beams over the surface, the water lay smooth, unmarred by the whitecaps stirred up in the day, when the wind was usually stronger and motor boats flew back and forth, creating crisscrossing and unceasing wake-patterns. The Carters' house was just a stone's throw from the water, their wide dock stretching perpendicular to the shore before turning two corners; Bull's sleek outboard and a pair of bright yellow jet-skis were tethered to its length.

"Hi, guys!" Elaine called. Tina and I joined her at the patio table on the upper deck while Mathias descended the wooden steps to the lower level, where the menfolk were drinking beer at the grill. Elaine poured us frothy margaritas from a round-bellied green pitcher and I felt guilty as I considered how exacting I was of Noah's drinking. Besides that, I wasn't quite twenty-one.

"Thanks," I told Elaine, accepting it nonetheless.

"Enjoy," she replied, with a grin that reminded me of Mathias. She sat to my right, bare feet propped on an adjacent chair. Her silky red hair had recently been cut short, falling to her jaws on either side. She tucked a strand behind her ear as she said, "You two are going to have such a great time on your trip. Dad's cousins out in Montana are really fun. We used to visit them every other summer when we were kids."

"They have horses, too," Tina said. "Or at least, they used to." She caught Bull on his way back to the grill, a stainless steel spatula in one hand, a six-pack of Leinie's in the other. "Dad, do Harry and Meg still have horses?"

"They do," Bull said. "Two or three, I believe. You and the boy can take all the rides you want. You ever been horseback, hon?"

"My dad took Tish and me one summer when we came up here from Chicago," I said, even though I'd thought immediately of Aces, Malcolm's horse. Even though Aces had died well over a hundred years ago, I was certain I'd ridden him—but of course I didn't mention this to Bull.

"The boy can help you," Bull said. "He's a natural."

Mathias was a natural at a couple of other very specific things, and a telltale flush stole over my face. Bull winked with his usual good humor—I prayed he wasn't a mind reader—and headed down to the lower deck, where the men were telling fish stories.

"Matty will want to show you all the places we used to stop along the way," Elaine said. "He's a sucker for those roadside tourist traps."

"I like them, too," I admitted. "I wish I could promise that we'll take great pictures to show you, but I'm so bad about that. It's all I can do to keep up with Millie Jo."

Tina said, "We all have that parental guilt about not taking enough pictures. Don't worry. Just have fun on your trip. Besides, you and Matty will have…*more than plenty* to do."

Elaine laughed heartily at her sister's suggestive pause.

"I was out at the cabin today," Elaine continued, poking me with her toes. "It's looking so good. We're all so happy you two are making it your own. It seems meant to be, you know?"

A shiver fluttered up my spine; maybe it was only the chill of the margarita. Thinking of what I'd discussed with Aunt Jilly, and determined not to fear my own happiness, I said, "I know exactly what you mean."

"I knew it last winter, I had a feeling," Tina said, refilling her drink. Her russet-red hair was the wildest of the three sisters, fluffed out in curls. Using Elaine's nickname, she demanded, "Didn't I, Lainey? You're not the only one with a sense of intuition."

"You did," Elaine acknowledged. Her eyes roved to her little brother, who was sitting on a barstool near the grill, relaxed and laughing, one elbow resting on the porch railing as he joked about something with Bull. Mathias looked our way and blew me a kiss. In an undertone, Elaine added, "I haven't ever seen him so happy. It's all you, Camille."

My lips were cold from the icy drink, but just speaking the words warmed my mouth. "I love him so much."

"Late March," Glenna reminded me, coming outside just in time to hear my comment, again provoking laughter. She displaced Elaine's feet and claimed a chair, setting a bowl of pretzels on the glass tabletop and reaching for the margarita pitcher. "I would absolutely *love* a little nephew."

"We're working on it!" Mathias called.

Diana served dinner outside, everyone crowding around the patio table. Bull lit the strategically-placed citronella torches, staving off at least a few of the mosquitoes, and we ate while twilight danced slowly across Flickertail, moving closer at the pace of a waltzing couple. The temperature was perfect, as was customary near the lake on summer evenings, no matter how heavily the humidity hung in the air all day. The last of the sunset burned across the top of the water in reflected flames. Orange was the dominant color in the west, streaked through with violet and magenta. To the east, Flickertail was cloaked in the silver-grays of advancing evening, the small bright lights at the ends of docks blinking on from that direction.

Mathias sat to my right and I counted my blessings for the countless time since I'd been welcomed into his family. My mind skipped through all of the *if I hadn't* things that eventually led to us meeting—if I hadn't gotten pregnant and stayed in Landon, if I hadn't found the picture of Malcolm Carter, if I hadn't taken the job at White Oaks. I leaned my shoulder against Mathias, who snuggled me close. I thought of what my life would be like if I'd moved home to Chicago at the end of that first summer, of where I would be now. And my soul seemed to shrivel, just imagining how close we'd come to never knowing one another at all.

I thought, *How many lives have we lived in which our paths were near, but didn't touch?*

I curled my hand around his thigh, holding fast.

See, he's right here. Mathias is right here. He isn't going anywhere…

He's all right. He isn't going to disappear.

We would have found each other, even still.

We will always find each other…

After supper Bull brought out the cards and the menfolk gathered around the dining room table, retreating inside. Diana stood at the kitchen sink, laughing about something with her oldest granddaughter, running water over a stack of bowls, while Mathias helped cart dirty dishes into the kitchen.

"Show off," Tina said, pestering her brother. She told me, "Don't expect this sort of thing all the time, hon. He's normally as lazy as those guys," and she indicated her dad and the other husbands, lounging around the table with fresh bottles of beer, fanning and reshuffling their cards in preparation to play some poker.

"Hey, I resent that," Mathias said, kicking at Tina's ankle. "I help out at home. Don't I, honey?"

"He does," I agreed, smiling as I thought of the many times and ways we made love in our own little kitchen, during and after he helped clean up from dinner. The counter was a perfect height for certain specific things.

"See?" he said to Tina, with undeniable smugness.

"Boy, we're holding up the game for you!" Bull announced in his roaring voice.

"Play through once without me," Mathias told his dad. "I'll be there in a few."

My phone, abandoned on my chair, caught my attention with its chirping ring, and I saw that Noah's mother, Marie Utley, was calling.

Shit, I thought. That meant something was up with Millie. I tried not to let the sudden burst of apprehension overwhelm me as I answered by demanding, "Is everything all right?"

"Yes, yes, don't worry," Marie said instantly. My shoulders drooped with relief, but then Marie went on, "I hate to ask, but could you swing out to pick up Millie? Noah has…well, he must have been sneaking drinks. He's—"

Not wanting to hear any more of this pitiful explanation, I interrupted, "It's no problem. I'll be there soon. Thanks for calling me."

A stack of dishes balanced in his hands, Mathias asked, "What's wrong?"

"That was Marie," I said. "I have to go get Millie. You stay here and hang out."

"What's going on?"

"I guess Noah is—" I stuttered a little, anger and irritation blocking my throat so that I was forced to clear it before finishing. "I guess he's *drunk* and can't bring her home."

"Oh," Mathias said, his voice carefully harboring no judgment. "We better go then."

I turned and studied the lake, curling my hands over the porch rail, restraining a sigh; I couldn't help but feel as though Noah had deliberately done this to ruin my night, which I knew was stupid. Behind me, I heard Mathias set down the stack of plates. I said, "I can go, sweetheart. You stay and play some cards."

"I'm not going to make you drive out there alone," he said, wrapping his arms around my waist, drawing my spine to his chest.

"You're so warm," I murmured, clutching his forearms. He was always so quick to understand things, to do what he felt was right.

"I'll warm you," he promised, lifting my braid to gently kiss the nape of my neck. "I want that in our wedding vows. 'I promise to warm you through all the days of our life' sounds about right."

"And nights," I whispered, shivering at the pleasure of his sweet words. "Don't forget about nights."

"Hell, yes," he murmured in my ear.

We left a few minutes later, after hugs and reminders to come back for dinner soon. I'd been hoping to stop by our cabin and see it in the moonlight, but that was out of the question now.

"I'm sorry we had to leave early," I said as we drove east, out toward the Utleys' farm on Jackpine Way. "Marie would bring her home, but she doesn't drive alone, and she said Curt's too tired to drive out to Shore Leave." I pressed my fingertips to my forehead, momentarily overwhelmed by irritation. "Why do they even have alcohol in the house? Don't they realize that's wrong?" Sinking even lower, I vented, "I suppose I shouldn't be surprised that Noah would do something totally stupid like drink enough at his niece's birthday party that he wouldn't be able to drive his daughter home. What was I thinking?"

"He's struggling," Mathias countered. "Even I can see that. He's a mess."

The radio volume was low, but I could hear George Strait singing "Cross My Heart" and allowed the familiar song to relax me. The last thing I should do was let Noah cause me any more stress.

"I feel a little sorry for him," Mathias said when I didn't respond. "I think he's truly regretful." He paused. "But I have to admit there's a certain way he looks at you that makes me want to smash my fist into his face. Repeatedly."

I looked his way, eyebrows raised.

"Longingly. He looks longingly at you," Mathias clarified, his gaze directed out the windshield. "It makes my skin crawl."

I'd never noticed Noah looking at me with anything but resentment, and found my voice. "I think you're misinterpreting that."

I sensed a slight relaxing of Mathias's powerful shoulders. He allowed, "Maybe," but there was a decided lack of conviction in his voice.

I realized what really troubled him and said softly, "You've already been more of a father to Millie Jo than Noah will ever be."

I'd hit the nail on the head; Mathias was silent for a few beats. The song switched to "The River and the Highway," and I shivered at the mournful opening notes. At last he said, with quiet vehemence, "I hate resenting Noah so goddamn much. I hate that I wish he'd leave Landon so I'd never have to see his face again. I know he's Millie's father, and I acknowledge that he's trying, but I hate it. I'm selfish as shit, I know this. I'm not trying to make an excuse, I swear."

I curled my fingers through his and squeezed, as he signaled to turn right onto the gravel road that led out to the Utleys' dairy farm. There was a lone streetlight shining on their property, creating a blue-white glow that highlighted the long, low-slung cattle barn. Despite the fact that this was my daughter's grandparents' home, I was rarely out here; usually Curt and Marie, or Noah, drove over to Shore Leave to collect Millie Jo. Their house was warm with lights and the front door opened as we climbed from the truck, revealing Noah's small, plump mother.

"Thanks for stopping out, Camille," she said. "Hi, Mathias."

"Ma'am," he said politely.

"Hi, Mama!" Millie called, darting outside into the gloaming light. I bent to collect her into my arms.

"Hi, sweetie," I said. I told Marie, "Thanks for calling me."

"You bet," she said shortly, clearly not wanting to discuss the matter any further; she had long ago stopped apologizing for her youngest son. The air out here smelled of the pines growing tall behind the house, and the nearby alfalfa field; the fainter scent of the cows was also present, but not unpleasant. There was a beat of purely uncomfortable silence.

"Give your grandma a kiss," I told Millie, setting her on the ground, and she ran to do so.

"Good-night, bunny." Marie hugged her close. "We'll see you soon."

I offered Marie as much of a smile as I could manage. Millie skipped to Mathias, who helped her into her car seat.

"How're you, little one?" I heard him asking her.

Marie observed all of this and her expression hardened; she took a step out the door and said, "Camille." I wasn't exactly sure how to gauge her tone, which sounded more like an order than I liked; maybe I was imagining the hint of censure. "Noah has been wanting to talk to you."

A resentful breath lodged in my lungs. "He can talk to me anytime he wants."

Marie pinned me with her gaze. "He's trying, you know. It's not easy for him." She clamped shut her lips as though to restrain further comment.

I wanted to scream, *Are you fucking kidding me?* My hands balled into fists, which I relaxed almost immediately—did I think it would solve anything to storm inside that house and aim a punch at Noah's chin? I muttered, "Good-night, Marie," and turned away without another word. My scalp prickled as I returned to the idling truck, suddenly aware that someone hidden was watching this entire scene. My footsteps faltered. *The barn*, I realized. The structure was cast in shadows but somehow I knew Noah was in there. The summer we dated, three years ago, in a rare moment of self-revelation he'd told me that as a kid he would hide out in the hayloft when things weren't going his way. Clearly he was hiding out there now, probably along with his stash of hard liquor.

Grow up! I sent the thought in his direction, with angry heat. *Grow up and get it together!*

Two hours later, at home, Millie was snoring in her room and Mathias and I were sprawled on our bed, the sheets a wild pinwheel of cotton beneath us. We were both naked, tangled together, my head resting lazily on his left shoulder. We lay studying the picture of Malcolm Carter in the glow provided by a single candle situated on the nightstand, our preferred lighting, the bottom edge of the photo resting between my breasts.

"I love Aces," Mathias said, his voice low and drowsy with satisfaction. He shifted slightly, cupping my right breast, his thumb moving slowly over my nipple. We'd spent the last hour talking in between bouts of making love and my limbs were weak from being wrapped around him; I didn't plan to move before dawn peeked through the window.

"Aces," I repeated, warm with contentment. "I love him too."

"There's so much about that lifestyle that appeals to me," Mathias continued. "Having to depend on your horse like that. Riding for the horizon, not knowing what you might find. Adventure. Danger." He paused and kissed the top of my shoulder. "Don't accuse me of romanticizing it at all."

I felt so secure in his arms, as though nothing in the world could ever hurt me again; I refused to get worked up at the mention of danger, especially in this context. Even still, I whispered, "Don't you go talking about riding away from me into danger."

"You'd be with me, of course, silly woman. I wouldn't go riding away from you. We'd have adventures together, unless I thought it was *too* dangerous."

"Searching for gold?" I murmured.

"Gold, land, the next card game," he replied, playing along. "I think it would be incredible to ride for the horizon all day and not come across any towns, anything manmade. That seems like true adventure."

"It does," I agreed. "To live in a time when parts of the country were wild and unsettled."

"What would you name your horse?" he asked. My nipple was full and round against his stroking fingers.

"I'd have to meet her first," I said, shivering at his touch. "I'd have to see what she looked like." I decided immediately, "She would be a buckskin, black mane and tail, golden body." I rested my nose against his jaw and then speculated, half-teasing, "I'd maybe name her something like Bluebell…"

Mathias snorted a laugh, hugging me around the waist. "*Bluebell?* What kind of name is that for a horse? She'd be embarrassed as hell."

"She would not!" I countered, giggling. "I had a stuffed horse as a kid. I dragged that thing all over the place."

"What was her name?"

I admitted, "Blossom. But that was the name she came with."

"*Oh my God*," he groaned, still laughing.

"Yeah, that's even worse than Bluebell," I allowed, tracing my fingertip over the picture, straight down the pale stripe on Aces' dark nose. I recalled all the lonely nights I had kissed Malcolm's face before I went to sleep, those years before meeting Mathias; I pressed a tender fingertip to Malcolm's cheek, remembering how this picture of him had pulled me through. In the photograph Malcolm appeared content, even happy, standing in the slanting light of a long-gone sunset. As I had many dozens of times, I thought, *I'll find out what happened to you, sweet Malcolm, I promise.*

Mathias whispered, "You love him, don't you?"

I loved that he understood this, that there was nothing but gentle acknowledgment in his question; my love for Malcolm was braided inexplicably together with my love for Mathias. It was almost as though they were the same man. It was not the first time I'd felt this to be true.

"I do," I whispered, a little choked up. "Or, I did…once…"

Mathias aligned his thumb over my fingertip, which still rested upon Malcolm's face. He said solemnly, "I promise to be worthy of him."

"He knows," I said, grateful anew that Mathias didn't think it was crazy that I spoke as though I was actually capable of communicating with his deceased ancestor. How I hated the thought of Malcolm, or Aces, being dead and gone, as abstract entities we would never be able to meet in this life; I'd wanted to hug both man and horse for so long now that I could hardly remember a time before I knew of them. I preferred to think of them as simply absent—waiting somewhere for us to find them, when the time was right.

Changing the subject, I whispered, "What color would yours be?"

"I'd want a black stallion," Mathias said at once, knowing just what I was asking, and his chest vibrated with a laugh. "With a tough name, like…*Renegade*," and my laughter almost drowned him out as he continued, with relish. "And I'd have a black hat, spurs, and boots, to match. Christ, I would be *such* a bad-ass. Gunslinger, gambler, six-shooter…"

Warming to this vision, I supplied helpfully, "And I'd be waiting for you in a dusty, remote little saloon. And you'd have been on the trail for a long time, without a woman's touch…"

He cupped both my breasts this time, with growing intent, nuzzling my neck. "And I'd catch a glimpse of you and tip my hat, and then I'd say, 'Ma'am, I'm going to need you to come with me.' See, there's a double entendre right there..."

I laughed even harder at his words, leaning to place the picture carefully on the nightstand and then returning to his embrace, resting my elbows on his strong chest, reaching to mess up his hair. The candlelight flickered over the angles of his face, his firm chin and sensual mouth, his black eyebrows, his seductively lowered eyelids. My ring caught the candle glow and glinted as I traced the outline of his lips, which sent desire knifing through my blood. I belonged with this man, it was that simple. When he was inside of me, held fast and deep, our names ceased to have meaning; we were simply *us*. Connected in ways I could not completely understand.

"Do you think we make love too much?" I whispered, thinking of how everyone teased us. I leaned to kiss the cupid's bow on his top lip, slowly, deliberately spreading my thighs over his hips, lightly grinding against his body. His blue eyes blazed but he remained still, letting me tease him. I loved the difference in the texture of our skin—he was so hard, his hands roughened by daily manual labor, his chest and arms and legs all covered in coarse black hair. He glided his touch down my waist and anchored around my backside. I shivered, my nipples grazing his chest, his rigid cock flirting with the slippery juncture of my legs.

"Now you're talking crazy, woman," he murmured, offering me a lazy grin that belied his true intent.

"Maybe just once more..." I breathed, licking his dimple.

He moved with fluid grace, knowing I could handle no more teasing, rolling me beneath him and surging back inside.

"Gentle!" I gasped, clinging to his shoulders. I was not being coy when I informed him, "Your cock is *huge*, you know."

He snorted a laugh at my words, still with a two-handed grip on my ass, but obligingly ceased all motion. He groaned a little, whispering, "How gentle? Show me..."

I kissed his chin, using my hips to set our pace. He moved accordingly, claiming my mouth as I gave over to his taste, his touch. Joy beat upon my nerves, radiating from my center as he continued on and on, slow and steady, until I was beyond all sense, crying out against his neck.

He gasped my name and I clung as he drove deeply one last time, and then fell still.

It was late. Mathias shifted us so that I lay cradled against his chest; he fell asleep almost immediately, as the candle dripped its wax and sank lower and lower. I drifted, caught in that almost-dream state in which I was vaguely aware of the familiar surroundings of our bedroom and yet half-sunk into another place. Somewhere far from here and far from what I knew as real.

Knives? Are you out of your ever-loving mind?

You'll be a sensation, girl, if you can just get over the fear of it. Trust me.

Sharp points thud against the wood near my head, but I know better than to shudder. Months of unending practice, that's what it took to quell an instinct that basic, the one driving me to shrink from blades being whirled through the air and toward my immobile body.

He's here, you know, the one that caught your eye from a distance last night, girl. Third row, with that same rowdy bunch. Them fiddle-playing musicians.

He's here? A hand curls unforgiving fingers around my heart. *What if…*

Waiting for my cue, as terrified as a child about to be punished, I listen to the excited buzzing murmur of the audience from where I hover backstage. I have heard it a thousand or more times before now. Through a small rend in the faded red curtain, stage right, I try to catch a glimpse, searching for the outline of a hat; I cannot let myself believe that it might actually be him. I've been destroyed by that thought too many times to count, already.

I see a hand mirror, small and wood-framed, lying on the floor near a discarded costume. I snatch it up and study my face, my slim pale face, with its eyes of two different colors, and the familiar loathing rolls in, swift as a springtime river.

Oh God, let him come back to me, let him come back to me, oh God, I beg of you.

Let him find me…please, I'll do anything…

I'll do anything…

Much later, I woke with a start. Suspended in sickening fear, it took me seconds to realize where I was, that I was safe and Mathias was near. I pressed both hands to my heart in an effort to calm my clubbing pulse. I was wet with fearful sweat, my chest tight. The dream had come crawling again, the sensation of being lost and alone, of being…

Of being without him.

Oh God, oh God.

My hands bunched into frantic fists. *It was just a nightmare, Camille, just a horrible fucking nightmare.* But I could not shake the sense that it was somehow more and would not be pacified; my fear only increased.

"Camille," Mathias murmured in his sleep and I aligned my body with his, pressing close, my face at his collarbones. He shifted, arms circling, and stroked my hair with both hands. He put his lips against my forehead; he was more fully awake now, and whispered, "What is it, honey?"

My tears were warm and wet on his chest, and I could not answer. He murmured soft sounds of love, comforting me, and at last I stopped trembling.

Chapter Five

THE EVENING WAS PERFECT FOR A BALLGAME; TWILIGHT cooled the air, and the sunlight was the sort that made my throat ache with its beauty, beaming across the freshly-shorn grass, radiating a brilliant, otherworldly yellow-green. Justin, Rae, and I joined the adults and littler kids lounging in camp chairs and upon picnic blankets rather than the small section of bleachers; those were typically left to the high school kids. In a town the size of Landon the teenagers saw each other often, even in the summer, but there was always an air of gossipy excitement surrounding them, one I remembered well from my own days of claiming the bleachers, giggling with Jo and the other girls as we admired the boys on the field.

Justin's little sister, Liz, and her husband, Mark Worden (known in Landon almost exclusively as Wordo) were already there and we settled beside them. Wordo had two kids from his first marriage, Lisa and Jeff; Jeff had long harbored a huge crush on Tish (one that, judging from their alleged make-out sessions, wasn't totally unrequited) and was a fellow member of Clint's baseball team.

"Hi, guys!" Liz said, leaning to grab us drinks from her cooler. Liz was petite and cute, with the same coffee-brown eyes as my husband.

"Hi, favorite sister-in-law," I said, as Justin set up our lawn chairs.

"Jilly Bean, you look like an angel, I'm dead serious," Liz said, shaking her head. "That dress makes your eyes as blue as the sky. When I was pregnant I looked like a goddamn hippopotamus."

"You did not, and besides, you were carrying *triplets*, might I remind you. Most of us just do one at a time."

Justin caught me around the waist and bent to kiss the side of my neck, which was bare, as I'd pinned up my hair. He said to his little sister, "Jilly is my angel, that's God's truth."

"You're a goddamn lucky man," Liz agreed, indicating with a beer can that I should sit.

"J.D., you gotta hear what Daryl thinks about..." Wordo said to my husband, but it sounded like maybe a sports thing, and I tuned him out; I settled beside Liz and accepted a can of lemonade. Justin crouched near Wordo and Daryl to join their conversation, cracking open a beer.

"Mama, can I go play with those guys?" Rae leaned on my knee to ask, crinkling up one eye as she regarded me. She meant a group of little girls on a blanket about twenty feet away.

"No hug for your Auntie Liz?" Liz asked, and Rae giggled, diving into her aunt's arms.

"Stay where I can see you," I told my daughter, and she scampered away.

I scanned the field, where the players were just warming up; I spied Clinty at once, number five for Richardson Plumbing, the sponsor of his summer league. They were playing Huber Auto tonight. I was a mother, but I was also more observant than most, and a girl standing near the tall section of chain link fence that separated the bleachers from home plate caught my eye; Claire Henry, Clint's one and only girlfriend in high school. They had dated for part of both tenth and eleventh grades, before Claire broke it off with him. Clint was devastated for a period of a month, near Christmas of that year, before his naturally cheery attitude finally reestablished itself. And now here she was, openly studying Clint. I could tell from his easy posture and the way he was laughing with another teammate that he had not yet noticed her.

"There's Claire," I said to Liz, indicating across the field.

Liz knew all about their history. "Regretting her decision, looks like."

"They were just friends all senior year, according to Clint."

"But he never dated anyone else," Liz reminded me.

"That's true. He's so shy in his own way. He's young for his age, you know what I mean?"

"He's sweet as could be," Liz said.

Claire settled near a group of girls on the risers as the game began. I watched Clint lift his ball cap to swipe his forehead with the back of one hand, still clutching the baseball, and right at that moment he saw Claire. I could tell just by the way his hand lowered too slowly back to his side and his spine straightened.

Oh, honey, I thought, wanting to run over there and hug him. It was never easy seeing your ex.

And it was *just* as I had this thought that Liz asked, "Am I seeing things, or is that actually Aubrey?"

My heart stuttered at these words, my gaze dashing in the direction of Liz's. Sure enough, Aubrey Pritchard was mincing across the ballfield and it was also apparent that she was coming to talk to us.

"God, Dad told me she was back in town," Liz muttered. She leaned and poked Justin's shoulder, as he was nearer to her than me, and still talking to Wordo. "J.D., I hate to tell you this…"

Justin looked our way with brows raised. Liz indicated and then he saw Aubrey; I watched how his shoulders squared as though preparing for a confrontation. He rolled his eyes and muttered, "Jesus, here we go."

He moved at once to sit in his chair beside mine, angling closer, almost protectively. Probably I should have found this endearing; instead it just made me all the more irritated. I wasn't afraid of her. I could hold my own. My heart clobbered my ribcage.

"Hi, everyone," Aubrey said upon reaching us, no more than fifteen seconds later. She looked totally overdone, even though you could tell she'd tried to look sexy; I assumed she was attempting to recreate her high school persona to some extent, as she wore jeans of the painted-on variety, a strappy black tank top, her auburn hair straightened to within an inch of its pitiful life. Heeled fucking sandals. She paused a few feet from my knees and angled herself with one hip jutting.

When no one immediately responded, she heaved the tiniest of sighs and shifted so the other hip was prominent. A small part of me marveled at her bravado. She was far too tanned and it didn't do any favors for her; that was not me being catty. It just didn't. Her eyeliner was exactly applied and extra black. Maybe she was going through a midlife crisis. I almost spoke this thought aloud to my husband, choking it back at the last moment.

Everyone in the vicinity, of course realizing that this was Justin's ex-wife, stared at this potentially interesting situation, some with outright curiosity. Finally Liz asked, with thinly-veiled sarcasm, "So, how's it going?"

"Great," Aubrey said shortly and then directed her mean little eyes at me, tilting her head to the side as though regarding a child. "You didn't mention to these guys that we talked in the store?"

Justin answered for me, which I really did not appreciate at this given moment, asking bluntly, "What do you want?"

I could tell from his tone that he wasn't exactly angry; unfriendly mostly, and I could sense his concern for me. He moved his hand gently over my left thigh, patting me and then settling it there as though to communicate that everything was all right. Aubrey's eyes zeroed in on this before flickering to my belly.

It was the second time today that I'd been rudely examined by someone I disliked, Zack Dixon being the first. Feeling as though Aubrey would win some minor victory if I didn't answer her question, I located my voice. "I mentioned it. And I am sorry for hitting your car. It was an accident."

"About that," she said, flipping her hair to the other shoulder and then focusing upon Justin. Her tone when she spoke to him made my fingers curl into cat claws; it was the same one I'd heard her use when they were still married, a cross between disdainful and commanding. "I need that fixed by tomorrow evening."

Justin leaned back in his chair and shook his head, a smile with no relation to humor crossing his face; it was purely hostile. "Dad told you it would be done this week. And that's the end of it."

I watched as her eyes narrowed and suddenly found myself confronted by an old, unwanted memory—this same field, but on a summer night now long past, way back in high school, when I'd seen Justin kissing Aubrey at the fence in front of the bleachers, gripping the chain link on either side of her. He was so passionate, and like it or not (and

I fiercely hated it down to the blackest, lowest, pettiest part of my soul) Aubrey had once been on the receiving end of that passion.

"It's not the end of it," she bitched. "I need my car."

"It's completely driveable," Justin said, retaining calm. I sensed that she wanted badly to agitate him, to cause a reaction.

Rae came running to us then, diving for her daddy, climbing onto his lap. Justin cuddled Rae close, ignoring Aubrey; I was the one who couldn't look away from her. Seeing Justin with his daughter seemed to dissolve something on her face. As I watched, a flicker of discomposure moved across the façade of self-righteous confidence.

See that? You lost your chance. He's mine now, I told her without words, sending the thought whistling through the air the same way I might have swung a bat toward her head. It must have connected pretty well, because Aubrey put a hand to her temple for a split second, before she resumed glaring at Justin.

"Dad will fix it up for you, no worries," Liz said, clearly trying to diffuse the tension.

"Aubrey, could you move?" Wordo asked, with complete politeness. "I can't see the game and Jeffy's on the mound tonight."

Clint jogged over from the field, coming to a halt at Aubrey's side and asking Justin, "Dad, you got the truck keys? Quick, I gotta grab my extra glove."

Justin hooked an arm around Rae's waist to anchor her while he shifted to unzip the side pocket of the backpack we'd toted with. Finding the keys, he handed them up to Clint, who responded with a quick thanks and raced away.

"'Dad?'" Aubrey repeated.

Rae tucked her chin on Justin's shoulder, facing me, and implored, "Mama, I gotta go potty."

Justin told me, "I got it, baby. You stay here."

His eyes held mine and he said without words, *Please don't let Aubrey upset you. Please, Jilly.*

I'm trying, I responded.

Justin rose, lifting Rae to his left forearm. In the evening sun I studied him momentarily through Aubrey's eyes, a clear picture of what she left behind and what she could never have again; it wasn't just that he was so incredibly sexy, with his long, lean build and powerful shoulders, his arms that rippled with muscle, his handsome face with its chiseled jaw and intense eyes. It was the sense of tenderness that he exuded as he carried his child to the brick restrooms on the far side of the field. He was a man who loved his family with his whole heart. A man who cared passionately for those he considered his. My eyes moved from following my husband and daughter, back to Aubrey's face, and I didn't need to be particularly observant to realize that something akin to regret was coursing through her as she also watched their progress.

The game got rolling; Clint located his glove and jogged to join his teammates as they took the field. Liz shot me a look, eyebrows raised, nodding at Aubrey, who was still blocking Wordo's view; he was craning his neck to see around her.

"I'll be sure to tell Dodge to call you as soon as the car's fixed," I said.

Aubrey turned back in my direction, shading her eyes against the last of the sun to peer down at me. Two bracelets on her right wrist clacked together. She all but hissed, "I'll call him myself, thanks."

This time I did nothing to disguise the anger that leached into my eyes. In high school I had been intimidated by her, terribly so, but that was long ago. I lifted my chin (Gran and Great-Aunt Minnie would have been proud of my assertiveness) and said, with venom, "Suit yourself."

Aubrey offered me an acidic glare before walking away, hips rolling.

"For fuck's sake," Liz muttered, and Wordo laughed. People around us were looking between Aubrey and me, and I felt uncomfortably hot in my skin, as though it had been steamed and shrunk. My heart began to ease down to a more regular speed but the clenching in my gut would not settle. Even knowing that it was impossible, it needled me on some level to realize that she wanted Justin back; that she dared to even think there was a chance of that.

Justin returned five minutes later, toting Rae, reclaiming his seat. He cupped the back of my neck, teasing the curls that formed there in the humidity. His touch sent little spikes of pleasure along my skin but I was not in the mood to be stroked, and twitched my shoulders; Justin recognized my frayed nerves and wisely refrained from commenting.

It's not his fault, I reminded myself, however grudgingly. *You can hardly blame him for what his ex-wife does.*

There was plenty of noisy bustling in the crowd as the game continued beneath the evening sky, darkening now to indigo; the field lights blinked to life. Clint was crouched low over second base, forearms to thighs. He rocked side to side, eyes intent upon the batter, Wordo's son, Jeff. The pitcher wound up, then released the ball in a flowing motion, graceful as a dancer. Jeff connected with a crack like that of a rifle shot in the distance and Clint became a blur. The crowd erupted as Jeff sailed past first base and flew for second, Clint rounding third for home.

"Go, Clinty!" screeched Rae, bouncing on Justin's lap.

Clint ran full-bore, arms churning; we were all screaming for him. I marveled at my little boy all grown up, a high school graduate, the same boy who'd slept in my bed for years after his dad died, the both of us comforted by one another; I would wake up during those nights with his heels pushing against my tailbone, forced to carefully unwind the blankets from him so I wouldn't freeze. He crashed into the catcher in a flurry of limbs and was a second later declared safe. I smiled, clapping wildly, as Justin whistled and Rae tried to imitate him, hooking her pinkies in her mouth. I giggled at the sight. Clint stood up and brushed dust off his backside, grinning widely, looking adorable. I saw Claire watching, standing now, closer to the chain link fence, her solemn eyes fixed on my son.

And I reflected again that it really did suck to have to run into your ex.

"Mom, can we get ice cream?" Clint asked after the game, lying on the grass at our feet, arms flung to either side. Jeff sprawled in a similar fashion, ball cap over his face.

"Ice cream!" Rae picked up the chant and Clint directed his grin at her. He knew well how to get her stirred up, and she was always on his side. Rae turned to Justin and caught his face in her little hands, patting his cheeks as she wheedled, "Please, Daddy-Daddy?"

Justin's eyes were soft with love and tenderness as he regarded our daughter, and I felt a familiar tug in my heart. I thought of the evening three summers ago when Justin and I had sat on the dock at Shore Leave, before we'd been a couple, and he'd mentioned that he wanted kids of his own. I smoothed my right hand over the lower curve of my belly, love for him overriding all traces of irritation. Justin looked my way and winked; he knew exactly what I was thinking.

"If Mama says it's all right," he allowed, kissing Rae's nose.

"Ice cream sounds good," I agreed. "We picked about five thousand strawberries today, didn't we, Rae-Rae? Should we go to the cafe and make strawberry sundaes?"

"Oh, Mom, for real? That sounds so good," Clint enthused, rolling to catch one of Rae's feet in his hand, jiggling her leg. She laughed and wiggled down from Justin's lap to climb all over her brother.

"You guys up for sundaes?" I invited Liz and Wordo.

"You know what, Dad is bringing the kids home in about fifteen minutes," Liz said. "So we better head back."

"Can I go, at least?" Jeff asked from beneath his hat. "I want ice cream."

"You're welcome to sleep over at our place," I told him.

"Isn't summer the best?" Liz reflected, rising and folding her lawn chair. "No school, endless sleepovers, and ice cream."

"Right," I agreed, stretching out my hands to Justin so that he'd help me from my chair; he would have anyway, but I was also communicating, *All is forgiven, I'm done being bitchy about Aubrey* with the gesture. He took my hands, dark eyes warm on mine, and bent to kiss my knuckles like a cowboy from an old movie. On my feet, I snuggled into his chest, hugging him close. He kissed the top of my head, clearly replying *I know, baby*.

"Boys, meet us at the cafe," I told Jeff and Clint, who'd biked to the field.

Ten minutes later we had parked at home and then walked through the woods to Shore Leave, where Mom, Blythe's step-grandfather, Rich, and Aunt Ellen sat having their evening smoke at a porch table, enjoying the twilight air. Flickertail was calm under the darkening sky, while a chorus of crickets about a million strong harmonized with the low-pitched, intermittent chirping of the pair of mourning doves nesting in one of the cedars near the cafe. A cardinal was perched somewhere, serenading the rising moon. Clint and Jeff pedaled up on their bikes and coasted in lazy circles around the parking lot.

"Grandma, we're here for some ice cream!" Rae announced, running ahead.

"I love this time of night," Justin said, swinging our joined hands, walking to accommodate my slower pace. He nudged my shoulder as we passed my old apartment, where we made plenty of love during past nights. "It reminds me of making out with you on that little landing up there. And then down on the dock." His voice took on a reverent tone. "God, I was so happy to find you that first night. I was praying as I drove, praying like I'd never prayed before, that you would be down there, alone…"

I giggled, vividly recalling. He'd confessed this more than once before. I teased, "I'm so flattered."

Justin was grinning, his teasing, naughty-demon grin that made fire burn along my skin, and would until the day I died. As we were closing in on hearing distance, he lowered his voice to whisper, "Dammit, my sweet, sexy little woman, it's all I can do keep from carrying you down there this minute."

Clint caught sight of us and angled his bike our way, and I bit back the reply I'd been intending to give my husband. Clint braced one foot on the ground and asked, "Mom, after dessert, can me and Jeff ride back to town? There's a bonfire out at the field."

"That's fine, honey," I said. "Just don't stay out too late."

"Justin, Jillian, you two want ice cream?" Mom called from the porch.

"Hell *yes*," Justin whispered fervently in my ear, and I shivered and then giggled more as he murmured, naming my favorite, "As long as it's caramel, with pecans," a sticky dessert he'd licked from my lips and various other parts a little farther south on my body, on many past occasions. And then, in a tone of voice that suggested he had never before harbored a dirty thought, he called over to Mom, "Thanks, that would be great!"

Up on the porch, I bent to hug Rich, as I hadn't seen him a few days.

He patted my back and asked, "How's the baby, honey?"

Rich was my second surrogate father, Dodge being the first; I'd known both my entire life. Rich smelled of tobacco and his aftershave, which was nearly as familiar to me as the scent of my mother's shampoo; she had used nothing but Prell since before Jo and I were born. I straightened and regarded Rich with both fondness and concern; he was looking tired these days. The baby kicked and I reached for Rich's hand.

"Feel," I offered, cupping his palm against the sudden frenzy of activity behind my belly button.

Rich's bushy white eyebrows lifted. "What have you been eating to get him so worked up?"

"He's just a night owl," I explained.

"Here, honey, have a seat," Rich said.

"I got a place right here," Justin, already sitting, offered, angling his right thigh for me to claim.

"I'm going to go help Mom," I said. I could hear Rae's chirping voice through the open windows, directing operations, and smiled. I told Justin, "Save my spot."

"Jillian, slice up a few more strawberries, would you?" Mom asked as I pushed through the swinging door between the dining room and the kitchen.

"Sure thing," I said, fetching a paring knife. The strawberries were washed, gleaming brilliant red in the wire colander on the counter. Rae stood on a chair, spooning whipped cream onto slices of pound cake; every other spoonful went into her mouth. Mom set forks in the first two bowls.

"Little one, bring these to Clinty and Jeff," Mom said, handing them off to Rae, who climbed carefully down from the chair. There was whipped cream in her bangs.

I'd wanted to talk to my mother alone and asked as casually as I could manage, "What do you think about that Zack guy?"

"Who?" Mom asked, busy slicing pound cake.

"That Moorhead student who barged in here today," I elaborated.

"Oh, he seemed nice enough," Mom replied, shrugging. "I got the impression he's a city kid."

I wanted to ask if he bothered her at all, if she sensed anything strange about him. I'd felt slightly off all day; again I experienced a sense of having been severed from something.

It's Aubrey, I justified again. *She's unsettling you more than you'll admit. And Camille—you're worried about her, too. There's so much on your mind.*

"Just wondering," I muttered, letting the matter drop, finished slicing the strawberries.

Back outside under the ivory moonglow I claimed my seat on Justin's lap and relaxed against him, resolved to chill out from this moment forth.

I woke to the thrumming of steady rain on the roof, a sound that would have been much more cozy and insulating if my husband wasn't getting up to go to work, rather than snuggling with me under the covers.

"Don't go yet," I murmured, still half-asleep, and then smiled as Justin thumped back onto the tangled sheets for one last kiss.

"You rest more, baby," he said tenderly. "I'll see you guys at lunch."

Our bed was deliciously warm and I drifted back to sleep after Justin left, curled around a pillow.

That's strange, I thought. *Summer shouldn't be over yet...*

But Shore Leave was decorated as though for autumn.

October probably, as the sky shone like polished cobalt, made all the more vivid by the contrast of the scarlet maples, the yellow-gold of the birches decked in their fall colors. The cafe was bustling with activity as I stood watching from the far edge of the parking lot. Somehow I knew I was supposed to be a part of the flutter but my feet wouldn't obey my wish to walk forward. For a while, on the outskirts, I admired the scene in the afternoon light. Dead leaves rustled around my ankles; I could smell their musty, damp-earth scent. People seemed to be dressed up for an occasion and then I sensed my niece behind me, and understood.

Camille's wedding.

I turned to smile at her and was instantly submerged in an icy wintertime lake, the freezing water closing over my head and stealing my breath. I floundered, helpless and terrified, unable to process the sight of Camille sitting on the grass with her spine curved like a wilted stem, wedding dress torn to shreds, the agony on her face catching me like a hammer to the heart. Beyond tears, beyond anything, her golden-green eyes ravaged by pain.

What could hurt me now? She choked on the words. *He's gone.*

I whirled toward Shore Leave, sick with desperation. But I spied the groom and a ribbon of relief twirled around me.

He's not gone, honey. He's right there. But then I squinted against the bright glare of the autumn leaves, and really saw.

Noah Utley leaned over the porch railing, fair and handsome in his black tuxedo, hands curled over the top, looking out to us. His happiness was apparent enough that I needn't be near him to see it; joy lit his face.

Milla! It's almost time, he called to my niece.

Camille was at my shoulder then, her breath on my cheek. *Aunt Jilly, don't let it happen. Oh God, wake up!*

Wake up!

"Mama! Wake up!" Rae blasted, almost in my ear, and I jerked to a sitting position.

"Mom, you all right?" Clint was in the doorway, eyebrows arched high. He was fully dressed, toting his work boots, and I remembered that he started his new job today; Mathias had put in a good word for him and Clint was going to be training with the township forest fire crew.

I pressed a hand to my clubbing heart.

Just a dream. Not a Notion. That wasn't real.

"I'm just fine," I told my son. Rae knelt on the bed and rested both palms against my belly.

"Can we call the baby Mickey?" she asked, fond of choosing names for her little brother.

Clint leaned on one shoulder in the doorframe, looking unconvinced despite my assurance.

"Honey, do you still have to go even when it's raining?" I asked, in an attempt to redirect his concern.

He didn't answer right away, still studying me with his blue eyes somber. "Of course. Rain or shine!"

"I suppose," I responded, catching Rae for a hug, blowing on her neck to make her giggle. Clint shoved off the doorframe and continued down the hall. I called after him, "Breakfast at the cafe if we hurry!"

As it was Tuesday, I wasn't scheduled to work lunch but Mom asked if I could pick up a shift almost the moment we clacked through the screen door. I shook out the umbrella, leaning outside to do so, while Rae shimmied out of her yellow raincoat. Jo and Matthew were already at table three, Jo sipping coffee and Matthew in his booster seat with a bowl of oatmeal. Blythe wasn't working at Shore Leave today, as he would have joined them; when not helping out in the cafe, he worked several days a week in a cabinet-making shop on the outskirts of town, learning the trade.

Clint thumped up the porch steps behind us. Almost before he sat down, Aunt Ellen set a plate of maple syrup-drenched pancakes, with a side of bacon, on the table in front of him. Clint was so spoiled; thank goodness his personality had never reflected that.

"Thank you," he said sweetly, digging in, and Aunt Ellen rested her hand on the back of his neck, bending to kiss the top of his head. Rae squirreled onto Clint's lap and stole a piece of bacon, crunched a loud bite, and then dangled it at little Matthew, teasing him.

"*Rae*," I scolded, taking the final empty seat at their table. I helped myself to a strip of bacon from Clint's plate, too, and he playfully stabbed at my hand with his fork. I leaned to kiss Matthew's plump cheek and appropriated Jo's coffee mug, stealing a sip.

"Morning, Jills," said my sister. Her hair was twisted up in a loose knot and she sat chewing on the end of a pencil, frowning at an open notebook on the table in front of her.

"What are you doing?" I asked. "Homework?"

"Making a list," Jo said, and then looked up to meet my eyes. She heaved a little sigh and elaborated, "Tish and I are driving down to the Cities to shop for college stuff today."

"Oh," I said, my eyes drawn to my own college-aged child, who sat shoveling pancakes into his mouth. Clint was usually in tune with my moods, even if he often appeared oblivious. But he was a good listener, an observer. Both he and Tish had been accepted to the University of

Minnesota, and as happy as I was that they would be near one another and at a good school, I dreaded the thought of their looming absence from Shore Leave. I said to my son, "I suppose we'll have to do the same here one of these days."

He nodded, watching me carefully, as though afraid I might burst into a frenzy of weeping.

"Good morning, everyone!" Mathias heralded with characteristic cheer as he, Camille, and Millie Jo hurried through the door and out of the rain. Camille's long hair sparkled with raindrops and the image of her from my dream, broken and despairing, came rushing back, unbidden. To distract myself I went to pour a cup of coffee.

"I'm nervous," Clint told Mathias, turning in his chair.

"You'll be fine," Mathias reassured him, helping settle Millie Jo on a stool at the counter before claiming the one beside her. Camille paused to kiss the side of Mathias's forehead before heading back to the kitchen to lend Mom a hand. Mathias held Camille's gaze, a smile soft on his lips, and the heat between them sparked almost visibly. The sight hurt my chest.

It was just a goddamn dream. It was not a Notion.

"I was really nervous my first summer," Mathias said, while Clint ate, listening avidly. "But you'll do great. Just pay attention and be ready to work hard."

"Hey!" Rae yelped, as Matthew succeeded in snatching the bacon from her hands, stuffing it in his mouth with glee.

"Serves you right," Clint told her.

"Matty-Bear, that wasn't nice," Jo scolded, but Matthew grinned around the bacon in his mouth, looking just like Blythe, and Jo melted like ice cream left on a sun-drenched picnic table.

"Yeah, he knows how to work his mama," I observed, stirring sugar in my coffee.

"Jilly, can you work for your sister today?" Mom appeared in the ticket window to ask.

"Sure, as long as Ruthie can watch Rae," I said, lifting my eyebrows at Jo.

"I'm sure that's fine," Jo said. "I suppose I better call them. They weren't even out of bed when I left." She caught up her phone.

Fifteen minutes later my nieces arrived, Ruthann to watch the girls while Jo, Matthew, and Tish left for their day of shopping. Clint was hitching a ride to work with Mathias, but he caught me for a hug before leaving.

"I know something's wrong," my son said, bending way down to put his chin on my shoulder. "You don't fool me."

Clint looked so much like his father, and always had, but it was the sound of his voice that caught me off guard; if I wasn't looking directly at Clint, I would have sworn that it was Christopher speaking just now.

Aw, Chris, I thought, holding my long-ago husband close right along with Clinty. *I hope you can see our son. He's such a good boy, and you would be so proud.*

"I'm all right," I whispered, even though normally I told him the truth. I added, as though justifying, "It's this whole pregnancy thing."

But I could never fool Clint; he was right on that count.

"It's that lady who was standing there when I came to get the keys last night, isn't it?" he asked. "That's who Dad used to be married to. I remember her from when I was younger."

Surprised, I nodded confirmation of this.

"Well, she looks legit skanky," Clint said, and I couldn't help but laugh. "What did she want anyway?"

"It's a long story," I said, realizing he needed to get going. "I backed the work truck into her car in the parking lot at Farmer's Market and she wants Dodge to fix it up for her. She's making a bigger deal than necessary."

"Did you hit her car on purpose?" Clint grinned at the prospect.

"Of course not!"

Mathias called, "C'mon, buddy, we gotta go!"

I hurried to say, "Good luck today, sweetheart, be careful, all right?"

"I will, Mom." He kissed my cheek. "Everything's fine, don't worry. See you later!"

I watched him and Mathias hurry across the parking lot in the sheeting rain, shoulders hunched, and reflected that sometimes it took a teenager to put things back into perspective.

Chapter Six

Rain, rain, go away, I THOUGHT AS I CLEARED A FOUR-TOP near the windows, hooking coffee mugs on my fingers, balancing plates. The pewter-gray sky had been weeping steadily all morning and I worried about Mathias out there in the downpour; the forest fire crew practiced and trained no matter the weather, and I hated the thought of him chilled and shivering without me there to warm him.

Oh for the love, Ca-mille, I scolded myself, separating my name into two distinct syllables, as Mom did when upset with me. *He's just fine.*

But I let my imagination run wild with the countless ways I would warm him tonight, in our bed.

"Milla, can you take the back booth?" Grandma asked, coming up behind me with a pale blue menu, laminated and single-sided, in her hands. "Jilly has her hands full at the counter."

"Sure, I'll get right over there," I said.

A minute later I flipped to a new page in my order book, looking down at it as I paused at the booth to get a drink order.

"Isn't this Jillian's section?" a male voice asked.

I glanced up and realized it was the grad student from Moorhead, the one who'd barged into the cafe so rudely yesterday, when we were closed. He sat alone, wearing a Cardinals ball cap and a t-shirt with rain-drenched shoulders, stirring creamer into his coffee; clearly Grandma had been here with a pot already. His gaze flickered behind me, in the direction of the counter, where Aunt Jilly was working.

"Nope," I said, trying to hide the impatience in my tone. He seemed like an asshole, which was maybe an unfair assumption, but something about him reminded me of the boys with whom I'd once attended private school back in Chicago, in another life I had absolutely no interest in revisiting, even in memory. A sense of entitled arrogance hovered about him. I all but snapped, "You need a minute?"

He looked up at me, clearly amused. Watching my face like a scientist anticipating a big reaction, he observed, "You're pretty young to be someone's mother. Got started early, huh?"

A frown drew my eyebrows together but I could tell my obvious shock only increased his amusement. For sure an asshole. This time refusing to disguise the acid in my voice, I announced, "I'll come back when you're ready."

"No, I'm ready now," he said, with what was meant to be a teasing tone, I could tell. "Number five, please, with fries." His eyes dropped from my face to my breasts and he leaned forward on his forearms. I took an immediate step away and he clarified, "I'm just trying to read your name tag."

"Well, *don't*," I muttered, wishing I could pour hot coffee right onto his lap. Without another word I turned from the table.

"Thanks, Camille," he called after me, emphasizing my name.

Behind the counter I caught up with Aunt Jilly and said, "What a *jerk*."

Aunt Jilly, in the process of making coffee, looked my way and raised her eyebrows, asking without words what I meant. For a second I admired the true blue of her eyes. She was so pretty; she and Mom looked very much alike but I'd always thought of Aunt Jilly as a pixie, probably because she was petite and always used to keep her golden hair short, like Tinkerbell. Her face was delicate, tiny freckles skimming her tanned cheekbones, her soft lips shaped like a pink rosebud.

"That guy from yesterday, I think his name is Zack," I elaborated, thumbing over my shoulder. "He's rude as hell."

Aunt Jilly's expression changed, just subtly, but I knew her well enough to see something negative cross her features. She obviously sensed something off about him, too. She asked, "What did he do?"

"He's a garden-variety asshole, that's what," I said, reaching for a fresh coffeepot. "He reminds me of the rich kids I went to school with back in Chicago, needing to feel superior to everyone else."

Aunt Jilly exhaled through her nose and seemed more upset than my words would warrant. "We can ask him to leave."

"Jilly, hon, can I get a refill?" asked a regular at the counter.

"Sure thing, Chuck," she said over her shoulder, and I put one hand on her elbow.

"No, it's all right," I said, wishing I hadn't mentioned anything. Aunt Jilly had seemed extra distracted the past few days and I didn't want to trouble her with nonsense. But I could sense Zack watching us from across the crowded dining room. Packing my voice with conviction, I insisted, "I can deal with him."

She nodded, saying *okay* without sound.

I steered clear of his table as best I could after that, delivering the food with no comment, hoping the cold shoulder would discourage him from returning here while he was in Landon. Shore Leave stayed busy with the lunch crowd and when I finally wandered back to check on him, I saw he was already gone. I breathed a sigh of relief as I cleared the table, noticing a twenty dollar bill placed squarely atop a napkin. Twenty was far more than his lunch would have cost and I glanced around the cafe, wondering if he was still here, expecting change; maybe he'd gone to the bathroom. Rain obscured the view out the window; everything outdoors resembled a blurry watercolor painting, and so I couldn't tell if Zack's car was still in the lot. Then I noticed handwriting on his napkin and lifted it up, confused.

The napkin read, *I didn't mean to make you uncomfortable. Thanks for lunch. Tell Jillian I said hi.*

I dropped the note as though it had burned my fingers. Before anyone noticed, I crumpled it into a tight wad and stuffed it directly in the garbage.

By late afternoon the rain clouds shredded apart and drifted away; the sun became blinding upon the multitudes of droplets clinging to the leaves. I went to collect Millie Jo from Ruthann, who earned plenty of money watching the girls on days when Aunt Jilly and I worked lunch, to find my daughter napping on the couch in Grandma's house. Ruthie told me she'd bring Millie home when she woke up, and so I walked over to my apartment to change out of my work clothes. I thought about doing some cleaning but instead found myself lifting Malcolm Carter's letter and telegram from the drawer of my nightstand, carrying these, and his photograph, to the kitchen table, where I sat and studied them.

"Where did you end up?" I asked Malcolm, angling the picture into the sunlight drifting through the west-facing window above the sink. As though he could somehow hear me. "Please tell me. I need to know."

I stroked my fingers over the surface of the photograph, touching the leather strip tied around Malcolm's wrist, the one with a woman's name carved into it; this detail was something I had noticed for the first time last winter. I imagined how Malcolm's voice would sound, could he reply to me. Then I touched the typeface on the telegram from 1876, with its desperate tone and heart-wrenching words. MISS YOU ALL SO MUCH I HURT, one sentence read, hand-lettered on the ancient Western Union paper.

Oh, Malcolm, I thought, aching at this evidence of his pain. *We'll find you. I promise.*

"What were you searching for?" I whispered, wishing he could magically appear to tell me; I glanced at the adjacent chair, imagining Malcolm sitting upon it, regarding me with the same half-grin that graced his handsome face in the photo. "If only you could talk to me. I wish we could take Aces out for a ride." Mathias and I joked about Aces all the time, as though he was *our* horse. In the photograph, which was not colorized, Aces appeared dark, his nose adorned with a long, narrow blaze marking. I imagined that his hide had been a deep reddish-brown, that I could step outside right now, cup his long face, and press my lips to the blaze. I *knew* I had done that very thing. Some way, somehow. Not for the first time, I imagined doing the same to Malcolm—cupping his face, seeking his mouth with mine.

I whispered, addressing the picture, "Would you know *me*, if I suddenly appeared in front of you?"

Through the open window I heard Mathias's truck rumble into the parking lot and I was out the door and halfway down the steps before I knew I'd even moved. I came across the yard just in time to see him climbing down from the truck, Clinty slamming the passenger door. Mathias caught sight of me and opened his arms.

"Hi," I whispered against his chest. He wore faded jeans and steel-toed boots, thoroughly caked with mud from the day's work, and the navy blue fire crew t-shirt that read CARTER in white letters across the back. His black hair was damp from the earlier rain, the stubble on his jaws raspy as he lifted my chin for a kiss.

"Hi, honey," he whispered. "I'm so glad to be home."

And then Clint leaned over the hood, bracing on his forearms, and announced, "Holy *shit*, Milla, Mathias almost died today, seriously."

Time seemed to pause, crystallizing the air around us.

Mathias said immediately, "That's not true."

"What are you talking about?" I demanded in a voice not my own, looking between them as the setting sun struck my eyes.

"I did not almost die," Mathias insisted, but Clint was shaking his head.

Clint supplied, "There was this tree limb overhanging the fire station that Chief Larson wanted removed, right? So he tells Mathias and another guy, Josh, to climb up there and take care of it. They showed me how to operate the ladder on the boom truck and then they climbed up to that branch. It was way up there, too, and—"

As much as I loved my cousin, his explanation was making me insane and I interrupted his prattling. "Then what?!"

Mathias took over, holding my gaze in his as he explained, "I climbed out on a branch beneath the weak one but then Josh stepped behind me, to hand me the saw, and then there was this cracking sound, like a gunshot, and—"

"The branch broke just like a fricking matchstick!" Clint concluded, his face stark white at the memory. He added quietly, "I don't think I've ever had my heart stop like that."

Mathias said quickly, "Josh grabbed my arm right away. He still had one foot on the ladder, it was all okay. But shit...my footing just fell away. In all the years of working on the crew, I've never had anything like that happen. And here we were doing chores, not even on a response. It took a while for my heart to calm down."

I realized he was babbling a little, still shook up, and understood that no matter how he attempted to reassure me, he'd been in serious danger. I clutched the material of his shirt in both fists.

"Hey," he said, observing my expression. "It's all right, honey. I'm just fine."

"I want you to call and tell them that you're done. Tomorrow. *Tonight.*"

"Honey, I can't do that. I've worked there every summer for years and never had something like this happen. It was just a freak thing."

Tears blurred my vision and I stalked away, aggravated at his continued stubbornness, just as I'd been furious when he wouldn't quit walking his trap lines alone. Behind me I heard Clint say, "She'll be okay in a minute," but Mathias dogged my steps.

"Hey," he said again, and the concern in his voice caused my feet to stall. He caught my elbow and gathered me close, resting his cheek on my loose hair, repeatedly smoothing its length with both hands. "It's all right."

The grass smelled sharply of the recent rain, the humidity of the day washed away. In the evening light, the quality of which was more precious than any jewel, I clung to him; a small part of my brain acknowledged it was irrational to demand that he quit the fire crew. Even still, I said brokenly, "It's *not* all right! What if Josh *hadn't* grabbed you? You'd be gone from me…*oh God*…"

He made a sound in his throat, concern and love. I pressed my cheek to his beating heart, holding him as hard as I could; at the center of my worst fears, I knew I had faced this before – I'd faced life after having been ripped from him, much different than a life in which we had not been allowed to find each other at all—and the loss haunted me even now, holding him close in the evening light, in *this* life.

"Camille," he whispered. He rocked us side to side, similar to the way I soothed Millie Jo when she was upset. After a time he dared to add,

"I'm always careful, I want you to know that. We're always careful on the crew, we check our equipment. We really do."

"You *think* you do, but I know you take chances," I rasped, my throat raw. "Last winter Jake McCall told me about how you went back into a burning house that one time…"

"That was crazy, even for me. I blame that on teenaged hormones." He added intently, "I would never take foolish chances, honey, not ever." He drew back enough to lift my chin. "I have never had so much to live for."

"Accidents happen so quickly," I argued. "You think I'm being unreasonable, but you don't take it seriously."

He used one thumb to brush away my rolling tears. "If we thought about all the terrible things that could happen, we would go crazy. Truly crazy, I mean. I know you better than that." He bent and kissed the skin beneath my right eye, then my left, softly as a bird's wing brushing my face. He whispered, "You're tired, I can tell. There's shadows under your eyes."

"I've been dreaming so much," I said, resting my forehead against his chest. "I wake up exhausted."

He said, "I know you do. C'mon," and stooped enough to lift me into his arms. He carried me up the steps and through our kitchen, then down the hall to our tiny bedroom. It was still early evening and I could hear the whine of outboard motors all over the lake, but he murmured, "Rest, honey, I'll hold you."

"What about supper?" I murmured, eyelids already drifting shut.

"Screw supper. Let me hold you," he whispered, and I pressed my face to the scent of him and was asleep within minutes.

When I woke again it was deep night. I lay tucked under the covers and could hear Mathias down the hall, in the kitchen making something to eat. I sat slowly, our mattress squeaking, and Mathias appeared in the doorway seconds later, backlit by the hall light.

"Hi," he whispered, in keeping with the stillness of the night.

"Is Millie sleeping?" I asked, disoriented from sleeping away the entire evening.

"She went home with Jilly and Rae." He joined me on the bed. "I packed her an overnight bag, and we remembered her toothbrush and everything."

"You're such a good daddy to her."

"That's about the best compliment I can imagine," he said, leaning to kiss my neck. "Are you hungry, hon? I had an idea while you were sleeping."

"What's that?"

"I thought maybe we could eat and then go for a swim. The stars are gorgeous out there."

Mathias grabbed the sandwiches he'd made while I changed into my bikini and dug the last two clean towels from the closet, along with the bug spray. The night was warm as we crept down our steps, the air alive with the sounds of crickets and frogs, the occasional owl. Barefoot, we made our way along the familiar path to the dock, fingers linked. Mathias sat on the glider and collected me onto his lap, keeping the towels draped to block out the mosquitoes as best we could, and for a sweet while we cuddled without speaking, eating our sandwiches, my head resting on his left shoulder.

"That's why people have babies," he murmured after a spell, as though we'd been in the midst of a conversation.

"Why's that?" I turned to rest my nose against his neck.

"To have part of the other person always with you," he whispered, and my heart panged, as though I'd been struck hard there. Try as I might, I could not get the image of the breaking branch from my mind. How quickly he could have fallen, been injured or killed. His words brushed my skin, low and intent. "You have my heart, Camille, and that's always with you, no matter what. I know you know that." He paused and I could tell he'd closed his eyes. "I've been thinking all evening about what happened today. It happened so fast. I was more freaked out than I was letting on. It scared the shit out of me."

"I could tell," I admitted.

"But I'm just fine," he said, sounding more like himself. "It's all right."

I slid my palms along his sides, his bare torso warm beneath my hands. "You have my heart, too. My heart is yours, for all time." I'd echoed the inscription on my ring without intending to, and a flash of déjà vu struck with enough force to create a dizzy ripple across my vision. Mathias took my left hand and kissed my knuckles, then my ring, the one he'd found as a boy and just last winter placed upon my finger.

"Then I'm the luckiest man alive," he whispered, dimple appearing as he grinned. "Will you swim with me?"

"I would do anything with you." Without another word, I stood and unclasped my bikini top, letting it fall to the dock.

"So that's the way of it," he said, a little hoarsely. Valiantly, he kept his eyes on mine rather than letting them detour south. I stood unselfconsciously in the starlight; I had long ago lost all inhibitions around him, and slipped free of my bottoms next, stepping delicately from them. The heat in his eyes nearly torched me alive.

"Come on," I invited, jumping into the lake, in part to escape the hordes of whining mosquitoes. It wasn't as warm as I'd anticipated but my shriek was muffled by the water. I surfaced just as Mathias, now also naked, executed a shallow dive and then swam underwater to me. I felt a burst of welcome laughter as his strong hands closed around my thighs. He surfaced near my breasts, the water lapping at my nipples, rising to his full height; his hair stood in wet spikes and he gave me a grin.

"Let's swim out to the middle!"

I nodded agreement and he ducked under, swimming just beneath the shimmering black surface. I took a moment to appreciate the heady night air, inhaling the familiar scents of the nighttime lakeshore—scents that were released in the night, no longer stifled by the sun's heat. The air was so calm I could almost hear the motion of the brown bats' wings as they flapped above us; as though to highlight the point, laughter floated across the lake from downtown Landon, a good half-mile away.

Mathias surfaced twenty feet out and I was about to push off the bottom and swim to join him when a horrible chill seized my spine. I froze, the same way I would have a split second before swimming for my life, as though a rattlesnake or some other equally deadly creature was approaching unseen beneath the water. I bit back a cry, willing myself to relax; the last thing either of us needed right now was more drama. I focused instead on Mathias, his head sleek as an otter's in the moonlight, treading water in the middle of the lake.

"C'mon, honey!" he called in a hushed whisper, and I kicked off the bottom and swam with sure strokes, my arms cutting through the dark liquid with hardly a splash; I'd adjusted to the temperature and the lake felt warm as bathwater, soaking my naked skin. It wasn't until we were more than fifty feet from the dock, the black-silk sky mirrored on the flat surface, reflected stars rippling with our passage through them, that the realization struck me.

Someone, hidden from view, was watching us.

Instantly I berated myself. *You're being totally ridiculous. No one is out here except for the two of you.*

Still, I wondered if I should tell Mathias what I suspected.

"Look at those stars," he enthused, rolling to float supine. His skin appeared silver-white against the ebony mirror of the dark water and reflected sky, his face lifted to the heavens as he hung suspended, naked and unconcerned. I continued to tread water, my arms moving in slow undulations, unable to keep from peering back toward the cafe. From this distance and vantage point, submerged to my neck in Flickertail, everything on shore appeared tiny. I scanned the familiar shoreline, inspecting every detail in an effort to seek out something furtive, someone hidden neatly from sight. Ever since becoming a mother, and certainly since the attack on Mathias last winter, part of my mind was on constant alert.

Quit it. You're out here under this gorgeous sky with your man, and nothing is wrong. No one is there.

With that thought in mind, I kicked out my toes and maneuvered nearer to Mathias, floating on my back alongside him. It was a giddy, almost otherworldly sensation, with the distinct thrill of the illicit, skinny-dipping under the starry sky, Flickertail silent and mysterious, a keeper of secrets, as it never was by day. I felt cradled by it, held as though in a womb, hearing the rhythm of my heart like a steady drumbeat, ears submerged under the water. The stars were so bright, so breathtaking and immediate, that a part of me believed if I willed it strongly enough,

I could somehow rise up there and drift among them, through space and time.

"It's so peaceful out here," Mathias whispered. "This is what I missed most when I lived in the Cities."

"This is the summertime equivalent of the northern lights," I whispered. Mathias loved to take us on winter picnics, where we would cuddle in the plow truck and watch the aurora on long December nights.

"For sure," he agreed. "Look at that cluster over there. I swear that as often as I've looked at these stars, I still find new ones. I used to swim at night all the time, only on that side of the lake." And he indicated in the direction of White Oaks.

"Same with us, every summer we'd come here," I said.

"It's so funny to think about all those summers you were over here, just around the lake." He brushed his fingertips against mine, beneath the water. "So close to each other, but we didn't know."

It was just what I'd been considering, the other night at Bull and Diana's.

So close...

What if...

But you found each other in this life.

You found him. It's all right now.

"It is, isn't it?" I whispered, and tears prickled, seeping from the corners of my eyes to the lake. I tilted my head to look at him; he looked my way at the same time, as we linked our fingertips. If I'd never believed in souls before this moment I now understood fully, beneath the stars of this sky, that they were real, interconnected in ways I could never comprehend.

And more than that, I recognized that mine and his were one.

Chapter Seven

A week had passed since I'd taken out the front headlight on Aubrey's car, and we'd not heard a word from her since the evening of Clint's baseball game. I didn't know if Dodge had found the time to fix her car, and I had not asked. Fixing it required a new headlight to be ordered and I cursed myself anew for not taking better care with Mom's big truck; the greater the delay in fixing her car, the longer Aubrey would be stuck in Landon. But I had bigger concerns than Aubrey Pritchard; after Clint's first day training with the forest fire crew, all thoughts of her were relegated to my back burner when Clint told us about Mathias's close call at the fire station. The memory of my nightmare about Camille's wedding loomed as Clint spoke; I reminded myself it was not a Notion.

I hadn't slept well the past week, blaming all of the things weighing on my mind as I wandered the darkened house while my family slept. More often than not I ended up on the porch swing, keeping rhythm with one foot, watching the pines and letting the sounds of the night-time woods lull me into a state of sleepiness. I remained more troubled than I could admit, even to myself; something was wrong. Large and amorphous, this knowledge stalked me, growing ever bolder. Even more troubling was the fact that I recognized something was wrong but could not perceive just what. My senses were noticeably dulled, altered some-how, and I was terrified—so terrified that I could not articulate the fear aloud, as though speaking of it would be equivalent to the final nail in the coffin.

Justin could tell I was struggling with something. He would not be pacified with my response that I was fine, just tired. Gently rocking the swing as I sat sleepless in the wee hours yet again, I thought back to the months after my car accident, three years ago now, when I'd moved back in with Mom and Aunt Ellen, unable to navigate the steep, narrow stairs leading up to my apartment. Mom had rearranged the living room to accommodate my near-invalid status, she and Aunt Ellen taking care of me during the day, while Justin was at work, and then he'd hurry over to Shore Leave to be with me all evening, spending the nights in a sleeping bag on the floor beside the fold-out couch; he'd been so worried to jostle my healing body that he'd not dared to sleep beside me. I'd sustained multiple broken bones and a punctured lung, on top of being pregnant. Instead, he lay as close as he could, reaching up to rest his hand gently on my leg, or my hip, curling his fingers around mine.

"I can't sleep unless I feel you," he'd explained.

Justin, sweetheart, I thought now, hearing the comforting, low-pitched growl of him snoring through the open window of our bedroom. I pictured the way he looked on our wedding day, late autumn of 2003; my recovery from the accident was gradual, and frustrating, but nothing could dampen my joy that day.

"Because of you, my heart is whole," Justin said during our vows. He'd been so excited, working on them before the wedding, using an old notebook he'd pilfered from the cafe, absorbed in his writing but refusing to read any aloud, despite my pestering. He'd insist, "You have to wait for the wedding, baby."

"Well, you are a poet, as I know well," I'd said; he was fond of creating poems of the impromptu variety, especially when we made love. "Just remember that children will be in attendance."

From his spot on the armchair angled near the couch, he leaned and kissed my right knee, saying, "Including our own," and patted my belly, where Rae was cradled at the time.

Clint and Jo stood up for us at the service, acting as best man and matron of honor. Justin carried me up the porch steps at the advent of the lovely, golden hour of sunset that evening, into the dining room at Shore

Leave. We'd both agreed we wanted the wedding kept small and simple, at the cafe; there was only one church in the Landon area, where each of our first weddings took place, and a ceremony held there did not appeal to either of us. One of Dodge's cousins was ordained and officiated for us, but even as Ike Miller spoke over us that evening, I was lost in Justin's intent gaze. An entirely unspoken set of vows passed between our eyes, an acknowledgment of the importance of the moment, the promise of our lives interconnecting from that day forth. After the ceremony our kiss lasted a good fifteen seconds. Then he'd lifted me into his arms and carried me straight back down the porch steps to his waiting truck, and we'd gone home and made love (carefully and so sweetly) before joining everyone a little later (amid much good-natured teasing) at Eddie's Bar for the lively reception, well in progress.

Our wedding was perfect in every sense of the word.

Out in the woods a gray owl hooted, answered seconds later by its mate, and the baby pressed at my belly. "Hi, son," I murmured, patting the little foot. I shifted position, wishing for a smoke, wondering if Jo was still awake and if she would sneak over to hang out if I called her. I knew she would, but she was tired these days, too, what with a toddler and two teenagers in her house. I heard the screen door ease open, just behind me.

"You don't have a pack stashed out here, do you?" Justin teased in a whisper, reading my mind.

I peeked over my shoulder, shaking my head even as I admitted, "I *wish*."

"Come to bed, baby," he murmured, scratching his bare chest. "I'm lonely in there without you. And I worry about you out here alone."

"It's peaceful out here," I said, though I rose to my feet and joined him where he stood holding open the screen door, fitting myself against his warm torso.

Justin rubbed his palms over my upper arms, as though to ease a chill. He kissed the top of my head and invited, "I'll rub your back."

"That sounds wonderful," I murmured, and he led me to our bed.

"Yay, Mama, it's sunny!" Rae announced the next morning, her little face right at my ear. She rejoiced, "Today's the parade!"

"You're right," I mumbled without opening my eyes. I could hear Justin in the shower, getting ready for work, though he and Dodge would close up early so we could take the kids to the parade downtown. The Landon parade was always held on the third of July, as the high school band was expected in Bemidji for a larger event tomorrow. Mom and Aunt Ellen had been planning their annual potluck party for the last week, which would take place tonight at the cafe.

"Get up, Mama!" Rae insisted, rubbing her hands over my back about as soothingly as a rug burn. She demanded, "C'mon!"

"Sweetie, go see if Clint's up. Mama's still tired."

"I'm up!" Clint said, pausing at the open door. "I have to be at the station in like twenty minutes. Mom, can I borrow your car?"

"Sure," I grumbled, tugging a pillow over my head, though Rae managed to roust me out of bed before too long. I showered and helped my daughter choose a red, white, and blue outfit, then sat on the edge of my bed wrapped in a towel, another wound around my wet hair, turban-fashion, holding the comb between my teeth as I worked Rae's silky hair into two braids. She was impatient with excited energy and I kept my knees around her torso in an attempt to restrain her bouncing.

"Hurry, Mama!"

"Hold still," I replied around the comb, tying off one of her braids with a sparkly blue rubber band. I finished my styling and she scampered back atop the bed, smiling at me with all of the joy that being two years old and anticipating a parade lent to a kid. Her eyes crinkled at the corners as she smiled, just like Justin's, and I smoothed a strand of hair from her cheek.

"I love you, stink-bug," I said, and she giggled at the nickname.

"Mama, get dressed!" she ordered, clapping. "Wear a pretty dress!"

I rose and opened the closet, gamely plucking a possible choice from its hanger. "What about this one?"

Rae rolled to her knees and tipped her head to one side, with a critical frown. "No. I like the pretty red dress, Mama."

I replaced the first dress and found the one Rae meant; I was fond of it, too, and had worn it a couple of times when pregnant with her. It was a gorgeous geranium-red, casually styled like a tank top with a long skirt.

"This one?" I asked, and she nodded, braids bobbing.

Rae raced to her room and found a few strands of plastic bead necklaces, blue and silver. I brushed out my hair and let her drape the beads over my neck; I discreetly adjusted the first necklace so that it wasn't lassoing my right breast. I giggled, thinking I'd have to keep watch for that all day. After getting ready, Rae and I walked over to the cafe to find everyone eating breakfast. Mom, Aunt Ellen, Jo, Matthew, Tish, Ruthie, Clint, Camille, and Millie Jo were all present when we clacked through the screen door, and I reflected, observing the usual morning chaos— Clint and Tish arguing, Jo trying to have a conversation with Camille and Ruthie that kept getting interrupted by the little kids, Mom and Aunt Ellen poring over an order sheet, coffee cups at their elbows—that I was pretty damn fortunate. We sure as hell weren't wealthy; we lived in modest homes and drove mostly old cars. Modern technology still had a long way to go to reach Landon; the nightlife here was basically non-existent; my son would probably never know that there was such a thing as jeans that cost more than twenty dollars. Would I ever want to live anywhere else? Hell, no. I had long ago learned the value of a simple life.

Besides, we had each other. And that was worth more than any riches in the world.

"C'mere, baby," Justin ordered with lazy contentment. We'd walked downtown after lunch and were currently situated at the far end of Fisherman's Street, under the shade of an enormous sunburst locust. Our town spread out before us under the afternoon sunlight, people we knew milling all around, talking and sidestepping excited kids, sipping lemonade and iced tea and beer; the scent of black powder, hot dogs and mini-donuts, tootsie rolls and bubble gum, diesel from the trucks hauling parade floats all intermingled in the still, hot air.

I settled on my husband's lap, kissing his jaw. He wore his swim trunks and a t-shirt from his baseball league, which would start up again in late July, with the word MILLER written across the back in black letters. I felt a swell of belonging and happiness, infinitely more precious than gold, as Justin kissed the side of my forehead and our kids sprawled on the curb near our row of lawn chairs. Rae, one of her braids coming unraveled, was crouched with steely-eyed determination, watching the street corner where the parade would start, clutching her candy bag. Clint was also wearing his bathing suit, along with a faded Landon Rebels t-shirt from his high school days, leaning on one elbow and appearing half-asleep behind his aviator sunglasses, one leg angled protectively behind Rae. He was barefoot but I didn't pester him about it, since I'd also kicked off my sandals.

"Life is pretty damn good," Justin murmured, lashes lowered to study my face, grinning as he rubbed his palms over my belly. "Sitting here with you like this, my sweet little woman, is such a blessing. You know how many times I used to watch you bring Clint to this same parade and wish I was sitting with you guys?"

I cupped his right cheek and stroked the scarring on that side of his face. "I would have welcomed you with open arms, just so you know."

"Next year the baby will be here with us, too. I can hardly wait." He nodded at our daughter and added quietly, "You think Rae will like being a big sister?"

"She won't even remember a time before him, after too long. Can you remember a time before Liz?"

He shook his head. "No, and speaking of the devil…"

I giggled, waving to Liz as she headed our way with her triplets in tow. Ruthie and Tish were with them, along with Clint's buddies, Jeff and Liam. Within a few minutes our whole clan inundated the sidewalk. Joelle, Camille, and Liz settled on lawn chairs, along with Mom, Rich, Aunt Ellen, and Dodge, while the kids flopped all over the threadbare blankets we'd spread on the sidewalk. Mathias and Blythe joined the kids on the curb, Bly with little Matthew on his lap. Matthew snuggled against his daddy's broad chest and stuck a thumb in his mouth, eyelashes fluttering. Mathias pointed out a team of quarter horses with sparkly blue ribbons on their harnesses to Millie Jo, explaining why the animals were wearing blinders.

"Good thing we came early to get seats, we take up almost the whole block," Clint said, resting his forearm on my knee, as though he was little again. I cupped my oldest child's face, struggling to accept the fact that he was on the precipice of leaving me for good. I knew he'd return to Landon to visit but it would never be the same after he went away to college; my heart shrank at the thought.

Justin ruffled Clint's hair and Clint grinned, again like a little boy, before reclaiming his place beside Rae; he wrapped an arm around his little sister and teased, "I'm getting all the candy! You better watch out!"

Rae squirmed away and crouched forward like a runner at the starting line. "Nuh-uh!"

The first stirring sounds of the high school band rang through the hot air, getting things rolling with "The Star-Spangled Banner," the color guard leading the way with flags lofted high. Justin shifted so that we could stand and my eyes flickered to Rae, making sure she stayed put, but Clint kept his hand on her head, corralling her. Everyone around us was in the process of saluting or placing their hands over their hearts, and I was about to do the same when something across the street snagged my attention. What exactly alerted me I was not entirely sure, maybe a certain unnatural stillness or just an uncomfortable shifting of the air, but I saw Zack Dixon then, watching me.

My stomach lurched. He wore a ball cap that left his eyes in shadow but somehow I understood that he stared with an unwavering gaze. He tilted his head just enough to acknowledge that he was aware I'd spied him. He remained otherwise motionless for another second before turning away, as though innocently engaged in enjoying the parade. I jerked my gaze from him, my chest tight, heart beating too fast.

Tell Justin, I thought at once. *Point Zack out. Who knows how long he's been standing over there watching you?* Somehow the thought that Zack could see my family, my husband and kids, made me all the more ill. But then I thought, *You're being ridiculous. He isn't doing anything wrong. Why cause a problem where there isn't one?*

And as though I'd imagined the entire thing, Zack was gone when I looked back.

The party at Shore Leave got rolling as soon as the parade ended. Eddie Sorenson and Jim Olson drove directly to the cafe, where they set up their chairs and proceeded to tune their guitars near the makeshift dance floor. I helped Mom, Aunt Ellen, and Jo tote food to the picnic tables, while Justin, Mathias, and Blythe carried more chairs from the garage and hauled wood for the bonfire. Dodge and Rich carried a beer cooler between them and settled near Eddie and Jim, the four older men recalling days gone by, the sound of their voices comforting in the background. Bull and Diana arrived next, bringing along two kegs of beer, and before long the parking lot was jammed, everyone double-parking, or pulling onto the grass, to join the festivities.

The little kids mobbed the dance floor for the first hour; Mathias was the first to brave the wild horde, bowing formally to Camille and escorting her into the fray. I could see him singing to her as they danced, holding one of her hands to his heart. He was such a sweetheart, and my niece's eyes were aglow with love as they swayed along to the music. *Oh God, let us be dancing at their wedding next*, I thought, watching them. I'd tried with all of my effort to force the nightmare of her wedding day from my mind, but it clung like oil. I'd not mentioned it to anyone.

"J, you're not getting out of dancing all evening," I warned my husband, as we claimed seats at one of the picnic tables.

"Who said I wanted to get out of it?" Justin teased. He carried a plate for Rae, which he set before her on the checkered tablecloth, and then helped her get situated on the bench. "Rae-Rae, you have to eat all your food before you get dessert."

"Grandpa said I could have as many roasted marshmallows as I want!" Rae announced.

"Is that so?" Justin replied drily, winking at me. "Grandpa better get

Mama's permission before saying things like that, if he knows what's good for him."

Clint slid onto the bench across from me, his plate loaded with two bratwursts, a double cheeseburger, a pound of baked beans, about half a bag of Doritos, and four pickle spears. He was balancing all this on two cans of orange soda.

"Hungry?" I asked.

"Gotta keep up my strength," he explained, eating half the burger in one bite.

"Daddy! Clint doesn't have any veggies!" Rae tattled, a frothy pink ice cream mustache decorating her upper lip. "*No fair!*"

"Pickles," Clint contradicted around a full mouth.

"We should probably make a trip down to the Cities one of these days," I told my son. "I made a list of stuff you'll need. Did you check the college website like I asked?"

Clint shrugged noncommittally; he had expressed zero interest when I tried to start this same conversation on two separate occasions.

"Honey, I know you don't really like shopping," I said, as Justin cut Rae's hot dog into manageable bites.

"Mom," Clint said.

"I don't really like shopping either," I reflected. "Maybe Jo would come with us. She actually likes shopping, and she's so much more organized than me. And she just went with Tish—"

"*Mom*," Clint said again, more insistently, interrupting my musing.

At the tone in his voice I fell silent. Justin looked between Clint and me, clearly wondering what was up.

"See, I've been thinking..." Clint slouched a little now that he'd claimed our full attention, pushing his baked beans around the paper plate the way he used to when he wanted to make it look like he'd eaten more than he actually had. He lifted his blue eyes to mine and finished in an urgent rush, "I've been thinking I don't really want to go to school in Minneapolis."

My lips fell open and Clint looked right back at his plate.

Justin caught my gaze and asked silently, *Should I say something?*

No, let me first, I said back, setting aside my fork and lining my fore-arms along the edge of the table. Rae appeared fully absorbed in eating her strawberry-banana gelatin, topped with whipped cream, but I sensed she was also paying close attention.

Clint's eyes remained downcast as I asked quietly, "Why are you thinking that, honey?"

A flood of earnest words rushed forth. "I don't want to leave Landon, for one thing. And I don't think I necessarily need a degree. I mean, maybe I'll change my mind but right now I want to get my certification and work for the fire crew. And it seems like a waste of money to pay for school when I don't even know what I want to do for a career right now. Tish wants to be a lawyer like her dad, and has this whole plan and stuff, but I don't." He heaved a sigh and looked to Justin, as though for encouragement, asking plaintively, "Dad, you didn't go to college, did you?"

Justin hooked a hand over Clint's shoulder, patting him. "You know what, I didn't. I thought about it. I actually got accepted to Stout State in Wisconsin, but then I got married way too young and that was a big mistake."

Clint nodded in all seriousness and Justin continued, "I know it's a hard decision to make, son. We all hate the thought of you moving away, but we don't want you to miss any opportunities, either."

Clint leaned his shoulder into Justin, who curled an arm and squeezed him close, understanding that Clint needed reassurance right now, more than anything else. Clint muttered, "I know."

"We won't make you do anything you don't want to do, Clinty," I told him. "There's still over a month before you have to go. You might decide you want to give dorm life a try, too."

Clint shuddered. "I would miss the lake."

"Hi, guys!" Tish heralded, plunking down beside me, her plate as full as Clint's had been; baked beans sloshed onto the tablecloth. She giggled and said, "Oops," scooping a bite of gelatin into her mouth. It wasn't un-til then that she regarded our serious faces; she paused in her exuberant eating and muttered to Clint, "You must have told them."

He sat straight again and nodded, blowing out a breath that puffed his cheeks.

"Make room!" Dodge said, headed our way now, Liz and Wordo just behind him, along with Jeff and the triplets.

I told Clint, "We'll talk later, all right, honey?"

Hours later, Rae had eaten her fill of roasted marshmallows and was snuggled on Aunt Ellen's lap, near the bonfire. Dodge, Mom (who held Millie Jo and Matthew, one on each knee), Rich, and the Carters were all seated around the fire, too, drinking beer and enjoying the gorgeous mild evening. Eddie and Jim played for hours with no breaks, an impressive feat, and were currently in the midst of a slow song. I was sitting with Jo on the porch steps, telling her about Clint's latest announcement, when Blythe approached us.

"Sorry to interrupt, ladies," he said in his deep voice, with gentlemanly formality. Almost shyly, he explained, "But I was hoping to dance with my wife."

Joelle smiled, reaching for him, and his answering grin could have heated the whole state in a midwinter blizzard. I elbowed my sister and muttered, "Remember you're in public, you two."

Blythe drew Jo to her feet and hugged her close. "How did I get lucky enough to become a part of this family, huh?"

"Well, you are kinda cute," I teased, squirreling in between them to steal a hug. I adored my brother-in-law.

He leaned down and kissed the top of my head, then ruffled my hair. "Thanks, Jills."

Jo stood on her tiptoes to kiss Bly's chin, tucking hair behind his right ear. She agreed, "Yeah, kinda cute all right. We'll talk more, later, Jilly Bean, I promise."

I went in search of my husband, determined to haul his ass onto the dance floor for a few songs. I tired too quickly for any serious dancing, but he wasn't getting out of it altogether. I found Justin sprawled comfortably in a sling chair near the picnic tables, where the non-dancing menfolk gathered, laughing about something with Wordo. I pit-stopped at one of the coolers and fished out a sizeable chunk of ice. Wordo caught sight of me approaching, but I put a finger to my lips to indicate silence and then slipped it straight down the back of Justin's shirt. He broke off in the middle of a sentence and yelped, leaping to his feet to dislodge the ice cube.

"*Darn* you, woman," he said, catching me close as I laughed and struggled. He pressed a kiss to my cheek and muttered, "If this is your attempt to get me on the dance floor…"

"You promised," I nagged, poking his ribs.

"Come sit on my lap instead," he invited in his most husky, sexy voice, the one he knew I could not refuse.

I caved. "For a minute. But then we're dancing, you owe me."

"Oh, I'll pay up," he promised, kissing my jaw, settling me in the sling chair with him; with our combined weight, I was surprised it didn't instantly collapse. Justin threaded his fingers over the fullest part of my belly.

"I never knew you were such a bully, Jills," Wordo teased, draining the last of his beer. "You need one more, J.D.?"

"That would be great," Justin said.

"And a lemonade," I requested, smiling at my brother-in-law.

"You got it." Wordo stood and stretched. There were dozens of adults dancing by now, most of the little kids having found laps to climb upon. I smiled at Jo and Blythe, holding each other close, and at Camille in Mathias's arms, listening to whatever he was saying with a soft smile on her lips. They were planning to leave for their vacation the day after tomorrow. I was watching my niece when Wordo's tone suddenly changed. He said, "*Uh*-oh," and I followed his gaze; my curiosity morphed instantly to bristling irritation.

"Oh, for fuck's sake," I muttered.

"She's loaded," Justin observed, with a sigh, and I supposed he would be the first to recognize it, as he'd lived with her in the same house for many years. He smoothed his palms over my belly and I was reminded, however ridiculously, of the way a person might soothe a pregnant cow. "Do you want me to tell her to leave?"

I felt my teeth go on edge, unable to peel my eyes from Aubrey as she leaned rather heavily on her cousin, Jen Lutz. She'd obviously arrived with Jen, whose husband was now playing guitar along with Eddie and Jim. Aubrey wore a very short, very tight jean skirt and a flowy white blouse, and she cast her eyes over the noisy crowd, finally homing in on us like a big, nasty, ugly pigeon. Except that she wasn't big or ugly. Just nasty.

"No," I said, answering Justin's question. My throat felt raw. "That would just imply that it bothers me."

"I'll tell her," Wordo offered. "Or Liz will. Liz hates her guts."

This was my home turf and Aubrey had the nerve to show up here; grudgingly, I acknowledged that about half of Landon was also in attendance. But it was still an insult of the lowest order, one that a part of me felt I couldn't let slide; I wanted to march over there and snatch a fistful of her long, shiny hair and tell her to get the fuck out of here. But doing so would only indicate to her that I was needled by her presence. Continuing to eyeball Justin and me, she rested her fingertips on her hips and flicked her auburn hair over one slim shoulder, and it was that familiar arrogant gesture which made my hands curl into fists.

Justin felt the tension in my body and murmured, "Jills."

With that one word I clearly discerned his worry for me and his quiet plea to let this go. I wished it was that easy. Aubrey's cousin redirected her attention, probably inadvertently, and Dodge headed over from the fire, hunkering down near our chair.

"You want me to make her leave?" Dodge asked, and I could hear the concern in his voice as he looked between Justin and me.

I whispered, "No, it's all right. I don't care."

"Well, I care," Dodge said, patting my knee. I'd told an obvious lie, but he let it slide. His presence was so reassuring; I reflected how much I loved my father-in-law, who'd been like an actual father to me for so long now, since my childhood. After Justin and Liz's mother left Landon, Dodge had held it together for his kids, and I had always admired him for that love and stability. Justin's mother had never even seen Rae and barely knew Liz's triplets, who were in their teens now, and though Justin was matter-of-fact about this I knew it still stung him deeply. Sometimes that was the trade-off, I knew well, as my own father had never been in the picture for Joelle or me. Perhaps having one good, solid parent was worth enough. Though he hardly ever spoke of it, I knew Justin depended a great deal on Dodge.

Dodge sighed. "All right then, honey. Tell me if you change your mind. I know she's only here to upset you, and that upsets me."

Justin's arms tightened around me and I understood he felt the same.

"No, it's all right," I said again, heartened by my family's concern.

"I'll get that goddamn car fixed and then I hope she leaves town for good," Dodge said. He caught Justin's eye. "You just say the word, boy."

"Thanks, Dad."

"I'll be at the fire with the little ones," Dodge said.

Wordo followed Dodge to collect fresh drinks for us, leaving Justin and I relatively alone, and I tried hard to keep my eyes from darting back to Aubrey, but she might as well have been flashing with Vegas-style neon colors, sequins and feathers and the whole cheap bit.

"I never would have guessed she'd pull this shit," Justin said, his chest vibrating against my spine as he spoke. "I'm sorry, baby. Don't let her upset you. It's what she wants."

"Who's upset?" I demanded, clearly upset.

Aubrey eased away from her cousin and waltzed through the semi-rowdy crowd, heading for the picnic tables. No one really seemed to be paying attention to her progress, except for me, and my heart crackled with electric anger as she skirted a few lawn chairs, stopping no more than three paces from our knees. I caught the familiar scents of both cigarettes and schnapps emanating from her. For a half-second I felt sixteen again.

"I saw you guys at the parade today," Aubrey said, her voice just on the border of slurry.

Good for you, I thought, exactly as Justin said, "Well, good for you."

"So *cute*," she mocked. "What a *cute* little family."

Neither of us replied to this comment but she was undeterred, telling Justin, "You owe me."

I sat straighter, my blood in a hot riot, prepping me to battle for my husband. Behind me, Justin remained calm and silent; he patted my belly again and though it was not his intent, I felt more like a mama cow than ever, big and fat and awkward, while Aubrey stood there all thin and leggy in her tiny skirt, reeking of booze.

When she failed to succeed in coercing a reply, she ratcheted up the whine in her voice and again addressed Justin, insisting, "I need to *talk to you.*" Her eyes snapped to me, as I had inhaled an angry breath, more than ready to let her have it. She lashed, "It's none of your business, Jillian *Davis.*"

Justin finally spoke up. "Anything you say to me is my wife's business."

"*I'm* your wife," Aubrey said, clearly without thinking, and then affected a horrible little laugh. She corrected herself, "Maybe not anymore. But you still owe me."

"What in the fuck are you talking about?" I demanded, and my voice was so loaded with hostility that I hardly recognized it.

"Wouldn't you like to know?" Aubrey all but purred.

I wanted to deck her in the mouth. I couldn't help but wonder how Justin would be reacting if this situation was reversed; if somehow my ex-husband was behaving this way in front of us. As though there was any chance in hell of that, but still. Justin would have dealt him a fist to the face by this point. Or at least seriously considered it.

"An…explanation," Aubrey finally said, stumbling over the word. "That's what he owes me." She looked back at Justin. "So you're Clint's dad now, too?"

"I sure am," Justin said, without missing a beat. I could tell he was not about to get pulled into her icky little ploy. I hated hearing Aubrey speak my son's name.

"You are not," she challenged, and then repeated, "You owe me."

"He doesn't owe you shit!" I raged, losing all cool. Despite the music and the noise of the crowd, a few heads turned our way.

Aubrey bent closer to me and I saw that her eyes were unfocused. Her breath was heavy and stale, ripe with peach schnapps. She actually dared to tap my nose with the tip of her index finger, whispering, "*Fuck you.*"

"Okay, that's it," Justin muttered, acid in his tone. He set me gently to the side before standing and indicating the parking lot with an outstretched arm. "No way do you talk to Jillian that way. Get Jen to take you home. *Now*."

Moving swiftly for being so drunk, Aubrey lifted both hands and caught Justin's t-shirt in her fists. I thought I might bite through my own tongue as she pleaded, "I'm sorry, Justin. I need you. Don't you remember how it used to be with us? You just need to *listen*…"

Justin took her wrists in his hands and forcibly removed her grip. She stumbled and he lowered her to a lawn chair; I could hardly see through the buzzing red rage in my skull. Justin was furious; she'd finally succeeded at that. He bent forward, firing his words like bullets. "You are the world's best liar, you know that? Jesus Christ, what a great performance. What is wrong with you? You can't handle that I'm happy without you? Are you fucking kidding me?"

I hated most that someone could make him so angry, to speak such things aloud. Aubrey retained that power over him and I hated her all the more for it, and for ruining our evening in this way. Joelle was suddenly there, and Jen Lutz, and things seemed to happen very quickly, and in a blur. Aubrey left with her cousin, tearful, making as much of a scene as possible. Justin's jaw was rigid with tension. Jo said, "Come on, Jills, let's go," and led me inside Shore Leave.

"You're shaking," Jo said, clicking on the overhead lights. She wrapped me in her arms and smoothed one hand over my loose hair. "I'm so sorry I didn't notice Aubrey was here. What a dumb bitch. Jills, are you okay?"

"I want to go home," I managed to say, clinging to my sister, my voice muffled against her familiar scent; she was right, my teeth were practically chattering.

The screen door banged open behind us and Justin said, "Baby, I'm so sorry. Come here."

He brooked no argument and Jo surrendered me to his arms. I wanted to cry but the heated emotions raging through me would not allow for tears. Justin bent his face to my loose hair. "You're shaking. Christ, I'm so sorry, sweetheart. That was so ridiculous."

"It's all right," I whispered. "I just want…to go home."

He nodded agreement, rubbing his hands over my shoulder blades as Clint was the next to barge into the cafe.

Clint cried, "Mom, are you all right? Holy shit, what happened? Did you almost get in a fight?"

I drew away from Justin and gathered myself together. "No, of course I didn't almost get in a fight."

"Then what happened?" Clint demanded.

"Will you please walk me home?" I asked my son, who nodded at once.

"*I'll* walk you home," Justin said. Immediately he throttled down his single-minded tone and amended softly, "Let me, please."

I looked up at him and my eyes sparked with a hot burst of fire, surprising me; I hadn't realized I was also angry at Justin.

"I'll be at home," I said, looking away as I ordered, "Come on, Clint."

Justin said, "I'll get Rae and be right there," and in my current mood I felt like he was attempting to do nothing but get in the last word.

Clint was uncharacteristically silent as we walked the short distance to our cabin, keeping my hand tucked in the curve of his right elbow. On the porch, I realized I didn't have my house key and fumbled for the one hidden in the planter to the right of the door. Clint finally asked, "So what happened? Grandma said Dad's ex-wife was being mean to you."

My dear son, always worried for me. I tugged on him so that he would bend down, and then kissed his cheek. I smoothed my hands over his close-cropped dark hair. "I'm so glad you want to stay around here. I couldn't bear it if you moved too far away from me."

"Aw, Mom." His voice cracked and he cleared his throat. But he wouldn't let me change the subject so easily. "Are you sure you're all right? Dad said he was coming right home."

"I'm fine," I said, unlocking the door. "You go back to the party and have fun. Tell Aunt Jo that I'm all right, or she'll be worried."

The trees seemed to be whispering as Clint loped back toward the cafe. The breeze had increased, shifting the air, and I could no longer hear Eddie's guitar tinkling through the night like a distant music box; its absence struck me as ominous. I wanted to sit on the porch swing and relax but as Clint disappeared into the woods a bolt of fear caught me unaware. A shiver seized the bones in my spine and sent the hairs on my nape prickling. It was such a terrible sensation that I froze, a mouse before a hawk, perceiving danger the split second before it presented itself. My gaze flew to the pines on the edge of our lot, their individual needles sharply accentuated in the moonlight.

Someone's there, I recognized, and the key fell from my wooden fingers. *Oh, my God. Someone's out there.*

I stared, riveted by certainty, heart thrashing, certain that a shadowed figure was about to emerge from the pines only yards away—a slow walk at first, gaze fixed on me, then bounding forward—

"Stop!" I cried, rasping over the word, lifting my palms to ward off the attack happening nowhere but within my head.

Jillian, open the door and get inside.

The reprimand, delivered straight to my panicking brain in the tone of Great-Aunt Minnie, served to center my focus. I scrabbled for the knob, rocketing into my house and slamming the door with enough force to rattle the dishes in the cupboard. Breathing hard, wild-eyed, I jammed the deadbolt into place and rushed to the window, peering immediately outside, only to see nothing. Not one damn thing. No stranger in my yard, no intruder striding across the grass. Only the pines. I closed my eyes, fingertips pressed to the cold glass, stretching out with the full force of my awareness, to be met by a maddening emptiness. The presence I'd sensed had vanished—or, I realized, my imagination had just played a mean trick. My fingers were unsteady as I slid back the deadbolt so that Justin and the kids wouldn't be locked out.

Ten minutes later, when Justin came home, Rae in tow, I lay curled beneath the blankets in our darkened room, troubled far beyond anything that had happened with Aubrey; fear had effectively taken precedence over the confrontation with her. My internal wiring, that which had always connected me to an extra set of perception, seemed haywire—and I couldn't shake the feeling that I was being messed with, on a level unknown to me.

But how? And why?

I heard Justin and Rae brush their teeth before he tucked her into bed and read her a book; the low murmur of his voice and her sweet, high-pitched lilting responses served to comfort some of my agitation. When Justin came in our room, quietly closing the door behind him, my first instinct was to tell him what had just happened—and how strange I was feeling in the aftermath. But something clamped hold of my tongue, a small resurgence of petty anger; I pictured Aubrey getting her hands around his t-shirt and my insides seized up all over again. She had told him she needed him. There was a part of me that wanted to kill her for thinking she had the right to say that. I heard Justin's clothes falling to the floor; he hadn't clicked on the lamp.

"Baby, I know you're awake," Justin murmured, drawing back the covers and sliding near. The temptation of his strong, warm, nude body was almost more than I could bear but I didn't answer, hot with stubborn petulance, pressing my cheek to the pillow. I felt all jacked up, for too many reasons to name, and craved a fight nearly as much as I craved our intense lovemaking. I sensed him on one elbow behind me, studying my back. He finally whispered, "I'm sorry. I understand that you're upset."

When I refused to answer, he stroked my hair, just lightly. He murmured, "All right, then," before lying down and rolling to face the opposite direction. Thoughts screamed through my head, each trying to win the upper hand.

Was there someone in our yard or did I just imagine that?

What in the hell is going on?

Do Aubrey's words mean something to Justin? Would he rather not know that she feels those things?

I sure as hell could have lived without knowing.

Jillian. Talk to him, right now. Tell him what you're thinking.

But in the end I fell asleep before saying anything.

Chapter Eight

By early evening on the Fourth of July, the truck was loaded to bursting. Though Mathias was as much of a slacker about housework as me, he was adamant about making sure we had everything we needed for our trip. In a flurry of impressive organization, he wrote two lists and together we had scoured Bull and Diana's big garage, helping ourselves to their array of outdoor gear. The plan was to camp for the first two nights, then stay with Harry and Meg Carter in Bozeman for two or three more before turning the truck back east to head home. Two sleeping bags, a tent, two low-slung camp chairs, one cardboard box of camping supplies and one cooler later, the truck was ready to make the journey west. Remembering well the long drive from Chicago to Landon every summer, I lined up two bed pillows in the back window, for use on the road.

Mathias jogged back from stashing the truck keys in our apartment; the whole clan was gathered down at the dock, deciding whether to ride in the pontoon or the speedboat to watch the fireworks. I could hear laughter and chatter, and the familiar rise and fall of Tish's and Clint's voices as they argued with each other. Millie Jo squealed about something and I smiled, feeling a beat of anticipation. I loved watching the fireworks explode over the lake. I called, "C'mon, love, let's go get a seat on the motorboat before it gets too full!"

Behind me, a car pulled into the lot; I turned in time to see Noah climb out and fix his gaze on the cafe. He was dressed differently this evening; normally he appeared about to attend a tennis match, or dine at a country club, never a golden hair out of place. Currently he wore a scruffy t-shirt and jeans. He glanced between Mathias and me, hesitating; I saw a sigh lift his shoulders before he approached. A few feet away from where I stood, he stopped and pulled off his sunglasses.

"Hey," he said.

"What are you doing here?" I asked, not exactly rudely, but a little startled. He hadn't called, and I definitely hadn't been expecting him. "We're going out on the boat in just a sec."

There were dark shadows beneath his eyes; it was an understatement to say that he appeared troubled. "I know. I just..."

"Just what?" Impatience, and growing concern, heated my nerves.

"I'd like to talk to you for a second," Noah said, not exactly a demand but his tone was much more assertive than normal. I sensed more than saw Mathias's shoulders square but he refrained from making any comment. Noah seemed to be holding his breath, his eyes weary but steady upon my face, and I was reminded uncomfortably of Mathias's words about how he thought Noah looked longingly at me; there was maybe a trace of that on Noah's face, I was not imagining it. I rarely thought of the summer Noah and I were together, preferring not to recall my own vulnerability, or how ridiculous I had acted in those days, like a puppy dying for any little affection he offered, but I suddenly remembered that Noah had first told me he loved me on the Fourth of July.

And like a fool, I'd believed his every word.

I looked at Mathias and his expression was patient, carefully hiding all traces of misgiving.

"Do you need his permission?" Noah asked, venom in his tone.

Mathias tensed, anger in his posture—but he knew he needed to let me handle this; there wasn't an overt threat on Noah's face, but challenge nonetheless.

Shit, I thought. *Why now?*

I cleared my throat and said quietly, "No, I don't need permission and I resent you implying so." I let that sink in before asking, "What do you need to talk about?"

"It's about Millie," Noah said. Then, seemingly to impress me with kindness, he changed his tone and used my nickname, "Will you please give me a minute, Milla? I want to talk about our daughter." He emphasized *our* just enough.

Mathias took those words like a blow across the face; I didn't have to be looking at him to realize this. I was not exactly in a position to disagree, as much as the thought of having to talk to Noah about anything, even Millie Jo, only exhausted me.

"Just say what you need to say," I said, sidestepping whatever game he was trying to play.

"It's all right," Mathias said. He smoothed a hand down my back, the briefest of touches, before saying, "I'll be on the boat." And without another word he strode across the yard, toward the lake. I watched him, the evening sun dusting his hair and his wide shoulders; it took about everything he had not to look back, I could tell.

"Listen," Noah said. His eyes were oddly intense in his pale face, which unsettled me. I had never in my life been frightened of Noah Utley—I'd been spurned by him, enraged and disgusted by his actions, but never afraid. And I would not start now. Without further preamble, he continued, "I don't like him making decisions for Millie."

I swore I heard the sound of my anger flaring to life like the business end of a struck match. "You have got to be fucking kidding me."

"I am definitely not kidding." Noah sounded like my father when he spoke in his lawyer voice.

"Mathias and I are engaged," I said, as though Noah didn't realize. "He loves me, and he loves my daughter, and he is…" At the last second I bit back the cruel comment, despite the fact that it was true that Mathias was far more a father to Millie than Noah, and instead spit out, "He is going to be her stepfather for the rest of her life. He and I will make plenty of decisions that affect her."

"I would like a little respect," Noah said heatedly, his expression taking on a fire I was not accustomed to seeing. "I am getting my act together and I want to see Millie more often. I want equal custody of her."

I would not let the roaring in my ears obliterate all sensibility; I would not grab the nearest heavy object and brain him. But my voice shook hard as I asked, "Since when?"

"Since now. I want—"

"Bullshit!" I interrupted furiously, anger borne of fear supercharging through me. I stared at him with open loathing and demanded, "Why all of a sudden? What's changed?"

He looked hard into my eyes and I didn't want to see what was present in his; I wanted him to get in his car and drive away, and I never wanted to deal with him again.

Before he could answer, I said, "Millie is *mine*. She is my baby and I will never let you take her from me, not even half-time." My chest ached with anger. "You left me and I didn't think I'd be able to make it on my own. But you know what? *I did*. I found Mathias, and *I love him*. I love him with all my heart!" I was yelling now and Noah was regarding me with the kind of grimacing expression a person might wear when being confronted by a lunatic.

"Camille," he interrupted, brusque with impatience. "Stop! *Jesus*. I fucking panicked, okay? And I'm sorry. When you told me you were having a baby, I couldn't deal with it. Maybe it doesn't mean shit to you now, but I just want you to know that I regret that. A lot."

"Well good for you," I muttered, glaring at him, breathless with consternation. "You can be the first to tell that to Millie someday."

"I *fucked up*," he said, and suddenly there was a naked desperation in his eyes, stronger than before. He continued in a rush, "I'm so sorry. I would hate myself forever if I didn't at least tell you that." He took my shoulders in his hands. "I'm at a point where I can take care of you now. You and Millie. I'm ready. I want that." He saw the disbelieving stun in my eyes and his hands dropped away.

"I think you should go," I whispered, recovering the power of speech. "Please, just go."

"Do you hear what I'm saying? I'm telling you I want to try and make it work. We never even tried…"

For a moment I was rendered truly speechless.

"Camille, did you hear what I said?"

I found my voice and spoke quietly. "It was never meant to be between us, Noah, that's all. We had sex a few times and I got pregnant, and I thought my world was ending, too, if I'm completely honest." He narrowed his eyes, as though he didn't understand, as though I might have an ulterior motive. I reflected that Noah had never really known me at all. "Even if I wasn't engaged to someone I love, I wouldn't take you back now. You think you can make your mistakes go away with an apology? No way. If you want to be a better dad to Millie, I'll let you. I won't stop that. But don't come here and tell me you're ready to take care of us now. Haven't you ever heard of actions speaking louder than words?"

"You really love Carter that much?" he asked after a pause, my words floating as though alive in the air around our heads. His voice was rough.

"I do."

Noah's chin jerked and he looked away. His lips twitched, jaw clenching, but he said with perfect calm, "I guess I knew that."

I suddenly had a horrible thought, one that made my blood ice up.

No—you're wrong, Camille. You're dead wrong. Noah would never spy on you and Mathias. There was no one watching you the other night while you were swimming. No one.

I tried to be nice then, to compensate for what I'd been thinking. I whispered, "I appreciate that you're trying more with Millie. That's something."

"I love her. I really do. I want you to know that." Noah's eyes filled with tears, which he did not allow to fall.

I kept my voice gentle. "Then *show* her."

"She looks just like you." He sat down on the porch steps, cradling his head in both hands. From that position he whispered, "I'm so sorry. I wasn't just using you that summer. I know you think I was. If I could go back and change things, I would."

"Don't," I begged.

Just as abruptly he stood, startling me. His eyes were red. "I won't fight you for custody. I only said that to hurt you." He cleared his throat, roughly, and added, "I would still like to see her on the weekends. I'd like to try to be her...dad." His voice choked on that single word, almost a sob, and my heart clenched in pity. I had no desire to see him in pain, despite everything.

With quiet firmness I said, "You are her dad."

"I do feel bad for him," I told Mathias much later, snug in our kitchen after the fireworks on Flickertail. We sat facing each other at the kitchen table with its mallard duck salt and pepper shakers, left over from when Aunt Jilly lived here. Millie slept soundly after the evening's excitement. I wore an old t-shirt of Mathias's as a pajama top, over a pair of lacy g-string panties. It was a strange combo, I knew; I needed to do laundry. Mathias, in his faded blue pajama shorts and absolutely nothing else, sat at a right angle to me. I'd told him everything that Noah said earlier, and he'd listened quietly. Roughing up my damp, loose hair with both hands, I sighed and concluded lamely, "I'm sorry."

"You have nothing to be sorry for." Mathias cupped my elbow. He was so warm, his touch so welcome on my bare skin. The back of his neck and the tops of his shoulders were sunburned, the rest of his powerful torso a rich brown, his thick hair wet from a recent shower, both on his head and chest. His muscular forearms were peppered in dark hair and if Bull was any indication of the future, one day his back would be quite covered as well; at the thought, I almost smiled. The gold flecks in his eyes shone in the glow of the light above the kitchen sink; he appeared uncharacteristically somber.

"Thank you for understanding." I smoothed my palm over his forearm, skimming the surface of his skin as I stroked the hair there one way and then the other, almost meditatively. "Thank you for not playing his game."

"Yeah, it hurt to leave you alone with him, I'm not gonna lie. But I could tell he was hoping to pick a fight. He wanted me to step in so he'd have a reason to react." He paused, searching my eyes. "I hate that he said those things to you, but I promise to try not to let it bother me."

I cupped his stubbled jaw, love for him expanding my heart, cracking it wide open; it was his unconscious way, opening me to feelings beyond anything I'd ever known. "I love you, Mathias Carter."

Later, I threw together a small bag of extra clothes and our bathroom things, including my glasses in their hardback case. We planned to leave at midmorning. Mathias had explained that it took a good ten hours to reach our first stop, a state park in eastern Montana.

"And that's not counting rest stops, and sightseeing stops, and stops to get out and smell the sagebrush. And make love," he added, his usual good mood restored, grinning at me over the unzipped canvas tote on our bed. I was about to close up the top when Mathias leaned forward to extract something from its contents.

"Honey, what's this?" he asked sternly, holding up a pair of transparent, turquoise blue undies. I leaned past him to root around in the bag, producing the matching bra, not much more substantial than dental floss. He swallowed hard and tried to maintain a strict expression. "I don't think these will protect you from ticks."

I said innocently, "They're rated number one in that outdoor catalogue you made me read."

He stepped closer, lowering his brows. I giggled and evaded, getting the bed between us. He offered up his slow, smoldering grin, twirling my panties around his index finger in a lazy fashion.

"Do we make love before or after we smell the sagebrush?" I asked wickedly. "And isn't sagebrush sharp? Prickly, I mean?"

"It's not sharp," he informed in his know-it-all voice. "It's soft, and smells incredible. The best is to rub the leaves between your fingers," and he demonstrated on my panties.

Oh, I said without sound, and my knees went a little weak.

"I can't wait for you to see the mountains," he said, grinning just as wickedly as he continued stroking my undergarments. "And we can ride horses."

"Bluebell and Renegade!" I cried, giggling. "Where are we camping tomorrow night? That place with the funny name…" I was thrilled at the prospect of real camping. I hadn't been on a camping vacation in years.

"Makoshika State Park," he reminded. He pinned me with his gaze and ordered, "Come here."

I shook my head, shivery with anticipation. "I'm not ready for bed yet."

He dove over the mattress and caught me close.

"Me, neither," he whispered.

In the morning, I cried more at leaving Millie Jo than she did at the prospect of me going on a trip without her. I hugged her for a third time, inhaling the scent of her curly dark hair, kissed her cheeks, and then took her little face in my hands. I said, "I love you, baby. You be good for Grandma, all right?"

"I will, Mama!" she said, cheerful as always. And then, as Mathias picked her up for one more hug, she added, "Bye, Ma-fias!"

He kissed her cheek and whispered around a lump in his throat, "Bye, my sweetheart."

By early afternoon we'd cleared the Minnesota state line and were well across North Dakota. I kicked off my shoes and propped my bare feet on the dashboard; Millie and I had painted our toenails a brilliant neon blue the night before last. Mathias cranked the radio and we sang along with the CD currently spinning in the player, Travis Tritt's greatest hits. The landscape grew ever more rugged as we cruised west, the long, flat expanses of wheat fields in central North Dakota finally giving way to undulating foothills and towering outcroppings of rock that suggested a hint of the mountains to come. I could not wait to lay eyes upon the Rockies. The ridges in the distance were rounded at their peaks, tinted by variegated shades of rich brown, dark as chocolate in one spot, streaked through with pale amber in another. We drove with the windows rolled down, not minding the rush of wind; the air flowing into the cab of the truck smelled fresh and herbal.

"Sagebrush," Mathias said. "I *told* you."

We stopped at five different overlooks throughout the day, snapping pictures with the digital camera that Diana lent us, Mathias bending down to my height, both of us laughing as we pressed our cheeks together and he held the camera high to capture yet another shot of ourselves.

"I love that you're such a good sport," I reflected as we drove on from the blue sign welcoming us to Montana, in the late afternoon. I felt a jolt of pure excitement at the sight of that state sign, the sense of wildness and wonder inside my soul stretching further outward. I clicked through the pictures we'd already taken, giggling at one where Mathias was licking my cheek instead of smiling for the camera. "You're such a goofball, and I love it."

"Sense of humor is vital," he said, lifting his eyebrows high and making a face at me as he drove. "And I love that you get mine. Most people just think I'm crazy, as you well know."

"You *are* crazy. But then you lick me and I'm totally fine with the craziness."

"Come lick me," he invited, and I scooted across the bench seat and got him good across the ear, so that he yelped and wiped it against his shoulder.

"If I wasn't driving you'd be in trouble," he warned, as I giggled and shimmied right back to my own side, propping my feet on the dash again. Out the windshield the sky was bluer than a jay's wing, streaked with a few thin, lacy, fair-weather clouds as the sun began its slow descent toward evening. The temperature was perfect, hot but not scorching, and there wasn't one blessed hint of humidity in the air. My hair was as straight as it had been since arriving in Minnesota three years ago.

"We should be at Makoshika in about a half hour, my sweet darlin' lover," Mathias said. "And then we can set up our tent and go exploring."

"It is so gorgeous and wild out here, I can't get over it." I set aside the camera to stare out the passenger window. The sight of the landscape caught me in the chest, not quite pain, but close. A longing rose within me, an ache almost like nostalgia, though I'd never before been this far west. I supposed everyone felt this way about certain places, maybe a familiar scent in the air, a particular tint to the sunlight striking the earth. But then I realized I knew the rock formations in the distance; I had seen them before, and a sudden twisting in my gut sent me bending forward.

"Out there," I heard myself say. "Aces and Malcolm are out there." I fumbled to open the glove compartment and retrieved Malcolm's picture, which I'd toted with; I didn't like to be parted from them. Clutching it, I studied the landscape in the distance and was pierced by certainty. I whispered, "That's where this was taken. Out there. Thias, I *know* it."

"I feel it, too," Mathias said, in a completely different tone; gone was all trace of lighthearted joking. The sun cast an auburn beam directly across his face, glinting in his blue eyes and somehow darkening them, highlighting the angles of his nose and chin, his straight black eyebrows. My heart clenched into a hard knot.

Malcolm, I thought.

He said, low and hoarse, "Come here, let me feel you against me."

I set aside the photograph and went to him at once, his right arm gathering me near. He shuddered, as though the cold shiver leaped from me to him, and pulled over on the shoulder of the interstate. Before and behind us stretched an endless ribbon of road, empty of all vehicles except for our truck. The Montana landscape sprawled as far as the eye could see in every direction, creating the illusion that the truck huddled in the exact center of a circle.

A circle that one could wander for days, for weeks, without reaching its end.

"Mathias." I clutched him as hard as I could, in desperation, over-whelmed by something I couldn't rationalize. I *felt*, that was all, felt the threat of loss all the way to the deepest trench of my soul.

"I'm here." He held me just as fiercely, as though I might disappear in a wisp of smoke if he loosened his grip. He said against my loose hair, "I'm right here."

"Don't go," I begged, in a voice not my own. "Don't go."

The sun slipped another fraction below the horizon and the angle of the light changed, however subtly. I leaned back enough to see his face, clutching it with both hands; he gripped my wrists. Our eyes held steady, both of us shaken, unable to explain.

"I will never leave you," he vowed. "Not ever."

I believed him; I trusted his words. But the loss had already hap-pened, beyond my control, out there in the foothills. The echo of it, the searing remembrance of pain, seemed powerful enough to smother me. *Don't you see, don't you see? Oh God, Malcolm, don't you see?*

I forced myself to say, "I know. It's all right."

He smoothed both hands over my hair and kissed my forehead, whis-pering as though to lighten the air, "Should we go get some food and then find our campsite, love? I'm starving."

"Same here," I whispered, though I was reluctant to move from his embrace; I kept my left hand in his right as we rolled on, our fingers tightly linked.

We drove first through the small town of Glendive, Montana, where we stopped to gas up the truck, hit a drive-thru, and buy some beer, and the normality of these things helped to dissolve the ball of ice in my stomach, at least a little.

"This town is so familiar. We always camped out here as kids," Mathias said as we shared chicken nuggets and fries, cruising along one of Glendive's main streets, a lovely route bordered by a thin blue strip of river to our right. The low-slung rocky ridges on its far banks were lit a warm caramel by the lowering sun. I kept the passenger window rolled down, my right elbow braced there, drinking in every sight as Mathias played tour guide.

"That's the Yellowstone River, there," he explained, indicating. "And there's the dinosaur museum where we always begged to go. There's a billboard of a T-Rex around here somewhere. Honey, keep an eye out for Snyder Street, that's where we want to turn left to get out to Makoshika." He pronounced it with the emphasis on the second syllable.

"Ma*ko*shika," I repeated. "Sounds Japanese."

"Lakota," he corrected. "It means something like 'big sky badlands,' I think. Isn't it great out here? I knew you'd love it as much as me."

"Of course I do. It's so hard to imagine you as a business major in Minneapolis," I marveled, which he had been once upon a time ago, as a college student before we'd met. "I feel like your soul must have been hibernating."

"That's exactly what it was doing," he agreed. "I understood it a little better when I came home to Landon last winter, but I didn't fully realize it until I saw you at Shore Leave that first night. My soul leaped and bounded then, right to yours."

I squeezed his fingers, clasped around mine. "Oh, sweetheart, look," I said, with reverence. I nodded east, where a nearly-full moon had just cleared the horizon. "Look at that."

"You just wait until we stargaze tonight," he promised, squeezing my fingers in response.

We reserved a night at Makoshika no more than fifteen minutes later, and were directed to a campsite. As the sun sank the air grew increasingly cold and I tugged a hooded sweatshirt of Mathias's over my head.

"Mom must have twenty pictures of us with that Triceratops," Mathias said, indicating the wooden sign near the entrance as we climbed back in the truck.

"Let's get one, quick," I said, and so we did.

The moon was splendid in the sky, a creamy ivory that gilded the edges of the rock formations as we found our campsite and proceeded to unload our gear. The very scent of the air here was wilder than back home, full of a sharp sweetness that I'd never smelled...and yet, I knew I *had*, at the same time. It made no sense. But as it had been since first meeting him, everything with Mathias seemed right. I fully intended to help set up camp, but he worked with swift efficiency, staking out our tent, hoisting the rain cover, setting up our two little camp chairs; he skillfully constructed a tepee of kindling, which he had burning even before the light fully faded from the violet and indigo-streaked sky. I did little more than admire him as I perched on a split log and sipped my second beer.

"You're incredible," I said as he crouched on the far side of the steadily-growing fire, the red flames highlighting the angles of his face from beneath. His grin was, as always, like a beam of sunshine.

"Didn't know your man was so capable, did you?" he asked in response, helping himself to a beer and cracking it open.

"You're a regular pioneer," I said, and looked around for our horses; surely they were tethered nearby, dozing contentedly after a day spent carrying us west. Of course they were. How could we travel without them?

Wait a second...

"I know, I feel like Aces should be right over there," Mathias murmured, indicating with his beer can. He looked beyond my shoulder, into the open country, as a log snapped and sent a small shower of red-hot sparks into the night. I shivered again, unable to shake the feeling that we had been here together before tonight. Near here, at least, in this area, and around a fire, exactly like this. Mathias whispered, "I swear he's out there, grazing."

"I swear it, too." I was hard-pressed to remember exactly what year it was. Maybe I was drunk. I reached for Mathias and he came around the fire.

"Come here," he said, tugging me onto his lap on one of our chairs.

"Do you believe in past lives, truly, I mean?" I asked as we studied the flames and the sky became spangled with an unfathomable magnificence of stars. I felt tiny and vulnerable under so much sky, and yet so very alive, washed clean and born anew.

Mathias caught my engagement ring between his thumb and index finger. So many nights I'd stayed awake, considering the possibility of reincarnation, vacillating between certainty and skepticism. I believed in Aunt Jilly's Notions with all my heart, and there was very little scientific rationale supporting the ability to sense the future; most people would just laugh, or outright scorn the idea. *There's so much more to life than you can see*, I heard Aunt Jilly say, and I was only beginning to understand the truth of this.

"A year ago I would have laughed at the idea," Mathias said, just as softly. "Even having been raised in the same house with Elaine, who's been reading the cards and trying to perform past-life regressions since we were little. When I think of where I was a year ago, in the Cities, trying to find a job. The scariest part is I actually thought I was fairly happy. I knew I wasn't *incredibly* happy, but I told myself that no one really is, I mean, come on. I figured life was about as good as it was going to get. And then I came home to Landon, but mostly I came home to you. I saw you and I knew you were mine, in every sense of the word." He whispered passionately, "And I believe to the bottom of my soul that you have been mine since the beginning of time."

"Thias," I breathed, turning so that I could press my face to the scent of his neck.

"How does it work?" he wondered. "How does a soul find its mate? Is there a celestial roadmap for souls, somewhere out there? I don't think… what I mean is, I don't think we've been allowed to be together in every life. I know we're young, I know we're healthy, but when I die, where will my soul go? Can it go somewhere to wait for yours? I can't imagine being apart from you for a few days, let alone a lifetime. Jesus, that scares me so much."

We'd talked of these things before, snuggled in our bed or swimming in Flickertail, but here under the open sky in a place that held meaning above and beyond what we knew as Mathias Carter and Camille Gordon, there existed an urgency that chilled me from the inside out. The thought of being separated from him, of death inevitably parting us, rendered me hollow and cold, elementally frightened. How many more lifetimes would we have to exist, kept apart from one another after that, until our souls could find each other again?

What if we never found each other again?

And the echoing cry of this dreadful thought seemed to lift from me and fly into the vast night sky.

"It scares me, too," I whispered. "But we can't think like that, sweetheart. We just can't. It's like you told me, back home. If we thought about everything that could happen, every terrible thing, it would rob all of the joy out of life. And I'm not planning to waste one second of this life with you, Thias, not one second."

"Camille," he whispered, and I could hear a lump in his throat. "I know you're right, honey."

For a time we watched the fire in silence, wrapped together beneath the old plaid blanket Mathias had grabbed from the truck. At last I murmured, "Look at the Milky Way. I've never seen it so perfectly clear."

"I remember lying on my back as a kid, in this same campground, and watching it. Feeling like I could maybe drift up there and swim, or something," he whispered.

"I thought the same thing the other night in the lake. About being able to fly up there and hop from star to star."

"That's where I'll wait for you," he said, half-teasing, but my heart seized at his words. "That one cluster of stars right there," and he took my right hand in his to indicate. "I'll wait right there for you. No matter how long it takes."

Tears filled my eyes. "Then I will find you there. Nothing will stop me."

He pressed his lips to my temple. "I want to make you pregnant, right now. I want you to have a part of me with you, always."

Urgency buzzed in the air, determinedly stalking us, about to pounce. Without a word I spread the blanket on the ground and then we were kissing, deep kisses that spoke of time running out, even as I rebelled against the horror of that thought. With hurried movements we bared our skin from the waist down, my thighs curving around his hips as I took him inside, fingers linked as Mathias drove almost violently into my willing body.

"Let me," I begged and he knew what I wanted, turning us so that I could straddle him. I kept our frantic pace. I didn't want to blink, afraid if I did he would be gone. In the moonlight he was achingly beautiful, strong and powerful, so hard inside of me, and yet there existed a gaping gulf of vulnerability in my soul; I felt as though I retained no control at all, that events were exploding out of my hands and I was powerless to stop any of it.

"Mathias," I gasped, curving forward over him, desiring to bring him into my body entirely, to cradle and protect him until the end of time, to force the universe to acknowledge that we belonged together, and could never be separated.

"Come here," he ordered, rolling so that he was on top once more. The onrushing intensity of him, the scent of his skin and taste of his mouth, the strength of his thrusting overwhelmed my senses, until the stars appeared ablaze in the sky, whirling faster and brighter, blinding my eyes. Just before he came I thought I saw a shooting star flare across the multicolored sky, breaking into two distinct tails before shimmering out of existence. And then he cried out, harshly, shuddering as we fell to the side and clung; the world around us all at once seemed hushed, expectant, and no words were necessary.

Later, when the fire had reduced to glowing embers, we curled together in our tent, kept from full darkness by the faint red glow. Mathias pressed his palm to my belly and kissed my forehead. He whispered, "There. Right there. Can you feel him?"

I managed a sleepy smile, naked and warm and all tangled together with my man. I murmured honestly, "I can."

When I woke—or was it a dream?— deep in the night, there was a third person in our tent. I gasped and tried to sit up, but was too enveloped in both Mathias's arms and the sleeping bag. My heart seemed to burst. I thrashed both arms as though I had the power to push aside the smothering darkness.

Please, a voice whispered, and its agony swelled in my skull. The faintest of outlines shivered beside our sleeping bag, on Mathias's side. I watched in silent shock, the pulse of blood gurgling in my ears, obliterating all external sounds. *Please find me, please, I beg of you. I've been waiting so long…*

Malcolm? I gasped. I leaned over Mathias's sleeping form, reaching wildly to grasp at the figure, desperate to contain it; I demanded, *Is that you?*

No, the voice whispered, its pain ancient and deep, and the outline trembled, allowing me to glimpse long, curling hair, much like my own.

It was a girl, I realized, and then for the space of one breath I could see eyes in her hollow white face, blazing into existence, one cedar-green and one with an iris so brown it was almost black. She stared directly at me and my internal organs simultaneously froze solid; a scent as of flowers filled the tent and in my mind appeared a sudden picture of a blossom with sharp pink edges. A name rose in my throat, emerging as both a gasp and an acknowledgement.

Cora, I whispered. In speaking her name, it all rushed back. Malcolm's desperate search had been to find her. To find Cora. Resistance built an immediate protective shield—I couldn't bear the razor of this truth; of what I'd already known on some deep level.

Malcolm had never found me.

I covered my eyes, blocking out the sight of Cora—of myself—of what I had tried so hard to forget.

Her pleading voice penetrated my defenses.

Please. There is no one else who can find me. Oh God, please, find me…
Find me…

Chapter Nine

I woke with an aching head the morning of July fifth, but I dragged myself and Rae over to the cafe to say good-bye to Camille and Mathias, who were leaving for their trip. Jo was there, Matthew in tow, and Grandma and Aunt Ellen, who were watching Millie Jo for the week.

I hugged Camille, whispering into the soft clouds of her dark hair, "Be careful, and find answers, all right?"

She drew back and I admired her beautiful eyes, her irises with a ring of darker gold surrounding them, her lashes fan-like on her cheeks when she blinked. I knew she wanted me to tell her that they would find all the answers they sought, and I wished so badly that I could assure her. But just now, I couldn't even assure myself.

She murmured, "We'll do our best," and kissed my cheek. "I love you, Aunt Jilly."

Later, Jo and I sat with Mom and Ellen at table three while the little ones played in a corner booth, Matthew trying valiantly to keep up with Millie Jo and Rae.

"You need sleep, Jilly Bean," Joelle observed. "And it's not from staying up watching the fireworks, I know it."

"Everyone needs to back off," I grumbled, hiding behind a long sip of coffee; I knew I was forcing my husband to walk on eggshells with my bad attitude, and I felt guilty for that, but was unable to relent. Though it had been fun out on the water last night, all of us crowded between the motor boat and the pontoon to watch the Fourth of July spectacular, by morning's light I was still fostering the tension, and Justin's patience was growing thin.

"Baby, this is getting old," he'd said before leaving for work. "We're talking when I get home."

"It's pregnancy that does it," Mom contributed, trying to be helpful. "I know when I was pregnant with you I wanted to pick a fight every other day." She snorted a laugh and concluded, "Maybe it's no wonder Mick left around then!"

Joelle shot Mom a scorching look. I set down my cup with a clack and demanded, "Is that supposed to be a hint?"

Mom rolled her eyes, not about to get sucked into my angry vortex. Just to my right, she reached and cupped my chin, as though I was about five. "Jillian Rae, what a ridiculous question. But here's a hint: Justin loves you with all his heart and you're hurting him by acting this way. As though he has any control over what his ex-wife does or says."

I felt the sting of tears, knowing she was right.

"But Aubrey said…" I stammered.

"Who cares what that dumb bitch says?" Jo asked, low. "She hasn't changed a bit. She should be ashamed of herself. I'm glad Justin told her off. He probably wishes he would have years ago."

They were determined to prove me wrong. I heard myself admit miserably, "I feel like I can't get a sense of things anymore."

None of them realized what I meant, the depth of my fear over what I'd just said. Gran or Great-Aunt Minnie would have understood, in a heartbeat; I missed my grandmother and great-auntie so much that I could hardly draw a full breath. I hated that I couldn't talk to either of them; right now, I'd have given almost anything. Aunt Ellen patted my forearm. "When Justin comes for lunch, you go hug him and tell him it's all right."

I swiped at my eyes and then nodded, determined to do just that. "I will, Ell, don't worry."

Lunch was busy, the tourist season mobilizing into full swing, sending city folk to the lake country in droves. Jo took care of the porch tables so I wouldn't have so far to walk, though that meant I was in charge of the entire counter and all the booths in the main room. And so it was that I was distracted enough that I didn't see Zack Dixon until he was already seated at the counter, on the far end, closest to the outer door.

"Are you ready?" I asked him, with no hint of acknowledgment or recognition that we'd been introduced prior to today. I was sweating, my temples damp, my Shore Leave t-shirt limp with the humidity, and he was openly staring at me, his creepy, too-close-together eyes taking their fill. I ignored this against my better judgment and insisted, "Well?"

"You have a minute to sit and chat?" he asked, leaning forward on his elbows on the counter. I took a small step away; his nose was far too close to my breasts, even at over two feet away. He informed me, "I've been out here a bunch of times, but you either weren't working or Camille took my table."

"Yep, that's right," I said rudely.

"I've been enjoying Landon," he said, choosing to ignore my tone, smiling as though we were having a pleasant conversation. "Even though there's not much to do at night. I get a little bored. What do you do for fun around here? Swim, maybe?"

I forced myself to look into his silvery-blue eyes, realizing that the last thing I should do was communicate unease. I clenched my jaw. "Are you ready to order?"

"Jillian," he implored, low and far too intimately. His eyes made me undeniably ill, though I could not otherwise get any sort of read on him. In the same tone of voice, he murmured, "You're so sexy. Sex just drips off of you. Does your husband tell you so?"

I blinked and then ordered in no uncertain terms, "Never speak to me again."

I walked away before he could reply, straight through the swinging two-way door to the kitchen, where I found Blythe. I pulled him aside and said, "There's a guy at the counter I don't like, a tourist. Can you take his order?"

Blythe frowned, studying my face for more explanation; this kind of thing wasn't like me at all. "Sure thing, Jills. Did he say anything you want to tell me about?"

Shit. Bly was overprotective and could not afford to get in a fight for any reason. I said quickly, "No, he's just really annoying. I don't want Jo to have to deal with him, either."

Blythe leaned into the kitchen to tell Rich, "Hey, Gramps, I'll be right back."

Huge, strong, intimidating (when he wanted to be) Blythe took Zack's order, and I studiously avoided his end of the counter after that, though he watched me with absolutely no outward qualms. When he finally left, I scooped up his basket and restrained the urge to chuck it directly into the trash. It was then that I noticed what appeared to be handwriting on his napkin.

What the hell? I wondered, turning it so that I could read the words, though probably I should have known better.

Jillian, please don't be mad at me. You're beautiful. I want to speak to you again. Thanks for lunch.

I almost gagged. As though he'd written something much more offensive, I crammed the napkin deep in the garbage and then went to wash my hands. In the familiar employee bathroom I studied the tension in my eyes, smudged beneath with shadows, and suddenly realized that Justin hadn't shown up for lunch.

Go to your husband. Finish up here and then go to him and make everything all right, and tell him about this shit with Zack.

First I packed a bag of food and then pit-stopped at home to change from my grungy work clothes into a maternity sundress, a pretty yellow one, and unpinned my hair, brushing it silken-smooth over my bare shoulders. Rae was still with Ruthie at Mom and Aunt Ellen's house, so I drove alone around the lake to the filling station, where my husband had worked weekdays ever since he'd graduated high school. The business had originally been his grandpa's, Dodge's father, Jacob Miller, who'd passed away back when Justin and I were in junior high.

My spine relaxed a little as I saw Justin's silver truck in the familiar parking lot, next to Dodge's rusty work truck. There were three cars in the customer spots, vehicles waiting to be repaired. Justin and Dodge worked on all engines, including boats. Out back, near the huge service dock, were gasoline and diesel pumps, where all manner of watercraft came to refuel when the station was open. I parked beside my husband's truck, feeling an unexpected glow of warmth as my eyes flickered to the red lettering on the white siding above the three service bays, reading MILLER SERVICE STATION, LANDON, MN. Halfway to the front entrance I realized I'd neglected to grab the lunch I'd packed for Justin, and was about to head back to my car when the sound of a voice from inside the first service bay met my ears. My footsteps faltered.

"If you'd just…" The rest of the statement was spoken too low for me to hear. But I needed no more than that to understand that Aubrey was here. A firebomb seemed to explode somewhere between my stomach and my throat.

"Leave, *now*," I heard Justin say, and there was a tone in his voice to which I'd never been privy, a flat, dark edge.

"Not until you listen. You never listened to me, you asshole," Aubrey cried, louder this time, and I rounded the corner of the open garage. Justin stood facing away from the door, his hands curled around the top edge of his workbench, wide shoulders taut with tension. All I could see, however, my gaze narrowing to a pinpoint of white-hot fury, was Aubrey, close behind him and reaching as though to put her hands on his back.

I felt capable of projecting flames from my eyes and was stunned to hear my voice emerge without a tremble. "If you speak to my husband that way again, you will be *fucking sorry*."

Aubrey spun around. Justin turned more slowly, imploring me with his dark eyes. He shook his head just slightly but I could not spare him a glance. I felt if I looked away from Aubrey I would lose some battle with her. I wanted to kill her even more fiercely than I had the other night, some small, detached part of me slightly startled by these bloodthirsty thoughts.

"I need to talk to Justin and it's none of your business," she said, enunciating his name, speaking the words with deliberate slowness, as though to a child.

Justin recognized that I was very near to causing her bodily harm; with that low, dangerous tone in his voice he said, "I am not going to ask you again. You have nothing to say that I care to hear."

"There's plenty I haven't said to you," Aubrey insisted, stumbling slightly as she turned back toward him, and I suddenly realized that she was drunk. I could smell booze emanating from her and I stood at the open door, a good five paces away. The afternoon sun made a hot oblong shape on the dirty floor at my feet. The air here smelled familiar, of motor oil and turpentine. The baby kicked at my belly and I wanted desperately to start crying, but I would not give Aubrey the satisfaction.

Justin let her comment slide and sidestepped her to come to me, but she snatched out her hands and caught his left bicep; he was wearing an old black t-shirt, one with the sleeves torn off, and that her palms were upon his bare skin created a buzzing force field of rage within my chest. Clinging to him, her voice shrill with insistence, she cried, "You screwed me over first, way before I screwed Tim. You know it's true." She started crying in little pathetic huffs and persisted, "I *needed* someone. It wasn't my fault you looked like a fucking circus freak."

With a great deal of dignity, Justin detached himself from her grip, but immediately she reached for him again; before I even knew I'd moved, my right fist clamped around a large hank of her auburn hair, yanking her head sideways. My husband responded like lightning, catching me against his chest and carrying me outside. He directed his quiet, intense words into my ear. "Jilly, she's not worth it."

I struggled furiously, anger clouding all sensibility, wanting nothing more than to be allowed to finish what I'd started with Aubrey, but Justin's arms were iron. He held me close despite my throaty, inarticulate protests. With no room for argument in his tone, he said, "Baby, I won't let you get hurt on account of me."

Tears gushed over my cheeks. I demanded breathlessly, "Let me go, Justin, *I mean it*."

Aubrey followed us and she wouldn't quit, standing with hands on hips, goading me, "I had him first, Jillian Davis, never forget that. I left *him*. And he begged me to stay. *Begged* me."

She delivered these words like white-knuckled punches, and I felt them in the gut. Behind me Justin tensed even further, but with quiet, if forced, calm, he said, "Jilly, she has no power to hurt me except through you. Don't let her."

"Fuck you, Justin," Aubrey snapped. "You know it's true. Look me in the eye and tell me it's not true."

At that moment I saw my father-in-law walking up the path from the lake, his aviator sunglasses in place, drying his hands on a frayed blue towel. He was whistling, but the instant he caught sight of the three of us the sound died on his lips. His steps stalled as he appraised the scene; perhaps five seconds passed before he resumed his route. He came to a stop near his son and me, pushing the aviators up on his head as he asked, "Justin Daniel, what's going on here?"

Just the simple fact that he used Justin's name rather than referring to him as "boy," which was his customary affectionate nickname, belied Dodge's concern.

Justin cleared his throat roughly. "Aubrey was just leaving."

"Dodge, this isn't your business!" Aubrey had the audacity to snap, but, like Justin, Dodge retained his cool.

"You've done enough damage to my family in the past that I do believe it is my business, young lady," Dodge said, and Aubrey's attitude deflated, if just slightly. Dodge continued, "You've clearly had too much to drink on this otherwise fine day, and so I will drive you back wherever you came from."

Justin gently released his hold on me. I moved straight to Dodge's arms, clinging to his bulk as I cried, hating myself for breaking down in front of Aubrey this way, too revved up at present to stop. Dodge made a sound of comfort and patted my back. I pressed my face to him, sensing Justin's aching concern; I was hurting my husband by acting this way, but I was too upset to deal with that knowledge right now.

Dodge said, "Jilly-honey, you head on back to the cafe and have a cup of coffee, all right? It's all right here. Go on now, honey. Justin will be along in a minute."

I did as he requested, refusing to look at Justin as I passed him. I drove home instead of going back to Shore Leave. I didn't want to see anyone right now, could not deal with explaining why I was such a wreck. Our cabin was occupied by nothing more than sunbeams and dust motes, far too quiet without the usual bustle of four people. I sat for a long time on the porch swing, smelling the pine sap as the sun drifted behind the peak of the roof. I watched the line of afternoon shade advance across the yard, keeping the swing in gentle motion with my right foot. As much as I truly wished I was a better person than this, I replayed Aubrey's words like a scratched record, my mind catching repeatedly on the word *begged*.

Justin, I thought painfully, cupping my curled right fist within my left hand, holding both under my chin. Tears leaked over my face like a faucet left running. I wanted to clutch his shirtfront and demand answers to the questions crashing through my head; at the same time, I didn't fully want to hear his responses.

Oh Justin. Oh God, I can't bear to think of how much you must have been hurting back then. Did you really beg that bitch to stay? Was it because you couldn't be without her? Or because you just didn't want to be alone? Oh God...

I thought of the August night close to six years ago, when Dodge first told me that Aubrey had left Justin. I'd found Justin that night, sitting on the boat landing dock; the memory of his bitter anger rushed back to me, the despair emanating from him like a heat wave. I told him what I really thought of Aubrey that night, and pleaded with him to come back to Shore Leave for coffee in the mornings, as was his habit before the accident. And still over two and a half years had passed before I even admitted to myself how I felt for him, that I was in love with him.

Jilly, stop this, I reprimanded. *You know he needs you. He loves you, never doubt that.*

It wasn't that I doubted it. But Aubrey's words stung deeply; of course she'd intended that.

What if he hadn't had the accident? Would he still be married to her?

Jillian. Enough.

He begged her to stay.

I tipped my forehead against my folded hands and gave way to sobs. No matter how I reassured myself, no matter how unfounded, I was jealous as hell. Thank God Ruthie was watching Rae at Mom's house, that Clint wouldn't be home until late evening. I didn't even want to see

Joelle. Anger and self-pity battled for the upper hand.

I want a fucking cigarette. Oh God, I want Gran.

The thought of my grandmother, with her brusque attitude and kind, observant eyes, made me cry even more miserably. She would know what to say, how to make me feel better. She would smooth her hands over my hair and set me straight, put everything into perspective again, and the pain of missing her made my ribs feel tight. I pressed the base of both palms to my closed eyes, fingers tangled into my loose hair, and so I didn't see or hear Justin climb the porch steps until he crouched on the porch beside me and gently stopped the motion of the swing with his right hand.

"Baby," he said softly. He must have walked over from Shore Leave.

I choked back my sobs, stubbornly keeping my eyes covered, refusing to acknowledge his presence with a response. Justin knew me well enough not to push; he didn't say anything else but I could sense him studying me, just as clearly as I could sense the way it wounded him to witness me in obvious distress. The baby kicked repetitively, as though to encourage me to quit behaving like a child; Justin waited with quiet patience, his hands curled around the edge of the seat on either side of my thighs.

I wanted to be in his arms. I wanted to feel his warmth and strength against me. I wanted him to tell me that Aubrey was lying, that he'd never once been so broken that he begged her to stay with him.

"I don't want to talk about it right now," I whispered, my voice a sandpaper rasp.

"Well, I do," he said, not so much a challenge as a statement of fact.

"Well, *I don't*." The edge in my voice could have honed a knife blade.

"Jills." I could tell there was a lump in his throat. My heart jerked and then took up a rapid thudding, but still I did not look at him. He whispered, "Don't be like this."

"Don't tell me how to be!" I flared, still hiding behind my hands. If I looked at him I would crack.

"I can't help what she does, let alone says," he said, quiet and reasonable.

I finally dropped my hands, using my fingertips to scrub at the tear tracks on my cheeks, keeping my eyes averted. Justin was kneeling near the swing; he shifted to cup my knees, caressing with his thumbs. I was still wearing the yellow sundress, my feet bare. I braved his dark eyes.

"How long had she been there before I got there?" I asked, my voice unpleasantly hoarse.

Justin's jaw tightened enough to communicate that my question offended him. He observed, astutely, "You're trying to pick a fight."

This comment only served to fan the combative flames. Pregnancy hormones may have been contributing a little, but I knew on some level that my own insecurity was also responsible; questions that I'd never asked him seemed to surge into my throat. I wasn't sure how I expected him to respond, even as I realized I was not only being unreasonable, but also a bitch. I demanded, "How long? Why didn't you come for lunch like always?"

Justin rocked back onto his heels, removing his hands from my legs and resting his forearms on his thighs. His dark eyes flashed with their own fire as he responded, "What are you implying?"

He had me there; I knew in my heart that nothing happened, or would have happened. At the same time, I craved a shouting match. I leaned forward. "Maybe you should have just fixed her goddamn car and been done with it. Why draw it out?"

"For one thing, I'm not planning to touch the car at all. Dad is taking care of it," he said, still controlled, but his eyes were aflame. "You *know* I can't help that she stopped at the station. I'm as surprised as you that she's pulling this shit. It's not even sincere, as you also well know! She's jealous of you and she's deliberately trying to upset you, and here you are, falling right into her trap." He used one hand to gesture at me, before plunging both through his hair, clearly something he'd done multiple times today.

"Yes, I'm that stupid!" I raged. "And you still haven't answered my question!"

"Jilly, goddammit! Because I'm not going to justify that with an answer! Because it implies that you think something was going on and frankly, that fucking hurts." His eyes drilled into mine and my heart knotted up.

"Tell me you wouldn't be angry if this was the other way around!" I cried, clinging to the shred of defense that I retained. I was way in the wrong, I knew.

"I would give you the benefit of the doubt," he said, taking the lofty ground though anger was almost visibly steaming from him.

"Maybe because I would never give you a *reason* to be jealous!" I yelled, fresh tears streaking my face. "There's nothing for you to be jealous *of*!"

"You have *no reason* to be jealous!" he yelled right back. "Which you know goddamn well!"

"*Really?*" I shrieked. "When she shows up *multiple times* to confront you and says those kinds of things to you!"

"I cannot help what she says," he said again, no longer yelling, the frustration in his eyes leaping into mine.

"I want to be alone right now," I whispered, retreating behind my hands. He heaved an aggravated sigh and pushed off against the swing as he stood, setting it into agitated motion.

"*Fine*," he spit out. And then, as though to hammer home the point that he was getting the last word, he muttered, "Pregnancy."

"Don't you say that to me!"

Justin stood with hands on hips, staring down at me with lips compressed in an angry line, his black eyebrows drawn together, creating a groove between them. I studied his handsome, scarred face, the face I loved with my heart and soul. Why did he also possess the damnable power to rouse such anger in me? Heat leaped and crackled between us, one part anger, a hundred parts attraction. I knew with just a word from me (as in, an apology), we would be in our bedroom, wrapped together. But I would not give myself, or him, the satisfaction right now.

I turned my chin stubbornly away and Justin stormed off the porch without another word.

I was too wound up to continue sitting outside, plus I needed to go to the bathroom. Probably I should walk over to the cafe and collect my youngest, think about something for supper. Maybe we could just eat fried fish at the counter; even though I wasn't particularly hungry at present, the idea appealed to me, as it didn't require any cooking on my part. I'd left my keys in the car and bent to retrieve the one hidden in the planter, only to realize it wasn't there.

Shit, I thought, digging through the dirt beneath the petunia blossoms. And then I froze. *You dropped it the other night, remember?*

The porch boards were bare, no key in sight. I chewed my lower lip, looking next to the pine trees on the edge of the lawn, where I'd imagined someone hiding. It had seemed so goddamn real—

Stop it, I thought next. *No one was there. The last thing you need right now is more stress.*

After grabbing the keys from my ignition, I unlocked the house, determined to chill out, pausing en route to the bathroom to lean over the kitchen table and inhale the white and yellow honeysuckle blossoms overflowing from the vase centered there; Justin had picked a huge bunch for me just the other day; he said the scent of them reminded him of me.

Justin, I thought, aching. *I'm sorry I'm being such a bitch. But I'm so angry.*

I stood there and let the sweetness of the flowers drift around me. The kitchen was peaceful in the late-afternoon light, comfortably messy with the trappings of our daily existence; Clint's baseball t-shirt and glove hung from the back of his chair, Rae's stuffed elephant slumped over beside a banana peel on the table. A pile of dirty laundry waited patiently near the door to our mud room, where the washer and dryer hunkered side by side. I straightened up and it was then that I noticed something out of place, even among the clutter.

What in the hell? I wondered, moving to the counter. My forehead furrowed as I regarded my panties, a sheer black pair I hadn't worn in a few months, which had been buried in my underwear drawer only this morning, now arranged on the counter as though for display in a department store; a single rock, round and gray, something perhaps plucked from the shoreline of Flickertail, was positioned directly over the crotch.

My vision blurred as my stomach seemed to bottom out. I had been the last person in the house today, I was certain, Rae and I the last to leave, and these panties were absolutely not here when we headed to Shore Leave. Shaking, I swept them from the counter with a vicious movement, the rock clattering with a dull thud against the wooden floor.

Didn't I lock the door? How could he have gotten in here? A window maybe…

Oh Jesus Christ, he has the fucking key!

The thought seized me by the throat and I whirled around, at once certain that he was going to be standing right behind me, smiling with his silvery snake eyes gleaming.

But there was absolutely nothing.

Anger swelled, swift and hot, filling me to bursting, displacing my fear. I found my shoes and marched over to the cafe with every intention of calling the police and demanding that they arrest Zack Dixon for…

For what? I floundered in my fury. There was no proof, nothing concrete, with which to accuse him. Did he look at me in a way that I found noxious and inappropriate? Yes. Did he make discomfort slither over my skin? Yes. But could I prove that he had somehow entered my house this very afternoon, leaving me a message in this fashion? I could not, and I knew it.

Justin has to know, I thought immediately. *You have to tell him about this.*

Mom and Aunt Ellen were on the porch rolling silverware when I came hustling (as much as I was able, anyway) out of the woods. Sweat trickled over my temples and I breathed with some difficulty as I mounted the steps. Mom lifted an eyebrow. She asked, "Honey, what's wrong?"

Aunt Ellen said, "Justin was here just a bit ago. He brought Rae over to Dodge's for supper, said you needed a little break right now. What is going on, Jillian?"

"I just…" I faltered, studying my aunt's familiar face, currently full of concern. Tears spouted from my eyes yet again, aggravating me to no end. I swiped at them, so frustrated, and even though I should have told them what I'd just found, I felt absurdly embarrassed to do so. Instead, I muttered lamely, "I'm just so upset with him right now."

"Well, then, you cool off and let them have supper somewhere else this evening," Mom said, though I didn't miss the look that passed between her and Ellen, the kind of sisterly look that I knew well, that I'd exchanged with Joelle more times than I could count. Mom leaned and smoothed a hand over my hair. "Why don't you go and sit on the dock for a little while, sweetie? It's been so hot today. I'll make you a sherbet tonic."

For a moment I was almost tempted to smile. It was Mom's old-time concoction, delicious and refreshing, orange sherbet with bubbly tonic water poured over top, served in a stemmed ice cream glass. She whipped up one for me and then I took their advice and made my way to the glider at the end of our dock, settling with a small sigh, determined to make sense of this afternoon. I calculated just what I could do about the possibility that Zack Dixon had actually ventured inside my house today and rifled through my underwear drawer.

Are you going crazy?

Even if he is creepy as hell, he wouldn't risk coming into your house.

But who else would do such a thing?

Aubrey…

No, God no, she's mean and nasty, but not crazy…

And she wouldn't have had the time today, anyway.

Could it have been Rae, messing around?

I'd sat on the dock for a good twenty minutes or so, sipping the sherbet tonic and reaching no satisfying conclusions, before my sister called down from the porch, "Hey, you wanna join me for supper?"

I peered over my shoulder to see Jo leaning against the railing. I felt a small splash of gladness and called, "Yes, I'll be right there!"

Inside the cafe it smelled of fried fish and onion rings, battered mushrooms and draft beer. I inhaled these comforting, familiar scents, moving to join Jo at the counter. It had been such a long and terrible day, I almost requested a beer from Tish, who appeared as though by magic to ask what I wanted. She and Ruthie were managing the dinner crowd, along with Sue Kratz, who helped out during the summer season. Tish's dark hair was twisted into a knot high on her head, curls escaping to drift down her neck, two green pencils sticking out from the bun at cockeyed angles. She wore raspberry-tinted lip gloss, two pairs of gold hoop earrings, and chewed gum a little too boisterously; she could have been Jo from our high school days.

"Honey, bring me an O'Douls." At least it was non-alcoholic.

Tish cracked her gum. "You got it, Aunt Jills. Mom, what do you want?"

"Just water for now, sweetheart," Jo said, and then bumped her shoulder against mine. She nagged, "So what gives? What the hell is bothering you so much, Jilly Bean?"

"Where's Matthew?" I asked, unwilling to spill my own problems at the moment.

"Christy's home with him," Jo said, reminding me that Blythe's mom was in town for a few nights, from Oklahoma; she had arrived this afternoon. "And it works out perfectly, since we've got the show at Eddie's tonight, remember?"

"What show?"

"*Oh my God,*" Jo groaned, exasperated with me. She flicked my earlobe. "You know, the one *you* were all excited about a couple of weeks ago? Jim Olson's nephew…his band played at your wedding reception, remember? He's playing at Eddie's tonight."

"Right," I said, recalling now. Shit, that *was* tonight. In the spirit of the Fourth of July holiday, the festivities continued in Landon through this weekend.

"Eddie thought standing room only." Jo dragged a couple of fries through the ketchup on her plate.

"I have to ask Justin," I said. "We…had a fight this afternoon…"

"About what? Aubrey? You're letting this upset you way too much."

"Easy for you to say," I snapped, and Jo sighed.

"Here's your drink," Tish said, reappearing. "You want a mug?"

"No, thanks," I told her and she darted away. I watched my nieces move expertly around the cafe, covertly scanning the place for any sign of Zack Dixon. If I saw that fucker I was going to confront him, doubts or no. He owed me an explanation. And with the thought of those particular words, Aubrey was right back in my head.

"Let's go out and have some fun," Jo said. "C'mon, Jilly. You look like you could use an evening away. Mom can watch Rae and we'll head over to Eddie's around nine or so."

And I grudgingly agreed.

Chapter Ten

"THE SPOKE," MATHIAS READ FROM THE SIGN BENEATH the flashing bulbs of an arrow. He grinned at me and decided, "It looks classy."

"It looks like a place with good fried food," I said. "You want to chance it?"

"Sure, let's try it," he said, swinging our joined hands. We had walked the quarter mile from our campground under a sky tinted bright pink with the sunset, a slim band of gleaming aquamarine along the eastern horizon. To the west, a group of sterling-silver clouds were jumbled atop one another like kids making a monkey pile. I pointed to the turquoise band. "Have you ever seen the sky that color?"

"Not back home, unless it's from the aurora," he said. "But I remember being out here when I was little and thinking that the sky had some really strange colors."

This morning, while still at Makoshika, I'd told Mathias all about my dream of Cora.

"Malcolm wasn't searching for gold or anything like that," I explained, as he'd made coffee and eggs on a cast-iron grill set over the fire. The sun crept from behind the rock formations in the east, casting soft light over us as he worked the fire. I insisted, "He was searching for her, for this girl. For Cora." It was on the tip of my tongue to tell him how, in the clutches of the dream, I'd believed that I was Cora—that in never finding her, Malcolm had also never found me. But the words wouldn't form; it seemed like a betrayal, and I would never betray Malcolm. I loved him, not only because he was part of Mathias.

"But he didn't find her?" Mathias asked, our eyes holding. "Jesus, that's so fucking horrible."

"She wants *us* to find her. But I don't know how. I have no idea what to do. Oh, Thias," I said, agonized anew. "She seemed so real. I saw her eyes for a second, and they were really strange. Two different colors."

"Where can we start?"

"Maybe…those letters in Bozeman. Maybe there will be something in those."

"We'll be there by tomorrow," Mathias said. "Or do you want to get there sooner? Should we forget camping out in Jalesville tonight?"

I shook my head, grateful that the sunshine and Mathias's good humor had restored a sense of normalcy. "No. I like being out here with you. It feels like we're the only people on the planet, and I don't mind that."

Mathias grinned, leaning to kiss me, tucking a strand of hair behind my ear. He whispered, "Thank you for last night. For every night, actually. For allowing me the gift of you."

I giggled at his formal wording, pulling his lips back to mine. "Well, it's a tough job…" And then a devil perched on my shoulder and made herself very comfortable. I murmured, "Taking your incredibly huge, hard cock into me…but *someone* has to do it…"

We had explored all over Makoshika this morning, before heading southwest, aiming for Miles City. We ate lunch there and then continued toward our evening destination, a little town called Jalesville; this place possessed a small campground that the Carters always favored on their journeys west, once upon a time run by an old friend of Bull's. Now, hours later and both of us hungry as hell, we made our way across the parking lot of the little bar and grill called The Spoke. On the walk from our campsite we'd passed a green sign welcoming us to Jalesville, population 823. Mathias held the door for me; already I could smell hot grease and my stomach rumbled in anticipation. I'd changed from hiking clothes into my favorite sundress, my hair loose and soft over my shoulders, and when Mathias looked at me I felt the love in his eyes the same way I would feel the sun breaking through a gray cloud-quilt, the heat and intensity and joy of it.

"Hi, folks," said the woman at the host stand. She was petite and pretty, with dark hair in two braids and scarlet cowgirl boots embroidered with fancy gold stitching, and bore enough resemblance to the woman tending bar that I thought, *Sisters.* The Spoke reminded me immediately of Shore Leave, but with a distinctly western theme; the jukebox in the corner was belting out a Tanya Tucker song, the barstools were fitted with saddles, the wooden walls decked in all manner of bridles, tack, spurs, fringed buckskin shirts, and a variety of ancient-looking rifles; a moose head the size of Rhode Island dominated the bar, its antlers strung with bare-bulb lights.

"Two, please," Mathias said, and she led us to a small round table, a lighted candle lantern centered on its surface.

"Oh wow, look at that," I breathed, indicating the table, which was constructed from a glass-topped wagon wheel.

"I want one for the cabin," he said at once. We checked out all the tables then; each was constructed from a different wheel. It was after eight and the crowd had certainly thinned from the dinner rush, allowing us the chance to inspect the variety.

"Duh, 'The Spoke,'" I giggled, back at our own table.

"Do you think these are legit? I mean, like actually from covered wagons? Ours looks about like it would fit on one," Mathias observed, opening his menu and indicating the table with it. "Imagine this rolling over the prairie a hundred years ago. That's a cool thought."

I stole a second to simply admire him, loving his natural enthusiasm and little peculiarities. How he lined his left index finger over his top lip whenever he read something, thumb hooked under his chin, the way his black eyebrows drew together in concentration, the effortless grace of the way he dropped his right shoulder in a half-slouch, comfortable in his chair. He looked up from the menu to meet my gaze and I smiled, certain he could see the stars in my eyes.

"What?" he asked softly.

"I just love you so much."

He reached and appropriated my right hand, bringing it to his lips and kissing my knuckles, and at that moment someone cleared her throat. We both looked up at the server, who regarded us with wry amusement crooking her lips; we were so apt to get wrapped up in our own little world.

"Newlyweds?" she inquired, in a teasing tone that reminded me of Aunt Jilly.

"Soon to be," Mathias said. "Our wedding is this October."

She winked at him and then asked, "Can I get you a couple of drinks?"

"I'll have an iced tea, thanks," I said; since I wasn't twenty-one I couldn't order a drink in a restaurant. And besides, there could very well be a baby growing inside of me at this very minute. I felt flush with warmth at the thought of last night, cupping one hand over my lower belly.

"Whatever you have on tap, I'll take a tall," Mathias said.

"Name's Pam," she told us. "You two got here at a good time. We'll be packed ass to ass in here in a half hour or so. My cousin Garth's band is playing tonight."

Her prediction was correct, as the place grew crowded soon after.

"I think this must be a townie bar," Mathias observed as we ate towering bacon cheeseburgers, drippy with delicious grease. He wiped his chin with the back of one hand. "You can tell everyone here is local."

"As local as tumbleweed," I agreed. "I have never seen so many cowboy hats outside of a country music video. It's pretty cool, if you ask me. Except that I feel a little naked without one."

The couple at the table to our left was decked in full western attire, the likes of which I would expect to see at a rodeo; the man sported an impressive handlebar mustache.

"Honey, you want to stay and listen to the music?" Mathias asked. Framed in the windows, the sky glowed with a silver twilight. The candlelight lanterns atop the wagon wheel tables gave the space a welcome glow, and I felt at home here.

"Sure, for a while," I said, and then gasped as a guy trying to squeeze behind my chair bumped the back of my head with a guitar case.

"Holy shit! I'm sorry!" he cried, bending down to inspect my hair as though I was spurting blood. "Are you all right? Jesus, it's so packed in here…"

"I'm just fine," I said as Mathias and I looked up at him; he appeared stressed, reddish-gold hair standing on end. He carried a guitar in a black case, a huge, overflowing backpack hanging haphazardly over one shoulder. He eyed the stage, far away across the bar, almost in a separate room, and muttered, "Dammit!"

"What's up?" Mathias asked, in a companionable fashion.

The guy looked back at us. "I knew I shoulda got here sooner. The table where we normally sit is full and I'll have to kick people off it. I *hate* doing that." He scrubbed a free hand through his hair and asked, "Shit, can I join you guys for a sec? I hate to ask, you're probably on a date, but I gotta take a load off."

"Sure, sit," Mathias invited, and I could tell he was amused by all of this.

The guy settled his gear on the floor with considerable relief; it spilled all over the place beneath the table. He plopped onto a chair and seemed about to say more, but was distracted by his phone. Catching it up, he turned slightly away and then proceeded to have a rather heated discussion with someone on the other end.

Mathias raised both eyebrows at me, sipping from his beer.

"Dammit," the guy said finally, ending the conversation and chucking his phone atop the table. The bartender immediately sent an incinerating look his way, drawing her index finger across her throat, and he called out, "Sorry, Lee! It didn't chip, I swear!"

"What's going on?" I asked, trying not to giggle.

The guy shot me a wholly embarrassed look, eyebrows lofted, as though he was concerned that I might be offended by his cursing. He explained in a rush, "Our lead singer crapped out on us just now and we're supposed to play in less than a half hour." He heaved a world-weary sigh, again swiping one hand through his hair. He was deeply tanned and lightly freckled, about Mathias's age; he lowered his face into both palms.

The thought occurred to us simultaneously; Mathias met my gaze and asked silently, *Should I go for it?*

A smile crept over my lips; I took a sip from my iced tea as I said back, *Hell, yes.*

"Hey," Mathias said, leaning to tug on the guy's t-shirt sleeve to gain his attention. "I don't know if it helps or not, but I'm a pretty good singer. I'd be happy to fill in, if you want."

The guy lifted his face, clearly surprised. He was really cute, lean and lanky and kind-of naughty looking, with brown eyes fringed in auburn eyelashes. I would have bet good money that as a kid he was the one to get everyone else in trouble with his ideas; he had the look of it about him, somehow. He cried, "No shit? God, that would be fucking awesome. Free drinks, on the house, for the whole set." He looked at me, again with the sheepish attitude, as he explained, "We play for beer."

"I better ask *what* you play," Mathias said, excitement beginning to radiate from him at this unexpected opportunity. I grinned to see it, excited, too; I could not wait to hear him in action.

The guy leaned over and grabbed something out of his backpack, then settled a chocolate-brown cowboy hat over his head. He tipped the brim, giving me a teasing wink. "Give you one guess."

"Good deal," Mathias said, relieved. "Country is my thing. You guys are in luck."

"Case Spicer," he said, by way of introduction, shaking our hands. "I'll say we're in luck. You just saved our asses! I mean, Garth and I *can* sing, but I'd rather play, you know what I mean? I'm playing bass tonight, but the fiddle's my personal best instrument." He grinned engagingly. "So, you guys like country music, huh?"

"For sure," Mathias agreed, just as I said, "It's our favorite."

Two other guys, toting instruments, threaded through the growing crowd, spied Case, and then headed our way; they resembled each other closely enough that they were clearly brothers, both lean as spareribs (as Gran would have said), with shaggy, medium-length brown hair and long noses that dominated their handsome faces; the older of the two sported a goatee and lots of stubble. He bumped Case's upper arm with a closed fist and announced, "So, we're pretty much screwed."

"No, guys, this dude just offered to sing for us!" And Case indicated Mathias, who rose and offered his hand.

"No kidding? You're serious?" The older of the two brothers shook Mathias's hand, the tension in his shoulders relaxing. He wore well-used jeans, a thin necklace of braided leather strips, and a dark brown t-shirt the exact color of his eyes. He exuded an open friendliness that put people at ease.

"I heard you play for beer," Mathias joked. "And I'll need a hat."

"Shit, we got a hat for you," he said in reply, and then introduced himself. "Garth Rawley. This is my little brother, Marshall."

"Mathias Carter. And my fiancée, Camille Gordon," he said, and I stood to shake hands as well, feeling drawn into their group with a sense of immediate welcome, as though we were, for this one night at least, all part of some big, close family. There was an air of merriment among the three musicians, a sense of past good times, and many more to come.

"Damn, you are one lucky man," Garth Rawley said to Mathias, shaking my hand and then turning it over to kiss my knuckles, but not in an impolite way; it seemed gentlemanly, a gesture from another era of manners. He nodded, releasing my fingertips. "Pleased to meet you, ma'am."

"Nice to meet you," I said, leaning to shake Marshall's hand next. I would bet he wasn't much older than me, probably not old enough to drink in a bar, but maybe around here no one cared. He was similar in appearance to Garth, but clean shaven and with eyes of a beautiful, rich gray, framed in long, coal-black lashes. Hiding a smile, I thought, *Ladies' man.*

"Ma'am," he said politely, giving me a wink.

Case asked, "Are you two on vacation? We'd know you if you were from around Jalesville."

"We're from Minnesota," Mathias said. He reclaimed his chair and I couldn't resist claiming his lap, subsequently freeing a chair for one of the Rawley brothers. Mathias hooked an arm comfortably around my waist. He explained, "We're out here visiting relatives in Bozeman."

The Rawleys straddled chairs at our table, leaning on their elbows, while Case rooted around until he found a cowboy hat, which he handed to me. "Here's one for your man. You want to do the honors, hon?"

"Sure thing." I turned to Mathias and settled the black hat over his hair. I slowly adjusted the brim. He saw the expression in my eyes and winked; he knew how damn good he looked.

"We do lots of old-school country," Garth was saying. "Like Johnny Cash, some Willie and Waylon, a little Hank, Jr. What's your range, Carter? You got any favorites?"

"I know a bunch of Travis Tritt, Garth Brooks, Toby Keith, some Charlie Daniels," Mathias said, his thumb making small circles against my belly, sending hot little pings straight south.

"We know a lot of that nineties-era country," Garth said. "I'm lead guitar and I'll chime in on vocals. Case here is bass guitar," (he pronounced it 'gee-tar'), "and little bro is our drummer."

Case tipped back his hat brim and then joked, "I know I look like a fucking greenhorn but I can't see what I'm writing otherwise." He held a short lead pencil and grabbed a cocktail napkin. He licked the pencil point and said, "Let's make a playlist."

"What's a greenhorn?" I asked.

The three of them laughed heartily at that, and Case gently nudged my shoulder with his beer bottle. Again, oddly, I felt a little like a beloved sister with them, comfortable despite the fact that we were virtual strangers.

"That's someone who's not acquainted with local customs," Case explained. "For me to wear my hat like this makes me look like I haven't got a clue how it's supposed to be. Carter," and he nodded at Mathias, who planted a kiss on my bare shoulder, his dimple deepening, "you gotta keep that brim level with the earth, just so. Take my word."

Mathias nodded gamely. "Duly noted."

"Let's start this crowd out right, do some fast sets first," Garth decided. The Spoke was really bumping now, people crowding the wagon wheel tables, the servers moving like worker bees through a noisy, neon-tinted field of honeysuckle. The woman who'd seated us appeared and asked, "What's the word, boys?"

"Our asses just got saved," Garth said. He grinned. "Netta, this here is Mathias Carter, of Minnesota, and his woman, Camille. He's gonna sing for us. Fuck Jason, for tonight, anyway!"

"Thank God," Netta said, rolling her eyes, hooking one hand on her hip. "We've got a full house and I was afraid it might get ugly if you guys tried to sneak out. I cleared out your usual table, just so you know." She looked at Mathias and me and said, "Good to meet you two. How about a round, guys? I'll grab a beer bucket."

Mathias whispered in my ear, "Shit, I just got nervous as hell."

I slipped my arms around his neck. "You'll kick ass. I know it." I studied the golden flecks that shone like treasure in his irises. "I happen to know how amazing you are, especially in the shower."

His dimple appeared. "You think they might let me keep this hat, for later…"

"You'll be wonderful." I rubbed his warm sides with both hands. "I can't wait to watch. I feel like I'm at a concert I didn't even know how much I wanted to see. I wish my sisters were here! Shit, and yours! They'll be so mad they missed this."

"You're right, we better not tell them," he said, grinning, looking slightly less worried.

"Are you kidding? I'm texting them right now!"

"At least I'm dressed a little like a country singer." He adjusted the hat. "Faded jeans, black t-shirt…"

"You look incredible," I adored, cupping his jaws. "You have just the right amount of scruff. I'll probably have to fight about fifty girls off of you once you start singing."

"Hey, I hope you know how grateful we are," Garth said, leaning to bump the side of his fist against Mathias's shoulder. He cocked his head to one side and looked between us, lips quirked in consideration. "You sure you two have never been out this way before tonight? Shit, it's strange, but I feel like we've met before. Like I know you from somewhere."

"That's fucking weird, I was just thinking the same exact thing," Case said.

"Same here, no fooling," Marshall said. "I thought that when we first walked up."

"I've been out this way as a kid," Mathias said. He added, half-joking, but I could hear in his tone that he was in agreement, "Kindred spirits? And hey, I'm glad I could help out."

"About that playlist?" Case prodded. "We got fifteen minutes 'til show time, men. The boys are almost done setting up the equipment," and he used the pencil to indicate the three teenaged boys running power cords, propping up amplifiers and arranging drums on the little pie-shaped stage in the far corner. In front of the stage stretched a smooth wooden dance floor, lit by the glow of an enormous neon moon, which clicked on with casino-grade brilliance.

"Jesus, my blood pressure just went way up," Mathias said, and beneath his tan he went pale.

"Thias," I said, slightly alarmed. "You don't have to do this."

"I really do want to. I'm all right. For the most part."

The guys created a list of about fifteen songs, while Garth tightened a guitar string. As each minute ticked by, I felt Mathias's heartrate increasing; his right leg, the one I wasn't sitting upon, had taken up a nervous jittering. I cupped his knee and squeezed. He polished off another beer and then wrapped me in both arms, kissing my temple, the hat brim bumping lightly against my hair. One of the teenagers did a quick microphone check, and Garth, Case, and Marshall began gathering up their gear.

Mathias said, "Let's do this before I shit myself," and the guys all laughed.

Case told me, "You get front row honors, hon. C'mon."

As we made our way through the rowdy crowd, Garth and Case toting their guitars, people took notice, lifting drinks to salute, cheering and whistling. Even I felt a rush of nerves at this evidence of anticipation; we reached a four-top to the right of the stage, front row with a perfect view of the action.

"I'll be right here," I promised. He looked a little like a man about to climb the gallows for his hanging.

"I'm all right," he whispered, but looked about to vomit.

"We're on, Carter," Case said, thumping Mathias between the shoulder blades, giving him a grin. "You ready?"

"Ready as I'll ever be," Mathias said.

There were two steps leading up to the stage, which Garth climbed with a spring in his step. The crowd erupted with excitement as he tipped his hat brim and took up the mic. He yelled, "Who the hell is ready to party? Who the hell wants to hear some good fucking music this evening?"

The roar was deafening; Case, carrying his guitar, and Marshall, with sleek black drumsticks in hand, mounted the stage, waving and grinning. Mathias squared his shoulders and followed, just as Garth continued in a tone that reminded me of a circus ringmaster, "We've got a friend from out of town joining us on lead vocals this evening. Sorry, ladies, he's about as taken as the morning train, so don't get your hopes up. But let's give it up for Mathias Carter! How's about a big ol' *Jalesville welcome!*"

I wished more than ever that Tish and Ruthie could be here to witness this moment. I clasped both hands and brought them under my chin, too exhilarated to sit down, as Mathias attempted to offer a grin, holding his hat to his chest as he gave a small bow; he straightened, looking my way, and I blew him a kiss. I tried to pretend I didn't hear the way all of the women in the crowd were screaming for him and instead just reveled in the fact that he was doing something he had long dreamed about.

"I wanna see asses on the dance floor!" Garth commanded, handing the mic to Mathias; for a second I thought he was going to faint. As Marshall lifted his drumsticks and tapped them together to count off the beat for the first song, I brought my folded hands to my mouth.

You're all right, honey, it's all right.

Garth and Case bent to their guitars, faces taking on expressions of absorption, giving over completely to the music. They had decided on "Should've Been a Cowboy" by Toby Keith for the first song.

Mathias closed his eyes. I held my breath.

And then his rich, true voice took up the first line of the song. It was one of his shower favorites, and though he kept his eyes shut until the second time he reached the chorus, I knew he was indeed all right. I exhaled and then a smile broke over my face, the warmth of happiness. For a second I watched the crowded dance floor, again noticing that cowboy hats seemed required wear around here, even for the women. But I could not keep my eyes long from Mathias, who overcame his stage fright and was now thoroughly enjoying himself, and I smiled all the wider. Probably all of my teeth were showing, but I didn't care.

You, I thought. *You are mine and I belong to you.*

Tears glinted, blurring my vision, and as everything took on a hazy outline I was blindsided by a rushing sense of déjà vu, a vision—*a memory?*—flowing across my mind. I saw us, all of us, Mathias, me upon his lap and held close, Garth and Marshall and Case, all sprawled around a crackling campfire, singing, sending our laughing voices into the everlasting night sky. There was a sense of wide-openness all around us, sparks rioting outward from the flames like scarlet fireflies. Our horses somewhere in the darkness close to us. And joy. I felt it as surely as someone pressing a red-hot branding iron to my ribs.

It's us, but not us.

We've all been together before, in the past.

I know it's true. It already happened.

The song ended and Mathias brought the mic closer to his lips. "Good evening, Jalesville, I hope you're in the mood to dance."

I could hardly hear over the roaring response. Mathias grinned, this time for real, and found my eyes in the crowd. "I want to say hi to my fiancée, my sweet darlin', my Camille, who's right over there…"

I blushed as hotly as the neon lights on the beer sign behind the stage, as just about every cowboy hat in the place turned my way. Mathias continued, "My only regret about being up here is that I can't ask you to dance, honey."

"I'll dance with her!" shouted more than one person, and I hid my face, giggling and shaking my head.

Garth led off with "Don't Rock the Jukebox," and the crowd went insane. Mathias launched into the vocals and I marveled again at what a good sport he was, how extremely sexy he looked, powerful shoulders keeping time with the beat. The dance floor was elbow-to-elbow, and some people were actually line dancing. I felt as though I'd wandered into an old-time saloon.

"Doll, I hate to see you sitting here all alone," said a male voice two feet from my elbow.

I looked to the left, startled, to see a tall, wiry older man with silver-rimmed glasses and a bushy gray mustache. He tipped the wide brim of his black hat and explained, "Those are my boys up there, Garth and Marsh. Two of them, anyhow, and Case is like my boy, too. May I join you?"

"Of course! Please, have a seat."

"Clark Rawley," he said, settling on an adjacent chair.

"Camille Gordon," I said, reaching to shake his proffered hand. I'd been this close to saying "Camille Carter" instead. Clark Rawley took my fingertips and kissed my knuckles, reminiscent of his son.

"And that's your man, up there singing?" he asked, indicating Mathias.

I nodded, flush with pleasure at the thought.

"Well, he's damn good," Clark observed. "He want a job?"

"I'm sure he would, if we weren't just visiting," I explained. "We're from Minnesota."

Clark nodded at this information, scratching his chin, studying me. "I don't suppose you two-step, do you, doll?"

I grinned at him. "I'm a quick learner."

Clark led me to the edge of the dancers, carefully steering clear of the flow of circulating couples, bowing politely before collecting my right hand in his left, his elbow gracefully elevated, right hand resting lightly against my waist. He was as lean and lanky as a scarecrow, dressed in a formal white shirt with a black string tie and faded jeans that fit like a second skin. He nodded at our feet, his in pointy-toed, western-style boots.

"I'll teach you the basic steps," he said. I moved awkwardly at first but Clark was patient and sweet; it took approximately two and a quarter songs before he deemed me knowledgeable enough to brave the swirling partners.

"I don't have a hat," I worried, feeling as if this was a large and unseemly fashion error.

"Don't fret," Clark said, nearly twinkling with good humor, leading us smoothly. "It would be a shame to cover up such pretty hair like yours, anyhow. Aren't I the lucky one? Loveliest girl in the whole place with an old geezer like me."

"Thank you," I giggled, and his eyes crinkled up at the corners, his mustache twitching as he returned my smile.

"Now, you said you're Camille. What's your feller's name?" he asked, nodding at Mathias, who was holding the mic perpendicular to his lips, singing like nobody's business, sweat trickling along his temples.

"Mathias Carter," I told Clark.

"Carter, you say?" Clark said. "Of Minnesota, you said?"

"Yes, near Bemidji."

"Will you two be in town long?"

"We planned to head over to Bozeman tomorrow," I explained. "We're here to see Mathias's relatives."

"Well, I'm right glad I came over to The Spoke this evening," Clark said. "My wife, my Faye, passed a few years back, and our boys are always saying that I should get out of the house more often. I surely am delighted that I found the time tonight. Faye and I have five of our own, and we had a fair hand in raising the Spicer boys, too."

We danced to one more song before Mathias passed the mic to Garth, who cupped his shoulder, grinning. They spoke for a moment and then Garth said into the mic, "I'm taking over on this one, folks, so grab your lover and get busy. *Dancing,* that is. Shee-it!"

Mathias hopped from the stage and came through the crowd with his eyes fixed on me; everyone seemed to want his attention, to compliment him, but he was a man on a mission. He caught me close and I wrapped my arms around his waist, kissing his jaw.

"You were wonderful," I enthused. He was hot as a log in the fire, radiating with excitement.

"That was a rush, holy *shit*," he said, and then remembered his manners, extending a hand to Clark. "Mathias Carter. Garth said you're his dad."

"That's right, son. Clark Rawley. Good to know you. Thanks for letting me steal your lady for a few dances," Clark said. "You are a lucky man."

"I couldn't agree more," Mathias grinned, holding me around the waist as the guys started up "Amazed" by Lonestar.

As Clark headed back to the table, I said, "I'm so glad we came here tonight. I don't know how to explain it, but I know we were meant to. I swear I had the strangest sensation while you were up there singing."

"How do you mean?"

"It was a good sensation. There was joy in it, a sense of belonging. I can't explain exactly..." My eyes moved up and to the left, to visualize past events. "We—all of us, I mean, you and me, and those three—were sitting around a campfire. We were singing."

"Kindred spirits," he agreed as we continued dancing, staying in an embrace rather than a more traditional stance.

I kissed his chin. "You're a natural up there. You should see yourself."

"I thought I was about to puke before we started!"

"I could tell, I was really worried for a second there."

"You know what could make this evening even better?" he asked. Before I could respond, he grinned and answered his own question. "*You* up on stage for the next set."

"Oh, no," I said. "No *way*. I sing for you at home, nowhere else!"

"And you're really good. I need your Dolly to my Burt," he said, grinning as he wheedled. "Or better yet, your June to my Johnny. We could sing 'Jackson,' Garth has the lyrics."

"Thias, no way," I said, eyeing the crowd of revelers.

"Please, honey? My sweet, sweet honey?"

"Maybe," I hedged, caving a little, his favorite nickname for me pouring warmly over my skin, just like it sounded. "Maybe just one." And then, a devil hopping on my shoulder for the second time today, I teased, "Only if I can be your sweet, sweet, *sticky* honey, you know, the kind you really have to lick off the spoon..."

His eyelids lowered and his dimple was deep enough for me to dive into, the gold in his eyes catching fire. He said in his throatiest voice, "Forget singing, let's get out of here right now. This minute, I mean. Damn, I'm already hard."

I shivered even as I giggled, pressing closer.

The song was ending. He murmured against my lips, "Please?"

"Please let's leave, or please sing with you?"

"Sing first, make love all night later," he promised. "I will lick every last drop of that honey, honey. You can count on it, but you have to sing with me first."

His promise literally made my knees weak. I heard myself say, "I will."

He grinned, taking my hand as he led the way through the crowd. Garth caught sight of us heading back to the stage and cried, "Give it up for Mathias Carter! Looks like he sweet-talked his woman into singing with him, so let's also give Camille the *warmest welcome you got, people!*"

I could hardly breathe as Mathias tugged me onto the stage and I stared out over the crowd from this unfamiliar vantage point; there seemed to be ten thousand pairs of eyes. Someone gave a shrill wolf-whistle and Mathias laughed delightedly, catching me around the waist with one arm as Garth passed him back the mic.

Garth, Case, and Marshall were all drenched in sweat under the heat of the stage lights, grinning at me, Marshall twirling one of his drumsticks. Mathias announced, "Camille agreed to sing with me and I just want all of you to know that this woman makes me happier than I've ever been in my life." There was a collective, rippling wave of *awwws*. Mathias curled his palm over the top of the mic and asked Garth, "You got those lyrics you mentioned?"

"Here, hon, I got those right here," Case said to me, sidestepping cords to get over to us, pulling a tattered half-sheet out of his pocket. My hand was shaking so badly that I couldn't grab the paper, but Mathias held it for us and he was so clearly elated that I was up here with him (I was, too, beneath the terror), that I felt a little of it drain away; he handed me the mic and curled his hand over mine, steadying it. Marshall tapped out the count with his drumsticks and it was now or never.

Mathias and I sang this song to each other all the time, to entertain Millie Jo at the breakfast table, or harmonizing in the shower either before or after we took care of other more pressing matters there, and so as a result I knew it well; it was just that I never sang in front of anyone else, other than my daughter and my little sisters. "Jackson" was also the song my own dad had been named for, once upon a time. I thought my heart might explode as our cue neared, and my voice wobbled before I lifted my chin and gave it my all. Dammit, how often would I have a chance like this again?

Mathias grinned as he recognized that I was all right, his voice rich and sweet; mine held pitch (mostly), and people were screaming for us, actually screaming, whistling and cheering, waving beer bottles and shots. I could hardly believe the reaction and for that moment felt like a star. I didn't even need the lyrics.

This is so crazy, I told him with my eyes.

It's crazy as shit, he agreed.

When we finished the song, I was hyper with laughter. Mathias was trying to say something to me but I couldn't hear him over the screeching crowd. He gave up trying to speak and kissed me.

"How about one more?" Garth leaned near to ask. "Shit, you two are good luck. Netta told me people are calling their friends to get their asses downtown. I don't think I've ever seen the place so packed. Pretty much all of Jalesville is here."

We ended up singing for the next hour. Afterward, the crowd demanded an encore and the guys obliged, playing two more before begging off for good. We all but collapsed at the table where Clark Rawley was still waiting, grinning and delighted. He said, "You two are naturals."

"Shit, tell me you'll consider moving here," Garth said, laughing and shaking his head before he downed a beer in about two gulps.

"What did we do without you two?" Case wondered aloud. "Jason is officially out!"

"Jason, who?" Garth agreed. "Carter, what'll it take to get you to stay through the weekend? We'll pay you. We have two more shows."

Mathias said, "I wish we could. I'd love to, but we're on a schedule."

"You gotta get back to a job?" Case figured.

"That, and our daughter," Mathias explained, and it was sweet that he would refer to Millie that way, without getting into the specifics. "She's staying with Camille's grandma while we're away."

"You got a baby girl?" Case asked, growing all mushy and doe-eyed. "Aw, I love little kids. I want a bunch of 'em but I haven't found the right woman yet. Someday, though."

"What's her name?" Garth asked.

"Here, I've got a picture," I said, fishing my wallet out of my purse. I noticed the green light on my phone blinking, undoubtedly with a wild array of responses to the text messages I'd sent my sisters, and Tina, Glenna, and Elaine. They were probably flipping out. I found the most recent photo, in which Tish and Ruthie were posing with Millie Jo on the dock, all of them grinning, dusted by the sunset glowing over Flickertail.

"Dang, you two have a lot of kids," Garth teased, taking the picture from my hand. Case and Marshall crowded closer to look.

"Millie Jo is ours," I explained, smiling, indicating her. "She's two."

"Holy shit, who's the girl with the gorgeous eyes?" Case demanded, tracing a finger just above Tish's face; his jaw had all but dropped open.

I giggled; despite hardly knowing him, I adored Case already. He was hilarious. In the picture Tish was smiling her exuberant, effortless grin, her eyes almost sparkling right off the photo. Her long, curly hair hung over one shoulder, perfectly gilded by the setting sun, and she wore a patterned halter top with jean shorts, which didn't leave much of her considerable curves to the imagination. She and Ruthie would both die if they knew good-looking guys were checking out this picture right now. I could just hear them.

"Those are my little sisters," I explained. "Tish and Ruthann."

"Wait, what's her name?" Case demanded, snatching the picture from Garth.

"Patricia," I explained. "Tish is her nickname."

"Is she eighteen?" Garth asked, clearly picking on Case, driving a shoulder against his friend's side.

"I'll wait, if not," Case said with half-drunken determination, and we all laughed at his earnest expression. He cradled the picture and begged, "Can I keep this?" And then, with true reverence, repeated, "*Patricia.*"

"Yes, she's eighteen, and no, you can't keep it! My sisters would kill me."

"Where you kids sleeping tonight?" Clark asked.

"Over at Green Springs," Mathias said, naming the campground.

"We walked over here to have supper."

"Well, I'd be obliged if you'd consider staying the night with us instead," Clark invited. "We'll help you collect your gear and you can follow us out to the homestead." When he saw our surprise at this invitation, he added, "I wouldn't normally ask two strangers to my home, you'll understand, but there's something I would like to show you. I hadn't thought of it in years, if you want to know the truth."

All around us The Spoke was slowly emptying of revelers, the evening winding down. The women named Lee, Pam, and Netta were busy behind the bar, cleaning. A few last customers lingered there at the smooth wooden counter, laughing and rehashing the show.

Clark Rawley smoothed a finger and thumb over his mustache in a gesture seemingly to collect his thoughts, and elaborated, "When I heard your name, son, I thought of it. It's not that Carter is so unusual, but it reminds me of something from way back, when I was just a kid. My granddad kept an old freighter trunk packed full of things from his own granddad, who fought in the Civil War, mind you. My brothers and me used to root in there like three pigs at a trough. There was a telegram, an old Western Union, from a man named Carter. Rung my bell when I heard the name."

I froze. Mathias leaned on his forearms and asked intently, "Malcolm? Was the man named Malcolm Carter?"

"See, now that's what I mean," Clark said, and Garth and Marshall were studying Mathias now, their intent gazes darting between him and their father; Case was still mooning over Tish, oblivious to the rest of us. Clark asked quietly, "How in the world could you know that?"

Mathias said, "We can be ready in just a few minutes."

Chapter Eleven

Justin and Rae got home about an hour after I'd finished eating supper with Jo at the cafe; I'd promised we'd meet her and Blythe back at Shore Leave around nine. I spent that hour cleaning the kitchen almost floor to ceiling. The dishwasher and the clothes dryer were both issuing muted rumbling, the air scented lightly with lemony bleach, when Rae hopped up the porch steps, all smiles.

"Hi, Mama!" she chirped. "Me and Daddy ate supper with Grandpa!"

"Hi, love," I said, holding her close and kissing her forehead. Justin followed more slowly, his eyes somber upon me as he entered, and then surprise lifted his eyebrows as he observed the squeaky-clean state of our kitchen and dining room.

"Mama, I gotta go!" Rae announced, and scampered for the bathroom. I watched her disappear in a flash of flying ponytails and then turned to face my husband, who stood behind my chair at the table, one hand curled over the top of it.

"You all right?" he asked, and I saw the concern in his eyes. He was still wearing his black work t-shirt and faded jeans, his feet in worn socks, as he'd stepped out of his work boots at the door. His black hair was wild and appeared to have been roughed up numerous times since this afternoon. Absolute need to be in his arms nearly took me to my knees, but I was still angry. And torn—my eyes flickered toward the counter, where my panties had been laid out this afternoon, and my heart seemed to cave inward. But I hadn't the wherewithal to mention this, not yet.

You're probably making something out of nothing anyway, I thought. *Probably Rae was just playing around. How stupid does it sound to be afraid of your own underwear, huh?*

I nodded in response to Justin's question and sensed his intense desire for us to get over this fight. He remained in the same spot, the table between us, unconsciously caressing the back of my chair.

"Jo and Bly want to go to Eddie's tonight, if that's all right with you."

"Oh yeah, Norm Olson's band is in town, aren't they?"

I nodded again. "You want to go?"

"Sure," he said quietly. "Let me clean up first."

We walked Rae over to Mom's an hour later; normally we would have held hands but tonight we walked with an icky little distance between us, and I hated this. I wanted to tell him I was sorry, that I was being stubborn and that above all, I was scared, but the words kept sticking in my throat like chewed-up crackers. Like cotton wads. Rae, oblivious to any strain between her father and me, danced ahead, clutching her elephant and yelling at us to hurry up.

Justin looked damn good, and I had tried pretty hard myself, changing into my favorite maternity sundress, a rich copper color that highlighted both my tan and my cleavage. While Justin showered, I spent a few minutes accenting my lashes and lips and brushing out my hair. Justin was unable to keep the smoldering heat from his eyes when he emerged from the bathroom into our bedroom, all damp and fucking sexy as hell, his hips wrapped loosely in a well-worn towel just to torture me. He knew well how incredible he looked with his powerful muscles on display; more often than not when he appeared in our room fresh from the shower, I yanked that same towel from his body and demanded his immediate and absolute attention.

"You look beautiful, sweetheart," he murmured, holding my gaze as I watched him in the mirror.

"Thank you," I whispered, but neither of us moved to the other. Instead I watched in heated silence as he dressed with quiet efficiency, donning his favorite jeans and a fresh black t-shirt, this time one with sleeves, shaking through his hair with both hands in a manly gesture I knew well. Damp, it hung in messy waves almost to his shoulders.

Now, in the intoxicating evening air, we came upon Shore Leave to see Joelle and Blythe waiting for us; Bly called over, "Hurry up, you guys! It's gonna be busy already!"

"You can ride with us," Jo invited, and minutes later Blythe had parked his truck about two blocks from Eddie's, which was already hopping a good hour before the music even started.

"You weren't kidding," Justin said to Blythe. The small, familiar bar was packed to the brim, full as a fish belly as Gran used to say. We settled at one of the few remaining high tops in the back corner, Jo and I claiming seats while Justin and Bly fought the crowd to go buy drinks for us.

"They won't be able to make it back here until the band starts," Jo predicted, fanning her flushed cheeks. Her long hair fell over her bare shoulders. She was wearing a rose-colored tank top and gold hoop earrings, a light sheen of sweat decorating her tanned skin. Eddie's didn't have air conditioning, which wasn't an issue when the crowd consisted of the ten or so regulars; tonight, with a full house, it was humid as a sweat lodge.

Jo said, "You look gorgeous, Jilly Bean."

I rolled my eyes.

"I mean it," she insisted. "Your eyes look bluer than the lake. And I think you're putting Dolly Parton to shame."

I giggled, my gaze dropping briefly to my breasts. "In my defense, they're about all I have going for me right now."

"You have never been anything but gorgeous, and you know it. You should see the way Justin stares at you. You're the crystal-clear water to his dying of thirst in the desert." Jo looked over my shoulder then, lowering her voice to add, "And not just Justin. Shit, that guy over there is totally checking you out." Speculatively, she muttered, "I don't recognize him." Her eyebrows lifted. "He's coming over here."

I turned just in time to see Zack Dixon headed our way, clutching a drink and smiling with just about all of his shark teeth showing. My stomach plummeted to the floor.

Oh shit oh shit oh shit. You can't confront him here.

But what if he was in your house today? What if he touched your underwear?

What if he has your spare key in his pocket, right at this second?

My insides curled over on themselves as he reached us. He said, "Hi, Jillian," and then actually hooked his free hand over my left shoulder. Jo's eyes widened and I shrugged irritably away. Unfazed, he gripped the back of my chair. Jo sent me a look that clearly asked, *Who the hell is this guy?*

"Jo, this is—" I felt compelled to say, but he interrupted me.

"You must be Joelle," he said to my sister, with far too much familiarity. I could smell the sharp reek of whiskey on his breath. "Zackary Dixon. I've met most of the women in your family, but not you."

"He's from the college in Moorhead," I explained to Joelle, sending her a message in return, *Discourage any conversation!*

"You look *in*credible, Jillian," Zack said, with unpleasant emphasis, and combed his fingers through my loose hair.

"*Don't,*" I ordered, with clenched teeth, angling my chair away from him, with some difficulty, as he stepped immediately closer.

"Did you get my note?" he asked. "I left you one today."

For a horrible, frozen moment I thought he was actually admitting to being in my house and placing my panties on the counter, but then I recalled that he'd handwritten a message on a napkin at lunch. I was speechless for less than a second; forcing myself to meet his slimy gaze, I ordered, "Get the fuck out of here."

"You're even sexier when you're mad," he said, possibly believing that this statement was humorous. Before I could move, he reached and drew a line straight down my cleavage with an extended finger, concluding, "Fuck, you're soft."

Jo's lips dropped open, her shock nearly as palpable as mine as Zack let his fingertip linger between my breasts. I shoved viciously at his hand, ready to outright kill him; a second later my husband appeared through the noisy crowd. Just the expression in Justin's eyes was enough that Zack took an immediate and large step backward. Furious as I was, I almost smiled at this.

Setting our drinks on the table and subsequently freeing his hands, Justin moved into the space Zack had just vacated and asked as though conversationally, "How much do you value your life, buddy?"

Zack smiled and said, "As much as you value yours, I'm sure. You got something to say, or what?"

Justin rubbed the knuckles of his right hand against his jaw and asked through his teeth, "You have a death wish, *or what?*"

I jumped in at this point, addressing Zack as I said, "This is *my husband*, you moron. And he will wipe the fucking floor with you if you don't get out of here."

Blythe was also back from the bar, and Zack, though clearly buzzed and maybe even spoiling for a fight, seemed to perceive the intensive threat to his wellbeing. He lifted both hands in surrender, still clutching his drink. He shot Justin a dark look but chose to say nothing more, and shoved his way back into the boisterous crowd.

Justin inhaled a deep breath through his nose, bracing both hands on the table. His eyes were as black as flint chips. "Shit, my blood pressure is off the charts. Who was that? I'd like to know his name before I go rip his head off."

I put my hands atop his, which were curled into hard-knuckled fists, and hastily explained, "That was the guy I was telling you about a few weeks back, remember?"

"That was the guy from lunch, wasn't it?" Bly asked. "You didn't want to take his order."

"The one you said you had a bad feeling about?" Justin asked, eyes further narrowing as he stared in the direction Zack had disappeared. "He's been back to Shore Leave? You should have told me."

"I know, I've been meaning to," I said lamely.

"He touched you," Justin said with grit in his voice. His wide shoulders and arms were taut, his powerful biceps tense and bulging. He would make good on his threat about killing Zack if I said anything else right now, I could see plainly.

"I'm all right," I insisted, not about to let him get in a fight. "I'm just fine. Don't let him spoil the night."

Blythe set their beers on the table and stepped nearer to Jo, gently gathering her loose hair in his hand, caressing her neck with his thumb. He said, "Jills, I would have kicked him out today."

Jo said, "Wait, I'm missing something here. Who is this guy? I can't believe he touched you, Jilly Bean."

A muscle ticked in Justin's cheek, and I mustered my sternest tone. "It's all right. It's done now."

Justin finally claimed his seat and I released the tense breath I'd been holding. He drew my chair immediately closer to his and lined his arm possessively along the back of it.

"Jills, is this the same guy that Camille has mentioned?" Jo asked. "What's the story?"

I curled one hand around Justin's left knee, which was closest to me, and backtracked, knowing I had to explain. "That first morning he stopped out at the cafe, I had the thought that there was something wrong with his eyes. Something just slightly off. He asked me to walk him to his car that morning and I said, 'Are you fucking kidding me?' and he seemed embarrassed, so then I actually felt bad for snapping at him."

"He wanted you to walk him to his car?" Justin repeated in disbelief. "What the hell?"

"And he's stopped out for lunch a few times. Camille's had to wait on him."

"He's the one she said was being an asshole to her," Jo said. "She mentioned that before they left."

"And then he was at the counter today," I said. "Before I stopped out at the station…"

Justin's eyes were tight with concern. As I trailed to silence, he concluded quietly, "And then you didn't think of it again." He shifted position, scanning the crowd in search of Zack, before his eyes came back to me. "What else has he said?" He was too good at reading my face. He insisted softly, "Jilly, I know there's more."

"He's been out of line," I admitted, which was the wrong thing, as Justin's eyes grew even darker with repressed anger.

"How so?"

"He told me that I was sexy…and asked me if you told me that enough." My voice trembled over the words, thinking of what else Zack had said. "That's when I asked Blythe to take the order for me."

They all spoke at once.

"This was just *today*? Why didn't you tell me?" Jo demanded.

"I would have put him out on his ass," Blythe said. "Jeez, Jills."

Justin's expression was outright dangerous; he said, with deceptive calm, "I'll be right fucking back," and pushed away from the table. I caught his forearm in both hands and could feel the fury flowing in waves from him. Despite my restraining grip, he stood and cracked the knuckles on his punching hand. He'd always been known for his right hook.

"You guys," I said desperately. "It's fine. I think he's just an asshole, like Camille said. He's the type that likes to make people uncomfortable."

Justin's voice was low and pained. "You've been going through all of this on top of everything else. You should have told me."

"I didn't want you getting upset over nothing!"

"It's not nothing," Justin insisted. "I'm going to go and have a little conversation with him right now."

"J," I said breathlessly. "No. Please, no. I won't have you getting into a fight."

"Baby, I'm not going to get in a fight. I'm just going to talk to him about what's appropriate and what's not." I knew he was doing what he sincerely believed was right, but I vividly imagined all the ways this plan could go south in a moment's notice.

I looked at my sister for help but she only shrugged; her expression said, *I think he has a point, Jilly.*

Blythe said casually, "I'll join you," and Justin acknowledged this with a nod. My husband and my brother-in-law disappeared in the shifting crowd and I stood, my chair scraping along the floor.

"Jilly, it's all right." Jo flew around the table as though I was perched on the edge of a fifth-floor window ledge, catching my arm. I shook free of her grip, but Jo clamped my elbow and tugged me back.

"Dammit, Jillian, you're pregnant! Don't make me sit on you."

"You're not at all upset that your husband is headed for a potential fight?" My nerves were raw and blistered. "Like that would be a smart thing for him!"

"Now you're just being mean," Jo said. Her voice rose. "He's not going to get in a fight!"

"I'm glad you can read the future now! Maybe you can tell *me* how this all turns out!"

"Maybe you should be glad we have men who *care enough* about us to *stand up* for us! Justin is doing the right thing. You're the one who's being ridiculous!" Jo's eyes flashed with brimming anger. We hadn't gone after each other this badly in years.

"Maybe I don't want to have to accept collect calls from my husband while he's *in jail!*" I stormed, and with that I'd pushed too far. Jo's eyes narrowed and her lips compressed; she'd been forced to do that very thing three summers ago, when Bly was behind bars in Oklahoma.

"Maybe you should shut your mouth!" Tears glinted on her lower lashes. "You're being *such a bitch* and I don't understand it at all!"

I was about to hurl a response at her, only to realize that Justin and Bly were already back to the table, both of them obviously a little stunned by this evidence of a heated argument. My face was flushed and Jo turned away from everyone, discreetly swiping at the wetness in her eyes. I felt terrible, not that I would admit it at the moment.

"He's gone," Blythe told us, moving at once to his wife's side, rubbing one hand along her back. She acknowledged this with a half smile, keeping her eyes from me. I heard him murmur, "Do you want to go, sweetheart?"

She shook her head, taking a deep breath and reclaiming her seat, lifting her drink for a small sip. "No, I'd like to hear the music."

Bly sat beside her and there was little choice but to rejoin them at the table.

Justin had about a thousand questions for me, as I easily discerned, but he said only, "He's not here anymore, we even checked the bathroom. If he shows up at the cafe, or *anywhere* near you for that matter, I want you to call me right away."

"I will," I promised, my heart slowly regaining a more regular pace. I leaned against my husband, so very grateful for his presence; he latched one arm securely around my waist and planted a kiss on my temple. I kept my eyes away from Jo as I admitted, "I appreciate that you were willing to talk to him. But I hate the thought of you getting in a fight. It makes me sick."

"It's not that I want to get in a fight," Justin defended himself. The music was starting and he leaned closer so I could still hear him over the din. "When I saw him touch you I just about came unglued. I thought the glasses in my hands might shatter, I'm not kidding."

"That's how *I* felt this afternoon," I said, referring to Aubrey. "Her thinking she could put her hands on you, and say that stuff to you."

Justin heaved a sigh and admitted, "Yeah, it pretty much sucks. But dammit, Jilly, I'm not vulnerable to her the way you are to this guy. That shit he said to you. What the fuck? Who talks that way and thinks he can get away with it? If you see him again, call me."

"I will," I promised.

We listened to the music for a good hour. When the band took a small break, I sent my sister a silent message that I was sorry for being a bitch. She met my gaze and nodded a little, about half-acknowledging that she accepted my apology.

I asked, "Have you heard from Camille and Mathias? Have they gotten to Montana?"

"Milla called us this afternoon," Jo said. "They were just crossing the state line."

Blythe said, "We should drive out there with the kids next summer, maybe do some camping. Do you think Matthew will be old enough to ride in the car that long by then?"

I studied my brother-in-law, with fondness; he was so handsome, and kind. I loved him for making Joelle happier than I'd ever seen her. I'd finally become accustomed to Blythe's facial hair—which he'd grown from a goatee into a full-fledged beard, complete with mustache; no one would ever guess that he was actually twelve years younger than Joelle. His long, wavy hair was tied low on his neck, as he preferred, and Jo gently stroked her fingers through its length as he talked. I knew, just like me, that she preferred when her man's hair was long enough to dig her fingers within.

"He'd probably sleep most of the way," I said.

"We could all go," Blythe said. "That would be great. You think the kids would be up for it?"

"Dad took us camping all the time at that age," Justin said. "We should take the kids over to the state park a few times first, see how they handle it. It's all fun and games until it starts to rain and everyone has to crowd into one tent."

"I'm in," Blythe said gamely, taking a long swallow from his beer. "We could go this next weekend maybe, what do you say?"

"That might work out," Justin agreed. I knew he liked Blythe a great deal, considered him a little brother. I recalled the day that Justin taught Bly how to replace some belt in his truck's engine, and smiled at the memory. Justin was a good teacher, and could be patient when he chose.

Jo's cell phone began buzzing on the tabletop. "It's Ruthie. I'd say that's our cue."

Ten minutes later Bly dropped us at Shore Leave to collect Rae, but she was sleeping in Camille's old bed at Mom's house, and Mom insisted that she would bring her home in the morning.

"You two go on home and have a nice evening," Mom insisted, kissing my cheek at the front door, and I wondered if she meant that as in, *Go have some amazing sex and forgive each other*, or was just offering a pleasantry.

The forest path was lit by the almost-full moon, which was terribly romantic. The crickets serenaded us, the moonlight throwing patterns all over our bodies as we walked side by side beneath the pine trees, along the familiar route back to our cabin. I was so aware of my husband that I could hardly catch my breath; he didn't try to take my hand and I felt horribly deprived.

Dammit, it's up to you to apologize, I thought, and took a breath to do just that, when Justin suddenly said, "I smell pot."

I did then, too, even though it wasn't something we'd ever partaken of with any regularity, even as younger versions of ourselves. I heard my son's laughter next, in chorus with a couple of other boys, and we came out of the woods to spy Clint, Jeff, and Liam all gathered on the porch and passing a burning joint. Instead of going apeshit, which was my first instinct, I said only, "Clint Daniel Henriksen, you get your butt inside *right now*."

Their laughter fell away as if a guillotine blade had dropped on it. Clint leaped to his feet and his voice cracked through about an octave as he cried. "Mom! I didn't think you'd be home for hours!"

"So that excuses this?" I demanded, drawing abreast of the three boys; Liam and Jeff could hardly meet my eyes. Clint, who had been holding the joint, chucked it to the grass and ground it into oblivion with the toe of his flip-flop sandal.

"Boys, why don't I take you home?" Justin said to Liam and Jeff, and I couldn't tell if he was angry or actually just restraining laughter. I thought the latter, but he wouldn't dare admit to it, at least not in front of the boys. To me, he said, "I'll be right back, hon."

"Uncle Justin, you're not gonna tell Dad, are you?" Jeff started in right away, and Justin shook his head at me as he herded the boys toward his truck, parked in our driveway.

"Of course I'm going to tell him," Justin said, laughing now. "Shit, you think I want him finding out that I *didn't?*"

I restrained the urge to take my son by the ear. I ordered, "Go sit at the kitchen table." Clint obeyed without another word. I stood in our yard and watched Justin climb behind the wheel of his truck. He rolled down the window and I called to him, "Hurry back."

"I will," he said, his voice softening, and then I followed in Clint's footsteps to find him slouched in his chair, watching me with wary eyes. The only illumination in the room came from the small light above the stove.

Instead of pleading with me, Clint said, "I'm sorry. We hardly ever smoke pot, Mom, I promise. We do drink sometimes."

I sat across from him. "I know, son."

"Are you disappointed in me?" The question was tinged with plaintive concern.

I reached to curl my hands around Clint's, experiencing a sting of awareness that his hands felt like a man's, no longer my little boy's. "I could never be disappointed in you. Don't ever think that, sweetheart. But I'm disappointed that you made this *choice*, especially on the heels of telling Dad and me that you don't want to go to college. Can you see how we might interpret that as worrisome?"

He exhaled a big breath. "Yeah, I do. But I'm not a pot smoker, Mom, I swear. I don't even know why we were smoking just now, except that it seemed like fun."

"Where did you get it?" I asked, releasing his hands.

"From Lisa," he admitted, naming Jeff's sister, Wordo's oldest daughter. Shit, it was just another thing we'd have to tell Wordo and Liz. As if they didn't have their hands full enough.

I sighed. "No more, all right? For one thing, it's illegal. Promise me?"

"I promise," Clint mumbled, knuckling his red-rimmed eyes. "I really do. I'm sorry." A half-teasing grin lit his face. "You won't send me away to college, will you?"

"Go to bed, I can't deal with you anymore tonight!"

Clint stood and walked two steps before turning back. He said, "Hey," and his eyes held mine, serious and steady. He looked more like a man than ever as he implored, "Mom, you belong with Justin. I can tell you're mad at him, but don't be. Please don't."

"Clint," I whispered, aching at his sincere words. "I'm not really mad at him. I'm just mad...at the situation."

"I've never told him that I can see how much he loves you," Clint whispered, and I heard a lump in his throat. "But I do see it. He loves you so much, Mom. I can only pray that I find a girl I love as much someday. Tell him you're not mad anymore, promise?"

Tears washed down my cheeks. "I promise."

It might have been the weed but I heard Clint snoring from his room no more than five minutes later. I slipped from my sundress and into the tank top I favored as a maternity night shirt, and then washed my face, water streaking down my neck. Free from any cosmetics, I studied my somber eyes in the mirror. So much had happened today I couldn't process all of it, but I knew Clint was right. I knew that I needed to stop being unreasonable; I was so sorry for how I had acted that my throat ached just remembering.

It seemed to take too long for Justin to get back from dropping off the boys, but probably he was stuck in a conversation with his sister and Wordo; I wondered if Jeff had spilled the beans on the way home and Lisa was now in trouble, too. I lay on my back on our bed, smoothing one hand over my belly, listening to the owls in the woods, the wind chimes softly tinkling, restless and sensitized; my thoughts kept circling back to the strangeness of finding my panties on the counter this afternoon. The rock placed on them. The missing key. I'd almost made up my mind that it was nothing; probably Rae had been playing with my things...

But what if it's not?

What if...

I was still hung up on the fact that I was unduly embarrassed to tell anyone I suspected my underwear had been used as part of a possible threatening message.

It's all done now, it's all right. It's nothing.

The truck grumbled along the driveway then and I rolled to one elbow. Less than a minute later, Justin came in through the door from the garage and I heard him washing his hands at the kitchen sink. Electricity lit my nerves while I waited for him. As he entered our darkened room and closed the door behind him, I sat, with some difficulty; a sob stuck in my throat as I whispered, "Justin."

Before my next breath I was in his arms. I clung, my cheek on his chest, imbibing his heartbeat as he swept tangled hair from the side of my neck to rest his face there. He lingered, cradling me.

"I'm so sorry," I whispered at long last. "I'm so sorry I let Aubrey make me that angry."

"Baby." His voice roughened with emotion. "I'm sorry, too. I hate that she upset you this much."

"It's because I let her." I swiped at my tears. "I shouldn't have let her."

Justin kissed my forehead. "She wanted to upset you. That was her goal all along."

"I wanted to kill her for touching you, for saying those things."

"Yeah, I saw that in your eyes." There was the faintest hint of humor in his voice. "And a part of me is even appreciative of that. But you're also carrying my son." His chest rose and fell with a deep breath. "Besides, do you think I was going to stand by and let you get in a fight with her, over me? Jesus, I just about had a heart attack when you lunged at her."

I cringed. "I wasn't thinking straight, not just then."

"I know what she said hurt you. I do, sweetheart, and I'm so sorry." He covered my right hand, which was still cupping his jaw, and kissed my palm. "I wish I could make you understand how little her words mean to me. I was in such a bad place back then. I was so fucking angry and bitter. I was scared that when she left I would be alone forever in the dark, scarred up, looking like a monster. Of course I begged her not to leave me with that feeling. But her leaving was a blessing, and I *know* you know that."

"I do," I whispered.

"Jillian, I can't even begin to explain what you mean to me, how I feel to know that you love me, that you're mine. I walked on that dark path for years, for so long it was familiar to me, the darkness. It was horrible. And then one day, not long after we talked on the dock that night after Aubrey left, I started to see a light. Pretty soon it was almost blinding me, telling me how stupid I was not to let myself acknowledge the truth. Oh God, Jilly, back in high school I remember thinking you were like this beautiful little wildflower, I had that exact thought. So sweet and sexy, and you were always laughing. I was so jealous of Chris. That night at your wedding when I danced with you, held you in my hands in your wedding dress, I knew I'd made the worst mistake of my life by marrying someone else, and I was so close to telling you so. I would have ruined your wedding, but I couldn't do that to you." He smoothed his thumb over my bottom lip. "After that I forced myself to believe I was wrong and that I had to forget those thoughts. And if I'm totally honest, know-ing that you loved Chris so much still rips my heart up."

"Justin," I whispered, loving him so much it was close to physical pain.

"No, let me finish," he said intently. "Please, let me tell you. I don't say that to hurt you. I mean that I understand jealousy. When I look in your eyes and see how much you love me, I can't describe how my heart feels. I could try, but it wouldn't do justice. With you, I'm just me. You look at my face and see me, not all the scars. With you I feel whole. I don't have to hide anything, even the darkest parts of me. I know that I have everything in this world that I could ever need. Jillian, you are my light and my wildflower and my heart. I can't bear to see you hurting."

"Justin," I moaned, tears hot on my face, and he made a sound in his throat as he collected me closer, cupping the back of my head with one hand. He bent his face to my hair. I pressed my mouth to his neck and held him as hard as I could. "I love you. I did love Chris, but I was born to be yours. You are the love of my life, Justin."

"I know it to the bottom of my heart, baby. I do." He stroked the tears from my face. "Do you see why I couldn't let some asshole talk to you that way? You don't want me to get in a fight, but you have to know that I would do whatever it took to protect you."

"I know you would," I acknowledged. I snuggled closer, whispering "Was your sister upset about the pot?"

Justin snorted a laugh. "Yeah, just a little. Did you talk to Clint about everything? What did he say?"

"He said he was sorry, that they hardly ever do that stuff. I believe him. Then he told me that he can see how much you love me. And that he has never told you how grateful he is for that."

"I love that kid so much. I've told him, but I hope he really knows it. I think...I really believe that Chris would approve of him calling me 'Dad.' The first time he said that, Jills, I just about broke down weeping. It was so...it just struck me right across the heart."

"Thank you for being such a good dad to him. I knew you would be. That night we sat on the dock at the cafe and you told me you wished you had a couple of kids." I kissed his right eyebrow and his hands anchored around my hips. "I wanted to tell you right then that I would be happy to have your babies. I was sitting there thinking that very thing."

"I sensed that," he whispered, husky teasing in his voice as his hands busied themselves on my lower body. "I really did. I should have kissed you right then, I wanted to so bad, but I was too chicken."

I kissed him, plying the tip of my tongue along the seam of his warm lips, my hands buried deep in his hair. A strand of my hair fell in the way and Justin tucked it behind my ear before claiming my mouth with a deep, all-consuming kiss. I spread around him, cradling his big, strong, nude body as we joined together in a sweet, flowing motion. Justin closed his eyes and uttered a deep, throaty sound of contentment, not breaking our kiss, though he lifted his mouth just a fraction to whisper, "I love you so."

And then we were lost to the rest of the world.

Chapter Twelve

"Hop on in," Clark invited, and Mathias and I climbed into the backseat of his two-ton pickup, a beast of a truck with dually wheels and a diesel engine. I scooted to sit on Mathias's lap and Case clambered in along with us; between the two of them in the cramped backseat, it smelled like a brewery.

"This is so exciting," Case said for the fourth or fifth time, and he was indeed grinning like a little boy. "I just love mysteries."

Our things were waiting patiently in the campsite that we'd set up before walking over to The Spoke, just a few hours before, never suspecting how this evening would turn out. *Fate*, I thought, and shivered as I climbed down from the truck. The men would not let me lift a finger to help, tearing down the tent and loading everything into our truck within minutes.

"I'll head back to the house," Clark told us. "Case can ride with you two and show you the way."

After he drove away, Mathias, Case, and I stood admiring the wide, starry sky, all of us caught up in something we could not explain. Our truck sat idling; I'd told Mathias I would drive us to the Rawleys' place, since he'd had so much to drink.

"I don't know why I'm just so happy," Case muttered, his words distorted from both alcohol and the angle of his throat, tipped back as he studied the heavens. He looked over at us. "Like, we're on the right path now. Isn't that crazy as shit?"

Mathias went over to him and hooked an arm about Case's neck, and this gesture chimed against a memory, a remembrance…something in my mind acknowledged recognition. "Nah, it's not crazy. I feel the same way."

"C'mere, Camille," Case invited, and I tucked myself against Mathias, holding him around the waist. Case reached and ruffled my hair. He said, "It's crazy. I get that. But I feel like you guys know everything about me and that's how it should be."

He was pretty damn drunk, but I understood he was being sincere. And I felt the same. Just as at Makoshika, I recognized at some instinctive level that we'd been here before tonight.

Mathias repeated, "It's not crazy."

"Fireflies," Case mumbled. "I can see a whole field of them."

I swore for a second that I could too—that the foothills were suddenly awash with millions of them, glowing green and gold, flickering like tiny souls. I held fast to Mathias. I thought the words, *Malcolm. Cora…*

You know what I mean, don't you?

The two of you have stood here, just like this.

You understand…I know you do…I can't bear to imagine the two of you without the other…

"Will you introduce me to Patricia?" Case asked, and there was something so serious and so hopeful, braided together in his voice. He murmured, "I can't stop thinking about her, I swear on my life."

"Of course I will," I whispered. "Someday."

"Someday *soon*," Case insisted. "Do you promise?"

"I promise."

Mathias said, "Would you look at that moon?"

The three of us held each other.

At last it was more than I could bear—a sense of sadness, of agony, lingered near the back of my neck, and I knew I must keep moving or it would latch a firmer hold, no matter how hard I tried to deny it. I whispered, "We best get going."

Back in the truck, Mathias slid in beside me and scooted to the middle, while Case took the passenger seat and directed us through the countryside to the Rawleys' homestead, a few miles from The Spoke.

"It's a hobby farm these days," Case explained, sitting with his forearms braced on his thighs. "The Rawleys used to ranch sheep. Clark's family has owned this acreage since the 1800s."

"Wow," I marveled, leaning over the steering wheel to peer at the rambling stone house, the two enormous barns; one was constructed of wood with a steeply-pitched roof, the other of steel-pole construction, much newer and sleeker, connected to a huge expanse of split-rail corral.

"Horses," Mathias breathed with excitement in his tone. "A whole lot of them."

"Park over there, hon," Case told me, pointing at a gravel lot to the left of the older barn. In the distance, the dim outlines of low-lying mountains lent the horizon a majestic and mysterious appearance, ancient and unchanging. It appeared that every light in the house was burning. A couple of dogs galloped to meet us, barking in furious excitement. Behind the older barn, in a stone fire pit the size of Flickertail Lake, a bonfire was blazing. A bunch of people, all male, came running to help us unload. I felt a little like the character, Millie, from the musical *Seven Brides for Seven Brothers*, which Tish and Ruthie and I had watched all the time when we were little; the part when Millie first arrives on her new husband's farm and is confronted by the reality of all six of his ill-mannered, backwoodsman brothers.

"Hi, ma'am," they all seemed to be saying, shoving each other around to be the first to shake my hand.

"Jesus, give them some space!" Garth ordered his brothers, laughing. "Mathias, Camille, these are my little brothers. You know Marsh already, and that there is Quinn, there's Sean, and little Wyatt over there, and this is Case's little brother, Gus Spicer."

I knew there was no hope of attaching names to faces. The Rawley boys all resembled each other too much to make distinctions between one another, at least for now, and Case's brother was also a freckled red-head with merry eyes.

"Boys, help carry their things inside," Clark instructed, resettling his hat and regarding this pack of boys with a smile lifting his mustache. "Come on inside and make yourselves at home."

I caught Mathias's hand in mine as we followed Clark to his house. Though I was no expert, it was surely designed with the local countryside in mind. The ceilings were constructed of gleaming logs, the light fixtures were made from antlers, the fireplace almost certainly built of a native stone. The furniture was substantial and bulky, in dark tones, lots of leather.

"This is like our cabin on steroids," I whispered to Mathias, who squeezed my fingers in response. Just thinking of our cabin jabbed a small splinter of homesickness into my heart. I pictured my little porch there, back in the north woods of Minnesota, the hammock that Mathias had hung for me between two oaks, and our plans to make it our year-round home.

The boys all piled in behind us, toting our luggage up a sweeping staircase to the second floor. Clark led the way to the kitchen and offered us seats at the dining table. Centered upon it was a long rectangular flower pot, overflowing with a plant bearing small, sharp-edged pink blossoms.

"What kind of flower is that?" I asked Clark.

"Bitterroot," he explained. "State wildflower and I'm fond of it, I admit."

I sensed Mathias's speculative look; he could tell my thoughts were whirling. I'd dreamed of this plant just last night.

I'll tell you later, I promised him.

"I need to dig out that telegram," Clark said. "You say that Malcolm Carter is your relation?"

"He was the younger brother of my great-something grandpa," Mathias explained. "They built my family's original homestead back in Minnesota, just after the Civil War."

"Our kin built this place near the same time," Clark said. "If you'd like to have a drink, relax a bit at the fire, I'll find that telegram directly."

I traced my fingertips over the petals of the bitterroot, admiring the tint of the flowers. I said, "That sounds good. I just need to change first," chilly in my little sundress.

"You two are in the guest room, third door on the right," Clark directed me.

This room, when I found it minutes later, was decorated with black bears. I giggled at the sight of the twin bed (there was little enough space in our full-size back home) decked in a red quilt with a bear's head centered upon it; the sheets revealed more black bears, walking in diagonal lines. Our bags were set neatly at the foot of the bed, and I rooted in mine until I found my jeans, a pair of socks, and one of Mathias's sweatshirts.

I jogged back downstairs to find Mathias drinking a beer at the table, grinning and amused as he watched Case, who sat holding the picture of Tish cupped in his palm; all of the boys, with the exception of Garth, were crowded behind him, listening respectfully as Case explained with awe in his tone, "This is my future wife, guys, see here." He traced a fingertip over her face. "Her name is Patricia. She lives back east. Isn't she just so *beautiful?* Look at her *eyes.* They're like sapphires. Like the morning sky." He seemed to be searching his mind. He grinned and concluded, "Like all the most beautiful blue things I've ever known."

Mathias hid a snicker behind his knuckles. I knew he was thinking of how Tish would react to Case's mooning. And, oh, how I wished my sister could see and hear it; she would flip out all over the place, snatch the picture back from Case, thump him over the head and give him a piece of her mind. This poor sweet guy had no idea what he would be getting into with my outspoken tomboy of a sister, and I giggled, unable to help it.

"Hi, honey," Mathias said as I approached.

"You got any more sisters?" asked one of the middle Rawley brothers, possibly Quinn. The boys ranged in age from about eighteen to twelve, with the littlest Rawley brother being the youngest. He was probably only eight or nine.

"Yes, that's my other sister, Ruthann," I explained, indicating her; in the picture, Ruthie leaned on her elbows on the dock between Tish and Millie Jo, her long curls pinned up in a twist. I'd taken the picture in the middle of Ruthie laughing about something, her face turned slightly to the left, and her carefree joy was obvious even in this immobile image; she looked happy and lovely, the sun glinting on her soft bare shoulders and highlighting the gold in her irises.

"Maybe I can marry *her*," Quinn said, but his enthusiasm was cut short as Marshall interjected succinctly, "Nope."

Quinn punched at his brother's arm, which Marshall neatly side-stepped; he explained to Quinn in no uncertain terms, "She's mine, little bro. Someday."

"Any others?" Quinn asked, undeterred, and I raised my eyebrows at Mathias, who hid another smile behind a sip of beer.

"You guys are animals," Garth said, coming from around the corner carrying two six-packs of beer, one in each hand. "Those are ladies. Ladies wouldn't give you bums the time of day!"

"Dad said you guys have a new singer," one of the boys said to Garth.

"We wish," Garth said, nodding at Mathias. "But these two have to be back in Minnesota. They can't stay out here."

"Shucks," said the boy.

"Shucks is right," Case mourned. "Maybe y'all can move to Jalesville one of these days. Is Patricia still in high school?"

"C'mon, let's go sit at the fire," Garth invited, and there was a thundering of bodies toward the door. I stepped closer to Mathias to avoid getting trampled in the crush of boys.

Outside, the stars were wild, riotous, despite the overshadowing power of the moon. I thought of last night, camping at Makoshika and making love while the sky seemed to explode with fiery brilliance. Mathias tucked me to his side, surely thinking the same thing; he slipped one palm over my belly and kissed my temple.

"Aw, let's stop for a sec," he said with hushed reverence as we passed the corral. The boys descended on the fire, where it appeared Clark had snacks waiting, but Mathias wanted to see the horses. We paused at the corral, resting our forearms along the top wooden beam. There were three horses in sight and more in the barn; I could hear muffled nickering and sighs, the occasional stomping of hooves. Mathias whistled, reaching out a hand, and was rewarded for this as one of the animals clomped our way and nudged at his palm with its long nose. I laughed, delighted, as the horse stuck its head over the fence and regarded us with somber eyes.

"Hi, Bluebell," I teased, stroking her neck with tentative fingers; she didn't shy away, instead scooting closer to my touch, the same way a dog would. In the moonlight I could not tell exactly what color she was (or if she was even female), though she was two distinctly different colors, light patches on a darker base color. Her hide was firm and warm, her hair short and bristly. She nickered at my continued scratching and I smiled, climbing onto the bottom rung so I could be closer to her face.

"Hi, pretty girl," Mathias said, patting her back. "What a pretty girl."

"Oh, here comes another one," I said, caught up in the excitement of it. The second animal, all one color, perhaps dark brown, joined us at the fence, nudging its head against the first horse's side to displace her from our attention.

Mathias laughed as the second horse bumped its nose lightly against his chest, as though searching for an apple. He rubbed its neck and addressed the animal with the tone of voice normally used for toddlers and puppies. "You want a belly rub, huh? You want a nice belly rub, huh, boy?"

"Yes, please," I teased, sliding a little closer to him.

Case yelled from the fire, "You two coming, or what?"

The fire pit was ringed with round stones, each roughly the size of snowballs we would roll for the base of a snowman, back home. There were frayed lawn chairs placed all around and Mathias and I claimed two of these. In the leaping flames, the tribe of boys reminded me of the kid from *Where the Wild Things Are*, or maybe Peter Pan's Lost Boys. They all looked a little ragged, and in need of a mother. I recalled that Clark said his wife had passed away and felt a sharp pang of sympathy. I thought of the way Grandma and Aunt Ellen would start packing them all up in preparation to haul them home to Landon, where they would be summarily spoiled within an inch of their lives.

"So, is your sister still in school, or what?" Case asked from across the fire, determined to get some answers. He looked so eager that I giggled again.

"She graduated this past spring. She's going to college in Minneapolis this fall, to start a pre-law program."

"She's smart," he understood. "Smart and beautiful. She would never see anything in me."

Everyone laughed at his words. Case was still cradling the picture in his palm. Beside him, Marshall punched his shoulder and demanded,

"Let me hold it for a second," but Case would not relinquish it.

"You guys up for a few songs?" Garth asked. He settled his guitar over his thighs and plucked out a minor chord, a slightly mournful note, inspiring a shiver along my spine.

"Are you cold, honey?" Mathias asked, opening his arms. "Come here."

I moved to his lap and the lawn chair creaked in protest beneath our combined weight.

"Let's hear some old-timey stuff," Case requested, slurring a little. He was halfway into his countless beer of the night.

Garth responded accordingly. I didn't recognize the melody; it was a song that had not been written in this century. After a second Mathias began to sing, low and sweet, and then I realized I knew the song after all. The boys all joined in on the chorus and "O Susanna" was lifted up into the Montana sky by our combined voices. Tears stung my eyes. I was just so happy to be here, singing with them. I looked around at the faces of people unknown to us before this afternoon, and again felt a sense of belonging, a *knowing*. Clearly, Mathias and I were meant to be here on this night. I only wished that my sisters were at the fire with us; I suddenly missed them both so much that my ribs ached. I looked across the fire at Case, his red-gold hair gleaming in the orange light, and Marshall, lean as a heron and with such pretty, dark gray eyes, the two of them all but fighting over the picture of Tish and Ruthie, and I felt a shifting, deep inside.

Something had changed, tonight.

"That's such a sad song, I always forget," Mathias murmured when it was over.

Case sat with his guitar braced against his chair and drunk as he was, still managed (after carefully tucking the picture of Tish into the neck of his t-shirt, *no* hopes of getting it back now) to maneuver the instrument onto his lap, strumming with no hesitation. Eyes half-closed, he ordered, "I want all of you to sing again. I liked it. 'Red River Valley,' here we go."

We sang and sang, connected by the old melodies (even though I only knew the chorus of most of the songs), the fire a reflective central focus, its orange, leaping light so conducive to speculation. I studied the flames, held close to Mathias, and pretended that we were sitting around a fire in another century—a century that belonged to Malcolm and Cora, a time period in which they'd been alive. Mathias traced patterns on the backs of my hands, or softly stroked the length of my hair, hanging over my left shoulder. Clark joined us as the final chords of "Shenandoah" rippled away across the midnight landscape. The air was cold and expectant, too quiet without the music; Clark carried a small, yellowed envelope, soft and worn from the passage of time. He hunkered down and placed it in my hands. "I found it."

There was a name scrawled on the back of the envelope in faded black ink: *Grantley W. Rawley*. I felt a jagged-edged jolt at the sight, thrown suddenly back to the winter morning I had first found the picture of Malcolm and Aces, in the Davis family trunk from our attic. With great care I withdrew the telegram, which looked just like the one Bull had found for me back in Landon. Pausing at the word STOP written on the old paper, rather than speaking it aloud, I read, "Back by spring thaw STOP no answers STOP God help me Grant STOP Regards, old friend STOP Malcolm A. Carter." It was dated December 24, 1876. Tears gushed over my cheeks as I spoke Malcolm's name. I didn't care if they all thought I was crazy as I choked, "Oh *Malcolm*. Oh, my God…"

Mathias hugged me close. I couldn't stop crying, even though everyone was staring with open stun on their faces. Clark reached and cupped my knee. "What does this mean to you? Tell me. Please, I must know."

"We hardly know most of it," Mathias answered softly, as I buried my face in both hands. "We have a letter and another telegram, back home, along with a photograph. My relatives in Bozeman have a few more letters, which we were on the way to pick up. But what we've pieced together is that Malcolm was searching for a woman, a woman named—"

"Cora," I said. "Her name was Cora."

Garth moved so swiftly around the fire that he seemed like a ghost. He crouched at our knees, staring intently at my tear-streaked face. He asked in a low voice, "Was she in the photo you found? Do you know what she looked like?"

"No," I whispered. But then I realized I did—and said, "Wait, her eyes…"

Garth finished immediately, "Are two different colors." We stared at each other, partly in disbelief, partly in simple relief that someone else understood; surely we weren't *both* crazy. Garth closed his eyes and confessed, "When I was a little boy, I used to dream about a girl named Cora. Dad, you remember?"

Clark nodded. "Used to scare you to pieces. Your ma and I were at our wits' end."

Case said, "I remember you talking about her."

"What did you dream?" Mathias asked.

Garth said, "At least, I *thought* it was a dream. It was too scary to think that she was a ghost. I remember that her eyes scared me to the bone. She would flicker at the foot of my bed and all I could see were her eyes, two different colors. One green and one—"

"Black," I whispered, and Garth nodded.

"Oh God, I saw her just last night," I said, trembling with restless energy.

"She wants us to find her," Mathias said. "But we don't know how… we don't have any idea where to start."

"Did she ever tell you anything?" I asked Garth.

"She never spoke, she just appeared. I was so young and it scared me so much. Shit, I haven't thought of her in a long time, to be honest. Once she seemed to be crying. I thought I was batshit crazy. She never even told me her name, I just *knew* it."

"Are you magic?" the littlest Rawley brother asked me. There was a certain amount of awe in his tone.

"Can we contact her somehow?" Marshall asked.

"I wish I was magic enough to find her," I said. "I wish there was some way to control when she appeared."

"By late 1876, Malcolm was back in Minnesota," Mathias noted, re-examining the telegram. "But your relative, this Grantley, was out here."

"How did they know each other?" Garth wondered. "How were they connected?"

"Dad, don't we have that whole trunk of stuff?" Marshall asked, his fingers drumming along on the arms of his lawn chair.

Clark sighed a little. "Most of those things were divided up when Dad passed. I wish I had saved more. I don't recall any additional communications, I swear. There were a couple of tintypes, clothes and quilts, a census report from the 1880s, but not much else that would help us now."

"This is the most exciting night we've had in a long time," reflected one of the brothers.

"Are you all right now, ma'am?" asked the littlest one.

"Yes," I assured him, offering a smile.

"We'll help," said another. "What can we do, Garth?"

Garth leaned and ruffled his brother's hair. "I wish I had a plan." He said to Mathias, "Our ancestors were old friends. What do you know about that?"

"That's too crazy to be a coincidence," Mathias said.

"I told you I thought I knew you," Garth said, with a grin.

"We were meant to meet you guys," Marshall added.

"We never even would've met if I hadn't hit Camille in the head with my guitar," Case said. "It was meant to be. *Shit*, you guys."

"It's late," Clark reflected. "I'll see what I can find in the morning, but I suggest we all turn in for now. What do you say, boys?"

"Do you and your brother live here, too?" I asked Case in the bustle of everyone heading inside.

"We stay here a lot," he said, indicating his little brother, Gus.

"Does your family live nearby?" I asked.

Case shifted as though uncomfortable, not meeting my eyes. "Something like that."

We said good-night and everyone headed for the house; only Garth remained around the fire, almost motionless, staring at the flames. At the foot of the stairs, Clark kissed my hand. "It's been a darn long time since I've had a woman to cook breakfast for. I'll spoil you, doll, just you wait."

Minutes later Mathias and I snuggled beneath the black bear-patterned covers in the guest room; he was blissfully naked and warm, while I wore his t-shirt, hesitant to sleep in the nude in a full house not our own. Mathias rolled to one elbow and regarded me in the moonlight spilling over us through the tall, rectangular window beside the bed. The telegram was centered on the nightstand, within arm's reach.

"That telegram about breaks my heart," he whispered.

I shifted closer, latching a thigh around his hip.

He murmured, "If you could only see the way your eyes look in the moonlight. Don't cry, honey, that truly breaks my heart."

I gulped and he gently wiped tears from my cheek. I moaned, "I can't bear to think about Malcolm alone and hurting, without her. He obviously loved Cora, Thias, and somehow they got separated. How? What happened?" There were too many possibilities to consider, a world's worth of potential tragedy.

"I wish I knew. Come here, honey, let me hold you." Stroking my hair, he murmured, "It's so wild that Malcolm knew the Rawleys. Knew their family, anyway. Talk about fate."

"I knew that our being here was right. Besides, you make everywhere home. You know what I mean?" My eyes drifted closed as I explained, "Wherever we are together, I feel like I'm home."

His chest bounced with a quiet laugh. "If I can smell your hair and your breath, then I know I'm home. And feel you beside me. That was so hard last winter before we lived together, to go back to the apartment and think about you in a bed without me."

I nodded agreement, kissing his bare chest, my eyes still closed.

"That night we watched the aurora for the first time, last Christmas, I wanted to ask you to marry me right then," he said softly. "But I didn't want to scare you away."

"I would have said 'yes' that night," I whispered.

"We'll have to invite these guys to the wedding," he murmured against my hair.

Though I was nearly asleep, I nodded agreement of this; I wanted all of them in Minnesota. I wanted my sisters to meet them—especially Case and Marshall.

"Sleep, love," he whispered. "I'll be right here."

Right here…

I want you to wait right here, do you hear me? I'll be back by dawn's light, I swear to you.

I knew that voice to the depths of my being. Hearing it now was akin to the striking of a finely-wrought tuning fork within my soul—a piercing need for the owner of that voice, whose life I had once come to depend upon far beyond my own existence. I'd heard it warm with laughter and tender murmurings, rife with joy, husky with the low, hushed sounds of lovemaking. Too had I heard it rasping through fear and disbelief, shouted fury and angry intensity; it was the voice of a man of strong passion and deep emotion.

Everything within me strained frantically toward him, but he was just beyond my reach.

Let me come with you, please let me come with you. I won't slow you down.

The desperate concern in his eyes stabbed a hole through my gut. The scar on my ribs seemed to burn.

It's too dangerous. Do you hear me?

Don't go without me. Please, I beg of you.

I love you with all of my heart. I will not put you in danger. Do you hear me?

Desperation sucked all breath from my lungs, clouded the air about our heads, the sickening tension of an impossible decision. From behind him, in the darkness, another voice called intently, *Carter! We'll lose them!*

I love you, too. You're mine. Don't go away from me.

There is no other choice.

There's always another choice!

Not this time, and his voice was broken with emotion. *It will be all right, love. It will. I will come back for you. I swear I will come back here for you.*

I drifted then, like a small and vulnerable boat washed out to sea, a cork on the waves, swept along in a tide not of my own making. Hovering just above a scene that my soul ripped itself inside-out to avoid witnessing; a soundless shrieking that hollowed out my heart.

Too late.

He came back. He came back for me but I was not there. The remnants of the fire, still smoldering. Trampled grass, tracks leading south and east. And his agony as a punishment I would bear forever. Agony never extinguished.

Don't you see?

Don't you understand?

My own voice called through a long corridor of time. *Tell me, Cora, please, I beg you! Where are you? What happened?*

What happened?!

I sensed I was on the edge of wakefulness and struggled away from it, desperate to hear her response. She was hardly a whisper now, faint as the smoke from a campfire in the distance. But she breathed, *Close. So close.*

And I woke to the scent of the bitterroot blossoms that grew in profusion out there in the foothills.

Chapter Thirteen

By morning's light our bedroom was aglow with a rosy dawn. Justin was still snoring and would probably be a little late for work today; I moved to kiss the back of his neck as he slept soundly on his belly, as was his habit. I could hear Clint rattling around the kitchen and snuggled my cheek into my pillow. I dozed for another half hour before Justin roused and gathered me close.

"Morning, baby," he said, planting a kiss on my lips and then straying beneath the covers to kiss my belly. "And good morning to this baby too."

I still hadn't managed to drag myself from the soft warmth of the bed by the time Justin left for work. I knew I needed to get up and go get Rae at Mom's, but I was so relaxed, my limbs pleasantly sore from being wrapped around my husband most of the night.

"Mom, I'm heading out!" Clint called from the kitchen.

"Have a good day!" I called back, and resolved to haul my ass to the shower. It was just as my feet touched the braided-rag rug beside the bed that I saw it, and everything within me went still and cold.

A lake rock, round and gray, very similar to the one that I'd tossed with all my strength into the woods yesterday evening, was centered on my nightstand.

Oh God, oh my God.

He's been here again.

When? How? Last night?

Oh God, Clint was here alone, before we got back.

This can't be happening.

I forced myself to draw a breath and then another, pressing both palms to my face.

Think, Jillian.

There has got to be a reasonable explanation for all of this.

It's a fucking rock. Probably Rae was playing with it and left it there.

But what if…

Oh God, what if…

I dressed without showering, in too much distress to do anything but be near my family. I knew I needed to tell Mom and Aunt Ellen, I knew I should call Justin right away. But there was a part of me that felt so damn foolish, completely ridiculous for even considering that a *rock* retained some ulterior meaning. I felt nuts. I had always possessed an overactive imagination, had always been a little bit attracted to drama. I could just hear Mom now, reminding me of these facts.

But you're not imagining Zack's behavior. He's been way out of line numerous times now.

But to the point that he's invading your home? That's way beyond serious. That's a fucking criminal act.

The sun shone warm on my shoulders, the day bright as a promise as I stalked through the woods; it was one of those rare July mornings when the air wasn't already drenched with humidity. I got to Shore Leave just as Clint was leaving for work; he waved out the car window as he drove away. Inside, Mom and Aunt Ellen had served Rae breakfast at the counter. Her golden hair was tied in two ponytails and she was coloring with a box of crayons.

"Hi, stink bug," I murmured, catching her close for a hug. "I love you."

"Hi, Mama!" she chirped. "Daddy was here, too, Mama!"

"Jilly, join me outside for a minute," Mom said then, while Aunt Ellen took a seat near Rae. The tone in Mom's voice was one I didn't recognize; I followed her out to the porch, where she led me around the far side, as though to make sure that Rae was not able to hear a word.

"Mom, what's—"

"Why in God's name didn't you tell me that this Zack Dixon has been making inappropriate comments to you?" Mom's familiar eyes snapped with concern. As was her habit when flustered or upset, she clutched her long braid and drew it over one shoulder, twisting it in her hand. Before I could respond, she carried on, "Justin was just here, adamant that we not allow him back on the property. I've never seen Justin look so angry. He said to call him if Zack showed up here again, and that he'd deal with him. And then he told me how this young man treated you last night. And the things he's said to you." Mom rattled through her words, clearly in distress.

"Mom," I began.

"Don't 'Mom' me in that tone, Jillian. I'm so upset that you didn't tell me what's been happening. Why didn't you? I would have told him exactly where he could go, and how to get there!"

Tell her about the rocks, the underwear. God, tell her right now.

But in the end I couldn't manage to vocalize my thoughts, still embarrassed at the absurdity of it. I only said, "I'm glad Justin told you. But I don't want him getting in a fight, Mom. I really don't. I would be horrified if that happened."

Mom pulled me close, rubbing my back with both hands. She whispered, "You're so little and sweet, honey, I worry about you. And you're pregnant. We all feel so protective of you, you know."

And here I'd always thought my family considered me pretty tough. Yes, I was the littlest, but I could deal with things. I could hold my own.

"I called the college in Moorhead and left a message with the director of graduate studies," Mom said. "I asked him to call me back as soon as he could. I also informed him that one of his students is a son of a bitch and needs to be reprimanded!"

I knew she would have phrased it just that way, no glossing it over. I said, "Mom, I'm all right. But thank you."

As it was Thursday, I worked lunch, glad for the routine. Ruthie came over with Jo and Blythe to watch Millie and Rae; Matthew was home with Blythe's mom, Christy. Just before it started to get busy, Justin called to tell me that he and Dodge were driving over to Rose Lake to check out a boat that Dodge had been eyeing in the classified ads, and wouldn't be back until late afternoon.

"Thank you for telling Mom about everything," I told my husband, balancing my cell phone between ear and shoulder as I wiped down a porch table. "I'm glad she knows. I wasn't sure how to tell her."

"Jillian. Woman. I would do anything for you," he said. "Joan and Ellen were pretty upset."

"Yeah, I heard all about it, believe me." And then, more softly, "I'm all right, honey."

"I still worry about you," he said. "You are more precious to me than anything in this world. You and our kids."

"Hurry home to me. I already miss you."

"I will, baby. See you later."

"Noah's out on the dock," Jo said after lunch rush, gazing over my shoulder. We sat rolling silverware on the porch, enjoying the hot sun. She mused, "I wonder if he tried to call and I didn't get it. Camille didn't know if he planned to see Millie this week, or not."

I craned my neck to see Noah sitting on the glider, his forearms braced over his lap, staring toward the far side of Flickertail. He was very still. It didn't take a genius to observe the sadness that hovered about him. Though I was still struggling to accept that my Notions seemed out of reach for now, that my awareness seemed altered (I prayed temporarily), I understood that Noah needed help.

"Do you think he would resent it if I tried to talk to him?" Jo asked as she watched her granddaughter's father. We were talking as though everything between us was peachy, which it was not; Jo was still mad at me, and had only spoken to me with small talk, the kind normally reserved for strangers, since the night at Eddie's. She was doing this to communicate that I had hurt her feelings, I knew.

"I'll talk to him," I said, on sudden inspiration. "He doesn't know me very well, but maybe that's a good thing. And that way Camille won't be upset with you for doing something like butting in where you maybe shouldn't."

Jo sighed a little, knowing I was right. She muttered, "Well, there's no time like the present. I'll finish up here."

I pushed back my chair and stood, tying my ponytail on the way down to the lake. The parking lot was empty of customer cars, but I noticed Noah's beneath the lone street light. He must have been deep in thought, because he startled almost comically as I walked along the dock boards. Though my footfalls were nearly silent, as I was wearing tennis shoes, the dock trembled in the wake of my passage along it, alerting Noah that someone was joining him, whether he liked it or not.

"Hi," he said, clearly flustered.

"Can I join you for a minute?"

"Sure," he said, and then, in a rush, "I'm sorry. I didn't ask to sit out here, I hope that's all right."

"Of course it is." I sat on the opposite end of the glider and followed his gaze across the mid-afternoon lake, gorgeous under the sunlight. Motor boats whined in the distance, kids on water skis cutting paths on its surface. The water rippled with blues and golds, lapping the moorings of the dock with tiny breakers. I could tell the poor guy was uncomfortable as hell, so I kept my tone casual. "No one cares if you sit out here. I just thought you looked upset. You maybe want to talk?"

He glanced my way as though gauging my sincerity. Sounding exhausted, he murmured, "I don't know."

I met his eyes, startled at the defeat present there. It made my gut twist up; gone was the confident, even arrogant, college student who had impregnated my niece three summers ago. Noah's eyes were full of suffering. I quelled the instant maternal instinct to wrap him in a hug and pet his hair. Surely he would not welcome such a thing.

"Hey," I said, and concern leaked into my voice. "Can I help you? Is this about Millie Jo, or Camille?"

His jaw clenched at my words, like someone trying to hold back a sob. He cleared his throat and whispered, "I fucked up so bad." He sighed and then apologized. "I don't mean to swear."

"It's all right," I said. "Fucked up with Camille, you mean?"

He closed his eyes and nodded, and then his words came spilling, "She hates me. No, she doesn't even have that much feeling for me. She just wishes I was gone, I can tell. So that Carter can be Millie's dad without me in the picture."

Shit. He was more perceptive than I gave him credit for and the longer I waited to respond the more he would know that what he spoke was for the most part true. Camille did wish Mathias was Millie's dad, I knew well. Trying to sound as though I wasn't fumbling for words, I said, "Noah. Hey. Listen to me. No matter what, Millie is *your* daughter. And you have a choice. You can be a good, decent, loving dad to her even if you aren't with her mom. Camille won't prevent that. She wants Millie to know you. And it seems like you're trying more than you have in the past. That's a good thing. You understand?"

He cupped his head in his hands and I could barely hear his muttered, "Yeah."

"Are you here to pick up Millie now?"

He nodded again.

"What are you two going to do?" I prodded, truly concerned for him.

"She's coming for dinner at our place," he said at last, drawing another deep breath. "She might spend the night, if it's all right with Joelle and Joan." Noah looked over at me and the sincerity in his eyes punched my chest. He whispered, "I love my daughter. It took me a while, I admit it. I was so scared. I didn't want to be a dad. But I love her now. I really do."

"I know you do." I rubbed a hand between his shoulder blades. I couldn't help it; I was too much a mother. I insisted, "And that's what really matters, you know?"

He nodded, scraping a knuckle beneath his nose. He said hoarsely, "Thanks, Jillian."

"If you need to talk, please feel free to find me. Anytime. I mean that."

Noah asked, "Is Millie over at Joan's house?"

"She is, with Ruthie. You want me to go get her?"

"No, I'll head over there."

I hooked an elbow over the back edge of the glider, watching as he walked slowly up to Shore Leave. I considered what Joelle would say when I told her about this conversation. She was no longer at the porch table; she probably felt too much like she was spying while I came down here to talk with Noah. He disappeared around the far side of the cafe and I turned back to the lake, processing what he'd just told me. I better call Camille and tell her about this, or at least tell her the minute she gets home from their trip; she needed to know what Noah was feeling, even if she didn't want to hear it.

No longer, though.

You aren't getting out of this one, fucker, I thought viciously, squaring my shoulders and throwing all of my anger into the air like a net meant to ensnare him. My heartrate increased, fueling my blood with adrenaline. I could tell the instant Zack spied me, as he sat a little straighter and then angled the bow deliberately in my direction. I watched him approach, hardly blinking. At the last second I stood, feeling too vulnerable to remain sitting.

He wants to scare you, I realized. *Don't show him any fear.*

When he was a few yards away, he quit paddling and hopped nimbly from the canoe, drawing it closer to the dock, knee-deep in the lake. The same sunhat shaded his eyes, his t-shirt dirty and stained. The stern of his canoe was loaded with a cooler, fishing supplies, and another, smaller tote. The afternoon sun danced over the water, disturbed by his motion.

"Well, this is an unexpected gift," he said, walking through the lake to stand as close to me as he was able, right at the end of the dock.

"Why did you do it?" My voice stayed steady despite the nauseous churning in my gut.

He cocked his head to the side, as though not comprehending. "Do what?"

I leaned forward, braving the pale flatness of his unwavering stare. "I know what you *fucking did.*"

I expected signs of immediate retreat. But he moved a step closer. "Yes, I wrote on that napkin. Yes, I touched you at the bar. And yes, I am drawn to you. I'm not apologizing for it."

Nervous sweat slicked down my spine; God, he was so horrible. It was the wrong thing to engage him this way, I realized too late, but still I said, with venom, "You know I don't mean those things."

"Then what *do* you mean?" he asked, perfectly composed, and I knew he was messing with me, I *knew* it, and at the same time I understood that I could never prove this; did I actually expect him to confess?

"You know exactly what I mean," I hissed, burning with frustration. "You were *in my house*."

His weight shifted slightly forward as the canoe bumped the backs of his knees. "I don't know what you're talking about."

Crawling with anger and unease, I insisted, "I know you were. And I want you out of here. For good."

"Thank goodness it's a free country then," he said. He was lean and strong, undeniably intimidating, and he took another step closer; he could have reached and gotten his hands around my thighs. His eyes slowly tracking all along the front of my body, he murmured, "But if you want me in your house, just say the word. I'm free right now."

I could not quite suppress the trembling in my knees. "Never come near me or my family again. You are *unwelcome on this property*."

"Or what?" he asked lightly, and there was a distinct edge of menace in his tone, even as he kept a smile pasted on his face. His unsettling eyes glittered. "Will you tell your scar-face husband? What would he think if I told him that you've been meeting up with me lately, while he's at work? What if I tell him that we fuck?"

I stared at him in blank shock. "You're insane."

He laughed at this and then said, "I think I could love you, Jillian. I think I could love you a *whole lot*."

"*Fuck you*," I whispered, numb and ill.

He winked at me as he stepped back into his canoe, sending it rocking. Catching up the oar, he said, as though we were old friends, "I'm sure going to miss you. I really am."

Before I could respond, he paddled away; his small green canoe moved swiftly over the surface. Rage, and simple disbelief that someone had actually spoken to me like that, erupted beneath my skin. He didn't look back as the canoe skimmed across the lake.

"Where's Mom?" I demanded upon entering the dining room no more than a minute later.

Jo, sitting at the counter with Christy, Rich, and little Matthew, looked up in surprise, startled by my tone. Without answering my question, she asked, "What did Noah say?"

"He said—never mind, I'll tell you later." I peered around the cafe, searching for Mom.

"Jillian, look at you," Christy was saying, standing to give me a hug.

Flustered, trapped in the necessity of being pleasant in this moment, I hugged Christy in return. She drew back and smiled, her pretty, smoky-blue eyes just exactly like Blythe's. She gushed, "Aren't you lovely? Look at you, so cute and pregnant! It's good to be in Landon. I'm so happy Junior lives here now."

"Jilly, you want me to make you a sandwich?" Rich asked. "You look like you could use something to eat, hon."

Dear old Rich. I drew myself together and assured him, "No, I'm not hungry. But thank you." I said to Christy, "It's good to see you too. Your grandson is pretty adorable."

"Isn't he?" she adored, smoothing her hand over Matthew's golden curls. "He looks exactly like Blythe did at that age, just exactly. And he's just as sweet, aren't you, precious?"

"Noah just asked if Millie could sleep over at the Utleys' tonight," Jo said, tugging me closer to her side. "I told him that was all right. Do you think Camille would mind? I couldn't get ahold of her just now. Of course she hasn't charged her phone."

"It's fine," I said, sounding more bitchy than I'd intended. "Let the poor guy hang out with his kid."

"So, what did he say?" Jo pressed, her arm around my waist.

"I'll explain, but where's Mom?"

As though conjured by my question, Mom appeared in the arch between the dining room and the bar, saying, "There you are, Jilly!"

I made my way through the dining room, leaving Jo with her mother-in-law, and Mom all but pulled me into the other room. The bar was empty of customers, but Mom still spoke in hushed tones. "I've been so upset about everything with Zack that I called over to the Angler's Inn, where he's been staying." There was only one hotel in the Landon city limits, run by our longtime customers and friends, Joe and Helen Thompson. Mom went on, "I meant to tell them that they needed to ask him to leave, at once, to explain that he wasn't welcome in our town any longer. But Helen told me there was no need, as he'd checked out this morning."

"He did?" I asked, nearly wilting with relief.

"Helen said she would have kicked him out the moment she heard he was being inappropriate. She was surprised, said he seemed like such a nice young man. She said he told her he was going out on the lake once more today, but that he needed to get back to a job in Moorhead tomorrow. So he's heading out. She said he packed up his car."

Good old small town gossip vines. I released a small breath, absorbing this news. He'd said just now that he would miss me; wouldn't that confirm that he was leaving town?

"So he's gone?" I asked. "He's leaving Landon?"

Mom nodded.

"Thank God," I muttered.

"Honey, tell me if anything like this ever happens again, all right?" Mom said.

I felt a small twinge as I promised, "I will," since now I didn't feel the need to mention that I'd just talked with Zack down at the dock. It would only make Mom more upset, needlessly, since he was leaving.

Thank God, I thought again. And then I said, "Mom, we need to talk about Noah."

Rae was sleepy, grumpy and out of sorts when I collected her from Ruthie, so I walked her home for a nap. Clint was at work and Justin was still in Rose Lake. I hated that I was ill at ease in my own house, on the lookout for *rocks*, for fuck's sake. The door was locked and dead-bolted, the windows shut, and there didn't appear to be a thing out of place.

Rae wanted to sleep in our bed, so I settled her there with her elephant and then covertly scanned our room, my eyes roving over every surface. Nothing was disturbed and my shoulders relaxed a little more. I bent to kiss my daughter's soft hair and then headed back to the kitchen, determined to make a good supper.

Zack's leaving town. It's all right now. But why can't I get a sense of things? Why do I still feel so disconnected?

This fact bothered me almost more than anything else, Aubrey and Zack combined. I inhaled slowly, trying to center myself. At last I pulled an old cookbook from the shelf near the fridge, opening to Gran's favorite lasagna recipe; though it was July I decided to make it. The recipe was everyone's favorite. I ran my fingertips over the page, food-splattered from decades of use, picturing Gran and Great-Aunt Minnie in the kitchen at Shore Leave, poring over this same book and deciding what to make for dinner, whipping up a batch of their special chocolate frosting that no one else ever came close to perfecting. I smiled, even as the ache of missing them cut into my heart, wishing so badly to see my grandmother and my great-aunt one more time, to stand nearby while they stirred the powdered sugar and cocoa and melted butter, handing me a whisk to lick.

Not too much now, Great-Aunt Minnie would say, cupping the back of my head, smiling at me with her horn-rimmed glasses riding low on her nose.

I called upon them now in my silent kitchen, begging softly, "Gran. Minnie. What's wrong?"

The empty house was soft with afternoon sun. I propped open the window above the sink and could hear a chorus of birdsong, thousands strong from the sound of them. Not a breath of wind stirred the pines outside. I listened hard, as though expecting to hear their voices.

"Tell me, please," I whispered. "Why haven't I had a Notion? You never told me that they would go away."

Of course there was no response, and I felt terribly abandoned. I shook myself together and clicked on the radio above the fridge as I worked making lasagna, searching the cupboards for the ingredients, clinging to the belief that somehow Gran or Great-Aunt Minnie would find a way to communicate with me.

"Doesn't that sound like fun, Mom?" Clint enthused, leaning around his loaded plate as though expecting one of us to try and snatch it from him. He was on his third square of lasagna.

"It does," I agreed, glad beyond measure to have my family surrounding the table. Rae resembled a circus clown, her little mouth ringed with tomato sauce as she continued happily eating, chin near her plate. Justin sat back, having eaten two pieces in quick succession, and regarded me with a lazy smile.

"That was delicious, baby," he said. He was freshly showered, as he'd been a mess when he'd gotten home from looking at the boat in Rose Lake. It was an old Evinrude outboard and needed a lot of work, but that was their specialty. My husband wore his swim trunks and a white t-shirt that accentuated his deeply-tanned skin, his black hair and dark eyes, and as always, looked a little like a dangerous pirate. A very sexy dangerous pirate. Mom had told him about Zack leaving town, and his own relief at this news had lifted the tension from his shoulders.

"Bly really wants to show his mom the campgrounds around here," Justin added. "He's so excited about taking the kids that I feel like I can't say no. He's like a damn puppy."

I giggled at this description. Blythe had asked if Justin would come camping with him, Christy, Millie Jo, and Matthew. Clint begged to join them (and so had Jeff, if Liz and Wordo would un-ground him), and of course Rae. Justin said they would leave tomorrow afternoon, if that was all right by me.

"Jo and the girls and I will have a sleepover," I decided. "We haven't had a girls' night in ages."

"Mom, what's for dessert?" Clint asked, polishing off the last of his food and then rising to put his plate in the sink. Rae leaped up behind him, not to be outdone.

"Ice cream," Justin murmured, winking at me.

Chapter Fourteen

"I FEEL LIKE WE NEED TO STAY HERE ONE MORE DAY, AT least," Mathias said Friday morning. We were still beneath the covers in the guest room bed where I'd told him about my dream.

"I agree," I whispered. The words spoken in the dream seemed etched into my mind; I could not shake the terrible sensations of ancient pain and loss. I pictured our little cabin in the clearing beyond White Oaks, where Malcolm Carter had once lived, where he'd dictated the telegram from Christmas Eve, 1876. Had Cora meant to live there with him? Had that been their intent? Homesickness for Landon bit into me, harder than before, and I said with undisguised yearning, "I really just want to go home. I want to move into our cabin and I want to forget all of this. I hate feeling so helpless, Thias. Cora wants us to find her but where can we start? It's impossible."

"Nothing is impossible," he contradicted quietly, stroking my hair. "A year ago, if someone would have told me that I would be living in the little homestead cabin in Landon with the love of my life I wouldn't have believed it. And yet here I am, with you. I can't even begin to explain how grateful I am. What brought us together, if not the impossible? How do you explain all of the things that have happened since we've met? Fate, destiny, past lives…I don't know exactly, honey, I couldn't explain it articulately, but maybe that doesn't matter. I think we can find her. I feel like…"

"Like what?"

"Like we should take the horses for a ride today," he said, with a slow grin. "Garth said something about that yesterday. What do you say we go have breakfast and then saddle up Bluebell and Renegade?"

Even before we opened the bedroom door, I could smell bacon. The kitchen, once we reached it, was a crowded, noisy, and altogether cheerful wall-to-wall wreck. Cartons of eggs, dripping pancake batter, melted butter, coffee filters in the sink, and boys all over the place. Clark stood at the stove with a cast-iron pan and a spatula, Garth was slicing onions and Case hiding behind sunglasses, even in the house, looking pale beneath his tan as he sipped coffee. A radio above the sink was tuned to a classic-rock station. Everyone wished us good morning and I asked what we could do to help.

"Now, I'm just plain offended at that, doll," Clark said. "You're our guest. I told you I was looking forward to spoiling a lady. You have a seat and let us wait on you."

I could not argue with this logic, feeling like a princess and wishing more than ever that my sisters were here; wouldn't they love being spoiled this way? Mathias helped with breakfast, whistling as he toasted bread while Garth added onions and peppers to Clark's pan of eggs and the younger boys hurried to pour coffee for me, offering cream and sugar and a spoon. Marshall set the table, singing along with the radio under his breath; he sent a grin my way, which I could not help but return, imagining Ruthie sitting here with me and how she might respond to this lean and lanky drummer who'd "claimed" her for himself. Surely thinking along the same lines, Marshall nudged my shoulder and angled so Case couldn't see, then pulled the picture from his jeans pocket, murmuring, "I stole it back."

Case nabbed the chair to my right, pushing the sunglasses up to the top of his head. His eyes were cinnamon-brown and slightly bloodshot, but he was as cute as ever, if a little worse for the wear this morning. I tried to picture Tish sitting across the table from us; what would she have to say about this guy's obvious infatuation with her? And then I almost giggled, just imagining. Tish was not one to pull her verbal punches. I remembered that I had a plan for introducing her to Case.

"Are you free in October?" I asked him. "Mathias and I want you to come to our wedding."

"For real?" Case asked, eyebrows lofted high. "Oh shit, that would be great! We're free, aren't we, guys?"

At the counter, busy buttering toast, Mathias said, "There's plenty of room at White Oaks for all of you. We'd love it if you'd come."

Clark said, "Of course we'll come. We'd be honored."

Case was ticking through numbers on his fingers, concluding, "That's three whole months away."

"Weddings take planning," I said, smiling at his obvious eagerness. He was so sweet; Tish would eat him for dinner. But…maybe he wouldn't mind that.

"What's your sister doing right now, do you think?" Case asked as if reading my mind, leaning on his elbows, knocking aside a set of silverware Marshall had just neatly arranged.

"Probably sleeping," I said. "You want me to call her?" I'd called home last night to talk to Grandma and Millie Jo, but hadn't yet spoken to my sisters. "I have my phone right upstairs."

"Oh God," he said, sitting straight. "Yes. Hell, yes."

I returned seconds later with my phone. Case was flushed and couldn't sit still as I pushed the icon to dial Tish. Mathias was laughing about something with Garth, who was trying to convince him to sing with them at tonight's gig at The Spoke. Marshall was using two forks to drum along with the beat on his dad's back, the rest of the brothers all singing along now; the tune was "Bad Medicine" and I giggled at their enthusiasm, adoring this big, loving family of menfolk.

"Oh God," Case said again, squeezing the lower half of his face; he could hear the phone ringing.

Tish answered on the third ring, sounding groggy and irritable. Motioning Case near enough to hear our conversation I chirped, "Good morning!"

"*Milla*," she complained. "Why are you calling so early?"

Case was all but hyperventilating at the sound of her voice, his head almost bumping mine to get closer to the phone. Maybe it wasn't exactly fair that Tish didn't know someone else could hear her words, but I wasn't too worried.

"It's an hour earlier here than Minnesota," I said. "Get your ass up!"

"My ass is perfectly comfortable *right here*," Tish grumbled.

Case's cheeks absolutely torched. He put his head on his arms atop the table.

"Who are you talking to?" asked the littlest Rawley brother, Wyatt, coming up beside my elbow.

"Who's that?" Tish wondered, sounding more awake. "I hear music in the background. And singing. Where are you guys?"

"It's my sister back in Minnesota," I told Wyatt, and then explained to Tish, "We're staying with some friends we met last night. They're really great, I can't wait for you to meet them."

"Mathias's family?" Tish guessed.

"No, we just met these guys last night, at a show. Did you get my message about us singing at the bar?"

"Yes, that's so wild! Ruthie and I were freaking out. Were you nervous?"

"Yes, but I'm so glad we did it. It was amazing. The musicians are from this big family that lives in Jalesville, and they invited us over because they actually *know* about Malcolm Carter. Can you believe it?"

"Wait, what?" she demanded. "How is that possible?"

I filled her in on the details, while Case regained control and leaned near the phone again; I angled it for him to listen, too. When Tish and I finally paused for breath, I covered the mouthpiece and whispered to Case, "You want to say hi to her?"

He shook his head, obviously terrified at the notion.

Clark and the boys had begun carting food to the table and I said to my sister, "Hey, I have to go, it's time for breakfast."

"I'm glad you called," Tish said, and I pictured her sitting up in bed, scraping a hand through her tangled curls. She added, "Hurry home, we miss you! Ruthie and I are having a sleepover with Aunt Jilly and Mom tomorrow, since everyone else is going camping at Itasca."

A sleepover, Case mouthed, and put his head back on his forearms.

Homesickness bombarded me. "That sounds fun. Give them hugs from me. I miss you, too. We'll be home by next week."

Breakfast was a noisy, messy affair, everyone talking and no one really listening; Garth was ecstatic that Mathias had agreed to sing at their show tonight.

"You, too, Camille, no excuses," Garth said, his mouth full of omelet. He gestured with his fork. "You two will move out here yet, just wait."

Case, who had not touched a bite on his plate, said for the third or fourth time, "I should have said hi."

"I can call her back," I offered.

"October is three months away," he muttered, as though he hadn't heard. "Three whole months. I'll never survive."

Despite Cora's presence in the back of my mind, I was determined to enjoy the day. Clark saddled horses for Mathias and me, and we were joined by Garth, Case, and little Wyatt. I'd only ever been on a horse once before, back in Minnesota with my dad and Tish, years ago. Clark decided that I should ride one of their mares, a small, gentle animal. He called her a sorrel; her name was Sunny and she was the color of a new copper penny, with a coarse, blond mane and matching tail. I loved her at once, unable to stop smiling at her as Clark walked me through the basics of mounting and sitting the saddle. Sunny was patient and hardly flicked an eyelash as I slipped my foot into the stirrup and climbed atop her back. I thought at once, *Aces. This is just what he felt like.* And again I missed the horse I'd never met.

I scanned the yard from this new vantage point, delighting in the feel of the animal beneath me; I envisioned her galloping across the prairie, racing toward the sunset. The sight of Mathias on a tall chestnut called Archer did things to my insides. He looked so right…he looked like Malcolm, I could not deny this. He was wearing the black hat from yesterday, sitting with both reins in one hand, chatting comfortably with Garth, their horses side by side. If I narrowed my eyes and hazed my vision, I could swear that this was who they actually were: Malcolm Carter and his old friend, Grant Rawley, and shivered with certainty. Case rode near them, as graceful on horseback as a dancer, his movements effortless; he'd told me that, like the Rawley boys, he'd learned to ride almost before he could walk. He explained his horse was one he'd raised from a foal, named Buck.

We rode into the foothills at a slow-paced walk, where the bitterroot flowers grew in low-lying profusion. I allowed Sunny to lag behind, quietly studying the landscape under the steady July sun. I wore a hat that Clark lent me, wide-brimmed and woven of straw, grateful for this as the day burned with increasing heat. Mathias looked back at me as I strayed from the group the first time.

"I'm fine!" I called. "I'm just admiring everything."

Mathias, Garth, and Case couldn't seem to stop talking, riding three abreast. Wyatt was doing the same thing I was, purposely stalling; he rode in a wide arc and then circled back, peeking at me and then shyly looking away. After the second time taking his horse in a big loop, he seemed to gain confidence and drew his lovely black-and-white mare alongside Sunny and me.

"Hi," I said.

"I'm eight-and-a-half," he replied.

I hid a smile. "I would have guessed ten, at least."

He flushed with pleasure.

"I have a little girl who's two years old. Her name is Millie Jo."

"That's a pretty name," he said politely. "This is my horse. She's a pinto. Her name is Oreo. Your hair reminds me of her mane."

"Thank you," I said, both amused and touched by these words; his tone indicated he meant them as a compliment. "She is a very pretty horse."

"My mom died," he said next, startling me.

"I'm so sorry." I didn't know exactly how to respond, but he continued as though I hadn't spoken; maybe what he really needed was someone to simply listen.

"Mama died in a car accident. She wasn't old enough to die, but she did anyhow. Dad explained that sometimes people die even when they aren't old and sick, but I still don't understand."

I wanted to tell sweet Wyatt that I didn't understand, either, that sometimes the world was a fucked-up place that robbed children of their mothers and separated two people who wanted nothing more than to love each other. That no matter how much time passed and how many well-meaning people tried to explain it to him, there was no good answer for why his mother was gone. I missed Millie Jo with an increasing ache, feeling every single mile that separated me from my daughter; suddenly it seemed as though we'd been gone from Minnesota for months instead of just a few days.

"Mama died right after Marshall turned eighteen, and that's why he hates his birthday now," Wyatt continued. "You know what's weird, I don't remember the day that Mama died, I only remember Marshall's birthday." He sighed, gathering tighter Oreo's reins. "Dad said that's all right if I can't remember it. He tells me about Mama whenever I ask. Sometimes my brothers tell me about her, and sometimes they tell me to get lost." As if concerned that I might harbor the wrong idea, he said earnestly, "But they watch out for me real good. They don't let anything hurt me, if they can help it."

"You're lucky for that," I said softly, watching him as he spoke; in the space of five minutes, this kid had already unknowingly claimed a spot in my heart. His narrow little face was shadowed by his hat brim, dark eyes solemn, his nose already beginning to dominate his face, just like Clark's and all his brothers'. Unkempt brown hair hung down his neck. I felt another pang, wanting to find a comb and some scissors, and trim him up.

"I s'pose," he said.

We rode in silence for a time, the guys perhaps fifty feet paces of us, laughing and enjoying one another's company. I studied Mathias as he rode, fantasizing what it would feel like to sit in front of him on his horse, riding together. It struck me as incredibly intimate and romantic, like our winter picnics to watch the aurora. As though sensing the heat of my thoughts, he looked back and blew me a kiss. I was so absorbed with the thought of riding double that I hardly heard the boy's next words.

"Wait, what did you say?" I asked.

"I see her, too," Wyatt said again, and my eyes snapped to his face.

"See who?" I whispered.

Looking at the horizon, he murmured, "Cora. I never said anything to Daddy or the others because I was afraid they would be mad and think I was just trying to get attention. But I'm not."

"What did she tell you?" I'd drawn on Sunny's reins without realizing, and the mare obediently halted, prompting Wyatt to do the same. The horses shifted their hooves beneath us, lowering their heads to nibble at the grass as I studied him intently.

"I've seen her two times now," he said, looking worried; immediately I softened my expression. "I know Garth said he was dreaming when he saw her when he was little, but I think he was just too scared to admit that she's not a dream. She comes and sits on my bed. I see her weird eyes, but they don't scare me. The first time, she touched my hair. She didn't say a thing. But then the next time she told me she was trapped. I think…I think she's been trapped for a long time."

"Trapped?" I demanded. "Where? How? Did she tell you anything else?"

"Somewhere around here. Far, but not too far. That's all I know."

"Anything else?" I was desperate for more.

He shook his head. "I'm sorry."

Dammit, Cora, I thought then, aggravated. *Dammit. Can't you be a tiny bit more specific?*

"I'm glad you told me," I said to Wyatt. "Thank you."

"I never believed in ghosts until I saw her," he said. "Do you think everyone who's died is trapped here, somewhere?"

His question tore at my heart. "No. No, of course not. I think that when there's a ghost, it's because there's unfinished business associated with it. Like with Cora." It was such a cliché answer but I wanted him to be comforted; certainly he was thinking of his own mother with this question; and to some extent, it really was what I believed to be true about ghosts.

He nodded, seeming satisfied.

"Case said my mama and his mama are in heaven together," Wyatt said. "That they talk together, up there, and can see what we're doing down here."

"Case's mom died, too? When was that?"

"Back a long time ago. Her heart was sick, that's what Case told me. And him and Gus's dad is white trash. That's what all the ladies in town say, anyway."

"They do?" I asked, indignant, and startled once again. Wyatt was a virtual font of information, go figure. Little kids always knew more than adults gave them credit.

"What's that mean, 'white trash?'" he asked next.

"Well…" I hesitated. Searching for a suitable response proved more difficult than I would have imagined. At last I settled upon, "It's a mean way of saying that someone is poor, usually."

"Daddy doesn't believe that they're white trash." Wyatt shifted in his saddle. "Case and Gus are the best friends we have. We love them. They do pretty much live with us. Their pa doesn't care what they do. He doesn't watch out for them. Daddy says it's because he's haunted."

"Haunted?" I thought, *Kid, you are full of surprises.*

"That's what Daddy says. Not by Cora, though, I don't think," Wyatt said in all seriousness. "By other things. Daddy says old Mr. Spicer has a demon, that's what."

I shuddered a little at this phrasing.

Wyatt whispered, "I don't know how you get yourself one of those, but it sounds scary."

"It does," I agreed. There were far too many demons in the world, real or imagined, as this young boy already understood. To lighten the air, I said, "So, we sang for quite a crowd last night! You should have been there."

"Garth and Marsh said you guys were really good. I bet that's fun, up on the stage. We sing at home, all the time."

"I guess we're singing again tonight." And I felt a ribbon of excitement at the idea, despite everything. "Maybe Clark can bring all of you to watch."

Wyatt bounced in his saddle. He cried, "Will you ask him, please? Please with a cherry on top? You're so pretty Daddy won't be able to say no to you, I know it."

I giggled at his confidence in my feminine wiles. "I'll do my best, I promise."

Late afternoon light dusted the landscape, the sunbeams tinted auburn by the time we got back to the homestead. My legs were sore from gripping the saddle all day, as I informed Mathias.

"I'm a little bowlegged, now that you mention it," he said, helping me down from Sunny's back. He kissed me flush on the lips, then brushed dust from my face. "That was great. You and Wyatt seemed to be having quite a conversation."

"We were. I'll have to tell you about it," I said.

"You up for singing again tonight?" he asked, and I grinned, removing his hat and roughing up his hair.

I murmured, "Yes, and tonight let's keep the hat, what do you say?"

His dimple flashed. "Your wish is my command, honey. I seem to remember making you a promise last night…"

"Hey, you two are gonna scare the horses," Case teased, coming to take Sunny's reins, leading Buck by a long rope.

"Showtime in two hours," Garth added, grinning happily at us, leaning on his forearms over Sunny's broad back. "Let's get cleaned up, shall we?"

The Spoke was as familiar as an old friend, warm and inviting with its wagon-wheel tables and flickering lanterns, the bar full to bursting. I dressed in jeans and a red blouse with short, fluttery sleeves, and kept my hair loose over my shoulders. Clark lent me a pair of hammered-copper bracelets, which he explained had once belonged to his grand-ma; they jangled merrily on my right wrist. Mathias was decked in his cowboy hat and faded jeans, as were Case, Marshall, and Garth, and I felt like a celebrity as we entered the little bar to deafening whistles, cheers, and hollers.

"Our reputation precedes us," Garth joked, waving and grinning, al-ready working the crowd, which grew until the double doors leading to a small brick patio had to be opened.

Clark had required little convincing to bring the entire family. We needed a table for ten to accommodate our group and as we sat in the glow of the neon beer signs, multicolored string lights, and flickering candle lanterns, I couldn't stop smiling, buoyed by the company and the entire joyful atmosphere. The Rawleys were the brothers I'd always wished I had. Wyatt insisted on sitting beside me, and so he was on my left and Mathias my right; Case sat directly across from us.

"Are you nervous tonight?" I asked Mathias, leaning against him so he would kiss my face. I loved that about him; whenever I leaned close, I could count on his kisses.

He kissed my temple. "A little. Nothing like last night, though. I didn't quite think I'd make it."

"I'll join you guys halfway through," I said. "I want to watch for a while."

"Thirty minutes 'til we're on!" Case said, flicking a french fry at us.

The show brought down the house. I joined the guys partway through, as promised, though my presence was much in demand on the dance floor; Clark's boys had clearly been schooled in old-fashioned dance steps, even Wyatt, and I took turns with each of them. They kept cutting in on each other to dance with me, and I felt more like Millie from *Seven Brides* than ever.

Tish and Ruthie should be here, I thought again, missing them. As I watched Mathias singing with Garth while Case and Marshall played, I was struck with the sense, strong and true, that our men were up there, and my sisters weren't even here to see. Ruthie would love the music— and my gaze darted to Marshall, grinning as he rocked out on the drums; he was completely at home on stage. Even Tish would have to admit she was having a good time—and I looked at Case, who was playing his bass guitar with a somber expression, eyes closed, totally into the music.

October, I reminded myself. *They'll all come to Landon for the wedding. Case and Marsh can meet them then.*

By the time we made it back to the Rawleys' house, it was near to three in the morning and Mathias all but carried me to bed. In the morning we would be traveling farther west, on to Harry and Meg Carter, and, I prayed, more answers.

Chapter Fifteen

"Let's plan tomorrow for the girls' night," Jo said Friday evening, a few hours after we'd bid our families farewell. They weren't headed far, as it was just over thirty miles to Itasca State Park, a longtime favorite camping destination of the Miller family. Jo swept her hair into a loose ponytail and fanned the back of her neck with its length, adding, "I'm beat. I need a night to myself, sunk in my tub."

"Can we do pedicures and stuff?" I teased my sister. I missed her, and almost asked if I could stay at her house tonight anyway. It wasn't as though it was very far through the woods from my own. But she needed time to herself, too; not that she would get lots of that with both Tish and Ruthann also in the cabin. Jo and I sat at a porch table as the sun slowly sank; there were a handful of customers in the bar, lingering over a last drink, but we'd both closed out all of our tickets and so were free to relax. The air was ashen with the warm dusk, as still as a photograph.

"Of course," Jo said. She tapped her lips with her index finger and I knew she craved a smoke as much as me at this moment. She murmured, "I've been thinking a lot about what Noah told you yesterday. I know Camille doesn't want to hear it, but she needs to. I understand where she's coming from, though. Noah abandoned her and Millie. She's supposed to leap back into his arms when he decides he's changed his mind?"

"No, of course not. I just feel bad that Noah understands Camille wishes she didn't have to deal with him, you know? That's not exactly something you want to hear."

"You think I don't get it?" Jo griped, taking a long drink of her beer. "Jackie tries to play the guilt card every time I have to be in the same room with him. Shit, like at Tish and Clinty's grad party. What a *joke*. Thank goodness Blythe doesn't let Jackie upset him so much anymore."

"Yeah, Jackie was asking to get his ass kicked that afternoon," I reflected. "I can't see Noah ever getting to *that* level. I mean, you and Jackie have a history. Noah and Camille were never truly together. They made a beautiful little girl, but they weren't ever married. Noah doesn't have the same motivation as Jackie. And I think Noah's finally just realizing his mistake."

"Can you see Noah and Camille together though, truly? I can't," Jo said. "It just seems wrong. I have never seen Camille as happy as she's been since last December. Mathias just loves her to pieces. And she loves him the same way."

"I know she does," I said; why did my heart feel the need to seize up a little, as though in fear? I shoved the feeling aside and whispered, "I just hope they find something on their trip. Some sort of definitive answer, so she can rest. She's so worried."

"She's always been a worrier," Jo noted, sighing a little. "It's being the oldest daughter that does it."

"Yes, we second daughters have nothing to worry about." I infused overt sarcasm.

"You know that's not what I mean. Gran would know what I mean," Jo said. She let her hair fall back over her shoulders, with another sigh, and I almost damned it all and went to root out the pack of cigarettes I knew was tucked behind the bar. Talking about Gran made me want to smoke more than ever.

"That's funny," I said. "I was missing Gran and Minnie so much yesterday. I always miss them, beneath the surface, but yesterday it hit me especially. It makes me want to be around the old house, you know?"

Jo nodded, her eyes misting with tears. "I miss them so much, too. And Gran passed so quickly, we didn't get a chance to say good-bye. I still sometimes forget she's gone, that she won't be sitting at table three in the mornings, drinking her coffee."

"Yeah, I know." My throat tightened with pain.

"We were lucky to have her as long as we did." Jo curled her hand over mine. "I love you, Jilly Bean. I'm sorry about everything. I know you were just worried the other night, speaking of worry."

I twined my fingers through hers. "I know. I love you, too. And I'm sorry I was acting like such a bitch."

"You've had a lot on your mind," she allowed.

"Well, if Justin *was* in jail for some reason, I would accept collect calls from him morning, noon, and night, just to hear his voice. It would kill me otherwise," I said, trying for a little teasing, though I meant what I said one hundred percent.

Jo leaned and kissed my forehead. "Thanks, Jills."

I found Mom and told her I was going to sleep at her house this evening if that was all right, and she replied, "Well, that's just wonderful. I made a pan of caramel brownies today."

"You know that was part of my motivation to stay over."

A few hours later I was snug in my pajamas, and Mom, Ellen, and I had eaten the entire pan of brownies. Contentedly drowsy, I lingered at the kitchen table with a last cup of decaf. The light over the stove still glowed, creating a cozy glow in the room; Mom and Aunt Ellen had retired to bed though it wasn't particularly late, only around eleven or so—but it had been a long week. I was just about to head upstairs to crash in mine and Jo's old bedroom when I realized my cell phone was still on the counter beside the till, back in the cafe.

Dammit.

I wanted to talk to my husband, to make sure they were settled in over at Itasca. I couldn't even use a phone here in the house, as Mom and Ellen decided just last year that they were sick of paying for land-line service in the house, when there was a perfectly good phone in the cafe. Mom kept a cell phone for emergencies, but I would bet she hadn't placed a call from it even once since purchasing it last year. I was pretty sure it was lying dead in a drawer somewhere, all but forgotten.

It's just a minute walk to Shore Leave. And it's beautiful out.

I grabbed a hooded sweatshirt and shrugged into it as I made my way over the lake path. Shore Leave was comfortingly familiar in the moonlight as I climbed the porch steps and used the key I'd carried in my pocket to unlock the door and slip inside. Even though I knew the space well enough that a light wasn't necessary, I clicked on one of the overheads. The dining room smelled slightly yeasty, of fried fish and beer, and seemed lonely in the perfect stillness of the night hours, devoid of its usual happy chatter and clutter. I glanced at table three with the overwhelming feeling that if I'd looked only a second faster, I would have spied Gran. A cold shiver rattled my limbs and seemed to explode in my nape—was Gran trying to tell me something?

Jeez, Jillian! Quit spooking yourself!

I'd done enough of that lately.

Even so, I collected my phone in a hurry and was about to scramble back to the house when I noticed that the message light on the answering machine connected to the cafe phone was blinking. My cell phone showed a missed call from Justin and I would bet that he'd tried to call me here, to let me know that they had arrived safely at Itasca. I leaned over the counter and pressed the playback button, a little reluctant to turn my back on table three. The first message was from a restaurant supply distributor with a solicitation, and I erased it at once. A man's voice I didn't know came on next, and my finger was poised to delete this call, too, but then I realized it was someone from Moorhead State University, returning Mom's call.

"…calling for Joan Davis. I apologize that I didn't respond yesterday but I was out of the office. Ms. Davis, I am quite disturbed by your message, for two reasons. First, we had a Zack Dixon here as a graduate student last spring. He was kicked out of the program, for reasons I can't disclose. But I assure you, he is a person to avoid. And secondly, I'm concerned that someone is in your area claiming to be from our institution. We have no students in Beltrami County conducting research. Please feel free to call me in the morning to chat further regarding this matter."

The phone fell from my numb fingers and clattered against the wooden surface of the counter. I was shaking almost too badly to retrieve it, but I managed, fitting it back into its cradle. My entire body felt immersed in ice water, my eyes frantically scanning the darkened windows. My own reflection peered back from the curtainless expanse of glass and a thousand eyes seemed to be watching. My neck prickled anew, in a seizure of horror.

He's gone, he's not here. He is gone. He left town.

Who the fuck is he? What does this mean? Is he really Zack Dixon?

My legs were almost useless, trembling as hard as they were, but I forced myself to walk out the front door, clicking on the porch light as I did so, determined to walk the short distance over to Mom and Aunt Ellen's and tell them exactly what I'd just learned. If they wanted to call the police, then we would.

Is that really necessary?

What would you even tell them?

I made it down the porch steps and an owl hooted just above my head. I jolted, gasping, pressing a hand to my heart to still the sudden frightful pounding, almost laughing at my own jumpiness as the huge bird flapped away across the black sky, no more than a few yards above the cafe.

It's all right, Jilly, it's just an—

It was at that exact moment he caught me from behind. I hadn't detected a sound, his footfalls silent over the grass, not even able to scream as his hand swooped around my head and clamped hard over my mouth. He carried me effortlessly to the far side of the cafe, closest to the lake, where he spun me around so that I could see his face, keeping my mouth firmly covered. The back of my head cracked against the siding as he pinned me.

"Don't make a sound," he ordered, his voice low and soft. As prey before a much stronger, faster, and cunning predator, instinct froze my limbs. In sharp contrast, my mind lunged and then streaked as though at light speeds, racing through a thousand thoughts and images in the space of a second.

Oh God oh God oh God...

He didn't leave.

You can't fight him.

He's going to hurt you.
Justin, oh God, Justin…
The baby. If I struggle, he'll hurt me worse.
Jilly, do something, for God's sake!
Move! Scream!

But only a gulp, a pitiful little whimper of air, emerged from behind his hand.

He braced my spine against the wall, the boards unyielding behind me. Even as I watched his terrible, pale snake eyes come closer, smelled his breath against my face, I was imagining impossible things, such as the wall magically becoming one of those revolving doors from a cartoon, safely spinning me away from this horror. I was trapped, a mouse in a cage, one of his hands gripping my mouth, the other lodged beneath my breasts, effectively pinning my upper arms. Sweat erupted on my icy skin, all internal sounds amplified, as though both hands were clamped over my ears. The baby kicked at my belly and my bowels liquefied with agony.

Oh God, baby, my baby boy, I'm so sorry…

Zack wedged a knee between my thighs. I was wearing loose pajama shorts and his hard bare leg felt more obscene than I could possibly describe. Bile surged and I gagged. Instantly he demanded, "Does this make you *sick*, Jillian? You don't want this? Don't want me?"

"You…*fucker*…" I tried to rasp, though I should have known better.

"That's big talk," he spat, shaking me with two violent jerks. He put his mouth against my cheek. "Where's your scar-face husband now? You're not so tough without him, are you? Will he still want you after I'm through with you? Tell me."

My breath came in frantic little gasps.

"He won't." There were notes of both aggression and triumph in Zack's voice. "He can fuck himself then." As he spoke, he lowered one hand down my body, over my belly and then farther. Tears flooded my cheeks and I heard growling sounds of hatred emerge from my throat. He only smiled, squeezing at both points of contact, though his voice bore an almost loving tone as he murmured, "But first *I'm* going to fuck you. I knew I was going to fuck you the second I first saw you, Jillian. I have never wanted a girl the way I want you. I just had to find the right time."

I closed my eyes to block out the sight of him but I could not likewise cover my ears. He pressed his face closer, directly against my skin, and continued speaking. "I know you want it. You can't fool me, you little pregnant slut. You're all little sluts. Camille swims naked in the lake, right down there. I saw her, but I don't want her the way I want you. I've been waiting and waiting for you, and finally here you are. I knew if I was patient I would get you alone. You're my reward."

I tried to bite him. My teeth scraped over his palm, uselessly, but he made a sound of muted rage, releasing his hold on my mouth and backhanding the right side of my face. Bursts of hot-white light exploded before my eyes. It hurt so much that I lost momentary focus; I'd never before in my life been purposely struck.

Seeing stars, I realized dimly, somewhere in the recesses of my mind.

"*Hold still*." His voice was clipped, breathless, his palm slick and rough against my mouth, his other hand resuming its course between my legs. He fumbled to the hem of my shorts and then there was nothing to stall his progress. His breath was heavy on my face. "You want it, admit you want it. You knew I was in your house, you found what I left for you. You want me. *Tell me so*."

"No," I begged, though the word was obstructed by his hand. "No."

He tried to force his hand beneath my underwear and I twisted so fiercely that he stumbled, enough that my countermovement caused me to fall to my knees. I tried to scramble away, on all fours, but he was on me in an instant, this time catching my hips and flinging me to my back, as though I was as floppy and malleable as a ragdoll. All breath fled my lungs as he braced over me, pinning me by the throat with one hand.

"Shut the *fuck up*," he hissed.

I sensed movement beyond Zack's shoulder and thought I was imagining things. Zack yanked my shorts down past my hips.

"Get away from her right now," said a trembling voice, just to my left. I was so overcome with terror that at first it didn't register that someone else was speaking.

Zack froze.

"Get away from Jilly right now," the voice repeated, wobbling over the words.

"Or what?" Zack asked, his tone black as death. His body blocked my view of the person connected to the timid voice.

In reply, someone fired a gun, perhaps no more than ten steps away from us. The shock of it sang through my ears, leaving behind a vortex of silence, filled an instant later by shrill ringing. Zack surged to his feet as though electrified and I rolled sideways, horribly disoriented, and vomited. There was a second gunshot, further rendering my ears useless. All I could see was my puke striking the dewy grass.

In the next second, someone was on their knees beside me and I fought to get away, choking on sobs and vomit, but it wasn't Zack. I finally realized that Noah Utley was hunched there with me, his hand curled over my right shoulder, his eyes wide with stun in the light of the almost-full moon. He was trying to talk to me, his mouth flapping. I made myself focus and heard him say, "Holy shit, holy shit, he just ran away. He's running away. Holy shit, Jilly, are you all right? Holy shit."

A pistol lay on the ground at Noah's knee. I drew myself to one elbow and managed to order, "Call 911."

"Oh Jesus, your face is bleeding. Oh fuck, are you all right?" He was beside himself with shock, I could tell, his voice traveling down a long corridor. "Here, Jilly, I've got you." Noah helped me to my feet, as gently as though I was made of something irreparably fragile, like tissue paper. "Can you walk?"

I nodded, clutching his arm, and then ordered, "Get...*that gun...*"

Noah nodded in response, crouching at once to grab the pistol; he held it awkwardly, as though it might bite him, aiming the short barrel at the ground. With his free hand, he helped me to the porch, where he seated me at a table. The baby was kicking furiously. My lap was wet; I'd urinated. Noah set the gun on the table between us and fumbled something else out of his pocket, dropped it, and fell to his knees to retrieve what I realized was his cell phone. He pressed its screen to make a call while I scanned the area with wild eyes, my hand near the gun; Zack

Dixon was nowhere in sight but I was not taking any chances. I was shaking so hard that my teeth rattled my entire skull.

"Please hurry," Noah was saying into his phone.

"Why…" It was all I could manage to articulate, but Noah understood what I was asking. He sank to the chair at a right angle to mine, as though his knees suddenly gave out.

"This is so c…crazy." His trembling words rushed forth like startled birds. "I was…I was out here to kill myself. I stole my dad's gun and I…oh God oh God…I was going to put the gun in my mouth down on the dock. And then…*and then*…I saw what he was trying to do to you…"

I blinked in slow motion.

And then I reached across the tabletop and clutched Noah's fluttering hands into mine. He was as cold as a rock dredged up from the bottom of the lake, shaking almost as badly as me, but I squeezed his hands, hard. It took almost all of my effort, but I steadied my voice. "Noah! Noah, it's all right. You saved my life. *You saved me.*"

"Jesus Christ, J…Jilly." He bent his forehead to our joined hands. He rasped, "You saved mine, too."

"*Jillian!*" I heard Mom's panicked voice, coming closer.

I tried to call to her but my ability to speak had been destroyed. Noah lifted his head and his eyes shone bright with unshed tears. Because I still gripped his hands, he staunched the flow of them with his shoulders, first one and then the other. Mom and Aunt Ellen flew into view from the direction of the house, jogging toward the porch in their bathrobes. Mom caught sight of us first and thumped up the steps. Somehow the image of my mother, barefoot, her uncombed hair loose over her shoulders, her eyes frantic, allowed me to fall to pieces. She was at my side then, cupping my head to her belly, as though I was a little girl. I wept, limp against her warmth. In the distance, moving fast, was the sound of a siren.

"What in the world is going on?" Aunt Ellen asked Noah, her palms resting on my shoulder blades.

I couldn't hear what he said. Mom smoothed one hand over the back of my head in a tense, repeated motion. Two police cruisers roared into the parking lot, top lights spinning. Mom bent to my ear and said with quiet authority, "Jill, tell me what's happening."

I drew back and observed the raw pain on her face as she regarded me, her lips dropping open. I watched the play of emotions cross her features, moving from shock and disbelief to outright fury. She cupped my chin and demanded, "Who did this to you?"

"It was…Z…" I gulped a breath and forced out his name. "It was… Zack."

Mom sank to a chair beside me. For a second I was afraid she might faint, but Ellen bolstered her.

"He had her on the ground," Noah supplied in a whisper. He was hugging himself around the torso, still shivering, but his voice had steadied.

"Oh my God, oh dear God," Aunt Ellen gasped. "Where is he now?"

Charlie Evans, Landon's senior law enforcement officer, and two younger deputies were advancing on the porch.

Aunt Ellen yelled, "Charlie, my niece has been attacked!"

"What the devil?" Charlie asked as he lumbered up the steps. Aunt Ellen bustled into the cafe, clicking on additional lights. I knew without a doubt that she would have coffee brewing in the next two minutes. Mom did not move from my side. I pressed my right hand to my belly, where the baby was performing energetic donkey-kicks.

"Jilly has been attacked, Charlie. I heard a gunshot not five minutes ago," Mom said. "It woke me from a sound sleep. And then I ran over here as fast as I could."

The two deputies flanked Charlie, all of them looking so official and out of place here on the nighttime porch at Shore Leave. I flinched as Charlie took my chin gently into his fingertips and examined my face. I'd known Charlie since I was a little girl and his eyes were full of concern, anger that this had happened to me.

"Tell me what happened," he said, taking a seat across from Mom, who drew her chair closer to mine. Catching sight of the pistol, Charlie said, "Boys," and one of the two deputies ran back to the car. Seconds later he returned and deposited the pistol into what must have been an evidence bag.

"First things first," Charlie said. "Whose firearm?"

"Mine," Noah said. "It's my dad's, I mean. I brought it out here be-cause…" He choked, looking at me for strength. I nodded, willing him to continue. He whispered, "I was planning to shoot myself. I stole that from my dad's desk drawer."

"And how does Jillian fit into all of this, son?" Charlie continued, calm and authoritative.

Noah said, "I had just gotten here. My car is out on Flicker Trail," and he pointed lamely toward the road leading back to Landon. "I heard what sounded like struggling and then I saw…*oh God*…I saw that guy holding Jillian by her neck. I told him to stop. He didn't seem like he was going to, so I…so I fired the gun into the air and then he jumped up and ran. And then the gun went off again, I didn't mean for it to shoot, but it did. And then I helped Jilly up here and called 911."

"Jillian, can you corroborate this?" Charlie asked.

"Yes," I whispered. I sat straighter. "It happened just like that. Z…Zack," I could hardly say his name. I started over. "I came down here just a little bit ago to get my cell phone and it was when I came back outside that he c…caught me…"

"Dammit, Charlie, she can't deal with this right now," Mom snapped, and I lifted my face toward the sky to contain my tears.

"I want Justin," I whispered to Mom, like a child, single-minded. I figured she could make this happen.

She nodded at once. "Let's get you cleaned up, honey, and then we'll call him right away."

"You want me to call him?" Charlie offered.

"No," I whispered at once. "Let me talk to him, please."

"I'll be right here when you're ready," Charlie said.

Fifteen minutes later Shore Leave was lit up like the Fourth of July. I had showered in scalding water and was wearing clean clothes, bundled into a flannel shirt of Justin's, one that smelled like him. I needed him with a rabid ferocity, and he was on the way to me, as we'd called him like Mom promised; I told Mom that I needed to be the one to tell him

I was all right because otherwise he would go crazy, totally ballistic with worry, but my throat was so blocked that I'd been forced to hand my phone to Mom.

Two feet away from Mom, I heard my husband answer with his warm, low voice, thinking it was me on the other end. "Hey, baby."

"Justin, it's Joan," Mom said, without preamble. "Jilly's been hurt. You need to come home right now."

Oh shit, I thought.

There was a split second of hellish silence and then Justin's frantic voice, "Oh God, what's wrong? What's wrong?"

Mom said firmly, "She's right here with me, Justin, but you need to come home now."

"Let me talk to her, let me talk to her *right now*," Justin ordered, and it sounded like he was choking.

I grabbed my phone from Mom, bringing my husband's voice to my ear, holding the phone with both hands. I mustered all of my willpower and whispered, "It's me, I'm here. Please hurry."

"Jillian." His voice harsh with fear. "Jillian, baby, tell me, oh God, tell me what's wrong..."

I started to cry.

Mom took the phone, wrapping me against her side as she explained quietly, "Just get going as quickly as you can. Call me back when you're driving and I'll explain."

"I'm coming," he said intently.

It was another fifteen minutes before I saw his truck. Justin barreled into the lot and almost took out the back end of one of the police cruisers. He slammed out of his truck and Mike Mulvey, one of the deputies, tried to detain him, but he barked, "Get the *fuck out of my way*," and then I was down the porch steps and in his line of sight. And then nothing else mattered because I was in his arms. He clung to me, touching my face, my back, my belly, his hands moving continuously over my body, assuring himself that I was in one piece. I clutched the material of his t-shirt, holding fast, crying again, this time in relief. He rocked me even closer, his lips against my hair. His voice broke as he said my name, over and over. "I am so sorry I wasn't here, oh God, I am so sorry. Oh God, sweetheart." He cupped my face and drew a painful breath, the expression in his eyes severe with contained fury. "Your mouth. *He hit you.*"

I clutched his wrists, for strength, and mustered the wherewithal to say, "He did, but I'm all right, we're both all right." Justin cupped my belly as I repeated, "We're both all right."

His eyes were beyond agonized. "Oh God, I will never forgive myself. Tell me. Tell me what happened."

Though I'd already explained the events to Charlie, told him that I hadn't been raped, despite the fact that this was Zack's clear intent, we sat down with him again, me on Justin's lap and held close, Justin crackling with the intensity of his anger.

He kept saying, "I want him dead" and "I'm going to fucking rip him to pieces," which perhaps weren't the kinds of things to be spoken in front of three officers of the law, but Charlie had known Justin his entire life as well, perceiving the justification for these statements, and so didn't comment. He told us, "We'll do everything we can to bring him in, don't you worry."

Already the woods were crawling with every on-duty officer in the area, in addition to a few who were not. Dodge was here, and Jo, Tish, and Ruthie. Blythe and Christy stayed at the campground with the kids, to keep them out of the activity for the moment. Jo was beside herself, fluttering around as pale as a sheet on a clothesline. Dodge also seemed unable to keep from moving, and he added plenty of his own threats on top of his son's; it was his way of offering reassurance, I knew. Curt and Marie Utley had been called, and both of them were sitting with their son, who was wrapped in a blanket and drinking coffee. My eyes flickered to Noah; I could not begin to consider what might have happened if he hadn't been acting out his plan to commit suicide down on the dock.

Oh God. Life is so crazy, I thought, clinging tightly to Justin's arms, wrapped around me from behind. *I don't even mean that in a bad way, but it's so fucking crazy. What if Noah didn't show up tonight? Would I be dead right now?* I thought of the way Zack's pale snake eyes looked, looming so close to mine. I knew, somehow, that there was a part of him that wanted to kill me, and suddenly, with the understanding of this knowledge, all of my extra senses rippled back into place, alive and pulsing, bursting forth as though dormant too long, requiring immediate recognition.

It's all right now, doll, I heard Aunt Minnie say, plain as day in my mind. *You survived and it's all right now. You've been delivered.*

Minnie! Don't go yet. Oh God, explain this.

"There's nothing more to be done tonight," Charlie was saying. "You two go home and get some sleep, if you can. I'll let you know if we discover anything before morning."

No one wanted to let us go home; Mom was adamant that we sleep in her house, Dodge wanted to stand guard over the bed. But in the end I wanted my own room, my husband beside me, and so Justin carried me to the truck after hugs all around, and drove us along the gravel road that curved through the woods and led back to our lot.

"Will you carry me to bed?" I whispered as he parked in the driveway, so exhausted I could hardly stand.

"I will do anything for you," Justin said. He cradled me to his chest as he carried me to our room. There, he placed me upon the bed, bending over me, cupping my belly and pressing his face. I dug my hands into his hair, holding his head against me as he said, "If anything had happened to you…Jilly, my Jillian, I would die." He shifted and took my face in his hands, his eyes ravaged, speaking around a choking lump in his throat. "Can you forgive me for not being here? For not protecting you from him?"

Of course he would feel that way; I knew he would torture himself with it, and I could not let him. "This is not your fault. Do you hear me?"

Tears flooded his eyes. With utmost tenderness, soft as cottonseed alighting on the lake, he kissed my lips. He smoothed hair from my forehead and whispered, "I'm so sorry. You can say you don't blame me, but I blame myself. It's my responsibility to protect you, to protect our family."

"Justin," I said, getting my arms around his neck. "Please don't do this to yourself. It's no one's fault. Please, never say it's your fault, not ever again."

He drew a shuddering breath and rested his lips to my forehead. I buried my face in his neck, inhaling his scent. "I need you so much, Justin." He made a sound deep in his throat, and I told him honestly, "It's all right now, I feel it. I really do."

He whispered, "I'll never let you from my arms again. I couldn't go on without you, Jillian, not for a minute."

He shifted us to the side, curling protectively around me. I could feel his heartbeat, steady and strong. He said, "I'll hold you while you sleep, baby. I won't let go."

Gran and Great-Aunt Minnie came to me in a dream, appearing as the versions of themselves that I remembered from my high school days, back when I helped Minnie dye her hair its original golden-blonde every few weeks. They came to me with their faces somber and smoothed their hands over my cheek as I lay against my husband, touching the bruising left there.

Jillian, it was too close, Gran said. *He would have killed you.*

His hatred is too deep to comprehend. Even he can't understand it, Great-Aunt Minnie said. *It's in his very blood.*

What do you mean? I begged.

Look at the boy, Gran said tenderly, casting her eyes upon Justin's sleeping form. *The boy has always been for you, Jilly. You just needed to realize it. You belong to him and he belongs to you.*

Is Zack gone? I wanted answers. *Is he gone? What about Mathias and Camille? What do they need to find out? Are they in danger?*

But as much as my grandmother and my great-aunt loved me, they could not answer.

Chapter Sixteen

Saturday morning dawned clear and golden, and we were still tangled together in bed as the clock edged past noon. We had two more days of vacation ahead of us and were no closer to any answers about Malcolm and Cora than we'd been a week ago in Minnesota. The only thing I knew for certain was that we were meant to meet the Rawleys here in Jalesville. Maybe that was the true purpose of our trip.

"Morning, honey," Mathias mumbled. He was still half-asleep, lazy and content after a very late night, first singing at The Spoke for over three hours, and then back here in our black bear bed, fulfilling my every naughty, wonderful request, as promised. A blush bloomed all the way to my hairline, just recalling. I hoped we hadn't been too loud. Mathias spread a warm hand against my belly, letting his fingertips trail lightly between my legs, and amended, "Well, afternoon, really."

"Good morning," I murmured. "Thank you for last night."

"Oh, holy shit, it was my pleasure. My very great pleasure."

I buried a giggle in the pillow. I supposed we'd have to get up and get moving; according to the little bedside clock it was quarter to one.

"Clark let us sleep right through breakfast," Mathias explained.

"I can't believe we slept this late…"

"It's all right, honey, we're on vacation."

"I'm going to shower," I whispered.

"I'll be here," he said with a grin, snuggling into the sheets. He looked so tempting I almost dove back into the bed.

After my shower I found him already dressed, sitting on the edge of the mattress and dialing his voicemail. His eyes lit with a smile at the sight of me. He said, "I love the sight of you all damp and steamy from the shower."

I blew him a kiss and then found my bag, rooting around for my own cell phone; finding it, I saw that it needed charging, of course. I moved to plug it into the wall as Mathias listened to his messages. I busied myself packing our things and didn't at first realize that he'd gone stone-still.

"Camille," he said, in such a strange tone of voice that I dropped the clothes I was holding.

"What is it?" I asked, alarm bells wailing in my head. He held the phone to his shoulder as though he couldn't bear to hear any more of the message. My heart ratcheted up to about a hundred miles an hour. I whispered one word, "Millie…"

Mathias shook his head at once. "No, no, she's fine. That was your mom. I don't even know…"

"What is it?" I cried, and Mathias tossed his phone to the side, standing and taking my shoulders in his hands.

"Last night Jilly was attacked by a man named Zack Dixon."

"Oh God," I uttered. "Is she—oh God—is she all right?"

"He hit her, but she's all right. Noah saved her."

"What?" I gripped his elbows to stay upright.

Mathias's voice was low with shock and concern as he explained, "Noah was out at Shore Leave last night because he was going to shoot himself on the dock. He had a gun. He saved your aunt by showing up. Zack was choking her and Noah shot the gun and scared him away."

It was too much. On top of everything else it was too much. I put both hands over my eyes and pressed hard, willing away these mental images. It was nearly the last thing I'd expected to hear him say.

"Honey, come here." He gathered me close, where I clung.

"Oh God," I moaned. "Aunt Jilly was scared of Zack, I could tell, and I didn't even do anything about it…"

"Who is he? Who in the hell is this guy?"

"Remember the guy whose canoe you helped load up a few weeks ago?" My voice wouldn't quit shaking. "He kept stopping out at Shore

Leave to sit in her section. He was such a rude asshole, I waited on him a few times, but I didn't realize he was crazy…that he would hurt her…"

"The college student from Moorhead?" Mathias sounded stunned.

"Where is he now? Did they catch him? I'll kill him myself," I raged, angry tears spilling over my face at the thought of anyone harming Aunt Jilly, my pixie auntie.

"I don't know, your mom didn't say. Everyone is with her right now. Millie is with your grandma. I guess Blythe and Justin took the kids camping at Itasca, and so they weren't there last night."

"We've got to go home," I said, in a hurry now, unable to remain immobile and helpless. "We can't stay here a second longer."

It was just my imagination; surely I couldn't really hear the wailing cry somewhere in the back of my head.

Malcolm, Cora, forgive me, I thought. *Forgive me*.

But then my thoughts circled back to something else that Mathias had mentioned and I faltered. "Noah was going to…shoot himself?"

Mathias swallowed and his eyebrows drew together, in abject discomfort at this fact; I could tell guilt was slashing at him the same way it was slashing me. "That's what your mom said. Honey, I'm so sorry. I don't know what to say."

"He wouldn't have gone through with it," I said, trying to believe this was the truth. I could not feel responsible for Noah's actions. But I did feel pity, and deep regret that he would even consider such a thing. He was my child's father, whether I liked it or not, and he felt terrible enough last night that he had intended to remove himself from her life, permanently. I shuddered. "I better call Mom."

Mathias sheltered me against his chest for one more minute. He felt so good, so warm and solid. He kissed the top of my head and whispered, "Let's get loaded up, love, and we'll get going, all right? I'll call Harry and Meg, too. We'll tell them there's an emergency back home."

"We'll miss you something fierce around here," Clark said, hugging the both of us. The boys were all lined up like stair steps, waiting for hugs of their own. "Kindred spirits need each other, so you come back soon, promise?"

"We will," I whispered, hugging everyone in turn.

"Tell your sister that I can't wait to meet her," Case said, with a smile, but his eyes were serious.

"We'll see you in October for the wedding," Marshall said. "We promise."

"Are you sure you can't just move here?" Garth asked.

"Don't stop looking," Wyatt whispered in my ear as I bent down to collect him close.

"I won't," I promised, brushing hair from his eyes.

"We'll miss you, too," I told Clark, hugging him one more time.

"You always have a place to stay here," he said.

"And you guys, in Landon," Mathias said.

The mood was so momentarily low that it was a relief when Case said, "Shit, it's not like we have to ride horseback to see each other. This is the modern age. It's just a day or so, by car, right?"

Mathias held the door for me and I climbed into the truck. He rounded the hood and climbed beside me, and linked our fingers as we drove east. We stopped in Miles City for supper, as we hadn't eaten yet today. I called Mom again afterward, sitting outside the little restaurant on a wooden bench, watching as a line of pewter-gray thunderclouds moved from the west, as though tailing us. Mathias was talking with Tina, no more than a foot away from me on the bench.

"Sweetie, there's no need to race home," Mom said. "Drive safe. Camp somewhere tonight if you're too tired."

"Mom, I'm just so upset. I feel sick about all of this. Is Aunt Jilly all right?"

"She's been resting today. Justin is at her side, don't you worry."

"Any news on…" I could hardly bear to say his name.

"No," Mom whispered. "But they'll find him. He can't hide forever. Apparently a man with the same name was a suspect in conjunction with the disappearance of a girl in St. Louis, two years ago."

"Oh God," I said. Mom hadn't mentioned this when we spoke earlier.

"Hey," Mom said, changing tone abruptly. "It's all right, baby girl. Millie is here with me, and Blythe and the kids are home, and it's going to be all right. You and Mathias drive safe. Don't rush. We're just fine here. Grandma and Ellen send their love." Mom didn't mention Noah this time, so I didn't either; she had told me before we left the Rawleys' that he was home with his parents, and that they weren't planning to leave him alone anytime soon.

"I love you," Mom said.

"Love you, too," I whispered, and hung up. Beside me, Mathias ended the call with Tina at almost the same moment. He wrapped me in his arms.

"We've had such sunny days, I guess we deserve a little soaking," he said, nodding in the direction of the approaching storm.

"It is gorgeous here, there's no denying," I said, resting my head on his chest. "But I am so glad to be going home. I miss Millie Jo, and I miss our little cabin."

"I wish we were sitting on our porch there right now," he agreed. "What did Joelle say?"

"She said not to rush." I realized something and cried, "Shit, I forgot to get that picture back from Case! The one of Tish and Ruthie."

"I'm sure he'll take good care of it, unless Marshall steals it from him," Mathias said, smiling at my concern. "But all the same, maybe don't tell Tish."

"Yeah, she probably wouldn't find that particularly romantic," I agreed.

"We can drive straight through if you want. That's what I was thinking."

"I'll take a turn driving, so you don't get too tired."

"Don't you worry about me," he said.

"I don't mind," I insisted. "You drove the whole way here."

Mathias surrendered the wheel and despite his words, was dozing within a half hour of leaving Miles City. It was July and the evening was long, but the rain closed in, overtaking us and creating an early darkness. I turned on the windshield wipers and dropped our speed; we seemed to be the only traffic on the slick, wet road, but still. The highway always worked to mesmerize me and my thoughts were so jumbled, snarling together as I thought of Aunt Jilly, and Cora, and Malcolm...

The truck rolled past a little road sign announcing *Terry, population 605*. It was just as this crossed my vision that I knew I needed to turn left. I *knew* it. I slowed, clicking on the blinker, and took the next turn, not allowing myself to question this action. The gravel road led us back almost the way we'd come, vaguely northwest, but I was overtaken by an intensity that I could not define. I looked over at Mathias, sleeping peacefully against one of our bed pillows from home, and decided I would let him rest. The first road sign I saw indicated I was driving over Highway 253. The countryside was rugged out the windows, obscured by a steady rain. I searched the landscape for any indication of something that could help me make sense of what the hell I was doing.

Camille, this is so stupid. Turn around. It's getting late and you're doing no good.

But there's something…

Something's here…

Cold fingers plucked at my heart. When a small animal, maybe a possum or raccoon, darted in front of the tires, I shrieked and stomped on the brakes, startling Mathias awake. He jolted straight and his left arm came across my chest at once, as though to hold me back from danger.

"Are you all right?" he demanded, fearful.

I clutched the steering wheel, my knuckles forming white peaks; the truck was halted in the middle of the road. Rain streaked the windows as though the sky was weeping in long, continuous sobs. It was dark as midnight. Mathias unbuckled and slid across the bench seat.

"Pull over," he said, and I did. "Where are we?"

"I'm sorry," I whispered. I had never felt less sane in my life but I could feel it all around us now, the intensity of the pulling. A line along the skin over my ribcage seemed to burn. I babbled through an explanation. "I took a left back near a town called Terry, I don't know why exactly, I just felt like I should…"

"I know the town," he said, holding me close in the dim glow of the dashboard lights. "Honey, what's going on?"

"She's here, she's somewhere close. *Oh my God…*"

Mathias didn't question how I knew this; he only asked, "Where?"

"She's pulling me. I can *feel her* pulling me. I have to go out there."

Before he could say otherwise, I opened the driver's side door and stepped into the rain. The air was rife with the scent of soaking earth, rich and loamy and overwhelming. The sky hung low and sullen; the scrubby brush in the ditch appeared sharp and menacing. Mathias followed right behind, catching me around the waist.

"You need different shoes!" he yelled over the sound of the wind.

He hauled me back into the truck, where I traded my sandals for sturdier tennis shoes. My hands shook so badly that I could hardly tie the laces, but I was in a hurry now, intent with purpose.

"Come on," I said.

"Wait!" he ordered, keeping me from forward movement with both hands around my waist. "I believe you, but this is country I don't know well and it's dark."

The burning in my side increased. "We can't wait! She's so close, Thias, I can feel her."

"Which way?" he asked, and I was heartened that he understood this was real. He considered another moment, looking out the windshield. Reaching a decision, he fished out our jackets and a flashlight and said, "We'll look, but you stay close to me. Stay right behind me."

"West," I whispered, and we braved the rain. Mathias locked the truck and tucked the key in his pocket, and we started forward. The going wasn't terribly difficult, much like walking through the woods back in Minnesota, a similar rise and fall to the land beneath our feet. Here though, there were no trees, the foothills full of rock formations, eerie in the darkness, turrets and ledges and indentations everywhere, giant, oddly-shaped stone fortresses. The rain stayed steady as we left the truck behind. I was pulsing with awareness. Mathias kept the flashlight beacon trained on the sodden ground five feet ahead.

Cora, I begged. *Show me where you are. Please, show me.*

The rain was nightmarish, steady and drenching, obscuring our long-range vision. Our shoes slogged through the increasing mud. I closed my eyes and reached out with my mind, my hand on Mathias's back as he walked just ahead of me. We didn't speak until the first bolt of lightning sizzled and then he stopped and ordered, "No. We're going back to the truck. I won't put you in danger out here!"

"But she's so close," I sobbed, tears and rain streaking my cheeks. "She's *here*. We can't leave her here anymore!"

"Camille, no! I won't put you in danger! Not for her, not for *anyone!*"

There was a tremendous, cracking roar and I leaped as though stabbed. Lightning flared in the wake of the thunderclap and Mathias was adamant. He yelled, "Back to the truck, now!"

The darkness was momentarily eradicated by the next brilliant flash and a skittering of loose rock tumbled down one of the silent rock fortresses to our immediate right. I saw something then; the falling rock directed my attention that way and I shouted, "Look there!"

I ran, stumbling in my haste, to the small opening there revealed, not quite a cave but close, a low crevice burrowing perhaps ten feet deep into the base of the rock. I fell to my knees and peered inside. My ribs burned wickedly, my heart cinched as though by a length of bristly rope as Mathias circled the flashlight around this ancient space, once, twice... finding nothing. It was an empty hollow, hardly big enough for two adult bodies, occupied by nothing more than small rocks and dirt. Rain sheeted. Thunder seemed to split the sky into chunks. Lightning pierced the night directly on the heels of another burst of thunder, appearing to strike the tip of the neighboring rock. I cried, "Where is she? She should be here..." I pressed my palms to the wet earth.

"Honey, come on," he said, dragging me into the small space and out of the storm. We were forced to crouch and the air was musky with the scent of dirt, but it was dry in this space. I felt a twinge of horror at the confinement but Mathias collected me close, setting the flashlight on the ground.

"I'm sorry, I'm so sorry. I don't know what's wrong with me. I thought she was here...she's supposed to be here!" I sobbed, hysterical with frustration, unable to get a handle on myself.

Holding me secure, rocking us side to side, he put his lips to my ear. "It's all right. It's all right, love. We'll be fine in here until the storm passes. I'm here."

The violent storm blew over within fifteen minutes, moving east; we could hear the grumble of thunder receding, leaving behind the quieter sounds of slackening rainfall.

At last Mathias said, "Let's go home."

I nodded agreement. I would put this insanity behind me, forever. I would hide away the picture of Malcolm and Aces, and the telegram and the letters, and I would pray that I never dreamed of them again...

"We'll go get in dry clothes and get some food, what do you say, sweet darlin'?" he asked, trying to restore normalcy to the situation, I could tell, running one hand through his damp hair.

I nodded, exhausted beyond measure. I bent to collect the flashlight, inadvertently nudging its beam a different direction, and it was then that I saw it, a rock that looked more like...

I grabbed the flashlight, aiming it at the very back edge of the cave. Without hesitation I crawled to the spot and used my fingernails to scrape the ground. When this wasn't enough, I scrabbled about for a small rock.

"Is that..."

"It is," I gasped. "It's a skull..."

Mathias helped me and the earth fell away as we dug, exposing something I'd only ever seen as a model in the science rooms at school, or as a Halloween decoration. And then suddenly it was in my hands, its top curve smooth and polished as a river rock. The entire lower jaw was gone; the empty eye sockets gaped as though peering at us.

"Oh, *Jesus*," I breathed, cold and trembling. Had my soul once inhabited this skull's body? Was I holding Cora—and therefore my past self? I almost dropped her, fingertips resonating.

Mathias put his hands over mine, atop the skull. "Is it...oh God, is it her?"

Before I could respond I heard a noise at the mouth of the cave, a dry skittering rattle. I turned just in time to see a small, pointed head glide over my bent legs, its long, smooth body following directly after. There was no time to process the sight before Mathias made a rough, strangled sound and it was only then I realized what was happening, that a rattlesnake had just slithered across me to sink its fangs into Mathias's left thigh.

Panic swallowed me whole.

Time seemed suspended, each second a buzzing eternity. I dropped the skull and thrashed at the creature, but it was already whipping itself away, fast and sinuous; the damage was done. Mathias bent forward and groaned, "Oh shit, oh *shit*."

Charcoal seemed alight in my throat. A thousand choices swarmed for attention in my head and yet I'd never been so helpless.

Mathias was attempting to remain calm. "That was a timber rattler. You've got to get help."

"I can't leave you here!" I fumbled with the flashlight, shining it over the bleeding wound on his thigh. He inhaled a harsh breath and I felt as though I was burning alive, tethered inescapably to a fiery pyre, my recurring nightmare unfolding literally before my eyes.

"Camille, you have to go get help." He clutched my arm in his free hand, understanding that I was about to fall off the cliff and into abject panic. His grip was noticeably weaker than usual.

I would not let this happen. *Fuck* if I would let this happen. My brain centered and focused, spitting out words. *Help. Hospital. Truck.* I couldn't carry him as far as we'd walked. I said, "I'll get the truck, I'll drive it back here!"

He whispered, "That's a good idea, I didn't think of that…" And then he tried to extract the key from his pocket and fell backward. I gasped, pulsing with agony, helping him to lie flat on the ground. I would rather die than leave him here alone in this narrow cave, but he could die if I didn't.

"Thias, oh God, I'll be right back, I promise." I held his face, kissing his mouth, before crawling out into the rainy night.

This was hell.

Hell was a rainy, rocky, no-man's land in which I was now forced to run, leaving behind the love of my life—this lifetime and many others.

Let him be all right.

It's what you feared most.

He'll die and you won't find him again…

And then there was no room for thoughts. I ran full-bore, falling once, sliding inches over the ground, scraping knees and palms, terrified that I had dropped the key. But it was still clutched in my fist. I came upon the truck and gunned the engine of the good old 4x4, thankful as hell that it was four-wheel drive. I cranked the wheel and drove back the way I'd come, avoiding boulders. The truck bounced like a pinball and lost a hubcap, but I had no time for anything but getting to him. For a horrific span of time I wasn't sure if I could find my way to the right spot. I braked where I was certain I'd left him waiting and was assaulted by visions of driving across eastern Montana and never finding him, of being kept apart from him, our souls never reuniting.

I'll wait for you right there, he'd said, pointing to the cluster in the Milky Way's expanse.

I leaped out of the truck and screamed his name, my throat raw. I could see the opening in the rock face now and raced to it; I had no idea how many minutes had elapsed while I ran for the truck and returned here. It could have been five minutes or thirty. I had no sense of time. My breath emerged as a whimpering growl as I saw him lying flat on his back, eyes closed. I scurried to his side and felt for a pulse.

"Thias, I'm here, I'm here...*be all right, I'm here*..."

His heart was beating but he was cold, damp from the rain, and his eyelids didn't flutter at the sound of my voice. Everything I'd ever heard about snakebites revolved through my head. Mom had long ago delivered the talk about venomous snakes, as we'd visited northern Minnesota every summer. I knew you weren't supposed to open the wound. What I needed to do right now was lift him into the truck and get him to a hospital as fast as humanly possible.

"I have to lift you up, Thias, I have to get you to the truck. Can you hear me? Oh God, hear me," I pleaded, sliding my arms under his upper body. He remained inert and I was frantic. He was so much bigger than me. "I have to lift you up, love, I have to get you up." But I could already tell that I wasn't strong enough, even with adrenaline pulsing through me. I would have to drag him and I would hurt him in the process.

There is no other choice. I understood this clearly. And then, reeling with helplessness, I heard myself sob out a name; I heard myself beg for Malcolm, over and over again.

Later, I would never be sure exactly what happened, though in the moment it was sterling clear, clear as glass, clear as water in the shallows of a lake. A sound like wind in a narrow tunnel rose from behind me and a crawling chill seized my spine; I turned to see a shadowy form hovering at the back of the cave, small and slight, long dark hair rippling over her shoulders. Her clothing appeared in tatters, arms and legs frail as twigs. The only substantial part of the entire being were her eyes—one green and one black, burning in a ghostly face. Her essence glowed in the cave, reflected in my wide and terrified pupils.

"Cora," I breathed. Shock electrified every hair on my body and made ice shards of my blood. She. Was. Me. I felt the very fabric of my soul—her soul—pulled by a tremendous force. Primal terror clamped hold – I pressed both hands to my chest to keep myself in once piece.

Before I could blink she flew to Mathias, the vibrating energy of her swelling to fill the cave.

You came for me, she sobbed, her glowing hands gliding over his face. *You came for me. I am so sorry, Malcolm, do you hear me, I am so sorry...*

Necessity overpowered my fear and restored my ability to move. "Help me! You have to help me, he's hurt!"

I should have trusted you. Forgive me...

"Cora!" I screamed. "Help me!"

Malcolm...

She seemed not to hear my words and I lost all control. Feral with desperation, as cruel as I'd ever been, I raged, "Goddamn you, Cora! I risked him searching for you! I love him as much as you loved Malcolm, don't you see?! We came here to find you and you will help me or I will smash your fucking skull into a thousand pieces and leave you here, forgotten forever, do you understand?!"

Time stalled, shrieking through my soul before voiding the cave of all sound—and then her soft, low voice filled my head.

It is me who should beg forgiveness. It's my fault, not his—I should have listened, I should have trusted. You are me but you are of Lorie, too, I know this. Her daughters and their kin were cursed to lose their men, the first men they ever loved. I couldn't stop it—I should have tried harder...

The whys of it mattered no longer in that moment; I didn't care anymore if I never understood what she meant.

"Then you owe us both," I whispered.

Chapter Seventeen

THE HOSPITAL ROOM WAS DIM, LIT ONLY BY A SINGLE LIGHT NEAR THE bed; the nurses had left us alone since midnight. They said to call if my contractions got any closer together. Just now I felt as though I may be in labor for the next week. I'd been on bedrest since Millie Jo's third birthday in February. Mathias smoothed tangled hair from my overwarm face and asked, "You want me to braid it, hon? It's coming all loose."

I nodded and he helped me ease forward; he'd had a lot of practice with this sort of thing, as he often fixed Millie Jo's hair. He finished his gentle ministrations and drew the long braid over my shoulder. I whispered, "Thank you, love," and he grinned, dimple flashing, giddy with excitement over the fact that sometime soon—maybe even by morning's light—we would finally get to meet our boys.

"Two," Aunt Jilly had told us back in September. She'd rubbed my belly and pronounced, "Boys, if I'm not mistaken."

It took a fair amount of time for Mathias to float back down from his elation at this news.

"Twins, on the first try," he kept saying.

We had returned home from Montana quite differently than we'd expected, back in July. My memory of the events in the foothills remained hazy, as something viewed through a smoked-glass window; I wasn't entirely sure if that was because I had been in such shock or because my mind was somehow protecting me this way. I believed, and would always believe, that I'd spoken to Cora's spirit and that she'd helped lift

Mathias into the truck. Much more clearly, I remembered driving hell-for-leather to the tiny town of Terry, Montana, wild-eyed as I searched for the hospital; the emergency room staff treated Mathias with antibiotics to counteract the rattler's venom. He'd been rendered unconscious the rest of that night while I waited in a stupor of terror, unwilling to take my eyes from him, despite the hospital staff's kind reassurances that he would indeed be right as rain. By dawn, Mathias's eyelids were fluttering and I restrained the urge to climb right onto the hospital bed and wrap around him. I touched his face; he reached and caught my wrist in one hand, his fingers curling around the bones beneath my skin.

"Did you see her?" he'd whispered. "Did you, Camille?"

I nodded slowly, cupping his face. His dear, precious face that I could not live without.

He whispered, "Cora was there. She spoke to me."

"She saved you," I whispered.

His fingers caressed my forearm with gentle motions, not yet up to his usual strength. He whispered, "*You* saved me. You saved me from so many things."

"Do you know how much I love you?" I asked. He had asked the same thing of me before we'd made love the first time.

"I do. My love, my sweet love. I've always known."

Mom and Blythe had wanted to drive to Terry and retrieve us; Mathias's sisters called about every ten minutes until we reached Beltrami County, so worried for their little brother, despite his reassurances. I promised all of them that I would get us safely home. The day before we left Montana, while Mathias rested in the hospital bed, I drove the truck back along Highway 253, slowly this time, and retraced my steps through the late afternoon, one last time. When I came upon the little cave it was lit by the orange fire of the lowering sun and I noticed what I hadn't in the darkness and rain—wildflowers, bitterroot blossoms growing profusely along the ground near the opening. I understood not even half the story, I realized this, but I understood enough. And there was only quietude here now.

I dropped to my knees and crawled across the dirt to retrieve the top of Cora's skull; all that remained of a young woman with tremendous strength and power, fierce devotion. I prayed she was at peace now, that all of her pain and anger had evaporated like dew with the morning sun. I cradled the skull—my skull—against my belly as I drove back to Terry, smoothing my palm over the dull curve that would have been the top of her head long ago, tracing my fingers lightly over the eye sockets, and my ring caught the glint of the dying sun; perhaps Cora once wore this exact ring. I would never know, but there was one definitive thing I could do for her.

"It's time you came home," I told her.

We buried her in the woods near the cabin. We decided that we didn't want to mark the place with a wooden cross and so Mathias and I worked together to find a medium-sized native stone with a smooth, flat surface appropriate for chiseling.

"We don't even know her last name," I said, tracing my fingertips over the rock. "Or when she was born. Or even exactly when she died."

Mathias considered for some time before he began chiseling, and the result was this: *Cora Carter, beloved of Malcolm A. Carter, 1876.*

"Do you think she'd approve?" he asked as we stood there later, her skull properly buried and the stone in place. I'd brought along a bundle of roses, which I felt she would prefer, tied with a silk ribbon. These I set carefully near the stone and rested my hand on its surface. I had spent plenty of time thinking of something Cora had said, back in the cave, about the curse.

Her daughters and their kin were cursed to lose their men, the first men they ever loved.

And this was true. I thought of my grandma, my mother, Aunt Jilly, even myself. Each of us had lost the first man we ever loved. Stretching back through time, this had been the case for the women in the Davis family. As a lightbulb flickering to life, I thought of Aunt Ellen and Dodge. Maybe she had never openly admitted her love for him for that very reason, even subconsciously. She didn't want to *lose him*.

But if we hadn't lost them, we would not have found our true loves, I realized. The curse was really a blessing. In complete disguise, it was actually a blessing.

"I think she would like it very much," I said, tracing her name on the inscription. As I stood, Mathias tucked me against his side and if he'd been wearing his cowboy hat, he would have held it against his chest in that moment. "This is where she always wanted to be, I think."

"I think so, too," he said. "She has finally come home."

Months later, in the labor and delivery wing at the Rose Lake hospital, Mathias was too excited to get any rest, even when the nurses warned him it could be a good while before the boys decided to emerge. He'd been anticipating this day since the moment we'd discovered we were to be parents, and I would always believe that the boys had been conceived that night at Makoshika, beneath the gorgeous starry sky.

"Are you hurting, love?" he asked, as sun peeked in the tall window to the right of the bed.

"You're asking again," I muttered. My good mood had long since dissipated but Mathias was undeterred. I'd told him if he asked one more time I would banish him to the waiting room.

"Matty-pants, if you can't handle a little pain, you better get your ass out of here," Tina said; she'd joined us a few minutes ago. Mom, Millie Jo, Aunt Jilly, and my sisters were just down the hall, along with Bull and Diana. Every few minutes one of them would pop over to our room just in case the action had started.

I giggled at Tina's words and Mathias said, "Are you kidding? You couldn't force me out of here at gunpoint. I'm going to be right here to play catcher when my boys come out."

Aunt Jilly stuck her head in the door, the morning sunlight dancing over her golden hair. "Can I join you? You don't mind one more body in here do you, Milla-billa? I'm too impatient out there."

"Of course not," I told my auntie.

She fluttered to the bed and kissed my forehead, smoothing her delicate hands over my belly in small, rhythmic circles, as though about to start a hypnosis routine; as always, her touch sent little spiraling shivers all along my nerves, an involuntary response to the electric energy of her.

"Morning, Jills," Tina said. "I saw your little guy with Justin at the grocery store the other day. Oh my God, he's adorable."

"I'll tell Justin you said so," Aunt Jilly teased. "He *is* pretty damn adorable, isn't he?"

Tina laughed. "Yeah, and so's your baby."

Riley Justin Miller was born last September; he possessed utterly kissable chubby cheeks and huge brown eyes, and I'd never seen a baby who smiled more than him. Possibly this came from being cuddled every second of every day. Rae was fiercely protective of him.

"By noon," Aunt Jilly said with certainty, patting my belly.

As of today, no trace of Zack Dixon had yet been discovered—not in Landon, or Moorhead, or anyplace in Minnesota—and there were no leads. Charlie Evans had conducted extensive searching, at last making contact with an old woman in St. Louis who claimed to have once had a grandson by that name, one she'd not seen in over four years. It scared me way down deep in my bones that another inexplicable crime had been committed in Landon, an otherwise sleepy little town with zero history of violence.

We'd speculated endlessly, reaching no conclusions—could Zack Dixon have been responsible for attacking Mathias in the woods last February? But again the *why* of it stumped all of us, even Aunt Jilly. Why would someone attack either her or Mathias? There seemed no clear motive, and though I resolved to stop losing sleep over it, the feeling lingered at the back of my mind. When I looked across our clearing in the light of the sunset and saw my man, the sun glinting in his black hair and the love in his eyes, I recognized I could never be grateful enough that he was still here, that I'd not been robbed of him; I still sometimes struggled to believe that Mathias was no longer in harm's way...that he and I could be so happy with no repercussions...

And then there was Noah, who'd become an unwitting hero. I talked to him at least once a week, satisfied that he was doing all right these days; he'd re-enrolled in college and was finishing up his undergraduate degree. He understood his life had been saved that night, too, and he believed in second chances, as he'd told me when I went to visit him shortly after getting home from Montana last summer. He saw Millie Jo as often as he could.

"You think?" Mathias asked Aunt Jilly, all but hopping from foot to foot. "By noon?"

Tish and Ruthie came around the corner from the hallway, Ruthie carrying Millie Jo and Tish with a tray containing coffee and donuts.

"I know you're not supposed to eat," Tish said, making room for the tray on the bedside table. "But I figured you'd be hungry."

"Thank you," I said. "There's enough food for five people here." To Millie Jo, who'd been worried all morning, I said, "Hi, baby. It's all right."

"Well, you *are* eating for three," Tish reminded me.

"She's been begging for you," Ruthie told Mathias, handing Millie to him.

"Your little brothers are coming today!" Mathias reminded Millie Jo, bouncing her on his arm as he carried her to my side. Millie wrapped her arms around Mathias's neck and clung, resting her forehead on his jaw; she disliked seeing me like this, on an unfamiliar bed in a room that smelled like antiseptic. Mathias assured, "Mama is just fine, sweetheart."

"Your brothers have to push out of your mom, just like you did," Tish said to her niece, trying to be helpful, nabbing a sprinkle-top donut and eating about half with one bite.

"*Tish*," I groaned, as Millie's dark eyebrows knit with confusion.

As Aunt Jilly and Tina both attempted to offer my daughter an explanation, I regarded Tish as covertly as I was able, thinking of my wedding back in October. The Rawleys had ventured to Minnesota, to our great delight, Clark bringing all of his boys, including Case and Gus. Mathias and I were so happy to see them; they loved Shore Leave as much as we'd loved Jalesville. My sisters met the Rawley boys; Ruthie was so shy she could hardly speak around them on what amounted to only a brief visit, hardly longer than the busy weekend. And Case had indeed met Tish. I sighed a little, wondering just what to do about what had happened.

It's not up to you to change anything, I reminded myself, not for the first time. *Tish can make her own decisions.*

But I remembered again the haunted expression in Case's eyes that night at the dance, and of the way he'd looked the next morning when they packed up to drive back to Montana…

Camille, it's not your business.

"Are you all right, Milla? You want a donut?" Ruthie asked, catching my braid in her hand and gently wagging it side to side. She was so sweet—she had no idea that Marshall Rawley, sexy drummer from Montana, had told his brothers if they dared to flirt with her that he'd bust their jaws; Case had told me all about it that October weekend—he'd basically issued the same order, about Tish. Even so, Marshall hadn't spoken a word to Ruthie the entire weekend, as though sensing it wasn't the right time.

"No, thanks," I said, touched by Ruthie's concern. Millie had started to cry and I tried to comfort her, and in the noise and confusion of everyone talking, I almost didn't realize that my water had just broken.

Hours later, two baby boys, just over five pounds each, were in my arms. The delivery room was once again packed with people, but I didn't mind. Our families were so excited that I could not deny any of them this opportunity to meet the newest members. Mathias and I had settled on names during my bedrest and two brand-new birth certificates read *Brantley Malcolm* and *Henry Mathias Carter*.

"These are my grandsons," Bull rumbled proudly, snuggling Brantley to his powerful chest. "My boy made twins on the first try, see there."

Aunt Ellen and Grandma regarded Bull with amused eyes. Grandma said drily, "Camille had nothing to do with it, I'm sure."

I'd never seen Mathias so giddy. He lifted Millie Jo up to see Henry, who was cuddled in my arms. "Look there, sweetheart, that's your little brother."

"Mama, are they going to live with us?" Millie asked, studying the baby with eyebrows quirked. She hooked a finger in her mouth, frowning like a little owl. Her expression clearly said *I don't know about this.*

Mathias kissed her cheek. "They sure are, sweetheart. You'll love them, don't you worry."

"You were this little once," I told her. "And Mama will need your help. These two need a lot of attention."

"Can they play with me?" Millie asked. "They don't look fun, Mama."

"Camille, you're hogging him," Ruthie complained, reaching for Henry.

"Me next!" Diana insisted, and Mathias sent me a knowing grin; he couldn't wait for us to be alone with our boys, but he also understood how much everyone wanted to see them.

I love you, I said without words, and he entwined our fingers.

I love you so damn much, honey, he said, and tears shone in his indigo eyes.

"We'll be home soon," I said, bringing his hand to my lips, kissing his knuckles.

"We are home," he whispered. "Wherever we are, as long as we're together, that's home."

And I tugged him close so that he could kiss my lips.

Excerpt from The First Law of Love

Rain was spattering the glass just a few inches from my nose as I sat there in the gloom of my apartment. I blew a long stream of smoke in the direction of the five inches of screen near the bottom of the window, cranked open in my attempt to ensure that no one would complain about the scent of the cigarette. I was stressed.

The city was dismal under the low, weeping sky, an hour or so from sunset. The streetlight a block away went through its paces in a repeating array of blurry color, starbursts of red, green, yellow and then back to red; I watched like one mesmerized.

I closed my eyes then, vividly conjuring up an image of fireflies at dusk, lighting the advancing darkness with their golden-green sparks of light. In the background I could see Flickertail Lake gleaming blue promises and my heart clenched on a hard note of longing.

Landon. Shore Leave. Home.

I hadn't been back to Minnesota in over a year. But what did I expect as a student in the JD program at Northwestern College? Free time? A boyfriend? The ability to see my family now and then?

I expected none of these things, as my father warned me over three years ago, after I'd been accepted to Northwestern Law. As I'd been staying in Chicago with them the warm and windy afternoon I'd received my letter of acceptance, Dad and his wife, Lanny, took me out for dinner at Spiaggia and I felt as though the universe was presenting me with an incredible gift, this chance to make something of myself.

Euphoric could not begin to describe me that evening, buzzed as I'd been on my own glory, real and imagined. The juris doctor program. Chicago and all its glittery, delightful bustle. Dad's beaming smile. Visions of myself standing triumphant before judges, handling and winning case after important case swirled madly through my mind as I sipped wine, too revved up for food. That was also the evening I first met Ronald Turnbull, a business associate of my father's, only a passing introduction as he'd paused momentarily at our table to chat with Dad.

"Ron, this is my daughter, Patricia," Dad had said.

Ron, silver-haired and stern-faced, intimidatingly confident of his place in the world, produced a smile for me as our hands met. "Ms. Gordon. I understand congratulations are in order."

"Thank you," I responded. "I plan to prove myself and then some."

He chuckled at this, and I felt my shoulders square in defense, but then Ron surprised me by saying, "I've got my eye on you, Ms. Gordon. Perhaps we can chat when you're on the hunt for summer work."

I was stunned by this pronouncement but I'd kept all of that from my expression, maintaining a professional mien. I responded smoothly, "I appreciate that very much. Again, thank you."

Dad couldn't keep from grinning as Ron was led to another table. He leaned toward me and murmured, "I would love to see you ground floor, Turnbull and Hinckley. That's promising, Tish, promising indeed."

"He sits on the appellate court?" I asked, peering discreetly after Ron. The appellate court was comprised of alumni and faculty; as a first-year student I would present mock cases before them, arguing against fellow students. The thought filled me with prickles of nervous anticipation.

"Alumni," Dad confirmed. "And Ron is an old friend. I've talked about you for years, honey, but you'll prove yourself."

That he thought so sent the warmth of pride through my heart. Dad was an expert schmoozer; a sincere compliment from him was a rarity and so I let myself bask in the one he'd just bestowed.

"Favors," Lanny said, caressing her wine glass. She had not yet touched the appetizers; she didn't remain a size two for nothing. My stepmother wasn't exactly the evil witch I'd once believed though I still found her as shallow as a wading pool, but I was mature enough to be civil to her. She elaborated, "Favors are what get you ahead. You scratch Ron's back now, he'll return the gesture." Her full, candy-tinted lips plumped into a speculative pout as she regarded me. I studied her false eyelashes as she added, "It doesn't hurt that you're young and beautiful, either."

I wasn't sure if I should thank her or consider this a smoothly-delivered insult. Implication: that's how a woman gets ahead in the corporate world.

Printed in the United States
by Baker & Taylor Publisher Services